The Zephyr Gene

E.K. Arden

Printed in the United States of America
Cover Design: Linkville Graphics

Linkville Press
linkvillepress.com
linkvillepress@gmail.com

ISBN-13: 978-1-947794-13-9
ISBN-10: 1-947794-13-2

A portion of all proceeds goes to Villalobos Rescue Center.
vrcpitbull.com

This book is dedicated to my mom for supporting my passion, to Alex for his listening ear, and to Julia for believing in my storytelling.

Death is a fickle thing. No one can see it coming nor do they realize its unforgiving nature. Humans are a vulnerable race and many times they forget that. I never imagined that death would have such an impact on my life. It both built and destroyed relationships while ripping away the people I held most dear. It hunted me with an eagerness that made me ill. It lurked everywhere just waiting to take another part of me, but it will never win. I will be the one to decide my own fate. After all, no one lives forever. Not even me.

Chapter One

"**L**ucy Faye Gaskin!" A frail, but loud voice called.

"What?"

"Get your behind out of bed before I come up there!"

Her grandmother's seriousness was projected through the halls and into her ears as she carefully opened one eye at a time. With a groan, Lucy pushed her bangs up out of her face and attempted to check the time. Slowly, as she readjusted herself, the digital clock's glowing numbers came into view. It was only nine o'clock the morning after high school graduation and she knew there was nowhere she had to be. Freedom was finally a reality and her plans to sleep past noon were dashed.

Grumbling incoherently, Lucy threw her comforter aside and shuttered at the cold wind coming from her window-mounted air conditioner. Goosebumps quickly formed and she sighed deeply as she stood.

"Lucy! Tryp and Rae are here. Hurry yourself, child," her grandmother's voice chimed once more. Lucy could only laugh.

Her namesake, Lucinda Morton, was an old-fashioned lady who tried her best to raise her only grandchild. They were the only family each other had after Lucy's parents died. Lucinda stepped into a mother role immediately to save her granddaughter from foster care.

As long as Lucy could remember, her Grammy had had a bun

of white hair securely plastered to her head, rectangle spectacles on the very end of her nose, and clothes that looked like they were from the 1920s. Everything about her screamed old and Lucy wouldn't have it any other way.

Cursing under her breath for nearly forgetting, Lucy flipped and folded her bedding, a required chore, before bolting across the hallway to the bathroom. She quickly pulled her hair up into a messy ponytail, washed her face, and brushed her teeth before applying the slightest amount of makeup. Afterward she gave the look a good once over. Lucy was proud of the blue eyes that her mother had given her and in the left eye was a single dash of green from her father.

Thanks to her grandmother, Lucy's parents had become more of a memory and less of a mystery. She was always free to ask questions regarding her folks and Lucinda promised to always tell the truth. Lucy asked very few. She had old pictures to remind her of their love and most of the time it was all she needed. Over the years, she acquired the stories of how her late parents met and of how their love had flourished. She also learned of her mother's love of rain and her father's love of cats.

"Your daddy would have had twenty or more had your momma been more lenient, but he loved you above all his pets, even over your mom, I sometimes thought," Lucinda had once told her. This was the memory she loved the most even if she didn't actually remember it.

Lucy soon finished her morning routine with a wink at her reflection. She quickly threw on a pair of jeans and a t-shirt before running downstairs. Her eyes scanned the windows in the living room as she passed. Blooming May flowers waiting to be planted filled their front porch. Lucinda would do that every year around that time. The sky was clouded and yet the sun shone through, warming the pavement and evaporating the dew. The town was busy that day, as many people crowded the streets and sidewalks. She found it unusual for a Monday.

As her eyes followed the people, Lucy's grandmother grabbed her wrist and caused a terrified gasp to escape before she jerked away.

"Lucy?" The old woman remarked to her granddaughter's strange behavior, but as the situation lengthened a wrinkled smile emerged and her expression softened, "good morning sleepy head.

Breakfast is ready." Though distracted, Lucy blankly scanned the table and atmosphere before a grin found its way to her face, "I'm not really hungry," she nearly whined.

"Humor me and have a seat." Before Lucy could deny her for a second time, Lucinda's wrinkled fingers found their way around her wrist again and, with a smile, she pulled her to the dining room. The old woman pointed to a seat across from Lucy's two friends.

Rae and Tryp were already seated and fighting over rights to the largest pancake. Fond memories of many suppers at that same antique wooden table flashed into Lucy's mind, but that part of life was closing quickly and the urge to hold on was getting stronger.

Rae's curly blonde hair was now streaked with a light blue dye that matched her eyes. She had always been an advocate of self-expression and was thrilled when she was finally free to carry out her dream. Their school would have never allowed unnatural hair colors. Graduation was an escape for her. The crippling hold that the school had over Rae's creativity was now severed and she was, in her own words, free. She had always been creative—a talent that had come from her parents. Rae's mom was a well-known photographer and her father recreated famous works of art for museums, libraries, and other places. He also wrote a comic strip in his free time for The Publisher, a popular local newspaper.

Rae had a good life and was lucky to have a large inheritance coming in the next year, which would keep her comfortable for the rest of it. Fun-loving and crazy, she was considered the friend of few, but Lucy loved her eccentrics. She could always count on Rae to be peculiar. Even this morning, she wore a cerulean blue dress with a large yellow belt, giant green hoop earrings, and red high tops. These strange styles were all too familiar to Lucy, as she could easily recall some of the odd outfits from the past.

Tryp was the son of an impressive family as well. His father flew all over the world for coffee beans and seemed to be a fan of being on the road. He was never at home for very long. Tryp's mom had died in childbirth and he quickly became used to seeing various nannies more often than his own father. In true rebellion, Tryp enjoyed spending his dad's money and, because of this, he always wore the best clothes. He had movie star looks that made most girls in their school melt at the sight of him. He never had to try hard for female attention.

They had always been the odd trio. Rae was weird and artsy. Lucy was shy and smart. Tryp was popular and athletic.

The two of them finally noticed Lucy and both greeted her before Rae stole the largest pancake and stuck her tongue out at Tryp. She smiled as she mocked him and batted her eyelashes.

"Well just look at you," Lucinda began as her granddaughter took a seat among her friends, "Lucinda, Renee, and Trypsin; my kids all grown up and graduated. I love you all so much!" She smiled lovingly as they all cringed at hearing their full names spoken aloud.

"Thank you for breakfast, Mrs. Morton," Tryp nodded politely just before they began to eat. Lucy groaned and simply gnawed on a piece of sausage as her friends gorged. They remained silent until Lucinda left the room.

"Are you going to the festival tonight?" Tryp blurted out at Lucy as he grabbed his glass of orange juice and took a swig.

"I'm planning to," Lucy answered, even though her mind was elsewhere.

"Good. You guys should come visit me. I'm face-painting in the bingo tent." Rae seemed overly pleased with her answer. They continued to eat for a short while until Tryp finished off the stack of pancakes that he had asked Lucinda to make.

Lucy could only listen to the mindless conversation going on between her two friends. It was a common occurrence for the three of them. Rae and Tryp were always talkative and Lucy was more than happy to just sit back and listen. After a few more minutes, each of them thanked her grandmother for the meal again before she excused them and they were able to venture out into the beautiful day.

The bright yellow sun had the sky to itself now. It was cool for May in Ohio, but then the running joke of Ohio weather was its unpredictability.

"It's going to rain tonight," Rae smiled and sounded so sure.

"Really? You should be on the news, Rae. You haven't been wrong yet." Tryp shoved her gently before they headed down the alley behind Lucy's house.

"No. If I go public I will start getting the weather wrong 'cause those weather people never seem to get it right." She shook her head and glanced at Lucy.

"What's the matter, Luce?" Rae drew attention from herself. It was then that they both noticed Lucy staring off into space, as she often did.

"Nothing, I thought I saw something," she blurted, which was a half-lie. Lucy had in fact been distracted, not by something, but by someone.

Lately she had been catching strangers staring at her, which truthfully wouldn't have bothered her at all if they had looked away when she caught them. Instead, they made eye contact and didn't blink until she looked away. Then she would look back and they would be gone. This had been going on for weeks and she hadn't told a soul.

It wasn't that she didn't want to, but the moment she looked away the features of these people vanished from her mind. She could remember seeing them and still feeling the fear they aroused in her, but not one memory of their appearance would remain. For this reason she hadn't told a soul of their existence. What good would it do if she couldn't remember their faces?

"Lucy," Tryp nudged her in the arm, "whatever's going on, you can tell us."

"It's nothing. Don't worry about me. Let's go watch this stupid parade, huh?" Lucy shrugged off their concern and watched their expressions of worry fade before they headed towards the main road.

Living in a timeless town might have seemed like a bore to most, but it was the neighborly closeness that Lucy enjoyed. She knew nearly everyone in the town or at least had seen them before. The atmosphere never seemed to change; the people only got older. She was proud to know that she could walk the streets blindfolded and still find her way around. They had one restaurant, a gas station, a grocery store, and a formidable park that hosted a large festival one week out of the year. Lucy's home was perfect for her.

As they got to the edge of the parade route, the high school marching band started up. It marched through the streets led by the only father figure Lucy had ever had, Charles Livonstervaff. To avoid mispronunciations, he was also known as Mr. L. She waved to them as they passed and then watched the remainder of the parade. Clowns from a nearby clown college honked by, along with several barking dogs and their handlers from the local humane society. There were also baton twirlers and various polished old cars, some with people on top and others with occupants who threw candy to young bystanders.

Together they observed and enjoyed the parade, although a feeling that she was being watched still loomed in the back of Lucy's mind. Finally, the emergency vehicles came with horns blaring and lights flickering. The noise quickly became an annoyance for Lucy and she covered her ears for a moment and backed away from the road. This part of the parade wasn't exactly her favorite.

Then, out of nowhere, a crippling pain struck her right wrist and she jerked it into her view. Lucy's disbelief nearly drowned her and shock quickly became overwhelming as she stared at a large gash in her wrist. It extended from the very bottom of the back of her hand to the center of her wrist and through several veins. Blood began to run down her arm in streams of warmth. Lucy had never been hurt so badly. She could feel panic take over and, though she tried, cries of help wouldn't come to her lips.

All eyes remained on the parade while she took a few steps back onto the sidewalk and marveled at the pool of blood that was where she had been standing. The pain was soon overpowering and Lucy wrapped her fingers around her wrist as she fell back onto the grassy hill of her neighbor's yard. Sounds from the parade faded out and she quickly became weak and cold.

Though her vision became blurry, Lucy watched as Rae looked over to Tryp with a puzzled look and then nudged him with a few words between them. After two more seconds of confusion, Rae happened to glance back and Lucy watched her eyes grow wide as her mouth moved to, "Oh my god! Lucy!" Moments later Tryp was at her side, along with a half dozen others.

One man took off his belt and made a tourniquet on her upper arm, while one of the ladies mumbled incoherently as she tore the hem of her dress and wrapped the fabric around Lucy's wound. They slowly tried to get her to stand, but the effects of blood loss were apparent and she could not remain upright.

After many tries, Tryp grew impatient and scooped Lucy into his arms before running off toward her house. Many people tried to stop him, but those who got in his way were plowed through until he got to her front door and slipped inside.

"What is going on?" Lucy's grandmother demanded as she entered their living room and took in the scene.

"Lucy's hurt. She lost a lot of blood this time." Tryp frowned with concern after setting Lucy on the couch.

"I will tend to her and you may go control the crowd," she snapped sternly before turning to fetch her medical supplies. Tryp nodded and hurried Rae outside before slamming the door.

Before long, Lucinda returned with an armful of bandage supplies. "Is anything broken?"

Lucy, though barely conscious, shook her head with a groan.

"What happened? Can you tell me that?" When there was no answer she continued to clean the wound.

After a pile of alcohol-soaked cotton was used and Lucy had stopped squealing from the pain, Lucinda slathered the cut with a sticky yellow balm and began wrapping it with stretchy gauze. Two layers of the gauze went on, along with self-adhesive tape that would keep the bandage snug. Finally, Lucinda helped her granddaughter up and handed her a juice box. The only thing Lucy had asked for was some form of pain killer, which her Grammy denied her. "We don't have any and even if we did I will not take the chance of it having some sort of blood thinner in it," she said with a smile. "Now, what happened?"

"All I remember is pain and then blood. So much blood." Lucy frowned and asked, "Can I still go to the festival tonight?" There was a long silence.

"I suppose, but only if you rest first," her wrinkles grew and faded as she spoke. Lucinda kissed Lucy's forehead before leaving the room and Lucy tried her best to sleep. She could feel the tension of that morning slowly leave and the calm of sanctuary enter, which was all that was needed to plunge Lucy into a dream.

Later that evening, Lucy found that the house had become dark and an eerie silence had invaded its walls. She sat up from the couch and rubbed her eyes before checking her wrist. Her memory returned to her in swift bursts. There was a cause for her injury—a long, curved knife. She remembered it well enough now and began to describe it to herself as she pictured it in her head. The blade was at least six inches long and was serrated, except for a smooth, curved edge at the tip. It looked like a hunting knife.

For a moment, Lucy was afraid to leave her spot and venture into the dark house, since the presence of an unknown assailant was still possible. Was it someone she knew or a stranger? Could the faceless people be behind the attack? The thought of those she couldn't describe launched her from her seat and to the nearest lamp. She flipped it on and watched as the sudden burst of light chased the shadows from the room. Lucy felt a sigh of relief. She was alone.

Her head pounded in unison with her growling stomach. It had been nearly ten hours since breakfast. A primal urge suddenly struck her and forced her into the kitchen. A high-pitched ringing filled her ears. With a swift pull, Lucy flung the fridge door open hard enough that the hinge threw it back at her with a snap. She snatched the left-over sausage with a groan.

Nothing was more sickening than cold meat, in her opinion. Wordless grumbling was all that filled the silence as Lucy literally threw the links in the microwave and punched in a few numbers. The countdown seemed to take forever and as her patience dwindled her hunger got to be sickening. Lucy found some cold pizza hiding in the refrigerator and ate it using as few bites as possible. She continued onto the sausages once the microwave beeped. They weren't the most pleasing, but she didn't care. When the ache of hunger had gone, Lucy changed her bloody clothes and removed her bandages before fixing her hair and makeup. She took another deep breath and let it go with a sigh. The house was dark and empty. She wondered if it got lonely while they were gone. The thought was amusing and she set her face with a smile as she left the hauntingly dark walls.

A rush of evening air entered Lucy's lungs as she stepped through the doorway and out into the night. The front yard was nearly covered in fireflies. The smell of dew already filled the air. It was at least nine o'clock and she assumed the festival was in full bloom even though guessing was unnecessary. From where she stood, Lucy could see a warm glow in the sky coming from the neon lights. They hovered over her destination like a beacon.

Then, without warning, the fear of night drifted through her. She knew that somewhere nearby the nameless, faceless strangers were watching. She knew that they were the same people who had hurt her. Even her advanced healing power hadn't erased her hatred of those who would cause her pain.

Lucy knew that she had no need to dread the slow healing process of normal people, since as long as she could remember her body healed itself unbelievably fast. It wasn't instantaneous, but cuts from hiking or scrapes from a bicycle wreck had always been gone within an hour or so. The wound she now carried had never been the source of her anxiety. It was the thought of a stranger hurting or perhaps killing her that was her cause for concern. When she saw the damage that should've needed stitches, Lucy didn't feel afraid. She hadn't seen the inside of a hospital since Lucinda took her on their first trip.

She fondly remembered the dumbstruck look on her Grammy's face when the pediatrician told her that her granddaughter was completely healthy. The broken ulna bone and various scrapes and bruises that ten-year-old Lucy had suffered after falling down the stairs had taken less than an hour to heal. Lucinda, however, was not convinced and requested x-rays just to be sure. There was an obvious healed break, but it appeared to be very old. After that day, Lucinda never took her to the doctor. She always bandaged Lucy up and let her body take care of the impossible healing that the doctors never could've done.

The warm lights of the festival were soon upon her face. There was an atmosphere of pure excitement that was very thick. Lucy entered the rear of the festival between the game booths and the rides, which were located on a gravel parking lot behind the parks. She looked fondly at the flipping and spinning cars before passing by the game booths on her way to where Rae said she would be. Lucy couldn't help but smile to herself as she listened for the invitations to play various games. She turned down the vendors politely and made her way into a sea of food stands. To Lucy, nothing smelled better than fair food. The combination of fried items and mouth-watering flavor wafted through the air and made her stomach growl. Every fiber of her being ached for fries and it was devastating to deny that urge. She soon passed through the bingo tent and began searching for Rae. It didn't take long to find her.

There was a long line of children at a very short table where Rae and her mom were sitting. Lucy walked up with a smile and stood behind them as they did some of the most elaborate face paintings possible. Not only did they surpass the common face painting usually seen, but they also decorated each child's face unbelievably fast and even made a stack of money in tips from grateful parents. Lucy watched several amazing paint jobs, which included a tiger, a fairy princess, and a dinosaur. She was constantly amazed at the full-face transformations and waited impatiently for the line to shorten. As Rae began a zombie likeness on a little boy, Tryp arrived and joined Lucy without a word. They waited in silence until Rae was done and the boy had hopped down from his chair.

"Ready?" Tryp asked to all who were listening.

"I can't leave yet. We're too busy. Come get me in an hour, before the fireworks start." She smiled and dismissed them as another little boy plopped himself in the chair and begged for a puppy dog.

Tryp and Lucy left the table and walked together back through the food stands and towards the games. As they strolled, Tryp took a large wad of money from his pocket.

"I'm buying tonight. Games and rides—let's spend it all," he said as he grinned wildly.

"Tryp, you've got to stop stealing from your dad," Lucy warned with a grin. "Eventually he's going to figure out that you hacked his bank account."

"He's never home long enough and he won't miss two hundred. Relax, Luce. I want to have a good time tonight. When I leave for college there will be no more fun."

"Really? Schools like yours have parties all the time. You won't get bored, trust me," she assured him and swiped the money from his palm with a smirk. "Enough scolding—let's play some games."

"Rides first. I don't want to have to lug all of my winnings around." He gauged her reaction and then laughed at Lucy's doubtfulness.

"Fine, rides first."

Together they walked past the game booths and rejected the many playing offers that came at them. The ticket booth was lit up in blue and green lights that blinked sporadically, which made it very easy to spot. Tryp retrieved his money from Lucy and left her briefly to join the line of people. She watched him disappear among the crowd and was briefly filled with a familiar sense of fear. It was the fear of being alone that left her paralyzed. Luckily it didn't last long.

Tryp returned shortly and attached a wristband to Lucy's arm. "Ready?" With a nod from her, they entered the gravel parking lot arm in arm and watched the spinning lights of the rides before them. Lucy immediately ran to her favorite ride, the swinging ship called 'Sky Voyage.'

For what seemed like hours they rode ride after ride and enjoyed each other's company. Besides the swinging ship there was a small Ferris wheel, a four-armed spinning ride, a large slide, a U.F.O-shaped contraption, and a child-sized roller coaster called 'Dragon's Wing.' Out of all the rides, they rode the four-armed one the most. Lucy enjoyed the sight of spinning lights that twirled before her. They lit up Tryp's face in a way that suddenly made her understand his ease with girls at high school.

Lucy had never noticed before, but he was truly a beautiful person. His eyes were the brightest hazel color that was brought out even more by the honey glow of his skin.

As they exited the same ride for the fourteenth time, Tryp glanced at his watch and cursed under his breath.

"What?" Lucy wondered aloud.

"I have to go and get Rae. The fireworks should start any minute now. Stay here; I'll be right back." Before she could stop him, Tryp had escaped her reach and disappeared into the crowd.

Lucy could do no more than stare at the disappearing gap he had entered. Her stomach became uneasy and the air around her soon became frigid. Goosebumps grew on her arms and legs, and suddenly it seemed as if time was slowing down. Then, she noticed something in the crowd.

A dark-haired man was standing amongst the moving people. They wouldn't come within a few feet of him and didn't even seem to notice he was standing there. It was like he was in a bubble that no one else could enter. Lucy knew exactly who he was.

One of the faceless people had come for her and unfortunately she was alone. He stood without blinking for what seemed like hours. She tried her best to stare back. For some reason, she wanted him to stay. She wanted someone else to notice him besides her. She hoped that Tryp and Rae would return before her eyes grew too dry, but in time Lucy could feel the fatigue growing within her and her eyes began to water. She allowed the tears to drip down her cheeks and onto the gravel below. Regret came swiftly as she realized that she couldn't keep her eyes open any longer. Lucy prepared to say farewell to the faceless man once again and deliberately closed her eyes. She knew that he would be gone just like always. She was ready and she only waited a matter of seconds before reopening her eyes.

A cry escaped her lips and she nearly lost her balance as she discovered that he had not fled. Time became irrelevant then. The lights blinked slower and the people barely moved. It was an impossibility that he was causing. Within a few seconds, everything around them had literally paused. Lucy lost all hope of being rescued. No one could come to her aid now. They had all been frozen at the will of the man she came to realize would be her murderer.

He was now standing less than two feet from her with a slight grin on his vastly changed appearance. The man's usually small, dark eyes were now nearly twice their normal size and completely black, while his features had gotten smooth and sharp. There were silver marks above his brow and his dark hair had become longer and jet-black. The transformation was subtle and still somewhat drastic. She was more terrified than she had ever been in her entire life. Lucy looked him over again. The whites of his eyes had vanished and the blackness that was left held her reflection well. His skin was pale white to the point of glowing. Above everything else, his eyes were the worst of his appearance. They bore into Lucy, making her cringe in anxiousness. The faceless man, though he was clearly stuck in her memory now, would always be a figment of the shadows. He would always be faceless.

With his blank expression nearly twisted, the man lifted one of his clawed hands, which were scarred and tortured with sharpened fingernails. Then Lucy noticed him grow more vicious in a way. His hand found its way to her throat and he squeezed until it became uncomfortable. He hadn't tried to yet, but Lucy assumed he would cause her death. The doom that she felt was reflected back at her in his bottomless eyes.

For a moment, she thought her life would flash before her or something, but it didn't, and after that disappointment, her fear melted away. She felt nothing. Lucy was left to his mercy with the cold sting of impending death close at hand. She could feel his fingernails pressing into her neck and eventually the constant pressure felt as if it was drawing blood. He did nothing else. It was torture.

The man looked at her closely as if he was unsure of something. He stared into her eyes for a long time. His breathing became harsher. His grip loosened slightly, which took the pressure away from his claws, but still held her in a way that she couldn't escape his touch. Lucy glanced away from him for a brief second. Tryp and Rae were nowhere to be found.

Finally, the man's face grew wild and Lucy realized that the time had come to die, but before he could continue in murder a strong gust of wind pushed between them and knocked his hand away, the force so powerful she fell to the ground. Lucy looked around for the source and found that it had not been the wind. A foreign arm had knocked the man away with such force that it even pushed him back a couple of steps. Amazed, she followed the arm up to its body and quickly drank in the person who had saved her.

His smooth and tan skin made his blue eyes ignite with the same ferocity as the cerulean color of Rae's dress that morning. Lucy watched him launch a spinning kick at the strange man. His wavy blonde hair danced as if loaded with springs rather than simple curls. He had the same beauty that Tryp was blessed with. His loose t-shirt and unzipped jacket flailed wildly as the fight progressed.

Though this new man was well versed in what seemed to be martial arts, the faceless man hadn't become helpless. He was blocking and dishing out the same amazing ability in the battle. The blonde man's fists moved like lightning. He pounded open palms in the faceless man's shoulders, knocking him off balance. Then, using a swift spinning kick, he forced him to the ground. Lucy watched her attacker glare up at the golden-haired man with a scowl that revealed more hatred than she had ever seen from anyone. The fight was over.

The faceless man sat on the ground, but remained as intense as before. Though the golden-haired man stood between them, Lucy could feel his stare. The power of his gaze kept her from moving. Finally the golden man demanded his attention and spoke to Lucy's attacker quietly for a couple of seconds. Lucy couldn't hear what he was saying, but it was effective. The faceless man nodded blankly and stood before sulking away into the unmoving crowd without another glance at his victim.

Lucy didn't know what to do. Her vision drifted back over to the man who had saved her. He stood firm and protective until he was positive that all threats had vanished. His shoulders were shifted backward in a defensive stance and his chest was pushed outward. All of a sudden, the lights began to come back on. They blinked slowly while the crowd remained motionless. People were paused in conversation, whether they had been standing or walking to places unknown.

The man looked down to Lucy. His expression was kind, but fierce still. She shuttered as the wind started to circulate again. She hadn't even noticed it had stopped until it blew her hair into her face, which she immediately struggled to remove. Hesitating once, she stood and moved to step towards her mystery hero, but he moved from her reach at once. The moment he did this, she became infuriated. Lucy could feel her cheeks begin to burn with frustration.

"Thank you," she managed to mutter through her teeth. Lucy had never had trouble speaking before. Though she was shy, it had never been a problem to say what needed to be said. She choked on her words for a moment and then waited for a response. The world around them began to speed up again until it returned to the pace she was accustomed to. The man didn't give her a reply. He ignored her as if he was deaf and wouldn't even turn around to acknowledge her thanks.

Maybe if she hadn't persisted, he wouldn't have left. What if she had waited for the thrill of the fight to run out of his veins before she approached? That, however, was not the case and there was no way that she could know what would have happened. Lucy attempted to see his face, but then when she tried, he left her immediately and vanished into the crowd.

Lucy nearly swallowed her tongue when she realized that he was gone. By the time she caught her breath, the crowd had begun to surround her. The pain and emptiness of being alone took almost no time to dissolve and to be replaced by every good feeling she knew. She could feel tears hit her cheeks, but couldn't muster the energy it would take to wipe them away. Lucy stood on her own in the way of the passing crowd for what seemed like forever before she saw Tryp emerge from the sea of faces. He had Rae by the arm and they were laughing as if nothing had happened. Lucy was disgusted by their laughter for only moments before she realized the situation that had nearly destroyed her affected no one else. In more ways than one, she was alone and that scared her more than anything. For them, nothing had happened.

"Luce? Are you okay?"

She heard Tryp's question and could only nod. She felt as if her voice would break if she used it. Rae's look of concern bothered her to the point that she forced a smile and wiped her tears. "I'm fine. It took you long enough."

"I was gone less than a minute, Lucy." Tryp now had the same look of concern.

"I'm fine. Let's go watch the damn fireworks," she groaned before storming off in the direction of the ball fields.

Behind the police station and gravel parking lot were a series of ball fields used primarily for baseball in the spring and soccer in the fall. In total, her hometown had six of them, four of which were just beyond the swinging ship. In Lucy's mind, six was far too many, but when the time came for those sports the town was busy. Besides the festival, those were the times out of the year when the most money was made, and though she tried, Lucy couldn't hate the fact that the city council kept the fields rather than building something she considered more useful.

The three of them made their way behind the swinging ship, watching it carry passengers through a stomach-churning ride. They entered the nearest fence and stood with a group of people waiting for the beginning of the show. After a few minutes, a loud pop signaled the beginning of the display. Then came a brilliant explosion of red that dispersed in all directions, which was joined by a louder boom. More flashes followed and Lucy found herself lost in the spray of colors.

In the farthest baseball field, she could see caution tape and watched as a team of people handled and launched the fireworks. A small sliver of red moon faded in and out with the man-made explosions. Lucy glanced over at her friends. With every pop of pyrotechnics, light hit their faces and cast unnatural shadows over their features. The same shadows forced her to relive the faceless man's confrontation again and again until she found the strength to look away.

The memory of that encounter burned in her and as she watched the fire explode in the night, Lucy saw the face of the blonde man again. Every time a firework lit the sky she saw him in the flash. His curly blonde hair, blue eyes, and fair features invaded her mind. She found it satisfying that she could remember him, but it also haunted her that she could now remember the faceless man as well. The light of the fireworks gave her this unknown man's golden face while the dark left the fearsome features of the monster that had attacked her. Lucy had become accustomed to the feeling of fear that the faceless people gave her, but now it was the uncertainty that lashed out at her. Every time a burst of light faded into black, it was like the attack was beginning all over again.

The trio watched the brilliant explosions carefully as Lucy overheard her friends attempting to guess the color of the next one. While they were occupied, she glanced around between the sound-shattering booms. Lucy knew that if another attack happened she wouldn't be able to save her friends, let alone herself. She looked at the faces of those around them.

All of the observers seemed to be interested in the festivities except for one. The distance between them was so great that she almost overlooked him. Lucy stared at the man for a few minutes before he glanced over. She felt her heart drop into her stomach. The golden-haired man who saved her hadn't left. He quickly looked away and nudged two of the people he was standing with. Both of them glanced at Lucy and together they turned and began to walk back into the crowd.

"Wait!" she screamed, to the surprise of her friends.

Before Tryp or Rae could stop her, Lucy was on her feet and running towards where the three people had disappeared into the firework spectators. She hadn't expected to see him again, so when the man did appear, Lucy had to at least try to talk with him. The crowd parted for her as she ran past them to catch up with the golden-haired man. It didn't take long for her to emerge on the other side, but he was already gone and so were the people he was with.

Lucy couldn't remain standing. She fell to her knees and the large chunks of gravel crunched under her weight. Her tears were no longer confinable and fell freely onto her cheeks and the rocks below. Lucy sobbed quietly and almost breathlessly until her friends came to her side.

"Luce," she heard Tryp sigh under his breath, "I guess the festival might have been too much after this morning."

"Tryp, we should take her home," Lucy heard Rae whisper before they stooped to lift her from the ground. After she got her footing, Lucy shook them off and headed toward the main road, followed closely by her friends.

It was a quiet walk home. She could hear their scuffing shoes behind her, but she tried concentrating on the sidewalk beneath her feet. Before long they had come to her street.

"You guys can go home. I need sleep." She grimaced as she turned to face them.

"Lucy, I don't know how to say this, but we've been talking. Lately you've been acting weird and we don't know how to help you, but we're here for you when you need us. Don't forget that," Tryp said then grinned before pulling Rae into a shoulder to shoulder hug.

"What I need is space, Tryp. I love you guys, but I want to figure this out on my own," Lucy shrugged as she turned back around.

"What is there to figure out? Tell us what it is. There is something there. We've been friends for a long time and we can tell when you are being bothered," Rae began to push, which was causing Lucy to withdraw even more.

"I'm tired," she whined as the tears began again.

"Tired?" Tryp mumbled before she could continue.

"Tired. Tired of fearing every person I come into contact with." She pushed the words through her teeth, "I'm tired of being different. I know that I am alone in the way I feel and I'm scared of that too." Without another word between them, Lucy entered her house as her friends helplessly watched.

The dark home was welcoming this time. It was security from questions that Lucy didn't have answers to. She wished that it could be as simple as telling them about the faceless hunters or her rescue and the pause of time. It would never be that easy. She knew that. Lucy could tell no one and be taken seriously.

Cold air passed her as she opened her bedroom door. On the second floor it was always hot and she left her air conditioning on, against her grandmother's wishes. The bitterly frigid air was a welcome comfort and just before she closed the door a noise came from the other side. She opened it and peered into the dark. Nothing was there.

She finally closed it with a sigh and turned on the light. Her room was simple and welcoming. Lucy took a moment to count her blessings before she took the rubber band out of her hair and let it fall to her shoulders. Then, as she went to pull back her blanket, a white cat leaped onto the bed and she nearly tripped backward.

"Avalanche! You scared me silly, kitty!" The cat's long, fine, white hair spread out in all directions as he curled up on the bed, his bright blue eyes following her while she changed clothes.

The young feline stretched himself across the foot of her bed and looked through the window to watch the passing cars below. Lucy had purposely pushed her bed up against the wall so that the foot of it was level with the window. Avalanche loved to watch the cars and this arrangement kept him from sitting in the dust that had gathered near the glass.

Lucy tucked herself in and watched him with a smile as he yawned with another stretch and revealed the sharp fangs hiding beneath his lips. No one ever believed her when she said that she had found him as a stray kitten and she understood why. He was a very beautiful animal and she would sooner think he came from a breeder than the streets.

Avalanche was a true friend. Lucy could talk to him about anything and he understood completely, listened until she was done, and didn't ask questions. She was happy that Lucinda let her keep him.

For nearly two hours, her faithful companion listened to her recount the events of that day without moving more than an inch. When she was finished, Lucy let out a sigh and, as if on cue, the white cat got up and walked to the head of the bed. He gently climbed behind her, laid down, and began to purr wildly.

"Thanks, handsome. You really know how to cheer me up," she cooed before settling into a sleep-ready state. After a while, Lucy fell asleep with the sound of a purring cat in her ear and the vision of a golden man in her head. What a dream it should've been.

Chapter Two

The night was long and memories of what had happened were still fresh when she awoke. Lucy not only had been seeing unexplainable things such as the appearance and disappearance of the faceless people, but she also experienced something impossible—the time delay that had taken hold of the moment she should have died. It scared her to know that she had been part of so many odd things that most people have never seen, and something inside her kept hold on those things. It was like the abnormal was being thrust at her and so far there was nothing she could do to stop it. She couldn't even dream—it was simply dark.

It was all she could think about even as a strange noise appeared in her head. It was a tapping of some kind. It was faint and growing louder by the minute. The tapping echoed. It was like a knock on a metal door that reverberated through emptiness.

Finally, Lucy opened her eyes and forced herself out of the dreamless sleep that she had been suffering through. The tapping continued even outside of sleep. It was coming from the window.

Lucy quickly pinched herself just to be sure and then sat up from her pillow. Her eyebrows drew together in concentration before she crawled forward to where Avalanche was sitting. He was watching something with a very intense set of baby-blue eyes. Lucy followed his stare and was shocked to see a familiar face perched just outside her window. Out on the roof that extended from the glass was the golden-haired man from the festival.

He was badly bloodied and beaten. His golden hair was soaked red from a gash in his head that had stopped dripping and his lip was cracked open as well. Though his wounds appeared painful, the man did not seem to be hurting. His eyes studied every inch of her that he could see and then they focused on her eyes. The connection was long and almost uncomfortable, but eventually it broke as he fixed his gaze on the bottom of the window.

Lucy quickly slid up the glass so that the screen was still between them, and before he could speak she flung a finger to her lips and asked, "What are you doing here?"

"I had to make sure you were alright," he said gently. His voice was calm and angelic. It nearly rang from his throat like bells. He had a subtle air to his voice and spoke with an accent. His voice completely matched the way that Lucy assumed he would sound: sophisticated and somber at the same time.

"What happened to you?" She spoke her thoughts before she could stop herself.

"It doesn't matter now. You're safe and I'm happy for that." The first emotion she ever saw from him lit his face. It was the feeling of relief.

With a brief moment of thinking, Lucy removed the screen and threw it to the floor as Avalanche hid under her bed. "Come in. Stay until whoever hurt you is gone."

"Thank you. I don't know where my family is. We got ambushed by—" He stopped himself immediately and cleared his throat.

"You can tell me, you know. It was the faceless man, wasn't it?" The man paused and considered his response.

"Yes, and his friends."

"What are they?"

"I can't tell you. If I wasn't afraid for both of our lives, you and I wouldn't be talking at all." The golden man glanced back at the window and shut it. He locked the top and pulled the shutter down, barricading that with pillows.

"What's your name?" At that question, Lucy watched his face grow pale and he shuttered before answering, "Sebastian. My name is Sebastian and that's what you can call me.

Though she tried, Lucy could see that he wouldn't give her

information that she didn't need to know, so she attempted kindness, hoping it would loosen his tongue.

"I'm Lucy. Thank you for saving me, by the way. I never did properly thank you." She smiled and stood from the bed as she headed to the door.

"Where are you going?"

"I'll come back. Stay here," Lucy ordered before slipping beyond the door. She saw Avalanche follow out of the corner of her eye.

She made her way to the large closet in the hallway where Lucinda kept all of the bandaging supplies. Lucy filled her arms with equipment and then made her way back into the room. She was pleased and surprised to find Sebastian sitting where she had left him. He simply stared at the ceiling at if it were a starry night. Lucy cleared her throat to gain his attention, but as he looked at her, his eyes dulled.

"What's that for?" His blue eyes followed her as she set what she was carrying on the bed and crossed her arms.

"Hold still and let me take care of those cuts before they get infected." As she said this he became hesitant, but Lucy wasn't afraid. After insisting, he allowed her access to his wounds with a sigh.

Lucy poured alcohol on a rag and moved it to the cut covered in dried blood. She grinned to herself in the anticipation of the pain it was about to cause, but the second it touched his skin Lucy made more noise than he did. Sebastian didn't even flinch. He sat still as a statue and waited for her to be done. She rubbed at his bloody forehead for a couple of minutes in search of the cut that had bled so profusely, but she couldn't seem to find it. She even searched through his hair and hairline without success.

"Where are you hurt? I don't see anything," Lucy whispered in his ear.

"I was going to tell you that you won't need those supplies."

"What about all of this blood? It isn't the faceless man's, is it?"

"Oh, no, it's mine." He grinned before removing the alcohol and wipe from her hand.

"Lucy,"—she nearly fainted when he said her name—"I was hurt and now I'm not. Don't worry about it."

"What are you?" she asked.

"A person just like you, and I'm more of a person than those 'faceless' people you fear. Like I said, you don't have to worry. I'm here to protect you; not the other way around." A grin found its way back to his face and he nodded before checking on the world outside through her bedroom window. "Lock this window from now on."

"How can you just confuse me like that and leave?" Her confusion switched to frustration instantly.

"Because it's what you need to hear. Lock the window, right?" He flashed a toothy smile and dashed out of the window and into the night.

Lucy bit her lip and did as he asked. Her mind was racing so fast that keeping up wasn't even in the cards. Dizzy, she lay on the bed and let a single tear fall from her eye. The rumble of her air conditioner was all that she could hear aside from her own breathing. She kept glancing at the window where her 'protector' had disappeared. It was strange that he was willing to risk himself for her life, and though she wondered why, Lucy wasn't bothered by it. She sat up with a shiver and opened the door for an awaiting kitty. The young fluff ball bounded into her room and jumped to his favorite sleeping spot at the foot of the bed. She watched him, amused as he spun in circles before settling down.

Without another glance, Lucy returned the bandage supplies to where she had gotten them and checked on her grandmother. Lucy could only see a tuft of white hair under the blanket and was satisfied that all of her excitement hadn't disturbed the old woman. She rubbed Avalanche's head when she returned and he purred happily. Lucy tucked herself in, and with a sigh she closed her eyes.

It was all real, she decided with a smile. The golden-haired, angelic man had a name and, even better, he was there to save her from the faceless people, the ones who had been causing her grief for months. Sebastian was everything she needed right now. He was the normality she was missing, coupled with the weirdness that had always followed her. Lucy knew that he had more answers than what he had already given her, and she knew that she could wait for them. She didn't need every answer, but a few more wouldn't hurt. He could heal himself even faster than she could. This one fact was the most puzzling. It was then she knew that he had the answer to the one question she had been asking for over eight years. Sebastian had the answer to her abnormal abilities and he alone might know why she was being hunted by the faceless people. All of these thoughts kept Lucy awake for a while, thinking of possible answers to her questions. But before long exhaustion overtook her and she drifted off to sleep.

Days passed slowly and even though she remembered the night vividly, Lucy was starting to believe that she had dreamed it all. She had yet to see one of the faceless people or Sebastian, and her hopes of doing so were fading quickly. Lucy had returned to her friends and grandmother without revealing anything of what had happened, even though they tried to pry out details. It was hard to keep the secrets, but she knew that, until Sebastian told her otherwise, they would have to be kept.

One day the house was quiet and remained so as the sky turned orange with licks of purple and pink. Lucy hadn't left the house all day and hadn't planned to for the rest of the evening. Her grandmother was out at bingo with her friends, and Tryp and Rae were out at a movie. Lucy had been restricted to the house. Lucinda wanted to be certain that no harm would befall her while she was away.

Understanding her concern, Lucy politely stayed put instead of giving her grandmother more reasons to confine her. She was more than ready to occupy her time and made a meal out of ramen noodles before heading up to her room. She leaped onto her bed and opened the window to allow the cool night air in. Lucy glanced out the window in both directions as far as she could see. The street lights illuminated sections of the road and sidewalk enough that she felt comfortable with just the screen between her and the world.

In her room, she spent the remaining time before sleep sketching out a picture of the faceless man. Lucy knew she would never be as talented as Rae was, but she managed to convey an accurate portrait. Her eyes studied his basic outline and, with a nod, she began to add the shadows of his sunken features and some of the tattoos above his brow. Lucy gave him the crazy, bottomless, black eyes that she remembered and the wavy black hair that was left to hang on his shoulders. Her pencil gently traced his jaw outline and her focus immediately hardened. She was determined not to make a mistake.

"What is that?" The voice came so suddenly, Lucy nearly rolled off her bed to escape it. She snapped her head back and saw Sebastian's familiar golden locks. He had a cocky look on his face and seemed to enjoy the fact that she was so easily startled.

"What the hell! Why would you do that?"

"I was watching for a minute or so until I saw what it was. Of all the beauty in the world, why would you draw that?"

"I didn't want to forget what he looked like. For the longest time I knew I had seen them, but couldn't remember their faces. Now I remember and I wanted to draw him before I forgot," she explained the drawing and ended with a smirk.

"There is no need to draw them. It will only torture you. You won't forget them now that you know me." He sighed and sat down on the roof, facing the screen that separated them.

"Why? What affect do you have on me? How could they be slippery enough to mess with my memory anyway?"

"It isn't them. Your mind, the minds of humans and those raised by humans, develop a defense mechanism to protect you from those people. The ones who forget usually remain untouched, but those who remember draw unwanted attention." He ran through the facts as if he was used to reciting them. The words came out flawlessly and he explained them in a certain way that made them understandable even though they shouldn't have been.

"Is that why they keep showing up?"

"No, you said that you couldn't recall their appearances until after the festival. They are interested in you for other reasons.

"Which would be?" She hoped for an answer.

"No idea, but you must be important because they have never pursued a human like this."

"So I'll just stay under surveillance for the rest of my life? Sounds fun," she laughed to herself sarcastically, though she was happy that Sebastian would be around for a while.

"Not even. My family has been deployed to find out what they're up to. As soon as we know, we'll put a stop to it and you can live your life in peace," the blonde man finished with a flashy smile.

"Family? The two people with you that night, are they part of your family?"

"Yes. The taller man was Cyrus and the dark-haired lady was Syrina. They are on offense in the field with me and another guy named Mitchell."

"Just the four of you?"

Sebastian almost seemed hurt by the shock in her voice, but he shook it off and cleared his throat. "No, Allegra and Kieron are scientists. They are the defensive team, but can become offensive if the situation calls for it."

"Are you a special branch of the military?"

"No, we aren't. The U.S. knows nothing of us."

"Does anyone?"

"Not many humans." That particular statement was a red flag to Lucy.

"What does that mean? You keep saying humans as if...are you human?" Lucy watched Sebastian's stunned expression and remained silent as he thought through his response.

"I was and, in some ways, still am. I think like a human and empathize as well, but I am not considered human by many."

Lucy's confusion was growing and she knew that Sebastian could see it in her face. He studied her carefully and she watched him watch her. Even through the screen, Lucy could see regret pool in his eyes. She knew what was wrong. "I haven't and won't tell anyone. What are you?"

"That is something I am not prepared to discuss and it is something you aren't ready to hear."

"Fine then; good night," she scoffed and reached for the blinds. Lucy felt that if she could be honest then he could be too.

"Wait!" Sebastian nearly shouted. "I will tell you anything else. Please, don't shut me out. Just don't ask me about what I am. Other than that, I will be totally honest with you, however, I would like some answers too."

"Like what?"

"I'm not quite sure yet. Let's take turns. You ask me and I'll ask you. Sound good?"

"Am I allowed to refuse questions since you are?"

"I will stay clear of a certain group of questions if you want, but if I need the answer then you must tell me."

Sebastian rolled onto his back and put his hands under his

head. Lucy watched him. His chest barely moved as he took in breath after breath. She watched him for a couple more seconds before clearing her throat, "I promise."

"Fine then, I'll go first. How old are you?" Sebastian grinned as he stared up at the night sky.

"I'm eighteen. How old are you?"

"Seventy-six."

"I call bull. You promised you wouldn't lie," she jumped on him before he could say anything else.

"That was me keeping my promise. I am seventy-six years old." His voice didn't give anything away. He was calm and understanding.

She knew that he was telling the truth. "But, how can you be seventy-six?"

Sebastian gave her no answer. He continued to lay on his back with a smile. Lucy became angrier by the second. She knew he was purposely ignoring her. They remained in silence for a couple more minutes. She was too angry to speak and he was watching the stars, waiting for the conversation to continue.

"Aren't you going to answer me?"

"It wasn't your turn."

"For what?"

"To ask a question. It is, in fact, my turn to inquire as to what exactly you know about the faceless people." Sebastian's eyes glanced back over to Lucy. His eyes met hers and he didn't break the contact until she cleared her throat.

"You are infuriating! Fine, I don't remember much about them before what happened at the festival. All I ever knew was that they had been there. I remembered seeing them and felt the fear that they made me feel, but I couldn't remember their faces and so I told no one." She rolled to face him and watched his expression intensify and then soften as if he understood.

"That must've been terrible to endure." He frowned and glimpsed to the street to ensure they were still safe. The awkward silence lengthened as he took in the deepest breath he could muster and let it out.

"What was your life like?" she asked him, finally taking her turn.

"That's a very complicated question."

"But it is a question and that is within the rules of our agreement." A grin found its way to her face as she waited patiently for his answer.

"I was born in a small town on the eastern edge of England. My parents were middle class. My father was a lawyer and my mother took care of me and my two little sisters, Annetta and Adrienne. The last time I saw them was the day I met Cyrus."

"That's all I get?" She groaned and glanced at him hopefully.

"Where are your parents?" He frowned in the seriousness of his question and waited patiently for the answer.

"I don't know."

"Your caregiver must've told you something."

"My dad was Craig Gaskin and my mom was Annie Wise. They never married and were killed in a car accident when I was young. My grandmother said she took me to see their graves when I was little."

"I'm sorry." Sebastian dropped the subject abruptly and rolled back to face the stars.

"How did meeting Cyrus change your life?"

"That has to do with what I am. I can't answer you."

Lucy frowned and sat up. His eyes followed her, but he remained silent. She leaned against the wall next to the window so that he could still see her and they sat in silence once again. The walls shook as a semi-truck passed with a series of grunts. When Lucy glanced back at him, she noticed that his gaze was on her rendition of the faceless man.

"Do you know him?"

"Yes. He is a terrible thing and the world would be better without him." His outright hatred of the nameless portrait subject made Lucy uneasy. His stare grew even more intense and Lucy finally felt it necessary to remove the notepad from his vision. She watched his eyelashes flutter and correct his vision before she asked him if he was okay. Sebastian didn't acknowledge her concern, but returned to watching the sky with a frown.

"What can you tell me about your team?"

"Well, Cyrus is the oldest and he recruits us as he finds us. Usually there are only two choices: join him or join the 'faceless people.' Once those creatures decide you are worth recruiting, there isn't a third option. Life is never the same and you never see your family again.

"Including me, we had a full team of six, and then not long after, the man you drew killed Kieron's biological brother. We went along with five for a while, but then found Mitchell and were once again a full team. We traveled rogue for a while and then were permanently stationed here in Ohio. Since then we became the strongest team in this state." He grinned at his story and watched her swoon under the spell that his adorable English inflections wove. The corner of his mouth crooked in amusement as he allowed her to process the information.

Lucy watched his eyes examine her and finally rest on the only thing left of the mystery attack from a couple days ago. Her scar was about two inches long and extended from the back of her hand to the middle of her wrist, where small blue veins had been cut. She allowed him to stare for a few more moments and then cleared her throat while pulling her hand from his sight. "After all that you've said, I still don't know anything about you."

"It might have to stay that way for a while." He grimaced and peered through the screen to get a good look at her features.

"You'll learn to trust me," she smiled down at him.

"Will I, now? What put that in your head?"

"You did the second you said that you were here to protect me. I trust you now and maybe you can feel the same way someday."

Even through the metal screen, Lucy could see his cheeks flush pink. She didn't even hesitate to remove the thin piece of steel between them and exit into the cold, cloudless night. She stood behind him on the small roof outside her window. His blue eyes shifted nervously and he tossed his blonde curls before clearing his throat. The orange street light made his skin glow with a bronzed shimmer. She caught a glimpse of a small tear in the corner of his eye as it was released and fell to his cheek. Sebastian quickly knocked it away and stood with a groan.

"Are you leaving, then?" Lucy blurted out the words before she could stop herself and he snapped his head back to look at her. He didn't seem startled, but instead of challenging her choice to leave the house, he did something that was completely unexpected.

Sebastian moved like lightning and was soon only inches from her face. The invasion of personal space was oddly familiar and reminded Lucy of the rudeness displayed by the frightening ghostly man that had nearly taken her life days ago. His breath was warm and had a musky undertone that made Lucy shiver. His intense stare made her stomach ache. With a steady hand, he brushed the free strands of hair from her face and tucked them behind her ear. "We never really leave the ones that matter to us." The moment was so intense that Lucy struggled to keep her knees from buckling under the pressure of his presence. Without another word, Sebastian leaped from the roof and landed one story below, completely unharmed. She watched him disappear down the street and then reentered her house and put the screen back in the window.

Feeling that the tension had gone, Avalanche emerged from under the bed and began to purr as he rubbed against her knee. Lucy sat back against the wall and started petting his electrified hair. The static-filled fur stuck to her hand and tickled a little bit, though she didn't mind at all.

Questions immediately flooded her mind to the point that her memory couldn't sort out what had been answered and what was still a mystery. She crossed her arms on her knees and sighed as she rested her chin on them. The young feline announced his disappointment when Lucy ended the massage, but soon calmed down enough to lay at her feet. She marveled at his sapphire eyes as she continued to sort out the events of that evening.

"He isn't human, Avalanche, or did you know that already? You hide whenever he comes around, so I guess you did know. I wish you could tell me what he is or if I should trust him. Maybe I should even be afraid of him. What do you think?"

The beautiful cat did nothing that would convey an answer. He only yawned, exposing the inch-long bicuspids that would send any prey scurrying for the hills. His smooth diamond pupils reflected the outside light and made them almost green. She grinned and watched him stretch across the bed and cover her cold toes. Avalanche always seemed to know exactly how she was feeling, both mentally and physically. He was a happily-added addition to her group of friends. He was the D'Artagnan to their three musketeers.

Lucy laid back down next to the window, as she'd become accustomed to, just in case Sebastian returned. The night air crept in slowly and gave her chills. Lucy had been leaving her window open and air conditioner off, but this wind seemed even colder than what that machine could produce. She closed her eyes and tried to keep his face in her consciousness, but the black backsides of her eyelids was all that she could see. The blackness drove her to sleep within minutes. Visions of Sebastian's life filtered into her mind and the dreams she pulled from his stories were so vivid, they could've been real.

Thunderstorms had already filled the skies by the time Lucy woke the next morning. Even as she tried to stand, she felt sick and collapsed back onto the bed. She drifted in and out of consciousness and her body temperature switched from hot to cold sporadically. Through brief glimpses of the world around her, Lucy saw her grandmother tending to her illness every now and again. She wanted to speak, but there was a weight on her chest that kept her from sitting up, let alone speaking. The day flew by and Lucy watched it pass by her window. She rested on her stomach and faced the outside world. Amish buggies passed along with cars and people out on walks with each other or their pets. Sleep became a welcomed friend.

After she awoke for the third time, Lucy realized it had become dark again. The entire day had been wasted, but she was feeling better because of it. She watched as yet another thunderstorm ripped the outside world apart. Lucy had pushed herself up and was trying to get a better perspective on the outside weather when an unexpected silhouette caught her eye.

"Sebastian?" The man's head turned and his dripping golden locks bounced slightly. His kind and yet halfhearted smile made her heart jump with excitement.

"You always seem so surprised when I show up," he chuckled and leaned back against the side of the house. Lucy watched the rain as it shot diagonally when the wind pushed it. The light post that lit the street in front of her house revealed the gusts of wind that twisted the branches of many small trees that lined the sidewalk. With a shiver, she watched Sebastian huddle under the small awning outside her window. Water dripped onto his beautiful face from his drenched hair and eyelashes. They glistened like tears before being released to leave trails over his cheeks.

Avalanche hopped to the top of the bed and purred at Lucy. He didn't seem bothered by the spray of rain coming from her window. She was surprised he appeared at all with Sebastian being around. The young cat made a bed by her feet and quickly fell asleep.

"You should join him. I know you've been sick all day," he suggested.

"I'm fine now. I've slept all day. Actually I'm hungry." She smiled and sat up from the bed.

"Go eat then," a woman's voice came from the other side of the screen. Lucy was clearly startled and pressed herself against the wet metal to see who it was. A dark-haired woman came into her view. Her bright blue eyes were the same color as Sebastian's, which momentarily led Lucy to believe they were related. Her dark wet curls fell over her shoulders as she resituated herself on the roof.

"Hey there, I'm Syrina. It's nice to meet you, Lucy. Go and eat. We have to go for the night anyway." With that she grabbed Sebastian's arm and they leaped from the roof. Lucy watched them disappear before she got up from her bed.

Suddenly an odd noise came from outside. Something wooden had been snapped and whispers were riding the wind. An ominous hum began, and without warning, Avalanche hissed and darted under the bed.

Lucy was so startled by his outburst that she had no time to react when a white cloth was forced over her nose from behind. At first she tried not to breathe, but soon the vapors of whatever was on the cloth began to sink down her throat. Immediately, weakness overtook her body. She felt exhausted and drowsy. The cloth was removed and she couldn't help but fall into the arms of her assailant. She tried to speak and found that either the words would not come to her lips or she couldn't think of what to say. Before the blackness completely enveloped her mind, Lucy took in the face of her attacker. He was a tall, dark-skinned man with sunken features and silvery tattoos along his brow and arms. His bright smile made Lucy uneasy.

"What are you doing in here?" Lucy heard her grandmother say before she completely blacked out and was lost to the darkness that had waited so long to consume her.

31

S

Chapter Three

ound was the first sense to return, and she heard crunching and rustling leaves from below. Birds were chirping. I'm outside. Her sense of smell returned next with the scents of pine and decaying leaves, the scents that she had come to associate with the autumn season. Her skin began to send impulses to her brain again and the damp, sticky air she felt around her was uncomfortable. Finally her sight returned. Lucy hadn't any idea what the strangers had given her, but it must have been strong enough to paralyze her temporarily. The tingling in her fingers and toes quickly began to drive her mad.

Someone was carrying her. His muscles rippled with every stride and his footsteps sent a small earthquake through her body. Lucy opened her eyes as little as possible, trying to look around without alerting him that she had awakened.

She could see many trees very close together and concluded that they were in a forest. The crunching leaves beneath them were the left-over foliage from last autumn. Her stomach knotted. Lucy knew that she didn't live near a forest this dense. They had kidnapped her and even if she did escape there was nowhere familiar to run to. She looked ahead of him and could see three other people walking through the brambles and large trunks. They made their way toward a visible clearing. She had no idea how far they had gone from her home, nor if there was anyone around who could save her if she called out.

At that moment the large dark-skinned man rolled her in his arms a moment and gently sat her on the ground. "If you are awake then you can walk." His deep voice was frightening. Lucy cried silently at the fact she had been discovered. She looked back at the man. His hateful green eyes bore into hers and immediately Lucy jumped to her feet. The three other people had stopped walking and had turned to face her. There were two women and another man all standing in a triangle before her. One of the women had even fiercer green eyes than the others. Lucy's attention was immediately drawn to her.

Her hair was the color of a rose and cut short, but angled in toward her face. Her bangs swooped until they dipped into her eyebrows. The woman's glossy skin made it seem as if she were made of porcelain. She glared for a few moments and then continued on the path while the two men helped Lucy to stand. They marched toward the clearing for what seemed like hours. Though her instincts told her not to, the urge to fight them grew with each step. It wasn't until she looked at the faces of the men next to her that Lucy became frightened. Their sunken features reminded her of someone. They both had silvery tattoos and pale skin. The man to her left had jet-black, long hair, but his eyes were green, unlike the faceless man of her memories. The group walked in silence for a while with only the birds and the crunching of leaves under their feet making noise. Though she knew they were walking toward it, Lucy felt as if they were making no progress toward the clearing. It didn't take long for her to doubt it was even there.

She watched the sun grow strong and then fade as midday turned into afternoon. This entire time the silence intensified. It was as if the people traveling together refused to speak to one another. Just as she had given up hope of seeing a full glimpse of the sun again, they entered the treeless clearing and strange shadows began to decorate the ground. Panic choked what words could've been said. These people had kidnapped her and taken her to a cemetery.

Though the surrounding graves were an obvious distraction, Lucy tried to keep up with the group and avoid unnecessary attention. The strangers around her made no eye contact or even attempted to restrain her. They only stood close by to block any possible escape route.

Without a word, the five of them traipsed through the maze of headstones and memorial towers. Of all the odd and creepy articles in the burial ground, the crying stone angels made her skin crawl. She didn't know why they had been designed to weep in a place that was meant to bring peace, and Lucy couldn't fathom why the simplest facts were distracting her from the situation. Nevertheless, she eyed the statues until they passed the last burial lot and headed toward the bank of a cliff. The grassy hill had been cut in half to create a steep, rocky edge. There was an unmarked path that led down the side of the bank and under the low-lying limbs of a few trees.

The strangers led Lucy toward the hill and soon they had all dipped behind it. Where they were going was still unknown to her, but just as she had asked herself a flurry of questions, Lucy got many of her answers. Like half of it had dropped into the earth, the hill cut off and revealed three large mausoleums.

The first two were part of the hill and incredibly older than the third, which lay twenty feet in front of the others. The newer one had bright white pillars and a double door that had been painted the same crimson color as the flowers that lined a cement path leading to it. All four of the strangers glanced at Lucy, sending a shiver through her body. Just as she thought they were headed to the beautiful mausoleum with the red door, the woman in front made a sharp turn and began to walk toward the oldest-looking chamber.

The black-haired man sped ahead to open the door and as soon as he did a moldy burst of wind flew out and nearly knocked Lucy over. The dark space was frightening, but before she could plead to stay in the light they had filed into the room and the door had been shut.

The chamber was very narrow and left hardly any room to move with the five of them inside and a brand new marble bench that appeared to have recently been installed. With the door shut there was hardly anything to see. She could make out the names of the people entombed and the faces of those around her, but that was all. Lucy studied the tombs. They all had the same last name, Havocen. She paused and allowed her fingers to trace the beautifully carved names. It didn't take long before the strangers had moved her through the chamber and to the back wall.

Beyond the marble alter, between name plaques, was a narrow door with a small knob. The woman with the red hair didn't hesitate and reached for it, but one of the men cleared his throat and she stopped with an angry twitch.

"Something to say, Charles?" She frowned and glanced back at him.

"No, Cecily. I only have doubt as to whether this human should be privileged enough to enter this door."

"That is none of our concern," the other woman in the room chided his doubt. "Eodin made his orders clear and you are to follow them. Your feelings toward the orders are irrelevant."

The man shrank at this woman's words and allowed her to continue. She opened the door and disappeared into the black cave behind it. Charles followed and the other man nudged Lucy to join him. The last person who entered shut the door, which drove out all of the remaining light.

Lucy shuffled her feet on the floor, trying to keep from bumping into any of her kidnappers. They walked a short distance before a small, round light appeared in the floor. As they neared it, one of the men warned her to watch her step. She did as she was told and threw her hands out to the wall, finding a railing there. Lucy's hand followed the railing and she used it for stability when she nearly fell down an unseen step. More steps followed and soon they were descending a spiral staircase into the white light.

The dark floor soon disappeared, revealing a room with high ceilings decorated in flame. Candles by the hundreds lit the area. It was adorned beautifully in earthy tones, and gold seemed to be everywhere, like they had robbed a dozen pirate ships. The spiral staircase made a straight line down the center of the room. It seemed to be the only way in or out.

During their procession down the stairs, the twenty or so people in the room gazed upward as they noticed the company. Lucy observed one man seated in a large, high-backed chair in a loft-like place above everyone else. His hair was black and short, but even before she saw his features, Lucy's gaze was drawn to the man's piercing green eyes.

It didn't take long for the company to reach the bottom of the tall staircase. As they left the last step, her four guards resumed their diamond-like positions. They wasted no time in heading toward the man on the loft. Most of the crowd had formed a tunnel only wide enough for the five of them to walk by untouched. She realized that her estimate of the number of spectators was wrong. There were at least fifty of them or more. They were all faceless people, but now the name that she had given them, the name that had once made the most sense, Lucy now deemed inappropriate. She didn't know who or what they were, however, it was now obvious to her that she could never forget their faces again. Once more, each presence bore into her and she was soon drowning in the fear and hopelessness that had become synonymous with these strangers. There was no escape.

Anticipation took hold of her and was gnawing away at the air, leaving only spare amounts to breathe.

Her kidnappers led her up a small flight of stairs to the top of the loft. The black-haired man who had captured her attention before was now out of his chair and prepared to greet them at the top. His black hair was jostled and his side burns elongated his face. He had a smaller nose and thin lips, which somehow made his eyes stand out and gave him an even fiercer stare. He wore a stylish red vest over a black shirt with black pants and loafers. However, his chilling smile took away from his charm.

The man gave Lucy his hand and she took it, afraid that if she refused he might be insulted. He escorted her to the edge of the loft and allowed Lucy to look over the crowd of people. She noticed no similarities among the ocean of faces except for their obvious sunken features and green eyes. She then realized that every face staring back at her had the exact same color eyes.

"My children and my friends," the leader began with a slight bow, "I am Eodin, but after today the word on your lips will not only be my name. Eodin will be coupled with savior and freedom. This girl will give it to us." The crowd cheered for a moment before he held up his hands and all fell silent.

"This little human has become a pet of our foe and right now they are on their way to find her. This is their mistake. Now that our family from the covens in the east and west have joined us, the wolves will easily be overwhelmed. We will finally be able to do as we please. We will be able to be what our ancestors were. We will hunt the zephyrs and become a mega coven before the order can send a team to replace them. We will be the most powerful coven in the United States, and after we destroy our enemy, the world will be next. No more weak humans to hide from. They will be our slaves and our prey." He finished with an obvious glance to Lucy before his family roared in acceptance of his plan.

Eodin made a point to look Lucy in the eyes before leaving her, but something stopped him in his tracks. He entered her personal space, stopping within only inches of her face. He groaned and squinted, trying to come even closer. For a moment she thought he was going to kiss her, but instead he raised his hand and snapped his fingers. The black-haired man who had escorted her into Eodin's presence stepped forward and immediately went to his leader's side.

"Lucian, I need a test done on our guest. Her eyes tell me

interesting things."

Lucy snapped her eyes closed immediately, which pulled a chuckle out of Eodin before Lucian's cold fingers wrapped around her wrist and pulled her to his side. The black-haired man forced her down the steps and then made a sharp left into another room. Compared with the dark and decorated place they had just left, this room was bright, white, and very clean. There was a tall-backed chair in the middle of the room that had leather arm and wrist restraints.

She felt her chest tremble and her heart begin to race. Without hesitation, Lucian shoved her forward and into the chair. He leaped at her and held her arms down as he fastened the restraints. Through the entire kidnapping, Lucy had done her best not to panic or show emotion that would encourage violence, but as soon as he forced her arms down she heard herself squeal and felt tears run down her cheeks. She watched in vain as he disappeared behind her. For a minute she could hear the sounds of metal rattling and Lucian mumbling to himself. After many nerve-wracking seconds, he returned wearing medical gloves and holding a syringe.

"Now either way, easy or hard, I am getting a sample of your blood," his chilling voice warned before he grabbed an alcohol swab and wiped her skin with it. "Don't move."

Reluctantly, Lucy flinched as she watched the needle disappear into her arm. She observed him as he pulled back on the plunger and moved the needle back slightly. The strap across her arm was so tight it acted like a tourniquet and Lucy could see her veins begin to bulge. It didn't take long before dark liquid filled the barrel of the syringe. After it was full, he pulled the needle out and wrapped her arm tightly with cotton and gauze.

Lucian pulled out a three-inch, rubber-topped vial and inserted the needle. He watched eagerly as it pulled the blood from his syringe. Lucy didn't look away from his face. His eyes slowly turned black and a silvery tattoo shimmered above his brow, catching her attention.

"Do you recognize me now?" He grinned and placed the vial in his shirt pocket.

"You're the man from the festival. I think I've known that for a while," she mumbled without averting her stare.

"Glad I left an impression."

"You tried to kill me." Lucy surprised herself by being unusually calm.

"More than once." As he admitted his involvement, Lucian seemed to take great joy in seeing the shock fill her face.

"The parade? That was you?" She watched as he bent and pulled a dagger from where it was sheathed on his ankle.

The six-inch, angled blade flashed the light into her eyes. It was an ancient blade that appeared to be brand new. The hilt was decorated beautifully with a carved design. Lucy blinked a few times and then squirmed, letting a cry escape, to his surprise.

"Are you scared? I would be too," he chided. "This won't take long, but before I go..." Lucian unfastened the right wrist restraint and pulled her arm into his view. Lucy's stomach turned as he used his knife to cut her skin. He took his time to inflict the longest amount of pain and drank in the screams that filled the room. When he was done, Lucian wrapped her wrist with more gauze and removed the wrapping from where he had drawn blood.

"What did you do to me?"

Lucian didn't answer her. He strapped her wrist back down and exited the room with her blood sample still in his pocket.

She watched in vain as he passed the window next to the door and then went out of sight. Though she couldn't see what he had done to her wrist, the pain was unmistakable. Lucy could feel the blood pooling under her arm and dripping onto her pants. The wound had bled through the bandage Lucian placed. The whole time she couldn't stop wondering how these people were able to do such terrible things to others. How could they be getting away with it and why would they do it in the first place?

It was silent for a while and though Lucy was scared, the stiffness in her limbs had worn off and she had started to wiggle against the loosening restraints. As half of her hand slid out, she sighed in exhaustion and satisfaction. Lucy watched her hand turn red and though it became painful, she still pulled against the leather, hoping that either the strap would break or it would become loose enough to pull her hand through.

Just as she thought her hand might come free, incoherent shouting came from outside the door. Her head snapped up and her eyes grew large. She searched the hallway outside through the one small window as best she could, but found nothing. After waiting a few more moments, she glanced back down to begin tugging again. Before she could, however, distinct fighting erupted from the other side of the door.

Lucy wasted no time in pulling on her restraints again and watched awestruck when Lucian was launched past the window as if thrown by a giant. After that moment, all hell broke loose. She could hear a riot beyond the door that was quickly growing in strength. Desperately, Lucy yanked against the leather straps. She could feel her heart speed up and her chest heave in order to supply her body with enough oxygen to support her. Lucy pulled on her bonds again, hard enough that she strained a muscle in her wrist, but didn't stop.

After every couple of tugs she glanced up at the window. Many times a pair of people fought past the door and she paused, hoping to go unnoticed. After they passed and the outside became vacant, she attempted to free herself once more and groaned in discouragement when the belts seemed to become tighter rather than continue to loosen.

Suddenly a click came from the door and Lucy froze again. She looked up slowly, feeling tears form in the corners of her eyes. Where she expected to see one of the strangers appear, golden hair came forth, followed by the angelic features of someone familiar and yet unexpected.

"Sebastian?" she stuttered in disbelief.

"Shh." He seemed preoccupied, but that didn't stop her questions.

"How? What are you doing here? What's going on?"

"Now is not the time, Luce." He was very stern and it was the tone he spoke with that stopped her questions. Sebastian looked the room over and inhaled deeply several times before coming to her side.

"Are you hurt?" His worried expression shone through as he gently released the restraints.

"Nothing serious," she smirked as he helped her out of her chair.

"Your wrist," he frowned and grabbed at her bound arm. Lucy pulled the wound from his sight and tried to find some answers. "Where are we?"

"I had hoped to explain at a better time, but we are in a coven."

"Like for vampires?"

"Yeah, for vampires," he sneered and inspected her arms, trying to stay away from her wrist. "They took blood?"

"And quite a lot of it too. Why would they do that?" She saw his eyes grow worrisome and that made her feel worried as well.

"Because they are monsters that have only two purposes in life: to kill and to breed."

"That can't be right," she refused to believe what he seemed so sure about.

"You humans have been convinced of their nonexistent good nature by the media. No such kindness exists," he accused as he continued to check behind her ears and the back of her neck.

"I wasn't assuming they were tame," Lucy protested and tried not to grow annoyed at his tireless worrying.

"Why not? Everyone else does before they're killed," he yelled back at her as he watched the progressing fight outside the window. She watched him lock the dead bolt on the door and take in another deep breath.

"Why are you here?" Lucy asked.

"To rescue you of course!"

"How did you know I was here?"

"Does it matter?" Sebastian seemed to shrug off every question as if it was no big deal.

"To me? Yes, it does. To you? I'm thinking not."

"It's hard to explain. Can we talk about it later?"

"You have to give me something. I'm far too curious now," she smirked, hoping that it would be enough to get an honest answer out of him.

"They kidnapped you and many others to lure me and my family down here. They were trying to ambush us."

"Why?"

"We don't know yet. Actually, I had hoped you might've heard something."

"They said something about being free of their enemy and bringing other members of their family here to kill someone."

"They did bring another coven to join the fight against us, their enemy."

"How did you overpower them?"

"We brought reinforcements just in case," he happily explained as he waltzed back over to her and took her hand. "That's why it took us so long to get here."

"Well, why are you locking us in?"

"I'm locking them out, actually," he tried to say through a laugh. Together they headed toward the back of the room. Sebastian offered her a seat next to the wall and she took it before finishing her inquiries.

"Sorry, but one more thing: why didn't they just bite me if they wanted blood?"

"I'm not entirely sure, but now that they have a blood sample you are in even more danger."

"Why?"

"Enough, Luce! Not now. I will tell you, just not now!" Lucy was taken aback by his assertiveness and though she felt the need to protest, she waited for him to "save" her as he had promised.

They remained in silence for a few more minutes, listening to the progressing battle beyond the thin walls. She didn't understand why he couldn't explain while they waited for something to happen, but still the urge to interrupt the silence was strong. However, the urge to keep him happy left her speechless.

All of a sudden a body slammed into the window, breaking through and scattering shards of glass on the floor. The motionless body lay unconscious while a second person stepped over it and toward them. This man was unlike the vampires that had kidnapped her. His skin was a crisp honey color and his short brown hair was highlighted in silver and allowed the light to bend shadows along his slender face. His bright blue eyes were the same color as Sebastian's and his muscles rippled over his shirtless form. The man's face was angled sharply, giving him a cat-like appearance, which reminded Lucy of Avalanche.

"You found Lucy, then?" A few of his teeth were jagged, which should've been even more frightening, but only intrigued her even more.

"Yes. Lucy, this is Cyrus, the patriarch of our family."

"It's nice to meet you, Lucy," he said with a smile.

Cyrus's voice was deep and, like Sebastian, had a small amount of a different dialect within it. He sounded a little bit German, like he'd been raised in Germany, but had long exposure to America. Lucy could do nothing but nod. The combination of speech and appearance left her no words.

"Let's get out of here, eh?" With that he took her hand and pulled her along to the window he had just broken with the face of another man.

The hallway was long and vacant now. They hurried to the opening that Lucian had dragged her through earlier and leaped up the steps to the loft where she had last seen Eodin, who was no longer in charge, and his snide outlook on humans was now replaced with hatred for his failed plan and those who had overpowered him. His smirk was nonexistent. He knelt with his head down as they passed. The vampires below them on the ground floor stared upward. Their eyes were green like his and yet blood-thirsty with the anger of their last fight. Each of them stood proudly with their hands nestled behind their backs and wounds bleeding to the floor. Many only had small cuts or scratches. One man was bleeding from a puncture in the ribs and another was missing part of his ear.

Cyrus stepped forward, his expression grim as he addressed the crowd. "You are not invincible, as we have shown you today. We never wished to do this and yet you continue to break laws. Every vampire has been left alive today, but I promise you this. If you've ever thought that getting to me or my family through the people we love is a good idea, forget it now. I want you to remember today and remember what happened. You are alive, if that's what you want to call it. However, if this ever happens again, a third chance will not be given."

Lucy looked over the crowd. Their expressions hadn't changed. Spaced evenly around them were nine people who had the same angled features as Cyrus. They eyed each other with brief glances, almost as if they were guarding each other. Every green eye in the room tracked them as Lucy and Sebastian followed Cyrus along the walls. The other members of his family abandoned their guarding positions to climb back up the spiral staircase. Lucy didn't release Sebastian's hand until they exited the mausoleum, which had doubled as the coven entrance. Waiting for them were some familiar faces.

Syrina immediately approached with a smile and gave Lucy a quick hug. As they embraced, she glanced around to see many other reunions taking place. Happy tears streaked the faces of most of the reunited. She wasn't entirely puzzled, but her cluelessness must've been enough to attract attention. Syrina took her arm and whispered an explanation.

"They will try again. Maybe not in the same way, but the thought of losing is shameful for vampires. They are very proud creatures, but in truth Eodin should've seen this coming. It was a bad idea to kidnap zephyrs. Cyrus is at his most dangerous and unpredictable when the people he loves are in danger. He was most worried about you," she smirked.

"Why me? He doesn't even know me."

"Sebastian tells us such stories of your life and it is like we have known you as long as him."

"Why would you care, though? You, well most of you, have never even met me."

"It matters not. You make a difference to Sebastian, and therefore, you have bearing with the rest of our family."

"I'm an outsider. Most people wouldn't invite someone like that in," Lucy argued, unsure if what Syrina said was really the truth or if it was what she assumed would make Lucy feel better.

"Oh," the woman's black hair blew in the wind and she seemed utterly surprised. She thought her response out carefully a couple of times and Lucy watched her eyes shift uncomfortably back and forth for a few moments. Finally Syrina cleared her throat and winced as she spoke, "What has Sebastian told you about us?"

"Not much. Your names and that you are a family of soldiers or something like that." Lucy tried to recall while talking with her hands for most of the recollection.

"Soldiers? He said that? Do I look like a soldier?" At her request, Lucy examined Syrina's lacey black tank top and jean shorts.

"I suppose not," she finally admitted with a smile and they laughed together before a young man interrupted them. He seemed about Lucy's age or a little bit younger. His face wasn't fierce like the others, but his eyes were the same brilliant blue. He had light brown, shaggy hair and sideburns that were angled over his jaw and shaved to a point. The rest of his face was clean-shaven, which gave him the angled appearance of his friends. He had a kind smile that was highlighted by a small silver ring in his lip. The man nodded to

Syrina and then to Lucy before he reached out to shake her hand. "I'm Mitchell. It's good to meet you, Lucy."

"Likewise," she said with a smile and was unable to do or say anything else. There was always something about Sebastian or his family that made Lucy doubt their honesty. She could feel something hanging in the open that didn't fit and she knew that they didn't trust her with the truth. Something told Lucy that she wasn't going to get the whole story by asking for it. Sebastian had outright refused certain questions and she had no doubt that the others would do the same. She hoped in time they would give her more information. It was hard to get by with what little there was.

"Is she coming with us?" the young man asked Syrina, which for some reason made Lucy feel annoyed and ignored.

"I think so. The vampires didn't kidnap her kindly." She shrugged and they turned to walk toward the others. Seconds of hesitation passed before Lucy joined them in strolling over to Cyrus and the others. It seemed as if her mind was never clear of questions. Now even more filled her conscience. They joined a large group of people who were being addressed by Cyrus. He was very charismatic and practiced at putting sentences together that made every person in the area feel important and comfortable.

"Thank you, my friends, for joining us today. I assure you that our success would not have been so without your help. However, I ask that you not spread word of this day. Laws were broken by the creatures we are sworn to control. Today should've been a blood bath and the beginning of a war, but I am old and have seen this never-ending battle that you all ache for. Killing doesn't give you pride. It leaves you with scars and memories that you don't want, believe me. I won't invite the responsibility of knowing that I caused that pain to be born. Remember your empathy and pity because that is what separates us from them. Return to your homes and be thankful that you do so because if a war had broken out today that feeling of love and warmth when you step across the threshold of home would not be there. Dismissed." His speech was long, but obviously resonated with those around him. They didn't show any sign of anger or killing drive. Instead they held the hands of those beside them and thanked the stars that they weren't too late.

Lucy watched the families split into groups and disappear in all directions. The trees swallowed them and before long only Cyrus and his group remained. Mitchell and Syrina stood side by side and Sebastian spoke with Cyrus for a few more minutes. They argued briefly, but still quietly and then parted.

Sebastian pushed his hair back and allowed it to spring forward again. He glared back at Cyrus, but continued to walk forward until he nearly ran over Mitchell when he didn't move. With swift turns, he maneuvered around him and went to Lucy's side. She stared hopefully at his face, which was filled with concern and a secret that needed telling.

"You're coming home with us, but Cyrus says I need to tell you what happened last night before we go." As he said this, Sebastian grabbed her hand and pulled her behind him and into the forest. They walked silently for a while, allowing the only noise to be the crunching leaves and the chatter of the forest. Finally, after a couple of minutes, he stopped at a large, moss-covered boulder. Lucy looked back at where they had come from. There was no sign of the clearing, just endless tree trunks that obstructed her vision.

She suddenly felt Sebastian's hands around her waist and he effortlessly lifted her to the boulder, which seemed to be only a couple of feet off the ground. She turned to face him and, hesitantly, he began. Lucy nervously obliged and gave him the time he needed to arrange his thoughts before they could go any further. Patience was hard for her as she waited for him to stop pacing. Eventually, Lucy got caught up in the world above her, the life of the forest. The canopy was full of small animals and singing birds that seemed to glide from branch to branch.

"The night we last talked, I didn't understand how to tell you certain things or if there was a right time to say them."

Lucy could hear the confusion trembling in his voice and though she wanted to encourage him, she only listened to what he had to say.

"I don't know how long you were asleep, but we are in a small forest in Ohio that sits behind an even smaller cemetery. They took you a long way. After my last visit, I stupidly went home. Please forgive me, but this morning I went to patrol and there were police at your house. They had the whole place taped off. Your grandmother was found that morning."

47

"She's dead?" Lucy choked out the words with disbelief. This was impossible.

"Back when I lived in Europe—back when I had just met Cyrus, vampires didn't just kidnap one family member. They tracked down whole families and killed the ones that refused them. That was what happened to my sisters," his voice became quiet and almost solemn. "I joined Cyrus and the vampires tracked down my family and killed my sisters and my parents just to be sure they didn't aid their enemy. I've never hated someone so much in my life. They killed Lucinda because of me. If I hadn't left you she might still be alive and you would've never gone through that." He frowned and gestured at her wrist. Lucy got exactly what she asked for—the truth—and a lot of it. What he was doing was cruel, but she needed to hear and understand it. She could feel the sadness pull her into depression and the feeling was oddly familiar. It was the same thing she felt when Lucinda told her how her parents died. It was the same feeling she encountered when Lucian confronted her at the festival.

"Are Rae and Tryp okay?" she asked quietly, and was relieved to find his head nodding. Although the same grim expression was on his face, there was something else there too—an emotion that she found hard to read. It was either relief or sincerity.

"Lucy, I'm not sure what you have figured out so far, but there is something else you need to know before I take you away from here. My entire family are what humans call werewolves. We just say canines or wolves, but you can call us whatever you want." He waited for the shock and fear to come, but it never did. Lucy could feel her body become warm and her surprise at the fact he was part dog was causing her to shake.

"What does this mean?"

"It doesn't change a thing. I am still me just not entirely human, but I used to be. I'll take you to meet Allegra and Kieron and then they can explain the facts. I, regrettably, am not as brilliant, but they can give you more details." With those final words, Sebastian reached for her hand and helped her down from the rock before they returned to the clearing. The three other wolves were waiting for them with a couple of cars.

"Welcome to the pack, Lucy," Mitchell greeted as he opened the door for her.

From the point when they left the cemetery, Lucy didn't know what to expect. She was riding in a car with a pack of werewolves

S after being kidnapped by vampires that were using her as bait. Life used to be simple. Rae and Tryp were simple friends who liked to do simple things. They had never been this unusual and Lucy was thankful for that. She watched out the window and tried to gain a sense of where they were going, but after several back road turns, there was nothing left to guess at. She was lost.

Chapter Four

omewhere inside her, Lucy always knew she was different. Whether it was straight A's in school without even trying or the speed at which her body healed itself, there was always something that made her feel different. As she watched the world fly by her window, a sudden urge to see her friends dropped into her stomach. In the back of her mind, Lucy knew that meeting with them was impossible now and that longing for a familiar face was tearing at her. She knew that Rae and Tryp would understand what she was going through. They always had.

Since the fourth grade, Lucy had told them nearly everything. They both knew why she couldn't go to the doctor like everyone else and they understood how different she was. Tryp had brought Lucy directly to her grandmother the day of the parade. It had become somewhat of a routine since Lucy healed so quickly and was prone to accidents. Lucinda had been a nurse for many years, and though growing a little older every day, her wrinkled hands were still able to patch her granddaughter up for a few hours until she was healed. Lately, Lucy had gotten used to being sick after certain injuries. They both assumed that she was so focused on the larger wounds that there was no defense left against anything else. However, she didn't stay sick very long either.

Lucy counted herself lucky to have the support structure that she did. Rae and Tryp would've always taken care of her and now that she had Sebastian, there could be more answers coming as to why she was so different. She wiped her tears away and nearly pressed herself against the glass to obstruct the view of everyone in the car. She didn't want them to pity her or see her crying. She might have been human, but somehow she was more. There was something inside her that made her less human and more something else. Deep inside she knew that the wolves might have the solution to her dilemma. It was only a matter of time before the truth would surface.

Suddenly, the cars came to a stop and without a word she watched Sebastian and Syrina exit the car. They met up with Cyrus and Mitchell before waving her outside. Lucy's jaw dropped as she closed the door and gazed up at the trees in their way. The road had ended at a small grassy field surrounded by trees that nearly touched the clouds. They reminded her of the sequoias from her trip out west. She had never seen trees that big in Ohio.

Lucy turned around to look back at where they had come from. The narrow one-car road had a line of smaller trees on both sides that opened up into the mouth of the field. She turned back around and found Sebastian, who was standing in front of her.

"No more cars," he grinned politely and took her hand. They were soon reunited with the others and the five of them began what Sebastian called a 'short hike' to their 'secret base of operations.'

The forest here wasn't as alive as the one she had been drug through earlier. It was eerily quiet. Not even the leaves seemed to make a sound as they broke apart when they were walked on. The wolves moved gracefully through the tree trunks like ghosts that were floating just above the ground. They didn't speak or even look at each other as the hike became lengthy and boring.

Sebastian seemed perfectly calm at first, but that quickly changed. He didn't allow emotion to show on his face, but his grip on Lucy's hand became painfully tight. With a slight whine, she squeezed even harder on his hand and he immediately released hers. They glanced at one another and said nothing. The number of trees slowly became fewer and finally the density of the forest had gone from harsh to nonexistent.

"Welcome home, Lucy," she heard Cyrus announce as they passed under an arch of braided branches. Lucy was prepared to see a lot of things. She wondered if they lived in caves or if there would be an enormous camp hidden among the trees.

A gasp left her lips as she got a good glimpse of where Sebastian had been living for so long. It was beautiful and still rugged in a way. A little waterfall trickled into a pond at her left and a weapons course sat on her right. There were many weapons hanging from a wall, ranging from swords to daggers, throwing stars, and even nunchakus. She gazed in awe at the arsenal, wondering if they really used those to fight or if it was just for show. Her curiosity had grown so much that she could feel Sebastian pulling on her wrist. Lucy blushed when she realized that she had stopped in the middle of the road with her mouth open like an idiot. He grinned and yanked her to his side.

They walked along the path, following the rest of the group for another minute before it ended. The carved road forked to the right and left, leaving only trees straight ahead. Lucy watched Cyrus take the left road and Mitchell and Syrina take the right before she looked up at Sebastian. "I'm lost. What's to the right?"

"Our homes. We used to live in a large house, but that got to be tiresome after a few decades. When we moved to this forest, Cyrus said that we would build a large place for everyone and have smaller individual homes too."

"Like what?"

"Cabins mostly, but the inside completely suits the person who lives there rather than living in one big house with many clashing styles."

"Can I see your house?"

"Maybe later." Sebastian grinned and nudged her towards the left road. "I think you ought to meet Allegra first. I think you'll like her."

With a little encouragement, Lucy took his arm and they strolled along the path toward a building in the distance. She watched the small building grow larger and larger until they finally arrived at the staircase. It had a comfortable and homey feeling about it and was oddly welcoming.

Sebastian opened the door of the house for Lucy and together they entered a large common room. It had a high ceiling and a big fireplace with a blazing inferno inside. The flames gave the room a warm glow, but also filled it with heat. Lucy looked around silently. She knew her mouth was gaping in awe and at that time she didn't care.

A large chandelier that was decorated with fourteen unlit candles adorned the center of the room. Two chairs draped in red sat across from each other with a glass table adorned with several old books in the middle. Sebastian led her through a high arch doorway to the left and into the kitchen. It was an enormous and incredibly clean kitchen that was completely modernized, which Lucy was not expecting. A plate of cookies sat on the counter. Before showing her into another room, Sebastian snatched two of them and handed one to Lucy.

"That was the kitchen and this is the recreation room," he announced and pushed open a double door to their left. He grinned at the shocked gasp that escaped her lips when she saw the room.

"We worked on this for a long time. On days off, we watch football and play video games, but if you like the older stuff we have cupboards full of board games too."

The room was painted dark and the shades were drawn. There were blue lights mounted on the walls that sent a glow throughout the space. An enormous flat screen television was mounted on the wall and on shelves beside it were nearly ten video games systems and a few other pieces of technology that would make the viewing that much better.

"Where did all of this come from?" Lucy mumbled in disbelief.

"I am seventy-six years old, remember? Mitchell is quite good with electronics and he is also quite young. Many of these things he grew up with and he created this entire room."

"I never would've expected to see something like this here." She sighed and traipsed around the perimeter, looking at the many forms of technology.

"Cyrus tries to make new family members as comfortable as possible. Mitchell was brought up with these things and to make him happy we sold many old artifacts to buy them and they will eventually become artifacts."

"Is that how you pay for new things?" Lucy snickered and was answered by a foreign voice. It was Cyrus, and though he was smiling, there remained a slight tone of disgust. "Of course. You buy something when it's brand new and then wait a hundred years." Silence pushed its way into the room and the three of them stared at each other for a few moments before Cyrus spoke up again. "Let's go down to the lab. We have some things that need to be addressed."

Without question, Lucy followed him back into the kitchen and across the entryway. They dipped into a small nook where a door had been hidden. Cyrus threw it open and told Lucy to watch her step before he led the way down a flight of stairs. The light gradually became brighter until it was nearly blinding and they entered a room that quickly reminded Lucy of the place from which she had just been rescued. Machines of all types lined the walls, and tables covered in pictures, microscopes, and charts sat in various places.

All of a sudden, a woman with pale skin, fair features, and red hair pulled back in a tight bun walked into their sight. She had a pencil in her mouth and didn't seem to notice them as she hummed and peered into the oculars of a microscope.

Lucy watched the woman for a few moments until Cyrus stepped forward and wished her a good morning. The woman's head snapped up in shock, but then a smile crossed her face and she made her way around the table.

The two met in the middle of the room and kissed passionately for a few seconds. They finished with a quick peck on the lips before the woman turned and hugged both Sebastian and Lucy. The unexpected contact was strange and surprising.

"Lucy, this is Allegra. She has been married to Cyrus for a hundred and fifty-two years and they still seem to be in love. She works down here with Kieron, wherever he is." Sebastian grinned as he introduced them. "Allegra is like my mother and except for the part that she looks my age, I would say that I could pass as her son." A light laughter filled the room.

"Yeah, you all have the same color eyes." Lucy smiled, but was disturbed by the roar of amusement that followed.

"What's so funny?" she grumbled when she didn't get the joke.

"All wolves have the same blue eyes just like all vampires have the same green eyes. It is one of the many things that make us different," Allegra explained as she took Lucy's arm. The red-haired woman led her to a chair and took her hand as she knelt.

"Lucy, Cyrus told me that that devil Lucian took a blood sample from you and though it could be nothing, I'm afraid we must do the same. It is vital that we know what they know. May I?" Allegra stretched Lucy's arm out and ran her fingers over where Lucian's needle had punctured her flesh. A large bruise had formed there. Lucy felt her breathing become stiffer as she agreed to the blood draw. She watched Allegra's smooth fingers trace her veins and then move to the other arm. "I will be quick."

Lucy could say nothing. She only nodded again and watched in horror as yet another needle came toward her. Thankfully, the stress of the first blood draw was absent and Allegra quickly had the sample she needed.

Out of nowhere, another blue-eyed man appeared and snatched the sample before disappearing again behind a machine. Allegra put pressure on the site for a couple of minutes and then wrapped it with some cotton and gauze.

"Why do you draw blood? What are you looking for?" Lucy couldn't help but ask when Allegra was done binding her arm.

"We are only making sure you're healthy," she insisted with a kind smile.

"But, why is that so important?" Either no one would or could answer her. It was as if the subject was taboo and they were going to burst into flames if they said a word about it.

Suddenly, out of the awkward silence came an unfamiliar voice. Kieron, though completely focused on his work, had heard what was going on and tried his best to begin what the others were going to say. His deep Scottish voice made his words blend together, but Lucy did her best to decipher them.

"Did you know that there are three subspecies of human?" he yelled from his microscope. "Tell her about that. It should explain some things." The attitude of the room quickly became tense and Lucy desperately watched the wolves glance at each other.

Finally, Allegra stepped forward, took Lucy's hand, and squeezed it before she began pacing the room. The red-haired vixen leaned against the nearest table and tapped her fingers in a bothersome way as she thought.

"There are three subspecies of human that we have discovered and studied. You won't find them in a book or on the internet because mankind knows nothing about them so far. They are werewolves, vampires, and zephyrs." She smiled and then paused as if she choked on her words. It was almost as if she didn't know what to say next.

Lucy wasn't about to let another long pause inject itself and she quickly spoke up. "Eodin said they would hunt zephyrs again if they ever were freed." The entire room looked over at Cyrus, expecting some form of reaction. There wasn't one.

"They used to hunt them, yes," Sebastian interrupted. "That is why we, as wolves, are involved. We've put a stop to the hunting and they hate us for it."

"In some humans there is a 24ᵗʰ gene," Allegra stated as she reassumed control over the conversation. "It doesn't have a big effect on them and most are unaware of its existence. Everyone is different. These humans aren't seen very often and most of them have a dormant or completely inactive gene. However, if there is a piece missing in it, the human is given the name 'Zephyr' because that missing part can be filled by something else. This makes zephyrs inhuman in a way. With the part of that gene missing, they are susceptible to two kinds of diseases—caninite and draculicous. These diseases are carried within the venom of other zephyrs that are already afflicted with it—vampires and werewolves."

"So there's a scientific explanation," Lucy thought out loud before letting Allegra continue.

"That's what Kieron and I have been doing for the past hundred years." At the sound of his name, Kieron's head snapped up and then sank back toward the microscope once more. His short brown hair was spiked with gel and he had a neatly trimmed beard that made his face appear thin.

"The speed that my body heals itself, does that mean I am a zephyr?" Lucy asked the room, but was briefly ignored.

She began to think no one had heard her until Allegra cleared her throat and said, "We are about to find out."

They all turned to watch Kieron. He had stepped away from his microscope and had a piece of paper in his hands, which he read with frozen concentration. He slowly walked toward them as he read. The suspense was thick enough to cut with a knife, but finally he looked up.

"You're positive, Lucy. You are a zephyr," he announced and a sigh of relief filled the room.

"What does that mean?" Of all of the questions in her head that was the only one that made it to her lips.

"This means that you've just started out on the road to discovering who you are and also that you are welcome to stay with us as long as you want to." Allegra's blue eyes shifted happily between Sebastian and Lucy. She could barely hold herself back and finally erupted into squeals of joy as she hugged her new daughter. They all took turns hugging Lucy, which quickly became awkward to her, but they didn't seem to notice. Kieron kept his distance and didn't even congratulate Lucy. He only turned around and strolled back over to his instruments.

A sense of worry overtook Lucy for only moments. Poor Kieron didn't seem happy that she was a zephyr and the only question that seemed to be in her head quickly became her focus. Why?

It was impossible and yet true. There was nothing that she could do to change it, but she still felt the need to try. Lucy had always been different and now she knew part of the reason. She wasn't considered human. A 24th gene had seen to it that she would never be the same or think the same as those around her. She had always been a burden for the people who cared for her because she was different. This realization answered so many things, but created even more questions. Thinking back, she could remember instances that having that extra part might have made a difference. Mostly she recalled the advanced healing that her body put her through. She wondered if every zephyr went through that or if it was yet another thing that made her special.

Encapsulated in thought, she soon realized that Sebastian had led her back outside and they were on the path that led back towards the housing.

"Are you alright?" Sebastian asked as he took her hand. The words woke Lucy from her trance-like thought process.

"I'm fine; just in a little bit of shock I think," she giggled and nudged him playfully. Lucy allowed her feet to scuff the dirt into clouds. As they neared the fork in the road, she could hear distinct clanking of metal and grunting. Though trees were in the way, she assumed that someone was using the weaponry course. It sounded as if they were doing quite well. The grunting was followed by shouts of victory, which made Lucy laugh to herself.

Soon the excitement was out of ear shot and the first of the homes appeared. A small path extended out from the road and to a small log cabin that had flowers in boxes on the windowsill.

"Syrina lives there," Sebastian whispered and looked back at Lucy, who had stopped a few feet back.

"This place is so big. Bigger than I thought. It seems like a lot for the six of you."

"We like our privacy and it is nice to go to your own place to sleep and not be bothered by the others. We also take in other wolves and newly discovered zephyrs like you. There are rooms above the main hall where they would stay, but you are rooming with Syrina. She insisted," he admitted with a grin, "I am the next house down. Will you be okay?"

"Yep. I got this. See you later." Lucy was more than ready to relax and she happily shuffled down the path toward the beautiful cabin. As she stood on the doormat there was a sense of excitement running through her and it was almost too much to turn the knob. Thankfully, she didn't have to. Just as she touched the cold handle, the door jerked open and Syrina appeared. She had a smile from ear to ear and greeted Lucy kindly before jerking her inside.

"So I guess you'll be rooming with me for a while, then?" Syrina barely waited for Lucy to nod before she squealed again, "I am so lonely all the time. The only girl around here is Allegra and she is always busy." Even as she spoke, Lucy took in the atmosphere of the room. It was mostly draped in dark purple, but wasn't gloomy. The room had two beds and there was a bathroom through the doorway across from where she was standing.

"There is running water, just don't over use it or Cyrus will get angry." Just as Syrina had finished speaking, a white cat jumped up on the bed and purred as he trotted over to Lucy and ran his paws up her stomach.

"Oh, and I believe this is yours. Sebastian saved him the morning he couldn't find you. The two of them didn't really get along so I've been watching him." Lucy couldn't say anything. She only smiled as she picked him up and tried to hold back her tears.

"I thought I would never see him again." Syrina sat on the bed and played with his tail. "He really is a sweetheart. I'm glad Sebastian saved him from the pound." Lucy removed her shoes and set Avalanche back on the bed. The floor was carpeted and the walls were covered in shiny strands of beads and colored fabric. It was just one large room with an adjacent bathroom. Lucy had expected more, but she said nothing. This could be her home for a while and that thought kept her from complaining.

"Are you stunned?" Syrina finally said as she sat up and brought her knees to her chest, "are you stunned about the test results?"

"How did you hear about that?"

"I already knew in a way. I've seen enough zephyrs to know the signs."

"I always knew something was wrong, but never did I imagine the answer was so complicated." Though Lucy could find no good in her situation, Syrina was ready to change her mind.

"First of all, there is nothing wrong with you. If anything, there is something wrong with the rest of them. You are a more advanced version of what they already are and I don't want you to think that those weak humans are any better than you! Understand this, I was like that too. I felt sorry for myself because I was different and it got me into problem after problem. Be strong in who you are; embrace it." Her words were shot like bullets and Lucy cringed every time she raised her voice.

"What are the signs?" Lucy wondered as she tried to become more invested in the truth of what she was.

"Subtle things usually, but your eye color and the spontaneous healing were giveaways. Zephyrs have blue eyes usually, but I've never met a zephyr that could heal themselves before transformation. That is very special, as far as I'm concerned."

"How old are you?"

"Wow, that came out of nowhere," Syrina scoffed and slid toward a fan-like door next to her bed.

"Please," Lucy begged. For some unknown reason, that was the only way she could believe anything the wolves told her. Their age made her feel secure.

"I lost count a long time ago," Syrina sighed and leaped off the bed. Avalanche followed her to the corner of the room, where she poured a small amount of cat food in a dish for him. She set it on the dresser and he leaped to the top effortlessly to begin eating. Syrina seemed to be thinking or maybe even remembering. Lucy tried to remain quiet so that she could search her mind to find what she was looking for.

"It was so long ago," she sniveled as the tears came to her eyes. "I don't even remember my parents' names, but I loved the clothes that we wore." For a moment, Lucy was utterly confused and waited for more information.

"My daddy was the king of England in the 1200's, but he was always away. I was a normal child and would've stayed normal if not for my love of adventure. I met a boy in my teens who didn't understand how special he was. We fell in love and one night we were kissing and one of his fangs cut my lip. That was all it took. My mother gave me two choices: leave and be considered dead or wait until the king returned and die then. It was the hardest thing for her to do, but I left at sixteen and was on my own. As far as I know, I have a grave with my name on it in Westminster Abbey. I guess that makes me seven hundred, give or take a couple years," she grinned and watched Lucy process the information.

After she put the knowledge where it needed to go, there was only one more question that Lucy could think of, "Then why do you look like you're in your twenties?"

"It's the wolf venom. It keeps us young."

"You don't age?"

"We age; just a lot slower than humans. I think the ratio is a hundred to one. Every hundred years, I get another year older or at least I am supposed to. Everyone is different." Syrina shrugged it off and returned to her bed.

Lucy couldn't believe it. In her mind, living over one hundred years was impossible, let alone existing for seven hundred. She couldn't even imagine what Syrina must've seen and done within that expanse of time.

"Do vampires age?"

"No. They're dead. They can't age," she mumbled gravely, almost wanting to resist answering the question in the first place. "That's why they're blood-suckers."

"So they are more like vampires from the legends?"

"Yes and no. They drink blood to sustain themselves. They don't care for sunlight but it doesn't hurt them, and don't go shaking a cross or garlic at them. You'll just embarrass yourself." Lucy couldn't help but smile. She wished that all need-to-know information was this easy to get from people.

All of a sudden, Syrina wandered over to her closet. She flung open the door and dug in the hanging clothes. Immediately she pulled a long green dress from the back and held it up. "This was what I was wearing when Kieron and his brother found me." The green dress had long, white, billowing sleeves and a golden cord that crisscrossed in the back like a built-in corset. A white sash was wrapped several times around the waist and then tied in the front, leaving the rest of it to fall past the knee. The fit was snug on the arm from shoulder to elbow and then the fabric opened into wide sleeves, with the elbow and cuff decorated with intertwined gold thread. It was the most beautiful dress that Lucy had ever seen.

"So they rescued you?" Lucy wondered as she carefully accepted the dress from Syrina and held it against herself in the mirror.

"There was no rescue. Six eyes are better than four. They offered to take me with them and at that time, I had nowhere to go," she explained and returned the dress to the closet. "Anything in here is yours. We are about the same size so I will take you shopping soon and find some more things. I might need a bigger closet." As Lucy laughed, Syrina grabbed her arm and pulled her into the small space. She moved the clothes and turned on another light. They walked through an archway and together entered the inner sanctum of Syrina's pride and joy. The inner closet was a healthy extension that seemed to be a whole other room. There was a small cushioned bench in the middle and four full-length mirrors, along with even more clothes, shoes, and accessories.

"This is incredible!" Lucy could hardly contain herself.

"Most of it I bought brand new and now it's vintage," Syrina laughed and gave Lucy a short tour. At the end, she revealed an empty rack and a couple of shelves. "I worked hard since we got back to clear you some room, but like I said, you can borrow anything for now, seeing that you don't really have baggage." As hard as she tried, Lucy couldn't be happy. She couldn't even smile. Her head felt heavy and without thinking she stumbled onto the small bench and looked around the room in awe.

"Are you okay?"

"I need to go home," Lucy admitted while she pushed the stray hairs out of her face.

"That is the only thing, at this point, you really shouldn't do and you know it." Syrina's curly black hair fell over her shoulders when she bent over the seat and rested on her stomach.

"I know, but I left a lot of things behind, and although I am so happy right now, I need answers and I need to say goodbye to my friends. After all that they've been through to support and help me, I owe them that much." With a sigh, she stood and watched Syrina do the same. Together they left the closet wonderland and each patted Avalanche's head before going outside.

The sun was barely showing through the trees now, but it was still light enough to brighten their path. Lucy felt like she was on a camping adventure. She had always felt comfortable in the forest. It was like nothing could harm her. She felt strong here and was glad that it could be called home for the time being. She wondered what would have happened if she hadn't been a zephyr. Would they have made her leave? Would she ever see them again? The thought was almost too much to bear. Lucy knew very little about most of them and in a strange way, she still trusted them.

Throughout her entire life, trust had never come easy. Maybe it was the strength she obtained from knowing exactly what she was, or perhaps it was the security she felt when she was around her new family that made her trust them. Though it wasn't obvious, at this point she decided that it didn't matter. Lucy was able to trust them and it was right to leave that alone. She wanted to be able to live in the moment and be happy.

Soon enough, the wooden family home came into view. It was a staggeringly gorgeous place and seemed to be even larger than before. They approached, walked up the stairs, and into the main hall. Instead of venturing into the kitchen, Syrina led Lucy into the room to the right. It was a living area that had all sorts of antiques on the tables and various places to sit. There was even a glass case in the back of the room that held invaluable items. Many paintings decorated the walls, none of which Lucy recognized, but they were all amazing just the same.

"This is the gallery room," Syrina said with a smile. As they turned the corner to see the rest of it, Lucy paused and greeted the others. Cyrus, Allegra, Mitchell, and Kieron were all sitting and chatting amongst themselves on the couches in the corner.

"Cyrus and Allegra know the value of closeness. Back in the 1980s we had a family expedition. They took Kieron, his brother, and me all over the world and we collected some rare finds to decorate this room. Almost everything in that case over there is older than I am!" She seemed to find that fact amusing, but stopped her grinning when she saw Lucy's face. It wasn't that Lucy didn't care, but she was far too preoccupied with thoughts of her friends.

"Aren't you ever worried that somebody will find you here or that someone will cut down this forest?" she asked and cocked her head as she waited for the answer.

"No, Lucy." Cyrus smiled and his eyes glistened. "I own this land. Trespassers are dealt with, but we haven't had any in a long time. You're safe here." The German in his voice made her skin crawl and his reassurance stopped all other questions.

"We are having dinner soon; any requests?" he asked politely. It wasn't until she thought about food that a crippling pain in her stomach began. Lucy tried her best to subdue any signs of pain and she suppressed the agony for a few minutes until it faded. It was then that Lucy realized she hadn't eaten since the night she was kidnapped.

"I could eat just about anything right now," she admitted in a chuckle and watched the family spring to life.

"Italian it is," Cyrus announced and led the way out of the room.

"I'm going to help them. Last time Cyrus tried to impress someone with food, he nearly burned the house down," Syrina said with a giggle before she followed, leaving Lucy alone in the room.

Immediately sensing the silence, Lucy's blue eyes searched the walls while she moved away from the couch. As if in an art gallery, she judged every painting. They were all signed by the same initials: C.G. Immediately, Lucy thought of her father. His initials were C.G. for Craig Gaskin, and she secretly imagined that he had done these great works. Lucy didn't know much about her parents, only the things that Lucinda had told her. She couldn't even be sure that those things were true. Unfortunately, her grandmother had trouble keeping facts straight.

Lucy made her way around the room, finally coming to the

glass case. Inside were many things, including a small chest of gold pieces, four bottles of wine from 1945, a piece of petrified wood, a pair of old spectacles, and other odd items that didn't seem special at all.

"If you knew where most of that came from, there would be a completely different look on your face," Mitchell stated as he came to her side. Lucy looked over at him and then back at the case, "Where did all of this stuff come from?"

"I only heard the stories. This family has been so many places and they've seen so many things. Those spectacles were one of the first pairs invented and the chest of gold came from Atlantis, which sank only a week after their visit. The petrified wood was found on top of a mountain where a huge ship was discovered, and those pieces of metal are from the Challenger explosion.

"Family members were on the Titanic the night it sank, and Kieron even witnessed the construction of the Sphinx."

"That's incredible! What amazing things have you seen?" Lucy's curiosity grew as she looked over the many unique artifacts.

"I am nowhere near as old as they are. I've only been a wolf for about 16 years. The only significant thing that's happened is 9/11, but that wasn't exactly a good time for a family vacation." He sighed and peered into the case with her. Lucy watched his expression shift from serious to excited and then back again. She watched him remember the stories, but then something else caught her attention and suddenly there was only one thing on her mind.

"How did it happen?"

"How did what happen?" She was unsure if he was serious or trying to avoid the recollection.

"Your change; the one that made you a wolf. How did it happen? Did it hurt?" Lucy waited for him to begin again, which took several minutes. For some reason, when the topic of transformation came up, no one wanted to discuss it right away. Unfortunately, these stories were the most important to Lucy and she would wait patiently if she needed to.

"In 1995, my human family and I had gone camping over in Pennsylvania. We had gone up there every summer since I could remember. My sister and I went for a short hike down a trail we were both familiar with and when we were on our way back, a doe and her fawn leaped across our path. We were so excited," he swallowed hard and pushed back the tears, pausing for only moments, "until we saw what was chasing them. It jumped onto the trail, but stopped when it smelled us. The creature stood like a man, but had large teeth that hung below his lip, long brown hair all over his body, and big hands with long claws. The creature looked somewhat like a large dog on two legs. I told my sister to run just before he leaped at me and knocked me to the ground. He immediately bit me in the shoulder as I found a large rock. Right before the pain took over I struck him in the head as hard as I could and he fell off me. It suddenly felt like my body was on fire. My skin was beet red, but I figured it was the adrenaline. The pain got worse and I soon passed out. When I awoke there was a naked man standing over me. He explained what he was and what I had become. I never saw my family after that and ended up staying with that werewolf for a month. Then I went rogue for a year before I met Cyrus."

"Did the change hurt?"

"It did before I passed out, but I'm told that it's quite painful if you are awake. Vampire bites are worse though, because in those cases your body actually dies." Mitchell's face became unreadable. He was quiet and she hoped that making him relive the night he lost his humanness wasn't too difficult to cope with.

"Did he ever say why he bit you?"

"Wolves are hunters by nature and without a more experienced one to help him through the cravings, I imagine he was living as an animal—scared and alone. The only miracle was that he didn't make me a meal." Mitchell sank onto the edge of one of the chairs with a sigh. He covered his face with both hands and groaned loudly as he rubbed his head, leaving his hair a tousled mess. Lucy looked over the items in the case again. It was amazing that they had seen so much and were able to collect evidence of it.

"I'm lucky, though. Most new wolves don't have a pack to rely on. I'm a first generation, just like my creator. Apparently we are the most dangerous, according to Cyrus. We are the most animal-like." When he had spat out the last word, Mitchell lifted back his lips so that Lucy could get a good look at his teeth. Both his top and bottom bicuspids were pointed slightly, like the canines of a dog, "Cyrus says that I will retain some wolf attributes out of the hunt, and the more

65

I allow the change to happen, the more I'll be able to control it. He says that eventually, with practice, a normal human won't be able to distinguish me from a dog and that some werewolves he knows have made that a permanent change."

"Would you ever do that?"

"Dog lives do seem easier, but I enjoy the company of people far too much to be silent around them." His smile was somewhat brightened by his frightening teeth. Lucy's head was swimming in questions. She didn't know what to ask first.

"Are there other generations besides first?"

"Of course, but only three are recognized. Second generations cannot become actual wolves, but they gain attributes like the angled face, sharp teeth, and super strength. Third generations get things like blue eyes and enhanced senses, but that's about it. When it comes down to it, you become like the one who created you, but there can always be variations. Cyrus says that we are all different."

"Are the rest of your family first generations like you?"

"Only Kieron and Syrina. Everyone else is second generation," he snickered through his words as if she should already know these things. Lucy knew she should be hurt, but her mind was too busy sorting through the new information to worry about feelings.

All of a sudden, Syrina reappeared in the doorway and cleared her throat. "It's done. Come on. We're having a family dinner, the first in a long time," she chimed. Without question, Mitchell nearly leaped from his seat and grabbed Lucy's hand. He pulled her along behind him and into the kitchen. They ended up passing into the room beyond, a small dining room with a large table in the center. Twelve wooden chairs that had been stained red surrounded the long rectangular table. It had a three-pronged candelabra as a center piece. Plates of tortellini in red sauce were set and ready to be eaten. Sebastian approached Lucy and invited her to sit down. The wolves waited for her to sit before they followed suit and dug into the meal that waited.

The first bite was unexpectedly hot, but when Lucy got past the heat of the dish, she found that it was the best pasta that she had ever had. Bite after bite, Lucy found herself enjoying the dish even more. It wasn't like the Italian cuisine she had had before. It was sweet, tangy, creamy, and cheesy all at the same time. As half of her portion disappeared, she knew that she wasn't just hungry and that the food was really delicious. It wasn't just her mind playing tricks on her. Finally the last twisted noodle was gone and she looked up at her company. Some watched her, while others finished their meals.

Lucy wiped her mouth with a nearby napkin and sat back in her chair. She looked at the ceiling and around to each of her sides. She hadn't noticed when they entered, but the dining room was really a library. The walls were shelves filled with books and there even seemed to be an upper level with even more books. Part of her was shocked that they owned so many, but then she realized that these weren't normal people and she should actually be shocked that they didn't have a lot more.

"Something on your mind, Lucy?" Cyrus grinned, bringing her back down to Earth.

"I'm just admiring your book collection; any particular genre?"

"Oddly enough, we collect the books and movies that depict us in them."

"You specifically or werewolves in general?" A trill of laughter filled the room and Lucy felt her cheeks flush with heat.

"It's hard to find material on us specifically. Mostly we like to see how accurate werewolf depictions are. It can be a source of humor in most cases." Cyrus seemed happy to explain their sense of humor and the inside joke that had been going on for years.

A short silence filled the room, one that was quickly interrupted by a sentence that would strip any humor from the house.

"I want to go home," Lucy announced. Even she seemed surprised that the words had come out in such a way, but the shock on the other six faces made her cringe. She didn't know how to explain and simply waited for someone to fight the statement. Mitchell was the first, saying, "What? Why?"

"My friends back home think I'm dead or worse. I need to say goodbye to them and collect some of my grandmother's things. Please take me back. I won't stay long."

Silence enveloped the room for a few long minutes. All of the wolves had their eyes on Cyrus. His solution would be the one they would take. His answer would be the one they acted on. It would be the alpha male's choice.

"I can see problems in this, so we must be cautious. Mitchell will go ahead and speak with Renee and Trypsin to make them aware of your arrival. You will enter the town at night and go through the house. Don't take more than necessary and be quick." When he was done, the wolves all stood and Mitchell hugged each of them before

T heading to the door.

"What can I tell them so that they will listen to me?" he asked Lucy before slipping out the door.

She thought briefly and grabbed his arm so that he would listen to exactly what she said. "Tell them that you know where I am and that I am coming back. That should be all that they need to hear."

A chuckle filled the room, but fell silent when Cyrus lifted his hand and said, "Be careful, my son." That was the first time Lucy had heard Cyrus's strong voice tremble. It sent chills down her spine and her teeth began grinding in nervousness. Mitchell soon disappeared and the others left in different directions.

"Lucy, Syrina and I will go with you," Sebastian said as he grinned and showed her out the door. "We need to grab some things." She followed the two wolves back to where the houses were.

"Will Mitchell take a car?"

"No, he'll go on foot. It will be faster that way. We will take a car," Syrina shouted behind her so that Lucy could hear. Although those facts didn't make very much sense, she didn't object and followed them to Syrina's home. Lucy could barely focus. All she could think about was seeing her friends again and letting them know she was okay. It was all that mattered.

Chapter Five

he sun had begun setting when they left and by the time the trio reached the outskirts of Lucy's hometown, night had fallen. The street lamps hovered over the pavement and briefly lit the car as it passed under. Lucy squinted into the dark, looking for anything familiar, hoping that something would jump out. Finally the car slowed down. She could feel her heart jump and then beat faster. They had arrived on her block. Within seconds, the two wolves were out of the vehicle. Lucy had never seen them move so fast; it was like lightning.

Sebastian opened the door for Lucy and helped her out. She knew where she was now. It looked different from inside the car. Her house was just around the corner and there was a mixture of excitement and fear brewing that had her weak in the knees. Though the land was shadowed, Lucy could make out the subtle glow of crime scene tape around the perimeter of her yard and on the door. Hesitation nearly knocked her over and she stopped two feet from the steps. Sebastian and Syrina didn't go much further before they turned to check on her.

"Lucy," Syrina returned and wrapped her in a hug, "We must be quick. You said you needed something, right?" She waited for Lucy to nod before continuing, "Well then let's go get it, so that we can meet up with your friends."

One by one, they crossed the tape meant to keep intruders out and snuck over to the door. Sebastian turned the knob slowly, and it clicked. The door was unlocked, which he hadn't been expecting. He closed the door after the others had followed him.

"Five minutes?" Sebastian suggested before they all agreed and Lucy led them to the second floor. The creaking stairs were louder than she remembered.

When they reached the top, Lucy heard a gasp leave her lips; it was one she couldn't control. There was a large bloodstain in the doorway between her room and the hallway. Lucinda had known of her granddaughter's absence, or maybe even the kidnapping, at the moment she died.

Lucy found herself wiping tears from her cheeks before Sebastian put his hand on her shoulder. She looked up at his understanding eyes. They nearly shook inside his head. He was either nervous or incredibly sad and Lucy was unable to see the difference. She watched his curls bounce as he passed her and entered the room where so much had happened.

Lucy remembered attempting to bandage him in that room, even though he knew that it wouldn't help. She smiled at the memories of their late night chats by the window and wondered if he remembered them as happy memories or if it was just a job to him. Lucy hoped that he cared, but was still unsure of what he really felt.

Syrina had disappeared into another room and they could hear her rummaging through it. The sporadic bangs and crashes made Lucy flinch as she realized that those noises were loud enough to be heard from the street.

"What are we looking for?" Sebastian finally nudged Lucy to bring her back to the moment. She hadn't seemed to notice how far away her thoughts had gone.

"It isn't in here," she suddenly realized and backtracked into the hallway. Lucy did a quick 180-degree turn and slipped into her grandmother's room. Sebastian didn't follow until he heard Lucy begin to throw things and mumble under her breath. Afraid to step into the chaotic room, he stood in the doorway and watched her for a few minutes. Soon Syrina joined him, and they stared dumbfounded at the mess that was being created.

At first, it seemed as if she was looking for something specific, but eventually the methodical sorting became tossing and cursing. They allowed her to go about her ransacking for a while longer before Sebastian cleared his throat and Lucy stopped as she let out a deep breath.

"What's missing?" Sebastian's angelic voice calmed her a little bit and even enabled her to answer him.

"A necklace; that was all I wanted. It was a necklace that my father gave my mother and then my mother gave to my grandmother. It was important and the only thing I wanted to keep from this house. Now it's gone. She always kept it with a box of important items. That entire box is gone. I don't know where else to look." Lucy's words had started to become sobs, but she pushed them back immediately and sighed, "Let's go."

Syrina nearly said something, but when Lucy glanced at her, the words stopped in her throat. The wolves followed Lucy back downstairs and out into the street. Sebastian replaced the tape on the door before heading back to the car. Just as they arrived, a familiar voice echoed out from the night, "I don't believe it!"

Lucy looked up and nearly screamed as she beheld the faces of her two best friends. Mitchell had found them and to Lucy's surprise, they had believed him. Hugs were exchanged more than a couple of times before the questions began.

"Where have you been? Who are they?" Rae was determined to get answers where Tryp seemed to be focused on keeping Lucy to himself. He still hadn't released her arm. It wasn't a painful grip, just annoying.

"I was kidnapped by vampires then rescued by werewolves. I am living with the wolves now and the vampires killed Lucinda. This is Sebastian, Syrina, and Mitchell. They saved me." Lucy tried her best to get them to understand, but it would've been better if they hadn't believed her at all.

Tryp's new mission was to get Lucy away from her new family. At first he pulled her behind him, but when she refused he lifted her onto his shoulder and trotted off in the direction of Rae's house. Though he was determined, Tryp didn't get very far. The pack was soon onto him and blocking his getaway path. Lucy heard Sebastian snarl and though she couldn't see him, she was certain that something bad was about to happen.

All of a sudden, Tryp moved under her and then put her back onto the pavement. Lucy looked back at the wolves. They had changed. Instead of three people coming to her rescue, there were two fearsome canines and a second generation werewolf. Sebastian's features had become angled and his teeth were bared in anger. His fingernails had grown into sharp claws and his body had become twisted into a force of nature. Lucy got chills just looking at him. She glanced up at Tryp. Any doubts that he had were now gone and there was a look of disbelief on his face, coupled with the terror in his eyes. The two wolves at Sebastian's side approached with ears back and hackles up. Lucy had had enough, "Stop it!"

Immediately the tension dropped and Syrina and Mitchell

scattered into the dark. Sebastian's appearance returned to normal and he stepped forward with his arm out in a kind gesture, saying, "Sorry." Lucy slapped his hand away and turned toward Tryp. "You can't fight them. They are important to me. His family has discovered what I am and why I was kidnapped. Don't you want to know?" She left the question hanging for Tryp, but it was soon answered by Rae.

"He may not, but I sure do. We've protected you all our lives, Lucy, and frankly I'm curious. I'll admit it. Are you human?"

"Sort of," she smiled and hugged Rae again as she joined them. Together they sat on the back porch of her neighbor's house and Lucy let them in on what she had been going through for the past week. Sebastian was unappeased when Lucy suggested that they relax, but she encouraged him, saying, "Father Kaylor lives here. He also has three other houses that he likes more. He isn't home; trust me."

Lucy took them through all the details when it came to her abduction, Eodin, Lucian, and the other vampires. She told them about the wolves' den and the various blood draws that she endured. They were on the edge of their seats for the tale of zephyrs and finally she revealed why she was different.

Lucy told them that she still didn't know why she could heal herself, but that she now knew what she was. The worst part was yet to come, however. In a solemn tone, after sweeping the bangs from her eyes, she revisited the truth of what vampires and werewolves were, and how she could become one of them if bitten.

Tryp immediately shot a glare at Sebastian and they locked eyes. The men stared at each other for a few minutes before Rae nudged Tryp and the connection broke. When the time to catch up was over, the four of them stood to leave.

Back on the street, Mitchell and Syrina were waiting by the car. Lucy was thankful that they were no longer wolves; that was still a strange concept for her.

"Now that you know, have either of you seen anyone go into the house after Lucinda died?" The concern in Lucy's voice made her tremble, but she tried to remain as calm as possible. She waited for their answer, and after a few moments both Rae and Tryp shook their heads.

"Only the police and coroner have gone in or out." Tryp frowned and glared back at Sebastian.

"Stop it, boys. Wait, did you say coroner?" Tryp nodded as his eyebrows crossed in concern, and said, "Why? What's wrong?"

"The police have my grandmother's keepsake box! They would've taken it for burial; her will was inside." The excitement in Lucy's voice soon had Syrina and Sebastian at her side.

Tryp became defensive immediately. "Lucy can't you stay with us? People will be so happy you're okay and you can live with me. My dad can afford us both. Please don't go with them." His words were touching, but Lucy knew what had to happen.

She sighed and waited for him to calm down before she took his arm and wrapped him in a hug.

"You know why I can't, and I didn't come back for you to convince me otherwise. My choice was made before I came to see you. This is goodbye, Tryp. I hope you can understand that. I didn't want you two to live with the thought that I had never been found. Mitchell's family is still out there thinking that." She heard the wolf snarl quietly at the sore topic. "I want you to know that I am alive and happy so that you can move on. I love you guys more than anything, but I can't stay."

As Lucy finished, Rae leaped to her and squeezed her in the hardest hug either of them had ever gone through. She could hear Rae sobbing into her ears as a mixture of saliva and tears stained her shirt. There were no words left. The emotions were thick and nothing could lighten the mood. It was destined to be a moment in time that could not be avoided or lightened by any stretch of the imagination. Eventually, Tryp pulled Rae away from their former friend and cradled her as she continued to cry.

"Don't remember her this way," he smirked. "She wouldn't want that."

"I know," Lucy agreed and touched his shoulder before abruptly turning back to the car. She couldn't look back. She was afraid of changing her mind. Tonight would have to be the last time she ever saw them and she wished more than anything that it didn't have to be.

Sebastian put his arm around Lucy and led her to the car. The sadness of the situation had left a painful lump in the back of her throat, and though he was persistent in trying to cheer her, Lucy could only crack a fake smile to appease him.

Time slowed down and all became silent as she suffered through the hardest thing she ever had to do. The last she saw of her friends were their silhouettes against the pavement as the car pulled away.

It would be a good two-hour drive to the morgue and that would give her plenty of time to refocus. She cried at the thought of completely forgetting her childhood friends. Along with Lucinda, they had been the foundation of her entire life and letting that go became near impossible.

Throughout the long car ride, Lucy could do nothing but stare out the window and will herself not to burst into tears. She watched the scenery pass by her window. It had begun to rain and the drops coming down streaked the glass with ribbons of water. It was dark out. There was barely any light on her side of the road. The highway was barren. She didn't know how late it was, but no one was traveling and that seemed odd. Their journey seemed to take forever and just as Lucy was getting impatient the car began to slow down.

They passed under a sign that read 'County Morgue' and a chill suddenly slid over Lucy's skin. They pulled around a circular driveway and parked right in front of the steps. To her it was odd and very conspicuous that they were leaving the car there, but the wolves didn't seem concerned. Lucy stepped out and looked over the property. There was a metal fence surrounding the perimeter and it was tipped with an arrow-like decoration. The building was large and square with rectangular windows. A flight of stairs led up to a porch that was a gateway to three different doors.

The calmness exhibited by Sebastian and the others was unsettling, as if they weren't concerned with getting caught. Lucy tried to appear confident with their decisions even though she wasn't.

As they neared the doors, Mitchell sprang ahead and turned the knob. It was secured against intruders. Without missing a beat, he pulled something from his pocket and began messing with the knob. Lucy couldn't see exactly what he was doing, but soon she heard a 'clunk' and the door popped open.

"Well done, Mitch," Sebastian congratulated him before passing into the lobby. Lucy followed close behind into a very dark room. The absence of sun left odd shadows against the floor, created by the faint streetlamps outside. There was a large desk that expanded the length of the back wall and several chairs that created a waiting room for the guests.

"Where are we? This doesn't look like a morgue," Lucy finally said as they ventured behind the desk.

It took a few seconds for anyone to answer her, but Sebastian cleared his throat before explaining, "The morgue was moved into the old hospital after the new hospital had been built. They kept all of the homey touches of a waiting room to keep the mood happy. I don't think they actually use this area." For some reason she found this funny, but then again it made sense. Lucy figured if she worked in a morgue these few features would make her job more enjoyable.

They took various turns through many different doors and hallways until a set of stairs appeared. The wolves wasted no time in descending them and they even appeared to know exactly where they were going. Finally they came to a long hallway of doors. Without stopping, Mitchell led them to the third one and he yanked it open.

The air inside was refrigerated and Lucy was certain that they were in the right room. The men made a beeline for the far wall that was lined with tall cabinets, while Syrina went to a computer and booted it up. Each of them seemed to have their own priority and Lucy was left alone to search the preservation chambers for her grandmother's name. Finally a note card that was stuck to the outside of a door caught her attention. "This one. She's here."

Although Lucy was talking to herself, Syrina's voice suddenly erupted in an order that left the room even colder, "Wait! Lucy, don't open that. Just hold on and let me find her in the computer."

"Why? I just want to see her face."

"Lucy, I'm warning you. If you open that you might not like what you find." Syrina seemed adamant, but Lucy was determined to find the truth. It was proof that she wanted. That was the only thing that could give her peace. Ignoring Syrina's warning, she gently pulled the handle and began to open the door. In a gust of wind, the female wolf was at her side and pushed the door closed with one hand, "I told you not to."

"What are you doing? Move!"

"Just wait. Trust me; we have time. Help the guys find that box, alright?" With a scowl, Lucy nodded and left the door alone. Syrina watched her walk to the file cabinets and wasn't satisfied until she started searching through them. Lucy glanced over every few seconds and sighed deeply as Syrina latched the chamber door and walked back to the computer.

"I found it," Mitchell finally shouted after a while. The young wolf pulled a cardboard box out of a group of other boxes and tossed the lid to the floor. Inside and plain as day was a small treasure chest that seemed incredibly old. It had metal fixtures that could've been used to chain it shut. Mitchell picked it up cautiously and set it on a nearby table. Lucy was hesitant to touch it.

There was a sense of breathlessness in the room. A tension built in Lucy's chest and with a trembling hand she lifted the lid. Among many documents and knickknacks was the very thing Lucy had hoped to find. An old heart-shaped locket the size of a silver dollar was strung on a long chain. There was only a moment of pause before she placed the locket around her neck and held it close to inspect the craftsmanship. There was a small design etched into the front with beautiful Celtic engravings around it. The back had obviously been worn over the years. It was smooth and discolored.

Lucy took a deep breath before she opened it and a sigh escaped as she began to tremble. There was a picture of Lucy as a baby in one side and a photo of two people in the other side. She didn't know them, but something was oddly familiar. They were dressed in old clothes. The woman had black hair and blue eyes. She was dressed in a knee-length, tight dress with boots, while he was in a black overcoat with a black vest and tie. He had kind, green eyes and wavy, brown hair. They seemed happy. Lucy knew right away that they were her parents. She couldn't help but smile. They were real. At some point in the past, her parents had both loved each other enough to be together and have a child.

Lucy closed the locket and held it tightly until her knuckles turned white. A sharp pain suddenly enveloped her hand and she opened it. A small puncture and red dot of blood appeared. The tip of the heart was sharper than she had noticed. Lucy wiped the blood on her pants and tucked the necklace into her shirt. She turned and scanned the room. Syrina was still on the computer, with the guys still going through boxes.

"I've got what I came for. We should go," Lucy decided as she closed the lid of the box. No one moved at all; not one inch. The men were watching Syrina. Moments passed and finally the eerie silence was broken when she said, "I'm not finished looking."

"For what?" Lucy's intrigue was sparked. She didn't realize there was an alternative motive for this break-in.

"I'm searching the files for unexplained deaths," Syrina said with a smile as she searched.

"Deaths caused by vampires?" Lucy wondered aloud.

"Usually anything humans cannot explain, mostly bites," Syrina explained without looking away from the screen.

"Oh." Lucy dropped the subject, afraid that she couldn't go much farther with her questions.

For the next hour, Syrina sped through case after case, but said nothing. Mitchell and Sebastian began playing cards with a deck they had found in someone's box of possessions, and Lucy went through her grandmother's belongings, pausing on the sentimental items. There weren't many things that she recognized. Some were baby pictures of either Lucy or her mom; she couldn't be sure. She had never seen pictures of herself that young, and part of her wished that they were pieces of her childhood. She gently set them aside and began going through the sheets of paper that were folded and crumpled inside the box; many of them were bills.

Then she came to a legal-looking document that appeared to be closed with a wax seal. With a deep breath exhaled, Lucy broke the impression and unfolded the paper. She scanned the words, coming to the realization that this text was Lucinda's will. It didn't bequeath much. She left most of her belongings to charity. Lucy wasn't mentioned in it at all, which, oddly, she understood. Even in death her grandmother was trying to keep her safe. One sentence in particular caught Lucy's attention.

Lucinda requested that she be buried in the family lot, which could be a clue as to where her parents were buried. She had gotten so enveloped in her discovery that Lucy barely noticed the men joining Syrina. She had said something that got their attention, and though it was difficult, Lucy stepped away from the box and joined them.

"There are two bites to take care of and then we can leave." Syrina's curly black hair bounced as she spoke, "We are looking for bodies numbered 54 and 31. Those are our bite victims."

"What is so special about vampire bites? It just drains their blood, right?" Lucy's assurance on the subject was met with scoffs from the wolves. Sebastian was the first to attempt a calm answer.

"No, vampire venom kills humans by shutting systems down. It takes the same pattern every time and leaves a green residue in the organs. Humans aren't smart enough to put the puzzle together half of the time, but we can't take any chances."

"Watch it! I'm human," Lucy warned and shoved her finger into his face.

"You aren't human anymore, Luce," he teased before joining Syrina at the wall of doors. By the time Lucy joined them, Mitchell was pulling open cooler number 31. A long table draped in a white cloth was pulled out. Lucy knew what was under it, but she couldn't concentrate on that. Her eyes were on Syrina. In her hand she had a long-needled syringe with white fluid inside.

There wasn't any hesitation or shock exhibited by the three wolves as the sheet was flipped over and the naked torso of a woman appeared. She was ghostly white, nearly blue, and her hair had been combed out of her face. Her body had been washed, but not opened. Lucy watched her closed eyes, waiting for them to open, but the lady was long dead and there was nothing left to force that movement. A hole the size of a small baseball cratered her right shoulder. It was bruised around the edges and extended into her body a couple of inches. The wound was smooth as if it was cut by a large melon baller. The injury was so distracting that Lucy nearly missed Syrina plunge the needle into the corpse's neck and inject half of the serum into her lifeless flesh. She removed it soon after and watched the reaction carefully.

Within only a few minutes the white color of the body began to fade into gray and then black. Suddenly the flesh began to disintegrate. Lucy watched the skin and muscle turn to ash around the bones. Eventually, even the bones began to splinter and then disappear into the pile of ash below them. Just as the remainder of the corpse dissolved, Mitchell covered it with the sheet and closed the door.

"What just happened? What is in that syringe?" was all that Lucy could get out before she covered her mouth with a free hand.

"We are erasing evidence," Sebastian explained while they searched for door 54.

"What is that stuff?"

"It is werewolf venom and the answer to your next question is: the vampire and werewolf venom react when they touch. In a living being they spontaneously combust. In bodies absent of life, the venoms disintegrate what tissue and cells there are. In the end, we use our venom to erase the evidence," Syrina explained as she found the second door.

"How long have you been doing this?"

"Long enough that we know how not to get caught," Mitchell replied as he grinned and opened the second chamber.

Lucy looked at the name on the door. She nearly swallowed her tongue. "No, please! Don't do that to my grandmother." The group was stunned for a moment and allowed Lucy to calm down before carrying on.

"We can't leave the evidence, Lucy. You don't have to be here for this if you don't want to be." Syrina wasn't about to let Lucy ruin the reason for their visit.

"Please don't." The thought of losing the face that had cared for her was keeping Lucy from what should be done. Her emotions were blinding her to what the wolves were trying to achieve.

"Lucy, it is just a body. The woman you knew is no longer there. Please, we need to do this." Sebastian frowned and forced her to turn around. He led her to the door and forced her to keep her back to the deed.

Lucy was empty. The disbelief of the situation left her cold and unaware of her surroundings. She crossed her arms and doubled over until she could sit on the floor. She buried her face in her hands and rubbed hard enough to remove a layer of skin. The refrigeration from the open chamber had snaked across the floor and was making the temperature decrease rapidly. Goosebumps covered her arms and legs. Syrina and Mitchell eventually arrived and helped Lucy to her feet.

"I'm sorry, Lucy, but we can't leave that evidence open to public interpretation. You'll understand someday. We can leave now," said

Syrina as she smirked sympathetically and began putting away the boxes that had been torn out. Reluctantly, the men helped her and in no time at all the room had returned to its former glory.

The journey back to the car was a long and quiet one. Lucy still couldn't wrap her mind around the exciting lives the wolves had, but she was less impressed with their responsibilities. The sun would be up in minutes and the world outside the building was cold, quiet, and wet with dew. Suddenly, the three wolves stopped and Sebastian took in several deep breaths.

"You smell that?" he announced to the group.

"It smells like an ambush," Mitchell yelled to the vacant property. Lucy was confused briefly until three of the faceless people appeared from the shrubbery that surrounded the walkway. They stood in an arrow formation, blocking the only easy exit.

The woman in front sported an evil grin as she allowed her hands to rest behind her back. Her black tank top fit snugly and was tucked into a pair of dark jeans. Her striking, fire-engine red hair was split by her shoulders, leaving strands to fall in the front. Her side-swept bangs shaped her face and made the angles of her cheeks appear even more flushed than they were already. The smirk on her peach-colored lips made her eyes glisten and her pale skin caused her hair color to look as if it was even brighter. She was very petite, but that didn't mean that Lucy would let her guard down.

The woman who flanked her left side was dressed similarly and had short blonde hair. She was incredibly skinny, but taller than the redhead. Even her face was small and reminded Lucy of a mouse or elf. Her complexion was very white and her ruby lips were the color of her leader's hair. Her gaze was intent on something. Lucy recognized the man to her right as the dark-skinned man called Charles, who had helped kidnap her. He seemed kinder in a way. His features weren't as fierce or as frightening as those of the women.

"Hello, Eliza." Sebastian grinned as he stepped in front of his family and took command of the situation.

"Oh, Sebastian, haven't you learned anything about taking in strays with our mark?"

"That doesn't make them your property."

Lucy had never seen Sebastian so tense. Whoever Eliza was, she clearly brought out the evil in him.

The woman behind her scowled and immediately spoke out in a thick accent that seemed to alter her words, "Do you want to make this difficult?"

"That's what I was hoping for. Viola, aren't you tired of being a runner for Eodin and jumping as high as you can whenever he asks it of you?"

"You know nothing of my relationship with Eodin, and how dare you criticize me when you have done the same for a human?"

"She isn't and has never been a human; you know that as well as I do." As their argument progressed, Lucy could see the color fade from the vampires' eyes and the angles of Sebastian's face tighten.

"We know. That's why we're here." Eliza smiled viciously and her sharp teeth became exposed.

"Come near her and you'll wish you hadn't," Mitchell growled at them as he stepped in front of Lucy.

"Little puppy want to play?" Viola teased him and batted her eyelashes as she laughed. Without letting another second pass, Mitchell dropped to a hunch and charged the vampires. As soon as he was close enough, Viola leaped over him and hissed at Lucy, which made her shiver. It almost seemed as if the vampires were here to kill her rather than kidnap her, or start a fight. Mitchell planted his feet into the ground and flipped around. He snatched Viola out of the sky with a clawed hand and flung her to the ground.

Though the blow was severe, she sprang to her feet and regrouped with her fellow blood suckers. Without further delay, the two groups charged each other. Sebastian tackled Eliza and, with his amazing strength, whipped her effortlessly into a nearby tree. Unfazed, the woman's head snapped up and she hissed. Eliza's appearance had reverted to the primal and frightening one that Lucian had taken the night of the festival. Her eyes were black and there were silvery tattoos on her temples and wrists. The fear that Lucy was used to feeling without Sebastian around had returned. She felt it snake down each of her limbs and restrict her motion.

Mitchell and Viola were also fighting, but in a different way. They both were using lightning-fast blows and blocks that Lucy figured was some form of martial arts. Syrina was up against Charles, but she actually seemed to be keeping him busy. Her swift attacks didn't have much effect on him, and she was too quick for his maiming attempts.

His hands were clenched tightly as if he was crushing tennis balls and he launched his towering form forward. Syrina dug her fingers into the bicep of his swinging arm and ripped at the muscle while striking his chest with her other hand. It was a thousand-year-old battle style from the greatest Kung Fu masters; first attack the arm that attacks you.

Syrina tore into his face with the claws of her right hand, raking along his nose and mouth. With the other hand she punched him as hard as she could in the chest, right above his heart. For a moment, Lucy was excited for the success of a kill. Syrina was an amazing fighter. There were no wind ups or wasted motion; each movement was designed to roll naturally into the next. To Lucy's surprise, blood spattered his nose and mouth. His eyes closed and he made a gurgling sound. Everything she knew about vampires seemed to be wrong. They could bleed and their hearts did beat, but whether or not it was necessary she didn't know.

All Syrina had to do was force her inhumanly strong hand through his chest, but instead she launched herself backward and kicked him twice in the chin. Charles stumbled backward. Then, with a robotic snap, his balance returned and his eyes fixed on Syrina as she completed a few back handsprings. The large vampire wasn't disoriented for long. To Syrina's surprise, he wiped the blood from his mouth with the back of his hand and calmly stomped toward her. Even from where Lucy was standing, the ground seemed to shake. With speed that had been empowered by the small defeat, Charles grabbed Syrina by the throat and lifted her into the air. Lucy watched in horror as her friend went limp and pulled helplessly at his fingers and wrist. If Charles had squeezed any harder he could've easily crushed her.

Lucy looked around to plead for help, but no one seemed free at the time. Sebastian and Eliza were tumbling around and throwing kicks and punches that didn't seem to make contact. Viola was keeping Mitchell busy as well. Lucy could see no other alternative. With a shaking hand, she tucked her hair behind her ear and took a deep breath. As every doubt in her head tried to hold her back, Lucy ran at the large man and leaped onto his back. Without thinking, she dug her fingernails into his ears until blood came out.

She was uncertain if it caused him pain, and prayed that it

would at least be distracting. As if the heavens had answered her, Charles dropped Syrina in midair and began clawing at his back. Lucy watched her friend gasp to life and scurry away from him before she released his head and jumped to the ground. An incoherent growl was all that it took to regain Lucy's attention.

The vampire turned to look at his assailant. His bloody ears were stained with red that was quickly drying. His green eyes found Lucy's blue eyes and they stared at each other for only seconds. He took a step forward and Lucy took a step back. It didn't seem like he wanted to hurt her. There was a sense of curiosity in both his manner and his eyes. Lucy was uncertain how long they would've continued on if Viola hadn't screamed his name. She didn't shout it as if it was a summons. There was fear in her voice. It was then Lucy noticed that Syrina had left them.

The three wolves had Eliza and Viola cornered against the arrow fence that separated the sidewalk from the yard. They were crouched defensively, waiting for the remainder of the fight.

"Just leave, Eliza," Sebastian ordered as he wiped the blood from the corner of his mouth. She almost seemed surprised that he had told her to go, but the wavy-haired vixen only glared at him with more hate than Lucy thought a being could control.

"We don't give in, Sebastian. You must know this," Viola sneered and spat at them.

"Then that is your mistake," Mitchell finished before they leaped at each other again. Eliza flew at him to tear at his face. As she sailed through the air, the young wolf managed to grab her closest arm and twist it behind her. In one swift motion, he flipped her over and pinned her to the ground. With his free hand, Mitchell took hold of her throat and held her to the pavement as he glanced back to see what had become of Viola. Lucy watched the color in his face fade, and though she had been watching his amazing feat, she now flung her entire body around to see what had made him lose his color. She could feel her limbs grow cold.

Viola had attacked Sebastian just as Eliza had gone after Mitchell, but in the tension of the moment their encounter had gone completely awry. Lucy examined in horror their unfortunate situation.

Somehow Viola had fallen onto one of the metal arrows. Sebastian stood over her. His arm was also punctured by the arrow.

The whole situation seemed impossible and although Lucy hoped for the best, she could tell by Viola's limp body that what "life" there was inside her had been stripped away. The arrow had impaled her through the chest right where her heart had been. Sebastian's forearm hid the sharp tip from view. It hadn't gone all the way through, but he still seemed to feel the pain. With a yank, his arm came loose. A squirt of blood erupted into the air and the wound pooled before he could apply the necessary pressure to stop it. Mitchell immediately released Eliza so that she could also see what happened.

Lucy had never witnessed death before. She had always expected her own and feared it above anything else, but the reality of a stranger dying in front of her was life-changing. She could sense the vomit-inducing misery coursing through the air, which had become thick and nearly unbreathable. She watched Eliza cry out in anger at Sebastian for killing her sister. His face was guilty. Lucy couldn't hear a word. The shock of the moment left any word exchange indecipherable.

Finally, Charles pushed through the crowd and lifted Viola from the fence. Her body was limp and her green killer's eyes were closed. Her small figure seemed fragile in his arms, like it would be nothing for him to break her in half. Lucy's hearing came back just in time for Eliza to shout a death threat at Sebastian before they vanished into the shrubbery.

No more than seconds after, Lucy heard a thud behind her and whipped around to find Sebastian lying on the ground and curled up. His entire body was shaking spastically as he nearly yelled in pain. It didn't take long for Mitchell and Syrina to check his situation and get him in the car. Lucy quickly slid into the back seat with him before she felt the car jerk to a start and skid out of the parking lot.

"What's wrong with him?" she yelled to whoever was listening. Both Mitchell and Syrina had chosen to sit in the front seat, leaving Lucy alone with a werewolf in pain. She suddenly found herself scared. She was more scared of him than she had ever been.

"I don't really know. Cyrus has forbade us to fight with vampires. I'm not sure what they did to him," Mitchell shouted to her. "Just distract him and keep him calm. We'll be home soon.

In a desperate effort to relieve his pain, Lucy grabbed his hand and began humming softly. His skin was cold and clammy, and the hole in his arm was bleeding onto the seat. She slid onto the floor and ripped the hem of her shirt. At the sound of ripping fabric, Lucy watched Syrina shiver. She had forgotten that she was wearing someone else's clothes. Though she realized that he would heal soon, Lucy wrapped his arm tightly to stop the bleeding and then forced him to rest his head in her hands. She watched his glazed-over appearance fade in and out with each breath. Something was terribly wrong.

Every so often, she watched the world outside pass. Syrina was going so fast that the scenery was blurred into the background. It was then she knew that they weren't telling her something. This was worse than what they were letting on.

"We'll be there soon," she smiled and glanced down at his pained expression while she tried to convince herself that he would be okay. As she went to look away, something caught her attention. His eyes were fading from blue to green. It was like his body couldn't decide what color his eyes were supposed to be. Lucy became mesmerized by the constant color change. She couldn't take her eyes off of him.

Suddenly, the road became rough and she realized that they had come to the meadow entrance of the wolves' den. Lucy's face suddenly felt wet. She wiped the tears away and realized that she had been crying for most of the drive. It seemed like only seconds before Mitchell threw open the door and grabbed hold of Sebastian. It appeared effortless for him to drag his brother through the meadow. Lucy had never seen one man bear the weight of another before and she wondered, even with the amazing strength he possessed, whether Mitchell would be able to carry Sebastian to their home.

With a grunt, Mitchell wrapped his brother's arms around his neck and used his back to support the weight. Soon enough he had taken off in a sprint. Sebastian's feet dragged across the ground and caused twigs to spring in the air. His blonde curls toppled over Mitchell's shoulder and into his face. Lucy and Syrina could barely keep up with him. They ran until the trees cleared and the large house came into view. At this point, Mitchell's arms and legs shook violently. He slowed to a stop and fought the urge to collapse.

"Not much further, Mitch," Syrina encouraged with a smile. This seemed to be all that he needed. With yet another grunt, his feet sped up and they ran the rest of the way.

Memories of what happened next were spaced, blurry, and slow. Lucy remembered Cyrus's face when he saw exactly what was going on. It was the only thing that was clear. His anger was buried by concern. Mitchell helped him carry Sebastian to the basement and Syrina stayed with Lucy. They sat in the gallery room where there were several things to distract their thoughts. However, with the spastic screaming that reverberated through the walls, nothing could take their minds off of what was going on below their feet. Sebastian was well aware of his pain now and by the unsettling shrieks coming through the floor, Lucy was certain that his condition was critical.

She tried her best to imagine something else. Syrina sat next to her. Light sobs were coming from her direction. Lucy wanted to comfort her so badly, but had no idea how to begin or what to say.

Suddenly, her thoughts were taken to the paintings on the wall. It was a relief not to be burdened with the pain of worry for a few minutes. She remembered the initials on the works of art hanging on the walls and wondered who had created them. Who could be so talented to be worth the time and wall space of people who lived for centuries?

Lucy's eyes wandered from one painting to the next. The emotion portrayed through this person's brush strokes nearly jumped off of the canvas. She could almost imagine that person's state of mind, whether it was excitement, anger, or love. The images made her feel a closeness between the artist and herself.

"It is true art," Lucy whispered to herself, but Syrina didn't appear to notice. With her amazing senses, Lucy began to wonder if she had said anything at all.

The sound of a closing door radiated in the adjacent room and both of them watched the doorway anxiously. Lucy hadn't noticed, but Sebastian's screaming had stopped and the house was quiet once again. Mitchell stepped into the room and nodded. Syrina was immediately relieved as she stood to follow him. Lucy did likewise, and he led them to the basement steps. There was an eerie silence that sent shivers up her spine. She wanted to ask if Sebastian was all right, but was afraid of what the answer might be.

They entered the lab and followed Mitchell around the corner away from all of the equipment and running tests. Kieron was behind one of the microscopes. His eyebrows were crossed in such a manner that Lucy feared they might get stuck that way. His brilliant white lab coat was sprawled out from his chair in all directions.

Lucy was so focused on him that she barely noticed where Mitchell and Syrina had gone. They were just around a second corner, which had been turned into a makeshift hospital room. Sebastian was lying on a cot with Allegra smiling at his jokes as she took his vitals.

"Are you okay?" Lucy muttered, which seemed to stop everything in midsentence.

"I'll be fine. I just need to rest."

"Don't lie to her!" Syrina scolded and slapped him on the leg.

"Don't hit me," he frowned, "I'm hurt enough already."

"Not in the leg you aren't," Syrina scolded as she hit him again.

"What is she talking about? You won't die, will you?" Lucy stuttered and sat at his bedside.

"No, Syrina is just overreacting."

"I am not!" she argued. As soon as the voices rose over normal talking level, Allegra intervened and shushed everyone back down to a whisper. Lucy looked back just in time to see Cyrus appear and tuck his arms around his wife's waist. They rocked together a moment before he kissed her on the side of her head. Even in the darkest circumstances they were still there to comfort each other. Lucy wished that she had a relationship like that.

In time, Cyrus left his wife's side and sauntered over to Lucy, asking, "Did it go well?"

"The beginning did," Lucy mumbled out of the corner of her mouth.

She could hear a faint rumbling laugh deep in his throat, followed by words that were utterly frightening. "Can I talk to you privately?"

In the shock of the question, Lucy nearly said "no," considering the fact that she had yet to hear of Sebastian's condition. With a quick judgment of her choices, she nodded and followed him away from the bedside. They reentered the main laboratory and he offered her a seat before disappearing behind a curtain. Within seconds, Cyrus returned with a bowl, some gauze, and a few other items. He sat next to her and gently lifted her arm, using his hand to support it. With his other hand, Cyrus pushed up her sleeve, exposing a gash that Lucy hadn't even noticed. Her speed healing hadn't stopped the bleeding completely, but it had slowed the leaking enough to harden it. With fluidity that Lucy deemed uncharacteristic, Cyrus continued to dip a piece of square material in the bowl of liquid and wiped the wound free of the partially dried blood.

"How did you know? I didn't even know," Lucy asked as she watched him tend to her arm.

"I simply saw the drips and figured that if it didn't require attention, your body would've taken care of it by now." His logic made sense. After finishing the cleaning, Cyrus wrapped her arm in gauze and self-adhesive tape.

"There," he said finally, "all done." With a smile, he patted her leg and stood up to dispose of the blood-stained squares.

"Did you hear what happened to Sebastian?"

"He got in a fight with Viola and she died. It's a pity." He frowned and returned to her side. They sat next to each other in silence for a few minutes. If it were anyone else, Lucy knew the company would have been uncomfortable, but with Cyrus no expected upset came. Sitting next to him was as easy as being with an old friend. It was effortless on her part to trust him.

"Why is he so sick?" Lucy finally asked as she turned to face him. The time for answers to come forth was short. He didn't have to think long. It was almost as if he was ready with the answer and all she had to do was ask the right question.

"Blood-to-blood contact between wolves and vampires causes a reaction. Viola and Sebastian were skewered by the same object. This broke his arm, which allowed her blood to get into his bone. Right now, he is making blood cells that are incompatible with his body and they are bursting. The vampire blood is killing him in a way, but his immune system will fight it off. He will be fine. It will just be a while before he is back to normal."

"Sort of like why you inject corpses with your venom?"

"In a way it's similar. We discovered a long time ago, during the war, that humans infected by two different zephyr hybrids will disintegrate. The reaction of two venoms in one body is and has always been death. Many zephyrs died this way back when I was still a young wolf. During battle, if we would try to change someone, a

90

vampire would bite that person too. The reaction of venoms would kill the zephyr and neither side would win." His expression grew bleak. "This is what my family is preventing, along with reducing the common knowledge of our existence."

"Is that why you erase bite victims?"

"Yes, that is why," Cyrus touched her shoulder as he stood.

"Um," she stopped him just before he could disappear behind the curtain again. "On the way here his eyes were doing something strange."

"It was probably just a reaction to the venom. Sometimes, with some people, the body can't decide what it is. Eye color fluctuations are startling, but they happen. Don't let it worry you." With a grin he offered her his hand and led her back into the makeshift hospital room.

All eyes shifted to them. Lucy didn't seem to notice and immediately sat next to Sebastian. His curly hair bounced as he followed her gaze down to the broken arm that had been set and wrapped. She let her hand trace the bandage, "What have they done?" She meant for her words to be accusing, but when she looked at him hoping that he would agree, Sebastian shook his head and placed a hand on hers. Sandwiched between his arm and hand, Lucy's fingers quickly became warm.

"No, Lucy, I did worse. I deserve this for causing her death." His seriousness worried her.

"She started the fight." Lucy was not convinced that he in any way deserved this sickness.

"Viola was a pawn and didn't deserve death. She was Eodin's first try at mind control that had succeeded. Whatever she did to Sebastian wasn't her choice," Allegra interrupted for a moment.

"Never mind that. It's over." Kieron sighed as he entered the room and handed Allegra a small stack of papers. "Move on. What is next?"

Kieron's adorable Scottish droll made him hard to understand sometimes, but somehow he always seemed to get his point across because at that moment Sebastian spoke up. "We were headed for a cemetery to look for Lucy's parents' graves."

"I had hoped to go soon," Lucy muttered and scanned the faces of those around her.

"You might have to wait," Allegra frowned and held out the papers Kieron had given her.

"Why?" Sebastian seemed to say what was on everyone else's mind.

"The reaction to vampire blood is subtle, but for the time being your healing speed has been reduced to that of a human. That broken arm could take weeks to heal."

"I can go with it broken," he reassured her, but for the first time, Lucy heard Allegra raise her voice.

"No, you could die if there is another ambush. Eliza wouldn't hesitate. You are grounded."

Lucy was briefly amused by her choice of words, but that humor was quickly replaced with disappointment. She didn't know if she could wait to find where her parents had been buried. If her grandmother had told her the truth, Lucy had been very young at the funeral and was too young to properly pay her respects. More than anything, she wanted to remedy that.

"I am willing to go," Cyrus interrupted with a certain grin on his face.

"Are you sure?" Allegra seemed surprised, but his response appeared to reassure her.

"I don't leave very often and I can't imagine what it would be like for Lucy to wait all that time with what she knows. That's enough to drive a person mad." He grinned wildly and took her hand.

"When can we leave?" Lucy wondered, still shocked by his willingness to volunteer.

"Now, if you'd like." Without another second spared, Lucy turned to Sebastian, squeezed his hand, and said, "Feel better." She smiled before kissing him lightly on the forehead.

"Be careful, and Cyrus, you'd better protect her!" he warned, but in a sort of cheery way. Soon after, Allegra and Cyrus spent a few minutes saying good-bye.

Then he led the way up the steps and to another door in the main hall that Lucy hadn't noticed before. Without hesitation, he tossed it open. For some reason, she was thankful that it was only a closet full of coats. Cyrus handed Lucy a short, pink overcoat and took a leather jacket for himself. "This pink thing is Syrina's, but I don't think she'll mind."

Like a gentleman he helped her put the coat on and then opened the door before following her out into the chilled forest air.

Chapter Six

ucy had never been exposed to cemeteries in her life and now they were becoming reoccurring scenery. She tried her best not to stare at Cyrus throughout the ride, but he had a presence that unwillingly stole attention. She attempted to watch the world outside pass just to avoid him catching her gaze. The sun had gotten higher since they had begun the journey. Lucy slowly began to realize that it had been days since she had slept for any length of time. She knew that resting would have been a good idea, but the effects of sleep deprivation were nonexistent. It was almost as if sleeping wasn't important anymore. She could allow the world to pass by without worrying about the necessities of sleeping, eating, or other human behavior. It might've been a zephyr trait, or just her gaining control over her body like Cyrus had said she would be able to do in time.

They had been on the same winding road for a good hour now. It had recently been paved and the blackness of the new pavement created the effect of glowing center lines. The road divided the forest into two halves and trees hovered over it as if they were waiting to reclaim the land for their own. She watched them sway in the wind, creating shadows that lined the road.

"How is it you always know where you're going?" Lucy asked without turning away from the window.

"Instinct," was all that he said. Lucy knew it was an answer given to avoid complicated conversations.

"But, you don't even know the address."

"Don't need one. I told you; instincts." He smiled and nudged her until she joined him in a laugh. Cyrus made his feelings about which turns to take sound like magic. The road appeared endless. It was just a long snaking path like a river that wouldn't stop until it got to the ocean.

Just as the scenery began to blur together, Lucy felt the car slow down. As they wound around another bend in the forest, a small sign came into view. It read Cemetery Road. Lucy was utterly dumbfounded when she realized that they had arrived. A knot immediately formed in her stomach. This is where her parents would be buried. This is where she might be buried someday.

The gravel road wound up a small hill. It circled around and was so narrow that Lucy could look down the side of the driveway to the bottom of a ten foot drop. Part of her became unwillingly frightened, but faith in Cyrus's driving ability kept her calm. After a few minutes of constant turning, they got to the top and crossed under an archway. At the top there was an old sign that read, 'Amistad Cemetery.'

The trees parted, and a small plot of land only a couple of acres wide appeared. There was a tiny house at the beginning of the drive for the caretaker and only a couple of rows of newer graves to the left. To the right and closer to the tree line were even more rows of gravestones that had been weathered and broken. They were brown and faded to the point that the names were nearly illegible.

Cyrus only drove a little farther before stopping and turning the engine off. With a sigh, his hand dropped from the keys and fell onto his lap. Lucy watched him out of the corner of her eye. She waited for him to open the door or say something, but nothing happened. She paused for a few more minutes. Lucy watched his chest expand as he inhaled, hoping for some other movement. Nothing came. He didn't even blink.

All patience lost, she opened the door and slammed it behind her. The ambiance outside was oddly comforting. Butterflies danced amongst the graves, which somehow made the cemetery seem alive. The grass was a vibrant color of green and there were even some purple wild flowers decorating the ground. With a sigh, Lucy went from grave to grave reading the names of those who had been buried there. Row after row, she looked for Craig Gaskin or Annie Wise. The older graves, that hadn't been eroded beyond the point of recognition, didn't give away any answers.

By the time she returned to the car, Cyrus had exited the vehicle and was leaning against his door. Lucy crossed to the other side of the cemetery toward the newer graves and watched him. The look on his face immediately made her worry, so she asked, "Cyrus, are you okay?"

"Just fine. Let's look, then." He sported an emotionless grin and ventured forward into the grass. Lucy tried her best to focus on the search, but found her eyes drifting to him more than once. There was something on his mind and it was strong enough to distract him from anything else. One by one, they looked over the graves, and with every unrecognized name, Lucy grew more depressed.

Finally, she could see the last two tombstones that they hadn't examined. She prayed silently. As soon as they entered her sight, Lucy heard a gasp leave her own lips. One of them was the Gaskin family headstone and the other was Lucinda's headstone. She hadn't been buried yet, but the plot of land was clearly marked by the monument's shadow.

"They're here," she mumbled, trying to hold back the sobs.

"No, Lucy. Look again," Cyrus said as he turned back toward the car and left her to read the stone. She did as he asked. When she read the names, Lucy nearly choked on her surprise. Where she had thought the name of her father was, the name of Cyrus Gaskin was engraved.

Lucy instantly felt her skin grow cold and clammy. Doubt padded her mind to absorb the shock of what she now knew. Lucy watched the wind blow her hair past her shoulders. With a shaking hand, she pushed the flying strands back behind her ears and turned to find him. Cyrus had returned to the car. He sat inside, staring out the windshield at anything that could distract him.

Lucy willed her body back into submission and strolled back over to the car. She could feel tears well up and begin to fall before her fingers wrapped under the door handle and ripped it from the lock. She fumbled her way into the vehicle like she was drugged and slammed the door with a grunt.

"Why didn't you tell me?" Lucy finally said and watched him flinch under the anger in her voice.

"I've been clear about asking the right questions before, haven't I?" His tone trembled as he spoke.

"Who are you?" Cyrus looked at her with smiling eyes to find that it was an accusing sort of question. Side by side in the front seat of his car, the werewolf began to divulge himself in a manner to which he was unaccustomed.

"I'm not as ancient as some of the members in this pack, but in terms of experience I suppose I am quite old."

"By terms of experience, you mean what?"

"War and death mostly. I was a Nazi general for most of my twenties and we would storm through city after city ripping through homes and murdering families. I gave the orders. Genocide was a result of the decisions I made. My soldiers would create a few lines of ten pedestrians and then open fire. They would laugh about it later like it was a game, their favorite game. I can still feel the spray of blood on my face. It always begins warm and then becomes cold and sticky. The blood of the innocent is impossible to wash off. Their faces are never far from my mind. I've seen too much and I hope that no one ever has to live as long as I will only to suffer the things that I have seen." Cyrus's voice had become lifeless. She could tell how haunted he was by what he had been through.

"That's awful. Does every wolf have stories like yours? Syrina, Mitchell, Sebastian; they all seem so sad."

"The change doesn't just take away your humanity. It strips you of your connection to humanity. You feel things differently. You walk and talk, or even think differently. It's a new set of ears and eyes to get used to. Often the change can be traumatic or even strip you of your former self to the point that you can't remember who you were."

"Would that happen to me?" She automatically became worried and for good reason. Lucy had never had an amazing life, but she wanted to remember it.

"I want you to know something, Lucy. You are special. I've never known someone to be able to heal themselves before the change. Also, you're incredibly smart. Beyond these things I am in the dark, but never forget that you are so important. You can do things that no other zephyr can. As far as I'm concerned, you could do anything if you tried. Believe in yourself," he smiled and put his hand on her shoulder.

As she came back into the moment, Lucy noticed Cyrus staring at her hand and out of instinct she covered the mark that Lucian had carved into her skin. The mark extended from the corner of the top of her right hand to the center of the bottom of her wrist. It resembled an incomplete hourglass. The z-like shape was the brand that a monster forced into her flesh.

"The scar is a mark that few receive," he finally spoke as his eyes averted so that he could stare directly into hers.

"Why did he do that to me?"

"Vampires mark zephyrs like that not only because it is cruel and painful, but also because that way they can identify escapees. It is also a way to lower them. The marked ones are seen as inferior by some."

"The blood sample he took hadn't even been examined when he did that to me."

"Lucian is very old and, like Syrina, he can see the signs before there is proof." Cyrus's voice grew cold, a tone that matched his face. "Eodin demands proof."

"Did you know my parents? Is that your name on the headstone outside?"

"Your dad is my brother."

"Their names aren't out there. They are alive then, right?"

"I was at your mother's funeral, as were you."

"My dad?"

"He had gone into hiding by then."

"Why do I have a feeling that you know so much more that you aren't telling me?"

"As before, I will respond truthfully to all questions." Cyrus moved slightly to make himself more comfortable and began to stroke his small goatee.

"Where is my mother's grave?"

"She was cremated and her ashes were scattered in the waters that occupy a small cove in Hawaii. It was a lovely ceremony. That was where your parents met. That cove was her favorite place in the entire world."

"Where's my father now?"

"I don't know."

"Why didn't he go to the funeral? Who was he hiding from?"

"A royal coven in Europe had their eye on him. He was an escapee that they were after. He had been under their control, but your mom helped him escape."

"What control did they have over him?"

"The royal coven is a very large coven that is controlled by seven leaders. Above them is one ruler who has a psychic ability to control all minds that let him in. Your dad gave them a run for their money."

"So he's still hiding somewhere?"

"I don't know. I haven't seen him in eighteen years." Just as he said that a thump came from outside of his door and it shot open. Mitchell stumbled into view and after panting a few breaths he stuttered through his message, "Blood banks are open. There is something you've got to hear."

"Did you run here?" Lucy asked the young wolf before he could slip out of view.

"Syrina dropped me off a few miles back and I ran the rest of the way," Mitchell managed to convey through his heaves. Cyrus didn't say a word. He started the car as Mitchell slipped out of view and reappeared in the back seat.

"How did your day go?" he asked as Cyrus spun the car around, throwing gravel through the grounds.

"Cyrus is my uncle and my father might be alive somewhere. You?" Lucy joked and held on to whatever she could as the car sped even faster when they got to the paved road.

"I don't think I can top that," he smirked back and howled wildly at the treacherous speed Cyrus was driving.

"Which bank?" The intense pack leader demanded without looking up at Mitchell in the rearview mirror.

"The one we've been watching. You were right about this one too."

"Right about what?" Lucy had been lost in her thoughts for several miles and felt it was about time to get caught up.

"The Forsaken, a royal coven in Europe, developed a ruse to accumulate stores of blood and distribute it among their family. It isn't necessarily legal in this country, but is better than the alternative I suppose," Mitchell explained as he pointed Cyrus to a street on the left. They had entered a small city.

"What's the alternative?"

"Completely draining a human by force." Cyrus glanced over to her. "We are actually trying to limit their food choices to animals."

"Lately, they've been stealing from hospitals or using blood banks to feed themselves, but they also test the blood and look for zephyrs. It is killing two birds with one stone," Mitch said with a frown.

"How could they possibly get away with that?" Lucy managed

to get out that last question as the car came to a stop in front of a brick building. There were two cherry blossom trees decorating the beginning of a small walkway. Under one of them stood two shadowed figures. Lucy's mind went blank with fear before memories of the faceless left her trembling.

As Cyrus exited the vehicle, she was nearly tempted to stop him, but then glanced back at the tree and was relieved to see that the strangers were Syrina and Kieron. Aware that they were heading into a vampire-run operation, Lucy's eyes shifted through the scenery, hoping that nothing would stick out as danger. Though distracted, she followed Mitchell and Cyrus to meet up with their pack members. As they approached, she was finally able to see Kieron in daylight and was amazed that he seemed to take in and express the sun like a moon on Earth. His bright eyes were bluer than anyone else's.

"What do we have?" Cyrus seemed eager for the update so that they could engage the false blood drive. The group circled under the tree and leaned inward like a sports huddle.

"There are four vampires inside. Cecily appears to be giving the orders. Eliza and Charles have bodyguard duty and Lucian is drawing the blood," Syrina spoke softly to avoid unwanted attention.

Lucy was immediately troubled and interrupted the conversation. "How could any person be comfortable with him taking their blood, of all people?"

"Vampires possess an ability that humans are vulnerable to. It makes them ignore their instincts. They believe what they are told and trust intentions. They nearly fall onto the needle. Even some wolves have trouble resisting him; right Syrina?" Kieron grinned and nudged her.

"One time and never again," she bit down hard and glared at him when he brought up the bad memory. Lucy didn't need to hear any more. She was well aware of how frightening Lucian was and no amount of charm would change her mind. He was her enemy—her one true enemy. There was nothing he could say or do to alter her perceptions.

Lucy waited and focused on the eyes of her family. They were calmly observant of the task at hand. She was unsure of just what that task might entail, but her newfound respect for the man whom she now knew was her uncle led Lucy to trust whatever they were about to do. It was a foolish assumption to think that they had any sort of plan, she was sure. Cyrus straightened and began to walk the length of the sidewalk. One by one, the group followed, leaving Lucy to bring up the rear. She wasn't sure that she wanted to see or hear the fight that was sure to ensue.

The doorway wasn't far. It opened and disappeared into the wall automatically. A frigid breeze swept past them and blew Lucy's hair out of her face. She immediately crossed her arms and tried to hold in as much body heat as possible. The room took her off guard. It seemed like a normal blood donation center with a waiting room, employees, and reception area. There were humans lingering in the lobby and reading magazines. They didn't seem afraid, nor were they apprehensive. The blood draws were routine for them. They reminded her of cattle waiting to be slaughtered, having no idea what awaits them.

The wolves remained in the entrance while Cyrus sauntered up to the front desk. The woman behind it appeared happy to see him and they began talking. The general kindness faded quickly as Lucy heard his words become harsher. Joy melted from the woman's face and fear replaced it. She wheeled her chair away from him and stood up. Everything about her body language was submissive. She wasn't about to resist his orders or try to fight, and somehow this made Lucy feel more confident in their endeavor.

After only seconds, the frightened lady came out from behind the counter and scurried through one of the doors in a small hallway. Cyrus returned to his group with a grin, and a reassuring wink to Lucy. She had never known much about her uncle or his persuasive speeches, but was thankful that he was here to negotiate rather than attempting a repeat of what happened at the morgue.

Within a few minutes, the door where the receptionist had disappeared flew open and a man stepped out. Lucy felt chills rush up her spine and down her arms. His green eyes were completely focused on her. She expected him to charge or fly demonically across the room like a shadow and attack, but instead he lowered his head and stared. In a few moments, he was joined by three of his coven members and they quickly completed a diamond shape behind him. Lucy felt her stomach drop into her abdomen. They always began their attacks in that formation. She instantly lost all hope in this encounter ending well.

Kieron and Syrina wasted no time in emptying out the lobby, saying anything that they could to get its occupants to leave. Lucy watched the people scurry past her. They were more annoyed than afraid and she was glad that they didn't know exactly why the evacuation was happening. She was happy to leave them believing a lie because that was what they needed to keep them alive. The truth that Lucy was now subjected to left her nervous and panicked most of the time, and she wouldn't wish those feelings on anyone.

Mitchell locked the door as the last person left, and Syrina drew the blinds. Lucy observed as Lucian watched them secure the area. His expression remained patient and curious, but she saw what lay deeper. His charming ways didn't change what Lucy knew he was.

"Finished yet?" he mocked with a tone that forced Lucy to stop breathing for a minute. The indifference he conveyed in his words was more than Lucy needed to want him dead. He didn't care if they hurt anyone or if the humans could see what was going on. Vampires seemed to live in the moment and were also oddly patient. This tolerance for wasted time was something that she didn't understand. It was like they were prepared to wait as long as it took in order to get the messiest, and most painful fight possible.

Lucy watched his reinforcements closely. The red-haired female from the morgue and her kidnapping was behind him, along with the kind-eyed, muscular Charles. Eliza had a small smile on her face and her head tilted slightly to look as if she was mentally unstable. The woman to her right stood powerfully and gazed across the room with a stare that could burn through iron. Lucy remembered Cecily's strange name and wondered if she was to Eodin what Allegra was to Cyrus. Her bangs were nearly covering her bright green eyes. The woman was something that Lucy couldn't get out of her head, and soon her name became like an earsplitting shriek, triggering an instant hatred within. It was a feeling she couldn't explain; not even to herself.

"You know that we always give you the choice. Leave, Lucian." Cyrus offered an escape route that the head vampire turned down immediately, to the excitement of his soldiers. Eliza couldn't seem to wait to dig her claws into someone.

"We do not back down so easily. We are the proper zephyrs.

You are mutts." His words didn't seem to penetrate very far. Lucy stepped away from the group. She knew that there was nothing she could do to help her friends if the fight didn't go in their favor. She wished that she could be a part of the fray and help in some way. As vulnerable as she was, there was nothing Lucy could do but get in the way.

"Let's do this then," Cyrus stated and just as the last breath of words left his lips, Eliza was nearly on top of him. She forced both hands onto his chest and threw him into the far wall. Lucy watched in horror as he slid down, leaving a large, cracked hole. With a spin he was on his feet and running at her. By then the others were fighting as well. Now that the humans had left the premises Lucy saw no reason to fight, but years of hatred and boredom can do wonders to beings that live for thousands of years.

Lucy watched Syrina and Kieron fighting back to back as Cecily and Charles attacked them. The speed at which the red-haired woman's fists were attempting contact was impressive, but Kieron could block every blow. His fighting style was precise and planned. With a scowl, she slapped him across the face and took hold of his neck with both hands. Though she tried, Cecily couldn't hold on tight enough to stop him from breaking her contact. Kieron wrapped his hands around each of her wrists and twisted them hard enough to break the small bones inside. Lucy shuttered when she cried out in pain and revealed her dagger-like, flesh-ripping teeth. Absent of hesitation, he used his foot to launch her across the room and into one of the chairs. Satisfied that he had stopped her for the time being, Kieron whipped around and began to assist in defeating Charles.

Across the room, Mitchell was doing a better job of out-maneuvering Lucian than he was fighting him. The young wolf was twice as fast as his vampire enemy and no matter what Lucian tried, he couldn't lay a hand on Mitch. Though all of the vampires appeared to be distracted, Lucy was still overwhelmed by the danger she was in and slowly made her way to the reception desk. After another quick glance at the room to be sure that no one had noticed her, she crawled behind it and hid in the corner to wait out the fight.

Every once in a while she could feel something slam up against the other side of the desk. Everything about the strike sounded and felt painful. She could only pray that all of her friends were doing well. Suddenly, a body crashed into the wall above her and fell to the floor with a thud. Lucy was terrified to find that it was Eliza. Her bright red hair was covering her face, but she didn't seem badly beaten.

Lucy watched her for a minute to be sure that she wasn't breathing and the brief glimmer of satisfaction was replaced by uncertainty when she realized that vampires might not need to breathe. Eliza didn't get up or stir. At best she was unconscious, but Lucy didn't want to be around when she woke up.

Her hands were shaking until she set them on the floor and pushed herself over Eliza's body. Just as she stepped over and knelt back to the floor, a hand tore into her shoulder, and in one swift motion flipped her back to the wall. Eliza had her pinned behind the desk where no one could see them and she had ample opportunity to end Lucy's life by any means she saw fit. All it would take was one bite to forever strip her away from everything she held dear and everything she wanted her life to be.

With a sigh, the vicious smile faded from Eliza's face and she moved her hand to Lucy's throat.

"You would be so dead right now," she mumbled and pursed her lips as her eyes shifted between Lucy and the floor.

"Why am I not?" Lucy asked, only to be growled at. It was clear Eliza didn't want her to talk. Instead, she watched the green vampire eyes shift in the shadows of a battle that was still raging behind them.

"Orders," was all that she said, followed by, "Eodin wants you to know that we have your dad and that he would like you to come with us, leaving your pets. We will retreat and you can meet us where you used to live, tonight at midnight. It would be in your father's best interest if you took the offer." Before Lucy could say another word, Eliza leaped back over the table and tackled someone to the ground.

Through the nauseating crashes and shouts behind her, Lucy struggled to come up with a plan to escape her adopted family. There wasn't any doubt in her mind that the vampires had captured her father, however she wondered why they were after her. There must have been so many other zephyrs in the world and to focus specifically on her seemed unnecessary, but if there was a way to save her father Lucy decided that she would try whatever it took.

She thought through the reactions of her friends when they would inevitably realize that she was gone and it broke her heart to put them through it, but she might have been his only chance.

After a few deep breaths, she peeked around the side of the desk. Eliza had rejoined the fray. She struck Syrina as hard as possible with her clawed fingers. Her movements were shockingly quick, but Syrina was able to push them away with a flick of her wrist. They were completely focused on the fight, which gave Lucy the opportunity to slip down the hallway and out of view.

The struggles in the waiting room drove Lucy to the farthest door at the back of the hallway. She barged through it and was nearly blinded by sunlight. Two large windows that spanned the height of the wall lit a short stairwell that led to a small metal door. With a quick glance over her shoulder, Lucy pushed the bar to force the locking mechanism forward. The metal groaned lazily as the door budged ahead and she nearly fell into a back alley. She closed the door slowly to avoid making too much noise, afraid that she might alert someone of her desertion.

Cars passed sluggishly as Lucy sauntered out of the alley and onto an actual road. She knew little about the town she was in or how to get back to her house. Adorable apartments lined the road as one street ran into another and Lucy finally came to a two-way street lined with store fronts and restaurants.

There were many people out enjoying the brief sunshine. Thoughts of stealing a car crossed her mind more than once and she wondered how easy it would be. She began scanning the parked vehicles for her victim and peered in the windows, hoping to find a set of keys carelessly left behind. Unfortunately, after a few tries she grumbled to herself and realized her stupidity in hoping for actions of trust against normal human behavior. As she studied a red Nissan parked closely between two large trucks, the locking device sprang to life. The sudden motion was startling and she jumped away from the car as fast as she could. Lucy turned around to hop back onto the sidewalk and nearly ran into a man standing directly behind her.

He seemed to be the owner of the Nissan and stared at her with interest when he realized that she had been snooping in his windows. His narrow face and kind eyes didn't judge her like she was expecting him to. His feathered hair flipped around in the slight breeze as he cleared his throat. Lucy tried to avoid judging him on appearances alone, but his odd clothes nearly forced her to look him up and down. The man was older than her, but not by much. He wore a brown vest that covered his suspenders and a bowtie, which made him seem more juvenile than he really was. His gray Converse Chucks were loosely laced and the bottoms of his pant legs were rolled into cuffs. The man's lips curled into a half-hearted grin and his posture bobbed as if he suffered from a small lack of balance or had had a few drinks. His pale blue eyes were unreadable.

"Are you all right?" Lucy heard him say under the powerful rumble of a passing motorcycle.

"No. I'm lost," was all that she could get out with her quivering bottom lip disrupting normal speech.

"I'm sorry to hear that. I have to teach a class in ten minutes or I would take you where you need to go," he said with a frown. The man's eyes shifted as he thought and promptly held up a finger when he had finished. He shoved his coffee cup into the nook of his left arm and used the other hand to dig into his trouser pocket.

With a grin he held out a handful of crumpled dollars and some change, "There is a bus terminal on 2nd Street and a deli on that corner as well. I don't take the bus often, but they're constantly moving in and out of here. If you ask, I'm sure that someone can get you in the right direction. What is left after the bus fee is for a sandwich. You look as if you haven't eaten in days." His eyes gleamed happily as he turned and pointed to the right.

Lucy was utterly shocked by his kindness, but took the money with a smile. "Thank you," she said. "There should be more people like you in the world."

The man seemed to blush as he nodded modestly and took another long look at her before getting in his car. Lucy returned to the sidewalk and waved at him as he pulled into the road. Just before he sped away, the man raised a hand to bid farewell. She watched and waited for his car to disappear before she continued on.

The streets were numbered and easy to follow. She passed by many places of business and was able to examine the goings on through the large shop windows. She watched people purchase things and have lunch or just enjoy each other's company over a cup of coffee. More than anything, she wished that she could trade places with them. Lucy wanted to be able to enjoy the company of normal humans for a change and believe that nothing was after her or the people she loved. She longed for the feeling of safety that seemed to be out of reach.

As soon as her distractive wishing was over, a green street sign that read 2nd Street came into view. Lucy's heart began to race as she turned the corner and saw a deli that wasn't far from a large bus terminal that appeared to be taking in buses of people as frequently as it was spitting them out. The scene was just as the man had said and Lucy was immediately grateful to have met him.

She strolled over to the deli entrance and let a sigh of relief escape as she felt the air conditioning pass over her skin. The people inside were occupied with their own lives and didn't seem to notice when she entered. She had missed being invisible.

The woman at the counter spouted a loud greeting to her and asked for her order. Lucy dumped her handful of money onto the counter and glanced back up at the woman, "How much is bus fare?"

Immediately, a frown crossed the woman's face, "Not from around here are you?" Though surprised by the question, Lucy shook her head and waited for the answer.

"A dollar twenty-five will get you out of the city. Looks like you have plenty."

"In that case can I have a sandwich?"

"Which one, dear?"

"Whatever three dollars will get me," she smiled as the woman nodded and disappeared through a swinging door that led to the kitchen.

Lucy leaned against the counter and watched a small television that was mounted on the wall. The news programs were the same here as they had been back home. There never appeared to be any good news.

Within a couple of minutes, she heard the door open and the woman from before appeared, humming a tune that she didn't recognize. She placed a brown paper bag on the counter and accepted Lucy's money.

"You have a good day, sweetheart," the woman spouted prior to resuming the cleaning she had abandoned.

Without another glance, Lucy stumbled out the door and

crossed the vacant street to get to the bus terminal. There were people of all shapes, sizes, and colors awaiting their buses and listening to a guitar player strumming for tips. Lucy tiptoed to a narrow wall and read the post of destinations that would be met from that station. Luckily she found her bus, one that would drop her off two blocks

R from her house. Excitement and dread passed through her all at once. It seemed like a lot for one person to deal with, but Lucy simply bottled it with the other emotions that she was forced to endure.

She wandered over to the line of buses and quickly found the one that would take the route she preferred. The change made a distinct metal clang as she dropped it into a dispenser just inside the door. The driver gave her a kind nod as she passed him and scurried back about three quarters of the way before finding a window seat.

She immediately ripped open the mouth of the bag and reached in for her sandwich, but was surprised to find so much more inside. She pulled out the food she had asked for, plus a bag of chips, some homemade cookies, and a bottle of juice. Lucy didn't know why, but she soon concluded that this city was perhaps the nicest place that she had ever been. Excitement raged through her and she tore the plastic wrap from her sandwich to take a bite.

Just as the bread touched her lips, someone ran into her view through the window. He was uncommonly fast and clearly out of breath. It was Kieron. Not long after, Syrina joined him. Lucy realized that they were probably looking for her and a stab of guilt hit her in the ribs. Her head told her to reveal what was happening and ask for their help to save her father, but her heart said differently. They could get hurt trying to save him just as easily as she would and that would be even worse than lying and running away. Lucy sank into her chair and only left enough room for her eye to snake the bottom of the window. She tucked her sandwich into her chest and watched her friends desperately call her name and ask pedestrians if they had seen her. A lump grew in the back of her throat.

Gradually, they began to check the buses. Kieron and Syrina would disappear and then reappear within a matter of seconds. She watched in terror as they came closer to her bus and nearly vomited when she saw Kieron leap up the steps and heard his sneakers scratch the floor. The noise progressed down the aisle, but stopped just before he reached her seat. Lucy wanted to look over at him. She wanted to see what he was doing or what he was looking at. She felt her hands shaking in anticipation. Did he know it was her? Could he smell her?

All of a sudden, he cleared his throat and spoke calmly and softly. There was worry trembling in his tone, "I am looking for a young girl with brown hair and blue eyes. She's very light in complexion and has a white shirt and jeans on." As he finished, Lucy was thankful that she had forgotten the pink overcoat in Cyrus's car, since that would have been an easy give away. No one answered him.

After a few more seconds, she could hear his shoes scuff across the floor again and then saw him leap off the bus and pass her window. Her anxiousness quickly disappeared and she waited until the bus pulled away before she sat back up in her chair. Lucy was suddenly struck with thoughts of Sebastian and what he was going to do when they returned without her. Nothing bothered her more than hurting him; however, this was something that needed to be done. She was going to find her father and she was going to save him no matter what.

Chapter Seven

emember what you're leaving behind, Lucy thought to herself. The safety that she felt and the protection of her new family were no longer in the cards. She knew that she could no longer depend on what they had given her. Being alone in a world that didn't know her and a town that wouldn't remember her was like living with a constant pressure that was trying to crush her against the ground.

The bus had puttered along between counties for about forty-five minutes now and finally the landmarks of her hometown were in view. The gas station and bank had passed by the window before the engines cut out and squeaky brakes brought the bus to a stop. Lucy seemed to be the only one leaving at the time and as she traipsed down the aisle, every eye followed her.

Outside, the air was thick with moisture that stuck to her skin as she moved through it. Evening had crept in while she was traveling and now twilight engulfed the whole town. No one was there to see her arrive, not even a passing car. The awning of the grocery store hid her from the street lamps and traffic lights that methodically changed color every minute or so. It would be two blocks to her front yard and two blocks to the strangers that waited to take her underground, to a place that she would have to escape from again. Nothing could keep her from volunteering for doom. She had to go there. She needed to save her father from them. He had always been a figment of her imagination, but now that he was so close, not even the threat of becoming a monster would change her mind.

The house's silhouette gradually began to stick out as she approached. All of the windows had been barred and the yellow tape from before had been reinforced by a fence. Obviously the police had noticed Syrina's searching job and appropriately secured the area. Lucy wondered if the coven had arrived yet or if she would have to wait.

Just as that thought crossed her mind a shadow appeared on the sidewalk ahead of her. Instantly, her head snapped up and she strained to see the features of the person making the ghostly image.

111

Cecily's small frame was lit by the glow of street light. She wore a frown that cast shadows over her face. A look of evil was present and she seemed to be willing to kill in an instant. Right away, Lucy's limbs lost their function and she was frozen, impaired in front of a lion. The hair on her arms stood and her muscles twitched as they tried to run.

In the blink of an eye, the vampire was only a few inches from her face. Lucy felt herself tense up and her eyes followed the dark figure in front of her. She felt the lump in the back of her throat return and hoped against all hope that they planned to keep their promises.

The woman's red hair was blown to one side in the breeze that had spontaneously erupted from the north. Cecily hovered like a hawk above helpless prey, but she didn't strike, even though Lucy could tell that she really wanted to. The vampire allowed the fear to build until the very last second and finally stepped away as Charles appeared at her side and let his hand rest on her shoulder. Eliza also became visible and she walked up to Cecily's other side. They didn't say a word. It was almost as if they were telling Lucy that she didn't have a chance to escape.

The three of them slowly surrounded her and led the way into a back alley behind Lucy's house, like escorting a prisoner to her cell. The near-lightless road made her stomach knot. Anything could happen and she wouldn't see it coming. She shuffled her feet and tried to hold her arms in to avoid touching one of the vampires. Lucy could swear she heard them breathing under the galloping beat of her own heart, but she couldn't be sure. Did they breathe? Did their hearts even beat? The presence of a heart must matter if Viola was so easily defeated by an arrowed fence.

The group didn't walk much farther before Lucy could see the distinct outline of a car. They then stopped in the middle of the alley. In faded light, she noticed Charles dig something out of his pocket and she immediately studied it and the way he was holding it. He had a syringe with something clear inside. Just as she realized what was going on, he turned and stabbed her in the neck with the needle.

"Just going to make you sleep. Relax," his deep voice reassured her. Before she could react to the stinging liquid, Lucy felt her legs grow weak and fuzzy. Her vision went blurry soon after and her balance disappeared. She felt someone catch her as she fell and soon she was on that person's shoulder. The last thing Lucy could remember before darkness crowded her mind was the ground below speeding by and the enormous feet of the man carrying her.

Consciousness returned before sight did. Lucy immediately knew they were indoors now. It felt warm, but she was strapped to a cold chair with restraints that felt similar to the leather ones from before. Her hope faded and she knew that they had taken her back to the coven and she was once again a prisoner. Her lips were dry and with a slight quiver she wet them and pulled against the ties. They were tighter than before. She also realized that a blindfold was in place when her eyelashes brushed against it. Lucy's vision soon returned. It was a red bandana they had wrapped around her head.

The room smelled like bleach, which was worrisome, and another faint odor was drifting around. It was a scent that she recognized. There was someone in the room with her. Someone she knew. Afraid of what her situation might be, Lucy tried to pull free again. The restraints had her glued to the seat. She could feel her locket shift on its long chain beneath her shirt and let go a grateful sigh; at least they hadn't robbed her. The metal sound of her sliding necklace must have gotten the attention of whoever was in the room because all of a sudden she heard a man clear his throat.

"Welcome back, Lucy." She shuttered at the sound of Eodin's emotionless voice. He had a way of causing nausea with just his dead words. Lucy felt anger erupt within her. She wanted to tell him how much she hated him. She wanted to curse him and tell him how much danger they would be in for their lies, but she couldn't say a word. All that left her lips were grumbles.

"No worries, young one. As the concoction in your veins wears off, the senses return. Speech will be the last. I imagine you're wondering what happened to our deal. It appears that you have been lured here under pure trust and the mutts haven't any idea as to where you are; how convenient for us."

She could feel his presence. It was like a winter wind, cold and desolate. His fingertips traced over her shoulders and Lucy did her best to jerk away. She felt his fingers on her neck and then the blindfold fell off and into her lap. The sudden light was strong, but after the spots in her vision faded, three people came into focus. The room was small and lit by one light in the ceiling. There was one door with a small window that could easily be obstructed.

Eodin was joined by two other men Lucy didn't recognize. One was a shorter gentleman with grey hair and the other a tall, debonair man with short black hair. They both studied her as she struggled and chuckled when the restraints did their job.

"It won't take them long, you know," Lucy threatened and was shocked to find that the drug had completely worn off.

"They will give us plenty of time, little duck," Eodin's odd words left her momentarily speechless, but she shook it off and tried to recall all of the stories she had been subjected to.

"Sebastian said that the more powerful covens live overseas. They won't get here before the wolves do. You'll be overpowered easily."

"See how you call them the wolves. Not family. Not friends; just wolves. You might as well call them 'mutts' as we do. They don't love you. They enjoy the thought of you. The premise of a zephyr that could either be harmless or devastating; if only the proper venom would be administered. When we take you away from them permanently, they won't come to save you anymore. Once you're one of us, darling, they won't love you. On the contrary, they will try to kill you by whatever means necessary." He was very calm in his words. Eodin's ability to scare the white off a ghost with just a sentence was properly used to gain his power. Lucy could see why he was in charge, but she forced herself not to fear him. She couldn't let him win.

"I won't let you," she cried out as he opened the door to leave. Lucy watched his spine curl when he stopped. She immediately regretted those words. In half a second the vampire had returned to her side and put his mouth next to her ear as if to whisper something. She couldn't see his face, but she could hear him breathing. Vampires do breathe. She could hear the blood pulsing through his veins and his slow heartbeat.

"You have no choice. The Forsaken have arrived and you're

out of time," he smirked and whipped around, nearly smacking her with a flailing hand. Eodin exited, followed by the gray-haired man. The other gentleman remained and the door was shut. They had left a guard in place this time and by the looks of it, he was one of the royals. His clothes had a beautiful Victorian feel about them and were unlike the other vampires' attire. Most of his outfit was burgundy or white, but the aspect that stood out the most was his necklace. It was a silver crest of two winged lions and a few words in a language she didn't recognize. The man didn't make eye contact at first. He was very standoffish.

"So you're part of the royal family?" Lucy asked, trying to make conversation. At first he didn't answer, as if he was under orders not to talk to the hostage, but after a few minutes the man cleared his throat.

"Yes, but not by blood."

"How then?"

"By mind. Not my choice," he didn't seem angry or afraid by the facts. To him it appeared to be the way of life. They were silent again for the longest time until he began on a different subject.

"You've grown up." Those words immediately started questions pouring through Lucy's mind.

"Do I know you?" Her eyebrows crossed in concentration.

"I wouldn't think so."

She frowned as he laughed through his words. "Then how do you know me?"

"I know Cyrus and I knew your mother a long time ago. You look just like her." His eyes watched the ground. Lucy was irritated by the lack of eye contact, but she tried to get more out of him.

"My mom? How do you know her?"

"My name is Craig Gaskin. I was married to her." The realization hit Lucy like a ton of bricks. She could see the resemblances between him and the locket photo now. She could place him within all of the stories and even some real memories returned. Lucy knew this man. She'd loved him without even realizing it.

"I'm your father, Lucy, and it's my fault that you are in this situation. I'm sorry. I am so sorry." He finally looked up. The eyes that she hoped would be full of love and acceptance actually reflected sorrow and regret.

115

"Why is any of this your fault?"

"I was on the run and hiding out in Hawaii before it had been claimed by America. Your mom grew up on what is now Oahu. I fell in love with her and she with me, but I was already a vampire. She wasn't one and we had you. You are a hybrid—an impossible hybrid—and if you are bitten by a vampire, there will be no one on Earth who can stop you. The Forsaken see you as a weapon and it is all my fault."

"Don't say that. You saved my life by giving me to your mom. She kept me safe."

"I'm glad, but she wasn't my mom. We didn't even really know her that well."

"You gave me to a stranger?"

"No, sweetheart. I wouldn't do that and neither would Annie, but we had to get you somewhere safe."

"Well then, who was Lucinda?" Lucy had completely forgotten where she was and what was around her. Finally the picture was coming together and her gut told her that to be truly satisfied, she would have to hear it from someone who was there.

"We ran when we discovered that you were coming. The Forsaken were able to read my mind and I knew they would come for you. Cyrus, Annie, and I went to live in a small house on the shore of Greenland. I remember standing on the ice watching the horizon for danger. I can't feel the cold so I was there for most of the day. At night we would come together and eat or sit by the fire and just talk. We would talk to you and about what would become of you. One night Cyrus barged through the door and told us that we had to leave. We fled that house and ran all the way to England. Your mom gave birth to you at a small hospital in the countryside outside of Penzance." He paused and cleared his throat.

"What happened to her?"

"We don't really know. She died that day, but was perfectly healthy after you were born. Cyrus spoke to our nurse about it. She was a lovely woman with golden hair and knowing eyes. She told me that she was sorry for our loss and hoped that she could help. That day, for the first time, I told a human the story of zephyrs and she took it surprisingly well. I revealed what I was and what you might be. Then I asked her how far she was willing to go to help. The woman said that she couldn't have children and feared only being alone in the world. With a broken heart and satisfaction in what your life would be, I allowed the nurse to steal you away to America, where vampires had not yet set foot. Not long after, Cyrus wrote me saying that he and his pack would move close to keep an eye on you. That was the last time I was in contact with anyone." The man looked up. His eyes were shining with the tears that had yet to fall and the glossiness of his cheeks revealed where others had been.

"I wish I could hug you," she finally cried and hung her head.

"I would love to remove those restraints, but my orders forbid me. It would be physically impossible," he frowned and appeared to search for more to say. "You can resist them. You are a vampire's daughter. There has never been anything like you. I would hate to stand in your way, and pity all those who do. Be strong." Little by little his speech began to jerk and his limbs locked into place. Finally, her father fell to his knees and yowled in pain before collapsing onto the floor. After that he didn't move.

Lucy couldn't free herself and it pained her to try. He had revealed his secrets and more. Now she knew why her senses were exceptional and her healing was so fast. Her dad might not have been there to raise her, but he gave her the ability to protect and save herself. She watched his limp body sprawled on the floor. Lucy didn't even blink until she saw him breathe. He was alive and that would have to be good enough for now.

She waited for someone to open the door and remove him, but after a while no one had even passed the window. They weren't going to open the door until they were ready to end her life. This was nauseating and yet it made her grateful. Lucy had time. She could break the restraints or maybe break the chair. The plan was simple. The leather straps wouldn't rip easily, but the foolish vampires had secured her to a wooden chair with wooden arms. If her father was confident in the strength that she had, it was worth a try.

As the thought of possible hidden strength crossed her mind, Lucy could feel the muscles in both of her arms tense up, as though just thinking about it was willing her body into submission. The tension pushed against the leather straps until it began to hurt and she considered releasing the control.

Finally, she gained complete power and wrapped her fingers

around the end of each of the chair's arms. She allowed a couple of deep breaths to calm her nerves and then began to pull against the solid slabs of wood. Discouragement welled within her quickly, but Lucy didn't stop. She slowly pulled harder and finally a snap echoed through the room. The underside of the left arm splintered under her elbow. With a little more pressure it completely broke away from the rest of the chair. The jagged part of the chair arm that was still attached to the seat scratched the fleshy back of her arm and Lucy winced at the marks it made. She pushed the pain out of her mind and began to focus on the other side. This time it seemed to make a clean break. Faith in ability came quickly and with a grin she bent both sides inward to break the small supports under her wrists.

With the planks still strapped to her arms at the elbows and wrists, Lucy bent in her seat and unbuckled the leather shackles that bound her ankles. Suddenly she felt light as a feather and launched from the chair before taking a moment to stretch out her arms and back. The planks of wood attached to her were no longer heavy. It was almost as if the freedom that she had given herself was coupled with strength that had previously been hidden. After a sigh of relief, Lucy hurried to her father's side and felt for a pulse. She wasn't sure if he would have one, but it was worth a try.

Lucy pressed her fingers into his neck and was relieved to find a strong beat throbbing below his skin. Immediately she stepped over him and nearly fell into the door. One of the wooden planks banged against the metal and she grabbed it to try and stop the echo. It vibrated into the walls, but no one came to investigate.

Glancing back down to her father, Lucy sighed in relief and turned the knob. It was locked. She examined the handle. There was a keyhole in the center of it. She shook her head with a frown and bent to her father's body. With a shove, she rolled him onto his back, which instantly revived him to a point. He stammered and opened his eyes. His lips were curled back slightly, exposing the fangs of a vampire. They were the teeth of a killer and reminded Lucy that he wasn't just her father. He was a monster too; less than a man and more than a beast. Craig Gaskin was a murderer.

"Where is the key?" she demanded as she began to check his pockets.

"You escaped," he sounded proud. "Good. The key is in my

coat. You cannot trust me now. They are assuming control of me. It takes a few minutes. Run." When he finished, Lucy whimpered as she watched the light leave his eyes and all of the trust and memories of her went with it. He was a stranger now. He wouldn't know her and she had to feel the same.

Lucy shook off her emotions and removed the key from his pocket. Just as he began to stir she unlocked the door and finally escaped the first of many obstacles that were sure to come. She entered a hallway that expanded in both directions. It was cold and empty. She pulled on the door behind her until she heard it click. Key in hand, she turned and proceeded to relock the door.

As soon as it was secure she heard a banging from the other side. The door knob jerked furiously as an ungodly shouting erupted. It was like the Forsaken had possessed him. The man she had come to know as her father was no longer present. If he escaped that room, she would be forced to defend herself by whatever means necessary.

The hallway left much to be desired. It was empty, foul, and frightening. She hoped that no one would hear him and come to his rescue. The room wasn't sound proof, but it did obstruct the noises so that they became muffled. Before she left the door, Lucy tested the tension of the leather straps on her arms. Although she could remove them easily, it might've been much more convenient to keep the extra protection for as long as possible. When it came to fighting vampires, she really didn't know what to expect and having wooden armor would do more to help than it would hurt. The straps were as tight as they had been when she broke the chair and would stay in place well enough if a fight broke out.

After allowing a deep breath to calm her nerves, Lucy explored to the left where she hoped to find a way out of the underground prison without attracting attention. She could hear noises coming from the doors that she passed and wondered what lay on the other side of them. Were there more zephyrs within who were prisoners like she was, or were there only more dangers beyond? Lucy jogged by every door, only slowing enough to see if the windows were obstructed. She couldn't see inside any of the rooms.

The hallway soon ended and, with hesitation, Lucy allowed a single second to pass before she was flat against the wall. She glanced at the ceiling and took a deep breath. There were too many thoughts in her head to sort through and worry about all of them. Only two desires came to her that she really focused on. She would do whatever it took to get back to the wolves, and she would fight for her life if necessary.

Another hallway intersected the one that she was in. It also seemed empty, but when she finally willed herself to turn the corner, she came to face the back of someone standing in the middle of the floor. From the person's tall stature, haircut, and color, she could tell that it was Cecily. Lucy gripped the part of the wooden arms that rested in her palms and took one step backward. She tried not to breathe as she attempted to slip back into the original hall, but she noticed the lady vampire take in a deep breath and cringe at what scent she caught. In a split second the woman turned and scowled at her. Lucy didn't know what to do. The look in Cecily's eyes had her frozen in place.

"You should know that I am authorized to detain you by whatever means necessary." She grinned and took a short step forward. Lucy wanted to run, but then another emotion engulfed her. It seemed to be anger and then revenge. She didn't know what the feeling was, only that it was shifting from fear, to anger, and to satisfaction. It took her only seconds to put the puzzle together.

She was experiencing Cecily's emotions as well as her own. Along with her new-found strength, Lucy must have released other abilities. She could feel the emotions of those who could not hide them. What else would she be able to do in time? With practice, could she control others? The sensation was unlike any other that she had ever felt. Lucy knew that Cecily would fight and it was this fact that helped her. She was instantly confident in herself. She didn't have the same weapons as her vampire foe, but there were other things to rely on.

Lucy had witnessed the way the wolves fought. They used intelligence as well as their abilities to win their battles. Cecily had become the enemy and though her emotions were strong, Lucy could peel them back and focus on what she was doing. There was a sudden calm in the air, which oddly made her trust herself and the choices she made. She could feel her spine straighten and her arms relax to her side. She could feel her senses open up and knew that she was finally in control of her body just as Cyrus said she would be.

There was no fear now. Cecily was quick to strike, but Lucy moved out of the way of her clawed hand, and punched her foe hard in the face with the support of the wooden chair arm that helped to crack Cedily's lip. As the vampire pulled away, scarlet blood appeared and dripped down onto her pale chin. With a growl she wiped the warm liquid and even seemed surprised that Lucy was as fast as she was. Her emotions were clear in Lucy's head—not that they weren't blatantly clear on her face.

Cecily immediately instigated the fray with another strike at Lucy's chest. The blows that seemed to be so fast in previous fights were now at normal speed and were easily deflected. The woman threw a clawed hand at Lucy's head, which she ducked to avoid. Then with the other hand she sliced open the belly of Lucy's shirt. There was immediately a shock of pain from the area, but it wasn't strong enough to worry about at the moment.

With that sudden pain, Lucy couldn't hold back any more. She gripped the wood in her palm to steady it and rotated her forearms slightly to use them in a strike. In less than a second, Cecily attempted another attack. She reached a hand out at Lucy's throat.

In anticipation of the hit, Lucy used the wood-enforced weapon to knock the vampire's arm downward and out of striking range. She watched her opponent's surprised face before using the wood in a final blow to the chin, which forced her to the floor. Lucy waited a few moments for Cecily to rise and fight more, but she didn't stir. She bent down and nudged the vampire gently. There was nothing. Lucy reached out for emotion. The hall was empty of it.

Without another glance back, she left the red-haired vampire's body lying in the hallway. She hoped that she was still alive, but couldn't be sure. The hallways snaked along and Lucy followed them, hoping to find something that she remembered. After a minute, something came into view.

She ventured out into the large room from her first visit and looked hopefully at the spiral staircase that didn't have a guard in sight. Her range of emotional sensitivity wasn't very large, so in regret Lucy had to trust her sight to judge whether or not the room was really safe. There wasn't any movement that she noticed, and other than the mellow sound of flickering flames, she couldn't hear anything odd.

After a reassuring couple of deep breaths, she took a few steps into the open. When no one moved to stop her, Lucy immediately let her guard down and ran to the steps. Just as she managed to curl her fingers around the railing another hand wrapped around her wrist and jerked her away from the stairs. Lucian's frightening appearance filled her vision then. He was menacing and full of what Lucy assumed was amusement. She couldn't feel his emotions like the others. He kept them hidden. His black hair was pulled back and his lifeless eyes had become green like the rest of his species. He wasn't the fearsome hunter that she had come to expect.

Lucy tried to pull her wrist free of his grip, but when that failed she swung her other arm at his head. The board had been an effective weapon against Cecily, but Lucian made it seem foolish. With lightning-fast reflexes, he caught her striking arm in midair and spun her around in an almost whimsical manner. He held her arms so that they crossed her chest. This made it impossible for Lucy to resist his commands. He nudged her back and with a groan she obliged and walked in the direction he led her.

The form of hold he had her in felt like an uncomfortable hug, and with her arms wrapped across her chest, Lucy was at his mercy. Some black strands of loose hair draped over her shoulders and the smell of honeysuckle filled her nose. She didn't know where he was taking her and there was no possible way to resist. Her head snapped up in the direction that he pushed her. Instantly her vision focused on the loft above them. There were several people seated next to Eodin and watching the proceedings with much interest.

"See them?" Lucian growled into her ear as he pushed forward again. "The Forsaken have been waiting for you longer than they'd like to admit. They've been patient for a hybrid since the theory of a weapon was made to be true. Now you will help them gain control."

"I won't." Lucian was not surprised by her refusal. In fact, he seemed to be amused by it.

As they approached, one of the royals stood and came to the edge of the loft. She was a woman with long black hair and dark green eyes. Her thin face was heavily shadowed and her stick-thin body looked as if it could easily be snapped in two. Her snug black dress was enrobed in a cape of red velvet that matched the color of her lips. She looked down upon them with interest whilst Lucian finally moved his hostage into the light.

Lucy gazed up at them. She could feel their stares even though she couldn't see most of them. The Forsaken could hide their emotions somehow and did so quite well. She couldn't feel them and hoped that they couldn't read her either.

"That's Ella," Lucian growled into her ear again. "She will initiate the change." The facts of the situation weighed heavily in the air. The vampires were moving in and there wasn't a rescue coming this time. Lucy had made a huge mistake. She had found her father, but the prize didn't outweigh the cost. With a sigh, she let the reality sink in and wondered if the bite would hurt or if her body would protect her from pain as it had before. She remembered one of the wolves telling her that vampire venom killed the body and she wondered if death would be the only exception.

A sinister grin appeared across Ella's face, but as quickly as it appeared, the look was replaced by confusion and curiosity. She seemed to be looking past them. Lucian didn't think anything of it until the other royals left their comfy chairs and joined her at the edge of the loft with the same expressions. Even Eodin followed them, causing tension to build in Lucian's chest. Lucy didn't know what had gotten their attention and impatiently waited to see for herself.

Finally, Lucian's grip tightened and slowly they shifted around to face the front of the room. As Lucy realized what had made the others act so strangely, she also stumbled into disbelief. Three snarling, four-legged wolves and two werewolves had come out of the hallway that Lucy had just escaped from. Two of the canines she recognized as Syrina and Mitchell, but the other she didn't know.

Sebastian and Cyrus had become their other selves and were ready for a fight. Their appearances had been altered to fit that of wolves on the hunt. Their eyes were fierce and dark. Hair covered their extremities and they had claws in place of normal hands. Lucy was in disbelief of what she was seeing. In her mind, it was impossible for them to be there and impossible for them to win against the most powerful vampires she had ever seen. Lucy was afraid for her family. She knew that they would have an unwinnable fight ahead of them.

"How did you get in here?" Ella instantly became enraged. "I personally oversaw the men who sealed that entrance." She seemed frustrated by Cyrus, but tried to retain her composure and allow him to answer.

"There is always a way in and if there isn't, you must make one." Lucy heard her uncle's reply before Lucian released her sore arms and simply wrapped his arm around her throat. She stumbled backward when he pulled her with him to the steps of the loft.

"Lucian! Give her to me. You have lost," Cyrus ordered while his pack surrounded the trapped vampires.

"How have I lost? We have what you seek to gain and our numbers are greater."

"Then I suppose we will start with taking back what belongs to no one. Then you will see that there is nothing to gain here."

Without another second wasted, Syrina and Mitchell leap over him and onto the stairs. Lucy was stunned at the height they were able to achieve and tried to follow them, but she was restricted by the strength of Lucian's arm. He held her tightly to the point just before choking, which had her gasping for air. Suddenly she realized that her arms were free. Without thinking, Lucy threw her armored forearms at his head and struck him hard with what was left of the wooden chair

For a mere second, he fell back and loosened his grip on her neck enough that she could slip away from him and deliver another blow to his chest. Following the escape, Cyrus was next to her instantly. With a strong hand, he pushed Lucy backward and into Sebastian's arms. It was a comfort to know that she was finally with someone who would take care of her and saw her as a person rather than a weapon. Lucy glanced over her shoulder at the wolves.

Syrina and Mitchell had joined their other wolf brother in herding the royals into a small ball, and Cyrus had Lucian by the throat. The fight appeared to be going in their favor until Ella straightened and took a step toward the pack. Lucy's stomach immediately knotted as she watched each of the wolves step backward and the vampires charge them. The sound of whimpering dogs tore at her ears and the last thing Lucy saw before Sebastian whisked her away was Lucian's clawed hand rip into Mitchell's face.

Like a tornado, Sebastian scooped her into his arms and ran back into the hallway. The commotion coming from the room had escalated into screaming and squealing that echoed down the hall.

The noises seemed to chase them until he pushed open a door and closed it behind them. Immediately the sound was cut off. The walls had been designed to be noise barriers, and they did their job well.

"Wait. We have to go back. We have to help them!" Lucy pleaded and ripped out of his arms to go back to the door. She wrapped both

T hands around the door knob and pulled as hard as she could. It wouldn't budge.

"We're locked in." He frowned and went to the back of the room where a large hole had been torn into the wall.

"Then break the door down. I know you can. We need to help them. They're outnumbered!" As she said this, Lucy could see tension spread through him. It traveled from his spine and out through his limbs. Then he looked back at her with an expression that would haunt her memory. It seemed as if he was already aware of the doom his family was in. Sebastian had gone into that room knowing that he would possibly be exchanging her life for the lives of his family. He wore an expression of worry that had been coupled with the devastation of losing the ones most dear to him.

Lucy could feel a knot grow in her chest. She had never felt sorry for him before and was shocked that he had made her experience this depth of sympathy. Without letting another second pass, Sebastian grabbed her arm and unfastened the piece of chair, allowing it to fall to the ground with a sharp and echoing bang. After doing the same with her other arm, he checked the abrasions embedded in her skin from where the restraints had been. Lucy rubbed the spots and was surprised to see that they were already fading. When she concentrated harder, the spots disappeared within seconds. Sebastian watched her with interest and then with a grin he finally spoke, "It's impossible for a zephyr to do that and you make it look so easy."

"I'm not just a zephyr. My father told me that I'm a hybrid." When she had finished, the look on Sebastian's face was unrecognizable. He seemed confused, but it was clear that he understood.

He then grabbed her wrist and led her into the dark hole that had been made into the wall. It was slightly damp and cold in the adjacent room. The dust that had settled left a gray blanket over the area.

"Where are we?" Lucy mumbled as she followed him through the room and to a staircase.

"We are in the basement of another mausoleum. Its walls are pressed against those of the coven lair. It only took a moderate amount of strength to break through."

With a nod, Lucy looked around the room at the beautiful, dust-covered décor. Candelabras of different sizes decorated the shelves on the walls and there were even some on the tables. None of them had been used in ages, but the wax on the candles had been hot enough to melt at one time. A set of stairs led to a hole in the ceiling. Lucy followed Sebastian to the plaque-filled walls of the mausoleum. They held the names of those buried in the room below.

They made their way around the marble bench in the center of the room and finally out of the old door into a night-stricken forest. It was cold and the air was damp with a fog that was so thick it was obstructing everything that was more than a few feet in front of them. The trees were silent and still. It was a daunting vision for Lucy to take in. She didn't know where they would run, but there was one thing that Sebastian had made very clear: they wouldn't be going back.

Chapter Eight

he forest seemed never ending and the fog heavier than ever as they trudged through the clingy brambles. Lucy could feel her legs weaken quickly and the pressure in her chest begin to weigh her down. They had been traveling for longer than she would like to remember and exhaustion was growing to the point of collapse. Sebastian, however, appeared strong enough to go another ten miles before becoming fatigued.

As they fled, she couldn't help but wonder how her father came to be under the control of the Forsaken. Lucy remembered the end of his story. He had been running from them and seemed to be the kind of man who could resist such evil. She couldn't shake the guilt of leaving her father behind in that terrible place, but Sebastian's constant pushing was helping to drive it from her mind. He was urgent in getting her far away from the coven as quickly as possible.

The fog had begun thick, and while they ran through the trees it slowly started to disperse. Finally, the cloudy haze disappeared completely and Lucy stopped in horror as they ran to the very edge of a sharp cliff. Sebastian threw his arm around her waist and whisked her away from the drop. He seemed as surprised by the cliff as she was. In complete reaction to the near-death experience, Lucy wrapped her arms around his waist and hugged him tightly as she looked down to the trees below. It looked as if an earthquake had ripped apart a hill into two separate pieces and one half had sunk into the Earth. Lucy held him with every bit of strength that she had and the near disaster they had just avoided wasn't even the reason.

They had been apart for so long and to her, being in his arms again was the best feeling that she had ever felt. Inside, she wanted him to hold her forever and was disappointed when he finally left her side. The chill of the wilderness replaced his warm body and Lucy let her arms fall as if she had lost something important. He didn't seem to notice.

Sebastian's eyes scanned the hills and finally rested on something. Lucy couldn't see what he did, but she took his hand and they walked along the edge of the cliff to find a way down. The path seemed never-ending, but as the border came into view, one fatal step sent the edge crumbling and Sebastian tumbling off the side. Lucy heard a scream echo through the woods and realized that it had come from her. She dropped to the ground and shimmied until half her torso was perched over the rock face. With a worried grin, she stared at him.

Sebastian had fallen about ten feet onto another cliff that served as the mouth of a cave. He had landed on his back and was staring up at her with a pained expression. As the shock of the fall wore off, they shared a laugh before Lucy yelled to ask if he was all right.

"I'm fine. We can stay in here tonight. Jump down; I'll catch you," he assured her as he stood and held his arms out. Hesitation reared its ugly head for a moment before Lucy made herself sit on the edge of the cliff. She took a deep breath and crept over the threshold. The wind that swept past as she fell seemed as if it would push her back up to the top, but in a split second she was in his arms. He cradled her, and instantly eliminated the force of the drop.

Lucy didn't know why, but Sebastian's arms gave her a sense of safety. The way he held her made her feel like she belonged with him and that every moment in her life had led to him. Sebastian let her legs drop after a few seconds and grabbed her hand before leading the way into the cave.

It was merely a dark pocket full of stalagmites and large rocks. To her surprise, there was a small amount of water trickling down the face of the cliff that was coming from a pool of clear water just beyond the rocks.

"It's so beautiful," Lucy murmured as she knelt on a rock and cupped her hands. With a grin, she dipped them into the icy cold stream. She stared at her reflection in the pool between her knuckles and sighed. If it wasn't for her mirrored image, Lucy would not have been able to tell that she was holding anything. She lifted it to her lips and took a drink before dipping her face in the water. It tasted amazing and felt like a cloud. Oddly, Lucy had never experienced water as pure as this. It was perfect.

"It's been naturally filtered," she heard Sebastian explain before he appeared at her side. She watched him repeat what she had done and after he had taken a drink, she grabbed his hand. It was still wet, but his strength and warmth sent chills over her body.

At times, Lucy felt as if all of this was unreal and that she might be dreaming the adventures that came with the wolves or the danger that accompanied vampires. However, it was the comfort and love that she felt for Sebastian that made her realize that there was truth to what was going on. He was the needle point in her life where everything came together and reason did not have an input on why him and why now.

Lucy didn't know when this would end, but she could feel it coming. Eodin had made it clear what the intentions of the wolves might be and she was unsure whether he had told her the truth. She hadn't been a part of this world for very long and it was possible that he was lying, but there was still doubt regarding the honesty of her uncle and his family.

Lucy's eyes met his while she was still deep in thought. His blonde hair fell into his face as he smiled and moved to sit on the rock that they had been laying on. He was unreadable. She couldn't feel his emotions either. It was like there was a wall between them that she couldn't break through.

Then, without provocation, he leaned in and allowed his lips to touch hers. It was electrifying in such a way that Lucy was unable to react. Her face was suddenly warm and she could feel her heart speed up, but she didn't move. Afraid of doing the wrong thing, she froze in shock and waited for him to proceed with whatever would come next.

Sebastian moved away with a sigh and placed both hands in his lap. He was almost disappointed, but still happy. To Lucy, reading him was impossible. She waited a few more seconds to take in what had happened before sliding into the same position he had taken. Her bottom lip began to quiver as she placed her hands in her lap and cleared her throat.

Finally, he broke the silence and spoke without the shock that she was feeling, "You don't know how long I've been waiting to do that." Satisfaction was released at last. His foreign inflections normally jumbled words in a way that made him hard to understand, but that sentence was clear as a bell. Lucy felt the same way. She had been waiting for that moment since his bloodied face appeared at her window and he revealed that he was there to protect her.

"I love you," he admitted with certainty before walking toward the mouth of the cave to give her the time she needed to understand what he was saying.

Lucy watched him sway in the dim light. Twilight was settling into the trees and pushing all light back into the sky to shine with the stars. She watched the wind toss his hair about. Sebastian seemed so certain in his proclamation and Lucy wondered how long he had had to sort through his feelings. She wouldn't lie to herself and say that she didn't feel for him, but what kind of relationship could they have? Being half vampire like she was, Lucy kept wondering if she would be able to stay with the wolves now that her bloodline had been revealed. Would they still accept and love her as if nothing had happened? Would trust be possible? As she thought on these things, Sebastian returned and sat on the ground next to the rock she was perched on.

"You shouldn't," Lucy finally replied to his confession. She watched the flush of red that remained from their kiss drain from his face. Sebastian didn't react at first. He hung his head and took a couple of seconds to think through what to say next.

"I can't help it," he frowned and turned to face her. "When I'm around you it's like my entire body is in pain. My heart races and I can't sort through my thoughts. You impair me."

"Is that really a good thing then?"

"It is the best thing." He grinned before standing and grabbing her hand. "Be aware that I know who and what you are, and that I don't care." His reckless attitude toward a love that shouldn't be was more amusing than it was endearing. Lucy saw him as a love-struck child rather than a rational seventy-year-old. It wasn't until the excitement left his face that she began to take him seriously.

"In all of my life, everyone I was born loving or grew to love has been taken from me in the worst ways possible." His voice had grown quiet as if he were whispering. "I don't want it to happen again." What color there was left in his face had completely gone.

"It won't," Lucy tried to reassure him.

"You ran to the home of my enemies in the shadow of a promise that could never have been kept. You let them fool you and didn't even bother to tell anyone."

"I can't defend myself against that. It was stupid. I wanted to see my dad and thought that I could save him alone." Lucy could feel tears coming to the surface, but she held them back and cleared her throat.

"They would never have let you leave and I think that you know why."

"I'm a weapon."

"You are an Envy," he corrected her as she went to sit on the ground beside him.

"What is an Envy?" The question was simple, but Sebastian still had to think on it. Lucy didn't know why he felt the need to sensor their conversations.

"It is a translated vampire term—Nelvotik Vashraka, which means 'bringer of death.' Shortened it translates to Envy. You would be unstoppable if a vampire bit you and completely controllable if that vampire was a royal. In theory."

"Is that why the others didn't bite me, then?"

"Lucian is old and able to control minds like the Forsaken, but he refused to join them. We think that's why he was stalking you. Eodin ordered him to change you the night of the festival and he was unsuccessful. That was when the call was made. In fear of losing you, Eodin made your presence known to the royals. We still don't know how your existence was discovered in the first place."

"Why didn't they just get it over with then?"

"Vampires like to draw out their kills and make their victims as scared as possible. They think it aids the potency of their venom, which isn't true." Sebastian grinned and patted Lucy on the knee before he stood. Again he walked to the mouth of the cave and took in a deep breath. He held it for a second and then released slowly. "We're safe for now. I don't smell anything peculiar. Do you?"

"What do you mean?" Lucy joined him to look out into the trees for signs of life. Small animals rustled in the brambles below and birds still sung their evening melodies.

"Close your eyes," he ordered kindly. She paused for only a moment before doing as he said.

"Do you remember what Lucian smelled like?"

"Yes," she mumbled and thought back on the honeysuckle smell of his hair accompanied by an odd musky scent.

"Take a deep breath through your nose. Allow the air to fill your lungs to capacity. Let it linger and then exhale through your mouth," he instructed and she did exactly what he said as he said it.

"Is he near?"

"No," Lucy grinned and glanced up at him, "he isn't."

"You really are impressive. I've never met a zephyr who could aromalize."

"What's that?"

"Once bitten, your senses change. The ability to decipher specific smells is called aromalizing. Wolves do it well. I've never met a vampire that could."

"Really?"

"Yes, just like werewolves cannot control the minds of others," his grin had turned into a frown.

"Can vampires control werewolves?" Sebastian scoffed at her question and then tried his best to answer it without offending her.

"No," his smile revealed more than humor. "Humans, zephyrs, and other vampires; never us."

"Good to know." She snuggled against his waist and together they watched night settle into the forest.

Eventually even the sky became lightless. It hid the trees in a blanket of darkness and suddenly there was nothing left to see and even more to fear. With a grunt, Sebastian broke away from her, returned to the center of the cave, and attempted to begin a fire. Small amounts of brush and bark around the edges of the cave served as decent wood to start with. They had probably been blown inside by the wind of a storm.

After digging a small hole, he smacked a couple of stones together several times before sparks began whizzing through the air. It didn't take more than a couple of minutes for the sparks to be transformed into flame. At long last he had finally built an impressive fire and Lucy found herself in awe of his inner boy scout.

"That was quick," she said with a smile as she sat next to him and began to warm her hands.

"I've had a lot of practice. You just need the right stones and the right kindling," Sebastian's toothy grin sent chills over her spine. Lucy didn't want to fall in love with him, but the more he said the harder refusing him became.

"Listen to me," Lucy commanded and watched his eyes grow wide. He seemed shocked, but did as she said and gave her his full attention. "When you kissed me—" she began, but was immediately interrupted.

"I'm sorry. I knew it might be a bad idea. I'm so sorry."

"Shut up," Lucy snapped at him, but allowed her seriousness to be lightened by a snicker before continuing. "That's not listening." A shocked smile grew across his lips and he chuckled a little bit as she tried to continue. "When you kissed me I was unprepared and I didn't react well. For that I am sorry."

Hope flickered in his eyes with the constant motion of fire in the background. They would be safe for the time being and this realization finally allowed Lucy to breathe a sigh of relief and enjoy his company.

"Do you want to see a picture of my parents?"

"Sure," Sebastian seemed surprised by the offer. After thinking it through, he continued with, "Then I can know which vampire to avoid killing." Although he joked, Lucy shot him a glare as she yanked the locket from inside her shirt. With a snap it opened and she let him examine the old picture of her parents.

It took Sebastian a while to be satisfied with his study. Lucy watched his eyes move from side to side and from top to bottom. He took in the photo and after a few minutes handed the charm back to her.

"They look friendly. You can hardly tell he is a vampire. I've never seen one so happy," he grinned as he commented and irrevocably sighed.

"He doesn't look happy to me," she doubted and studied the photo even further.

"Trust me; he is. It's in his eyes. Eternal life is nothing unless you have something to live for."

Whatever accessory light there was left in the cave had been sucked out by the sunset and now the glow of their small fire was all that lit the area. The shadowed corners left much to the imagination. Lucy couldn't help but snuggle in close to him for warmth and safety.

"The other wolf with you in the coven, who was that?"

"Kieron insisted on coming. He felt guilty for letting you slip past him on the bus."

"He knows about that?"

"We pieced together what happened." Sebastian didn't seem mad. There was a tone of disappointment deep in his voice, but he didn't try to make her feel guilty.

"Did the fight at the blood bank go well then?"

"Yes. Mitchell suffered blows to the face and chest that might take a while to heal, but there was no permanent damage." He chuckled through his words as if remembering the fight in his head. "They fled, but will try again eventually. We can't do anything to prevent it, only stop it when it happens," he explained and moved down to hold her waist.

"Ouch; that hurt," Lucy snapped as she jerked away from him. Sebastian was as shocked as she was and immediately examined the hand that he had touched her with. Lucy watched his eyes grow wide in disbelief and was left to wonder why for only a few moments.

He turned his hand to allow her eyes access to his blood-coated palm. "You're wounded?" In disbelief, Lucy lifted her torn shirt slightly and revealed three slashes, one of which was quite deep. Whenever she moved a drip of blood was released to trail over her abdomen.

"Cecily and I fought, but I didn't think anything of it. I figured it would heal eventually," Lucy tried to explain as she watched him tear a piece of cloth from his shirt and press it against the gash.

"Relax. Your mind has been clouded lately. Just clear it of everything and concentrate on healing yourself. If you don't let your body heal then you won't be able to at all." Sebastian seemed calm and it was the absence of urgency that allowed Lucy to finally relax and focus on the wound in her stomach. She longed for the day that it would come naturally, but for now she would have to take his advice.

Though it was hard, she slipped into a meditative state and concentrated on healing her entire body. They were safe and she felt secure enough to let her guard down for the healing process. A tingling sensation began to agitate her veins and it was almost as if her entire body was aching and itchy at the same time. The prickly stinging didn't last more than a couple of minutes and Lucy felt that the process had been completed. With a sigh, she removed the cloth and was satisfied with the scarless adhesion of her skin. She checked the abrasions on her wrists where the leather straps had been and was happy to see that they had gone as well. However, as she examined herself, Lucy noticed that the zephyr mark that Lucian had carved in her flesh was still an ugly scar. A shock of disappointment went through her mind and she wondered if she would ever be rid of the constant reminder of that day.

"That was amazing. You never cease to surprise me," Sebastian interrupted her thoughts. His kind smile couldn't hide the impressed skepticism in his eyes.

"What now? Do I have to be different for one more reason?"

"It seems so. No zephyr can heal themselves in that way and not even I can do it that fast."

"What's going to happen now? Obviously I can't join my father and I'm a liability for you. What will I become?"

"I don't know. Cyrus supposedly had a plan, which he has yet to divulge." Sebastian shrugged his shoulders and let the topic fizzle.

The heat from the fire expanded into the cold of the cave and made it quite cozy. There was time for sleep and right now it seemed to be a safe choice.

Lucy knew that she was tired and that she would do well with some rest, but something was weighing her down. Her father was a vampire under the control of the Forsaken and she didn't have any ideas as to how to save him. She was in love with a man who had saved her life more than once, but he was more than a man. Inside, Sebastian had instincts and strengths that Lucy had yet to fully understand. Although she was trying to discover what exactly there was within her own heart, Lucy didn't have any certainty as to whether or not she could trust herself. There could be dangers in her that had yet to be revealed and maybe there was a beast below the surface just waiting for a time to come forth. Nothing was certain and she couldn't even rely on herself at this point.

As all of these thoughts circled in her head, Lucy was able to relax in his arms and finally close her eyes. She listened to the call of the night beneath the wispy flames in her ears. It was soothing. Without much effort, she was quickly roaming within a dream that had no backbone, in a place where she was completely safe and in control. Anything could happen there and nothing could harm her. It was perfect. A place of beauty where the silver leaves fell from the trees and onto a river that rolled into a waterfall. Where the fields of red grass swayed in a sourceless wind and orange clouds hid two different suns in spurts of shade. Lucy didn't know where she was, but the peace that she felt nearly brought her to tears. It was fantastic.

As reality sank back into her consciousness and the dream of paradise faded into the background, Lucy's senses returned to the world around her. Sebastian was no longer laying at her side, but he had left his jacket as a makeshift blanket that was surprisingly efficient at holding in warmth. The ground she had slept on left aches in her body where pebbles had carved dents in her skin. With a groan, Lucy wished that she could just return to her dream and stay a little while longer. It would be impossible now. She could barely remember the place let alone create it to be the same once more.

As she inhaled deeply, an unfamiliar scent drifted into her nose and triggered her curiosity. Lucy could smell meat and the scent instantly caused her stomach to ache. Somehow, she didn't realize how hungry she had been. Her last bite of food seemed like several days ago and for an unknown reason the aroma of cooking meat had sent her hunger into meltdown.

With another groan, she propped herself up to find the source. Lucy winced at the invading light as she opened her eyes, but as the spots in her vision faded, she was greeted by Sebastian's glee-filled face. He seemed overjoyed with his morning task of finding a suitable breakfast. Lucy squinted at the large black skillet in his hands. Sebastian held it painstakingly over the small fire and poked at several items inside. Upon closer inspection, she noticed a couple of large eggs, some slabs of bacon, and a few sausage links. It was an odd sight and Lucy was unsure what to say. On one side, he had found them a wonderful breakfast that made her stomach churn with excitement, but there was also a question that she couldn't seem to shake. Where did it come from?

Almost as if he had heard her thoughts, Sebastian's head snapped up and he gave Lucy the widest smile he could muster. She had never seen so much joy on his face before.

"Come on. Let's eat while it is still hot." He laughed and handed her a fork before snagging a sausage for himself.

"Where did all of this come from?" Lucy couldn't help asking as she pawed at her bacon and glanced up at him.

"Does it really matter?"

"No, I guess not," her defeat was well displayed. Lucy was still curious, but if he wasn't keen on telling then she wouldn't push any farther. Just as she had taken a bite of the bland, but succulent meat, Sebastian cleared his throat and took a slice of bacon.

"There is a camp site about five miles from here. They won't miss these things and won't suspect a werewolf either."

"How do you know?"

"I made it clear that a wild animal had ransacked their camp," his cheeky smile returned. Sebastian was proud of his deed, but Lucy seemed disappointed.

"I guess one did," she made her disgust for his actions clear.

"Lucy, don't be that way. It was either this or roasted squirrel. I figured you would appreciate a human meal over what I've eaten nearly every day for most of my life—bloody and raw sometimes." Sebastian tried not to reveal his anger as it built. Lucy remained quiet and watched him struggle with his inner beast. She let him regain control before thanking him.

"It is fine," he reassured her through what Lucy knew was pain, "I'm fine. Resisting the change can be painful when you're young. Kieron has been working with us to control our bodies and he will work with you too as soon as they come to get us. We will return to the den and all will be as it was." Lucy swallowed hard. She didn't know if he was serious or if it was just hopeful thinking. With a slight hiccup, she bottled up whatever sadness and regret were coming to the surface. Lucy didn't want to be responsible for more death. She had already caused so much and it was time for things to go in her favor.

Together they finished what was left of the breakfast. It wasn't a filling meal, but would suffice for the time being. Lucy watched him carefully. Somewhere between breakfast and extinguishing the fire there had been a change in his behavior. It was a side that she had never been able to see before. Sebastian was worried and this emotion came through loud and clear. Until now, Lucy was unable to feel anything coming from him since he kept his feelings buried deep and hidden well. Something had obviously changed. The amount of worry that penetrated her mind was sickening and she couldn't shake the weight of his guilt any longer.

Suddenly, she could feel a knot in her stomach and with the thought of burying the pain of Sebastian's worry, Lucy focused on it with all that she had. Somehow, the unfriendly feelings were being pushed out by whatever she had focused on. There was hope in this. Until now, Lucy relied on learning from others the means of controlling newfound strengths. However, there was a renewed confidence in her that said she could learn the skill of discipline for herself and use it whenever necessary. Lucy was finally able to breathe a sigh of relief. She had pushed his worry away for what felt like the thousandth time and it was a good feeling.

With a satisfied breath, she stood and brushed the caked dirt from her clothes. Sebastian glanced over, but said nothing. She wondered what he was thinking and wished for just a moment that she was able to read minds like the bloodline from which she was sired. Lucy was unsure if she would ever be able to use that specific gift and wasn't positive that she wanted it either. Oddly, she wanted to try and prove that she couldn't do it, but didn't even know how to attempt such an impossible feat.

A stray wind wisped through the cave and caught her attention. It shook the branches outside wildly and caused low-flying birds to rapidly change direction. It tossed the fallen foliage from last autumn and whipped it into small tornados on the ground. The breeze was enjoyable and a reprieve from the guilt and worry that flooded her thinking, but there was an undertone of something else within the wind. It was something her former self wouldn't have noticed, but with new guns come new triggers. It was a familiar smell that she had coupled with something bad. It only took a moment to remember the source and that was when a devilish chill swept over her skin.

"Lucian is nearby," Lucy whispered to herself and in less than a second Sebastian was at her side.

"Are you sure?"

"Of course; I can smell him. Musky honeysuckle; that's what he smells like." Lucy didn't have to say any more. Sebastian whipped her around by the waist and ordered her to hide. She didn't need much convincing. Lucy wasn't sure how close he was, but Sebastian had an idea because he crouched just inside the mouth of the cave and took hold of a sharp knife in his belt.

Except for the wild wind brewing outside, there were no other noises. Inside the cave was silent. Even the trickling water didn't make a sound. Lucy could barely breathe. She was more scared than she had ever been. She didn't know where Lucian was and that was probably the most nerve-racking thing of all. They waited a few minutes and just as she began to think it was a false alarm, a figure dropped from the cliff above and stood slowly.

It was Lucian, but he had changed. His long black hair had lost a significant amount of length and his clothes were old Victorian like the Forsaken had been wearing. His eyes were still the coolest green color and his features were normal. She remembered his appearance before then and how it had always changed when he was hunting. Lucy was unsure what these odd changes did, but she coupled them with danger. Until now, Lucy hadn't considered the possibility that the wolves had lost their fight. Lucian's presence brought forth the unforeseen shock of losing the people she held most dear. It was a crushing pain and as the vampire stepped into the cave and looked around, Lucy felt the urge to rip his eyes out or cut something off. All the hatred she had ever felt for him was instantly doubled and nothing would keep her from revenge if he had harmed her family.

Lucy watched Sebastian as he considered what to do next. The light in his eyes shone brightly as they shifted through the scenarios playing out in his head. She didn't know what his plan was or even if he actually had one. She only hoped that he did have an idea of what to do.

The ground seemed to shake as Lucian strolled toward the back of the cave. He took in long breaths just like the ones Sebastian had taught her to take, but his sense of smell wasn't as keen. He couldn't smell them over the heavy aroma of cooking meat. Lucy did her best not to breathe as he wandered over to where the fire had been and with a scowl scooped Sebastian's jacket from its place on the ground. Lucy could hear him growl. She wished that she could feel what he was feeling and know what he was thinking. His frown grew as he inhaled the scent from the fabric and then let it fall to the dirt.

"I can hear you breathing, Lucy Gaskin," Lucian's voice rang over the walls of the cave and out into the trees. Birds flew for cover and squirrels jumped into trees as the low boom of his voice radiated through the cave and out into the woods. There was an obvious change in him. He was deadly and confident. His voice was deeper and it boomed in power without effort.

"Is this the part when I taunt you and tell you how easy it was to leave your pathetic family in the hands of some of the most powerful vampires in the world? Is this your moment to confront me? Heroes don't usually win, my dear. That is a place in fiction that everyone is used to. Bring the same circumstances into our world and they will never measure up. Now come out and let's finish this." His hissing words struck at her nerves, but when she looked at Sebastian, Lucy was calmed enough to stay exactly where she was. Lucian wanted this to be easy and that was the last thing she was willing to give him.

"Lucian, you wouldn't be so foolish to think that Lucy was on her own." Sebastian scoffed as he came out from hiding and sheathed his knife.

"How admirable." The vampire glared as he turned away from the rear of the cave to face his enemy. "And no; I'm not that thick." His mocking words made Lucy's limbs tremble.

"I thought you were against the Forsaken," Sebastian frowned as they began to circle each other.

"I am."

"Still, you let them do that to you? What were their promises?" Sebastian frowned and scolded Lucian on his treachery. The vampire wore Victorian-style clothing and his hair had been cut. He was a hypocrite and Sebastian had no problem pointing it out.

"I'm no fool. There were no promises. I accepted their power in order to return Lucy to where she belongs. That's all," he shrugged off the questions and his green eyes flickered in the invading sunlight.

"You won't be able to resist them forever."

"I don't plan on living much longer so there will be nothing for them to control." His emotionlessness was chilling. It reminded Lucy of Eodin. She watched them interact like old friends rather than enemies. It was chilling to see this shadow of a man confront the only person she trusted. Lucy wanted to stand in his defense, but also realized that would be a big mistake. She felt helpless as she crouched like a coward behind a boulder and watched Sebastian exchange sentences with their enemy.

"You think that I will kill you, then."

"No, someone else will. It won't be you, my brother. Your heart is too soft." Lucian smiled and opened his arms in a kind gesture. Lucy wasn't sure if she had heard him correctly at first, but replayed the sentence in her mind and discovered that, in truth, he had called Sebastian his brother. Whether it was just a few kind words or a serious admittance, she did not know. Could they be brothers? She studied both of their faces and noted that they didn't look very similar, but there wasn't any shock on Sebastian's face. Lucy was dumbfounded.

"Don't torment me. We aren't brothers anymore and haven't been for a long time," Sebastian snapped with a glare in his eye that she had never witnessed before. He was beyond angry now and Lucy could only watch the events unfold, unable to do otherwise.

"Aren't you going to attack?" Lucian seemed to be getting impatient.

"No," Sebastian's answer came so quickly it nearly interrupted his brother's words. Lucian's green eyes shifted with aggravation. He stood with vigor as his livid nature shone through. Then he leaped forward with a clawed hand and sliced it across Sebastian's face. Lucy couldn't hold back her gasp and tried to catch herself by covering her mouth with her hand. It seemed to do the trick. Under Sebastian's screaming no other sound could break through. Helplessly, she watched him fall to his knees and cover his face. Lucy wanted to run to his aid and help him escape, but she remembered his eyes. She focused on them. Sebastian wanted her safe and it would kill him if she died trying to aid him.

Lucian decidedly kicked him in the shoulder and Sebastian fell to the ground. Lucy's eyes followed him to the cave floor and watched hopefully. He didn't move and she couldn't even be sure that he was breathing.

"Now you can see, Lucy. I have been given the power to return you to your kind, where you belong. Your stay with these creatures was an arrangement, nothing more. Your father entrusted you to the

mutts because of your uncle, but as you can see, family means nothing once the change divides you. They are your enemy, Lucy. Come with me." As he finished, the vampire turned and reached toward where she was hiding, like he had known her whereabouts the entire time. Lucian's hand dropped to his side and he took a step forward before

T clearing his throat. "You shouldn't fear me. We are family."

"Family," Lucy stated in disbelief as she emerged from her hiding place, "you think we're family?" Her calmness quickly changed to shouting. She couldn't believe he assumed they were anything alike. Lucy knew how deadly he was and how much he enjoyed killing. She didn't know what part of her he was referring to. Could there be a deadlier version hiding just inside her consciousness? "You can assume whatever you want, but I know who I am and I don't kill people. That is a life that I don't want." She refused his offer without hesitation.

"Give it time and nothing like that will bother you." Lucy took a second to drink in his offer once more and although he was well trained in persuasion, she was able to deny him again.

"You have my answer," she growled and took a step forward. Lucy didn't know why, but she felt herself being forced to confront him. This was something she had wanted to do from the beginning and now there was a strength that gave her the ability to do so without fear. Lucian didn't move, but appeared confused. In his mind, the offer must've been easy to accept and Lucy's rejection did not make any sense. After a few moments, he straightened and a chilling grin made its way across his face. "Are you going to fight me, Lucy?"

"I was thinking about it," she growled again and took another step forward.

"I know. It is written all over your face; the strategy and the fear. This is not a good idea."

"You don't need to be afraid of me," Lucy found herself taunting the monster in her path. She didn't know where all of this anger and cockiness was coming from, but she couldn't stop it. At her words, Lucian scoffed. He let his head hang in a snicker before it snapped back up. In those two seconds, his features had changed. The mask of draculicous had shrouded what was left of a man and transformed him into a hunter. The black eyes that Lucy had come to fear stared at her like she was prey. Surprisingly, regret never settled in. She didn't wish against what had been said. She was ready for this. Every cell in her body wanted him dead.

Lucy craved his last breath and anticipated his death more than anything. It would come soon. If not by her hand, then the claws of the wolves would rip him to pieces. Lucian's time was over and he knew it, but she couldn't feel his uncertainty. He might have been unsure of the person who would strip his life away, but Lucy was determined to be that person and would try whatever it took to kill him.

Chapter Nine

he trickling of water behind them became the only sound heard. Outside, the wildlife had gone into their respective homes and the wind had stopped blowing through the trees. It was nearly silent, quiet enough that Lucy could hear Lucian breathing. She could see the blood pulsing in his neck. Just as she wondered how his death would happen, movement caught her eye and she managed to evade his first strike. It was a punch to her blood-stained abdomen, which Lucy avoided with the slightest bend to the left. Lucian's other arm hastily swung at her head and she easily ducked under it and threw a punch at the ribs under his arm. She nearly collapsed when she felt his bones give way under the force of her fist. Disbelief that it was even possible to cause such damage flooded her thoughts.

She could barely breathe as the vampire stumbled away from her, cradling his side and coughing up a small amount of blood. Lucy watched him collapse against a rock and wipe the blood from the corner of his lips. He grinned as he looked at the redness that coated his palm and coughed once more before standing again. "Didn't see that coming. You've discovered most of your abilities, I'd gather. Can you read minds? Will people to do what you tell them? Have you tasted blood yet?" His words were more accusing than they were actual questions.

"You know I haven't, so why ask?"

"Just letting you sample what is waiting for you. It's time to join your kind, Lucy. All of these gifts and more are just waiting for you. The sky is the limit and the Forsaken will not take 'no' for an answer. I'm telling you this for my brother's sake. If you refuse, they will cut down his family and the ones closest to you. The wolves will be slaughtered."

"The Forsaken are outnumbered. They could never win," Lucy was sure of her words. A group of five vampires could never defeat the thousands of werewolves that resided in America. Lucy had witnessed their numbers before when they raided the coven to save the kidnapped victims.

"They aren't so small. Ella and her guards make up only one small portion. The royals control most of Europe. Your wolves wouldn't stand a chance." A solid knot formed in the bottom of Lucy's stomach that made her sick. There was no proof that what he was saying had any truth in it, but something in his face revealed what his voice had hidden. He was serious. There was power overseas that could rip her away from her family with such force that mending the break would be impossible. Lucy admired the fact that Lucian still cared for the well-being of his brother. She wanted to comfort him. She could see the sadness in his eyes and even some emotion was coming through. It felt like a bee stinging her temples, a constant annoyance that she couldn't get rid of. His feelings toward Sebastian were confusing. She could feel them swirl in the air.

Lucian was losing control of himself, but it didn't take long for him to realize this and regain control. She watched him struggle before shaking his head and causing the vampire features to vanish. His black eyes had returned to their familiar green and his face became more human. He continued to fight within himself and Lucy could do nothing but watch as he heaved and cleared his throat a few times. The rock he had fallen onto became a crutch once more. Lucy didn't know it was possible for him to be in such pain or that she could be the one to cause it. Every time he took in a breath, she could see him wince. It was a subtle confession of the agony he was in. It was sufficient revenge for her grandmother's death and Sebastian's defeat. Lucy was satisfied with his pain.

Lucian took a few more moments to shift himself in odd directions and reset his ribs. Lucy didn't want him to feel better, but his healing was as advanced as hers. There was nothing she could do to stop it. After a couple of minutes, he straightened and stepped away from the rock without pain. As a grin emerged, Lucy could see the clotted blood in his teeth. In his breathing she could hear wheezing and decided that the broken ribs had probably punctured a lung, which was taking longer to heal. He was still impaired and would not be able to fight effectively.

"I still won't abandon them. I'm not you and I can learn from your mistakes." Lucy didn't know where the defiance in her voice had come from, but she stood behind it and watched rage fill his face. Without any further provocation, Lucian let go of an outraged yell that exposed his fangs. Lucy felt herself become anxious. He had terrified her for the first time since the festival. As his outburst faded, Lucian strolled toward her and stopped only inches from where she was standing. "I did not have a choice and there weren't any mistakes. You are one of us and I will prove it to you."

With that final word, he blew a small stream of air in her face. As it struck her nose, Lucy felt herself begin to choke and then become light-headed. He was like an aphrodisiac. Whatever he had done left her dizzy and ready to accept what would happen whether it be good or bad. She knew that he had done it on purpose and did all she could to fight the drowsiness.

In vain, she watched him edge closer and move her hair behind her ears. She couldn't ignore him and even tilted her head to the side for reasons unknown. The realization that she didn't have the power to stop him finally sank in and his hot breath fogged over her neck, leaving moisture that felt like lava. Then the pain began.

It started like a mere pinch and grew into what felt like a hot poker that was skewering her through the shoulder. Lucy was helpless and all she could do to combat the attack was scream. She studied him out of the corner of her eye. His eyes had become bottomless pools of black again. It was as if her blood was forcing him back into hunter mentality. Agony swept her body again. It was a crippling pain that caused Lucy's legs to shake. If Lucian hadn't been holding her up, she would've collapsed to the ground. Her thoughts felt thick and pulsed slowly in the shadow of his venom. She could feel it pushing through her veins and coating her insides. Finally the light-headedness began. Lucy didn't know how much blood she had lost, but it was enough to loosen what control she had.

Just as she began to fade away from what was going on, Lucian growled and stopped his attack. Lucy glanced up at him. His face was filled with doubt and she didn't know why. Only seconds passed before a clawed hand appeared over his shoulder and grabbed hold of him. The strong arm whipped him around and picked him up before throwing the bloodied monster to the edge of the cave. He flopped like a rag doll out onto the cliff just outside. With just a little more effort, Lucian would've sailed out into the trees.

Lucy watched him try to lift himself off of the ground. As she observed his struggle, Cyrus's face came into view. She let go of a relieved sigh just before the most intense pain she had ever felt ripped through her body like lightning. It was paralyzing as she convulsed.

"What is happening?" Lucy roared through her teeth as she doubled over.

"Your body is dying," Cyrus explained before grabbing her hand and holding it tight. He didn't say anything further and just put pressure on the wound to stop the bleeding. The pain was worse than anything Lucy had ever been through. As she struggled under the sickening venom, she could see her attacker out of the corner of her eye. He was getting up. She tried to warn Cyrus, but was unable to speak or even gesture concern.

Lucian shook off his hunter features and calmly stepped in their direction. He crouched like a gargoyle before speeding at them. Lucy winced in preparation for his strike, but after a couple of moments without an attack, she glanced back to look for him. A thrill of hope shot through her body and pressed out all pain for a minute. Sebastian had come to their rescue.

He was still bloodied, but had Lucian by the throat, squeezing as hard as he could. The vampire didn't allow him to do so for long and quickly grabbed both of his arms, twisting them until just before the breaking point. Sebastian's fanged teeth emerged and he growled as he pulled an arm loose, drew his knife, and held it at Lucian's throat. She couldn't push the pain aside, but still forced herself to watch them in pure fear of losing Sebastian. Confidence in him built with the addition of an actual weapon, but in anger of the advantage, Lucian immediately knocked it from his hand.

Lucy watched in vain as the blade slid on the ground to the mouth of the cave and off the edge of the cliff. With a grin, the empowered vampire grabbed Sebastian by the waist and sent him contorting through the air, nearly causing him to collide with Cyrus.

Although the crippling pain still coursed through her limbs, Lucy managed to crawl to his side and brush the hair out of his face. Suddenly, something unexpected hit her and for the first time, Lucy felt as if she was really meant to be with him. Led by the best feeling in the world, she knelt next to him and bent over his motionless body. Without any further hesitation, she kissed him, pressing her lips firmly against his and exhaling slowly through her nose. The contact remained for what felt like a couple of minutes, and, finally satisfied, she pulled away. As they separated, Sebastian opened his eyes in shock, "Aren't you hurting?"

"More than you can imagine, but if I'm going to become a monster then I needed to do that now. I love you," Lucy revealed as she began to sob.

"Never! You could never become a monster and I love you too! Let me borrow this," he smiled and yanked hard on the locket around her neck. Without much resistance, the clasp broke and it fell into his hand. Leaving no more words to say, Sebastian leaped to his feet and stood defiantly in the path of his brother.

As they glared at each other, he released the charm and it unraveled to the ground. The heart that had once punctured Lucy's skin caught on the larger end of the chain and Sebastian held tight to the other side. Like she had seen Mitchell do with nunchakus, Lucy watched him twirl the necklace at his side like a weapon. He crossed it before his body and slowly began to advance as he became comfortable with the control. Lucian didn't appear afraid and he quickly disregarded the twirling bronze piece. He took a step forward and let go of a devilish grin as he revealed a dagger that he had retrieved from his belt, "You aren't the only one that comes prepared."

In one swift motion, Lucian snagged the blade between his fingers and threw it with great force at his brother's chest. Although it was a gut-churning try, Sebastian made it seem like a wasted effort. With one swing of the chain, he snapped the knife out of the air and it hit the cave floor with a clang. As if the charm hadn't even hit anything, it flew through the air and was easily manipulated by just a small twitch of his wrist. For most of the twirling, Lucy's necklace was a mere blur in the dim light. Sebastian maneuvered the chain as if he had been doing so his entire life. The sharp heart danced about in a sudden beam of sunlight and broke through the air with such force that it created a bright whizzing sound. It was now that Lucian's attitude changed. The cocky look that always seemed to be on his face was replaced with agitation and a little bit of panic. "You won't be able to save her."

"You shouldn't have done that. Biting her was a mistake."

"Then kill me. You will always be pathetic. You couldn't save our sisters and you won't save her." Before he could say anything else, Sebastian twirled the trinket for a last time, over his head and out its entire length. Lucian stumbled back as it hit him and he fell onto one of the larger boulders at the edge of the cave. He glared up at Sebastian with more fury than Lucy thought was possible. It didn't take much longer for a line to appear at his neck as blood began to pour onto his chest. Lucy watched his eyes roll back into his head as he slumped over into unconsciousness.

Relief at the sight of his death was short-lived, and like a bullet, pain from the bite returned. It coursed through Lucy's veins and made her sick. She took hold of Cyrus's hand and squeezed hard as the viciousness of the toxin pumped throughout her body. In less than a second, Sebastian was at her side and hovering over to look in her eyes.

Suddenly, blackness filled her vision and just as she was about to panic, Cyrus began to speak, "Lucy can you hear me?" She opened her mouth to answer him and found that her ability to speak had gone as well as her sight. With a groan, she closed her mouth and with a whimper nodded a couple of times.

"Okay, the venom hasn't stopped. I'm not sure why, but it hasn't. He's dead and that should've ended the change."

"Lucy, I love you and I'm sorry," Sebastian apologized desperately.

"Don't lose yourself, son." Lucy could hear Cyrus reassure him before he placed a hand on her wounded shoulder and pressed. "Listen to me, Lucy. The pain is going to get a lot worse. Don't be afraid. I know that you can get through it."

Even though he told her not to be afraid of death, it was a fear that she couldn't shake. In her life, Lucy had always been able to cheat death and pain, but now it was something she couldn't get away from. It was that fact that terrified her to the core.

"Do you remember when we were talking in the car back at the cemetery and I told you how special you are?" With another whimper, she nodded again. "They weren't just words, Lucy. I meant it. You can do the impossible. We've seen you do it and I know that if you really try the toxins in your blood will break apart. Concentrate and force your body to attack the venom."

Although it seemed useless, Lucy took a couple of deep breaths and a knot formed in the back of her throat. As she concentrated, something in her chest fluttered. It was a feeling that was almost impossible to describe. It was like some form of energy coming out of the smallest cells. As unlikely as it was, she didn't resist. With a reassuring and painful breath, Lucy thought about what Cyrus had said. She believed, for the first time in her life, that she could do something incredible and concentrated on the feeling within as it began to do what she willed it to. Finally it was obvious that she was actually in control of it.

Lucy tested her ability to move the energy before splitting it into five pieces and sending it through each of her limbs and up to her head as well. The infectious liquid that pulsed in her veins was instantly eradicated. She could almost feel it fizz, like she had been injected with something carbonated. The strength it had taken to cause such a miracle left her out of breath, but after finally calming down, Lucy opened her eyes. She didn't have to look far to find Cyrus. His beautiful blue eyes filled her vision and his arms cradled her as they rested on the cave floor. Sebastian was there too. His teary-eyed grin was all that it took for Lucy to realize what she had done. It was obvious to both of the men that her pain was gone and that Lucian's venom had not done its job.

"Are you all right?" Sebastian asked as she sat up and hugged each of them.

"Yeah, the pain's gone except for my shoulder," she frowned and attempted to see the damage from under her uncle's bloodied hand.

"Best not, I'm afraid," Cyrus reassured her. "It is quite gruesome and will take several hours to heal. Let's wrap it up; out of sight and out of mind." It appeared that Lucy really didn't have a say in the matter. Cyrus was going to wrap it up with compliance or kicking and screaming. Either way he didn't seem to care. Without hesitation, Sebastian stood and pulled his shirt over his head, revealing a toned body that Lucy hadn't expected to see. He wasn't a body builder by any means, but still the steel muscles under his skin rippled as he moved.

There were long moments of staring before he knelt back to the ground and began ripping the cloth into pieces. One long strip after another was torn from its frame and laid neatly on the rock behind them. When enough had piled up, Cyrus used one to blindfold Lucy and then lifted her arm in the air, "Hold it up while I bandage the bite." His order was kind, but serious. Although the bite was still painful and had become itchy due to the start of the healing, Lucy held her arm in the air as he worked. She could feel layer after layer of soft cotton as he applied them. The bandage was light as a feather and after a few minutes and an aching arm, Cyrus removed the blindfold. He had finished and the dressings were immaculate. Lucy didn't have any idea where this skill had come from, but she was thankful for it, even though she still wanted to see what Lucian had done. Human curiosity was an awful thing, but seeing it made it real.

"Are you ready?" He grinned and stood before helping her stand as well. Lucy couldn't find any relevant words to say and with a sigh she nodded and walked toward the mouth of the cave. Lucy looked down at Lucian's body. It had become pale white and his eyes had become blue. His black hair had begun to turn gray and lose its luster. Lucy stopped before they passed him. She never imagined the vampire to be any more than a killer, but now he looked almost human.

"What happened to him?" She struggled to avoid letting the words escape. Now that her thoughts were known, Lucy realized that for some reason, she really did care about him. The creature that was once a vampire had been a man before the disease took him. He had, at one time, been Sebastian's brother.

"He's dead. The venom doesn't have anything to feed off of so it dies and his body returns to its former self. His age is catching up to him. He will be bones and dust within the hour," Sebastian explained as empathy filled his face.

"I didn't think vampires could die."

"There are two kinds of vampires, Lucy. He is the kind that dies," Cyrus explained before helping her toward the mouth of the cave.

As they neared the edge, Sebastian scooped her up into his arms and told her to hold on tight. Without question, she did as he said just moments before they leaped fifteen feet to the ground below. A brief moment of weightlessness was followed by the crunch of foliage below. The men spoke quietly about which direction to travel before speeding off in full gallop. Lucy didn't know how fast they were going, but by the sound of feet pounding into the soil she assumed it was quite fast. She buried her face into Sebastian's shoulder to keep the wind from torturing her senses, and waited for them to slow down. Lucy listened to him breathe. For the amount of energy he was using to run, Sebastian's breathing was uncommonly slow as if he were merely walking through the woods. As the men sprinted, she couldn't forget what Cyrus had told her about vampires. How could there be two kinds of vampires and why hadn't she seen the other?

Just as this thought wrapped her brain in curiosity, Sebastian jerked to a stop and let her legs fall to the ground. With some difficulty, Lucy got her balance and stood with a slight wobble as he left her side. An impossible sight brought tears to her eyes. Mitchell, Kieron, and Syrina were leaning against an SUV awaiting their arrival. Although they were alive, there were clear signs of battle present.

Syrina was bruised, but not badly wounded. The look on her face revealed relief and exhaustion like she had just run a marathon.

Lucy could see various cuts and bruises on Kieron, however, the bite on his arm was drawing the most attention. She wondered how vampire venom would affect him and if there was a possibility of it crippling him.

Though she was worried about the puncture wounds on Kieron's arm, everything was pushed from Lucy's mind when she saw Mitchell's battle scars. There were three large slashes across his face made by vampire claws. They had already begun to heal, but it was obvious that there would be scars in place of the gashes. They extended from the hairline on his temple to the middle of his cheek. It looked as if he had jerked away to avoid the attack, which left a slight curve in the mark.

Lucy knew that there should have been feelings of joy and relief, but all that she could rest on was doubt. They shouldn't have been standing there. Three wolves had fought their way around incredibly powerful vampires, and to her, it was an impossibility. Suddenly the pressured burning in the back of her nose, which was always a precursor to tears, arrived. Her eyes became wet and eventually released drop after drop down her cheeks. She couldn't feel anything else except the sinking feeling that came with doubt and thoughts of what could have happened.

Instantly, Syrina was standing in front of her, looking down with a solemn grin on her face. Her blue eyes gleamed as she studied Lucy's emotions, and after a few moments offered her a hug. Like she hadn't seen love in years, Lucy launched herself into Syrina's arms and fought back the urge to sob. The wolf's long curly hair fell onto her face and they held each other for a couple of minutes. The embrace allowed Lucy the time she needed to gain control of herself. Kieron and Mitchell each hugged her when Syrina had finished, before they all piled in the car.

As soon as the last door was closed, Cyrus hit the accelerator and the car fish-tailed in the leaves before shooting down a desolate back road. Lucy was lucky enough to be seated next to a window. She observed the passing forest with a critical eye, wondering where they could possibly be. The sun's rays beamed through the tight canopy of leaves and formed into blotches of light on the ground. They highlighted tiny meadows of tall grass that patched the forest floor.

Lucy was hypnotized, but she couldn't seem to shake the questions that Cyrus had forced upon her. What was the other kind of vampire? Why hadn't she encountered it before? She tried her best to answer them in ways that made sense, but without a true answer, Lucy was left to wonder.

Time passed slowly as if a grain of sand was occluding the passing zone of an hourglass. The trees became blurs that were actually causing nausea and eventually forced Lucy to look at the floor of the car in hopes of easing her stomach. Sebastian's blue eyes suddenly caught her attention. He had been watching her attentively.

"I'm fine," she reassured him with a grin.

"Sure you are," he doubted with a smirk and took hold of her hand. His grip was firm. It was comforting to know he was there. Lucy didn't know if relying on him was a good idea or if her new-found strength would be enough to feel safe.

The trees faded in numbers after a while and the rocky road that led them out of obscurity had turned into a solid asphalt road. Cyrus was finally able to speed without the threat of losing control of the vehicle. Lucy didn't know how fast they were really going and decided that it was best she didn't know. The endless fields on either side of the road were dotted with cattle. Their car traveled smoothly along the freshly paved road as Cyrus wove through the various Amish buggies that were out. They had exited the woods and entered the middle of nowhere.

As if he actually knew where he was going, Cyrus skidded down various roads, making Lucy cringe with every tire squeal. She was just about to complain when the car slowed down and stopped at an intersection. They had gotten to the outskirts of a town. In vain Lucy searched for a welcome sign. The name would be enough to satisfy her curiosity, however there were no signs to be found. The village was small but busy and reminded Lucy of where she had grown up. Cyrus stopped at a gas station momentarily and both he and Kieron left the vehicle. Gusts of wind blew past them and into Lucy's face. She could smell a lot more now and could decipher specific scents within the breeze. The doughnut and hotdog smells whipped through the air as the automatic doors opened for patrons. The heavy smell of gasoline was also present, but filled with undertones of perfume. As Lucy concentrated more, she realized that picking apart the components of perfume was as easy as picking the noodles out of spaghetti. It became an unusual talent that was oddly amusing. She wondered if the wolves could always aromalize this way and how she was able to do so.

The men piled back into the car almost as quickly as they had departed and Lucy was able to take in the smell once more before the car sped off. They didn't stop again for a long time. Watching the world outside pass was causing a strength of nausea that kept Lucy from admiring the scenery. She laid her head against Sebastian's shoulder and yawned as if she was tired. In truth, she was wide awake and her thoughts sped through her head faster than she could keep up.

It seemed like she was drowning in her reflections for hours before Sebastian stirred. He glanced down like he hadn't even noticed she was laying on him and wrapped an arm around her shoulders. "We're almost home," he said. Though she was unsure how he knew, Lucy was grateful to be near home. It was time to regroup and focus on healing.

Like an answered prayer, their vehicle plunged into the bumpy meadow and slowed to a stop. Relief sent chills over Lucy's skin as she exited the car and waited for Sebastian to follow. With a grin he took her hand, closed the door, and led the way into the towering trees. The other wolves followed closely. In the shadows, Lucy began to notice familiar landmarks that led her to feeling anxious and safe. The archway of trees was welcoming and they had soon passed the training area that Mitchell used very frequently. Finally the fork in the road came into view and the group split in two. Mitchell took the path that led to his individual home and Cyrus, Syrina, and Kieron accompanied Sebastian and Lucy to the large house filled with expensive wonders.

Everyone was silent, but she could barely contain herself. There were questions that still waited to be asked and there were answers that could stand to be repeated. The threshold of the home sent another wave of chills over her as they passed under it and the men marched to the door of the hidden laboratory under their feet. Lucy wasn't so anxious to return there. She had memories of bad news in that place and had no desire to return. Cyrus waited at the top for her, but after noticing her hesitation, made a quick excuse to stay upstairs.

"You all right, Lucy?" His concerned tone hid away any suspicion.

"I'm fine. I just have a lot on my mind."

"I have ears," he chuckled. "Do you want to talk?" He didn't move forward and waited patiently for the answer.

"I have so many questions, but when I ask them I get watered down answers that don't really solve anything."

"Sebastian is just trying to protect you," Cyrus tried to rationalize for her.

"I know, but it isn't just him."

"I see. What do you want to know?" Cyrus's grin made Lucy feel warm. He gradually led her into the gallery and closed the door. Though he sat down, Lucy was unable to join him. She paced slowly in front of the glass case for a couple of minutes before gawking at the various paintings on the walls.

"Who is C.G.?" Lucy felt confident in her first question. There was very little wiggle room. He could either tell the truth or lie.

"It is either your dad's or mine. As boys we did a lot of traveling. In our actual twenties, we met a man called Van Gogh while in southern France. We worked at a pub that he attended regularly. Craig became taken with his use of paint and eventually did quite a few works himself while we were hidden away with your mother waiting for you to be born. Your dad was quite the artistic man; he enjoyed instruments also. His favorite invention was the guitar and he played very well." As Cyrus explained pieces of her father that Lucy had never known, she could feel tears build and tried her best to push them back. "I wish you could've known him before the Forsaken sunk their teeth in him, figuratively."

"Was he a good man?"

"Oh, the best!" Cyrus managed to utter before clearing his throat of risen emotions. "And he loved you. I think it is best that you know. Your dad loved you more than anything and it broke him into pieces when he realized that he couldn't have you. In all my time, I have never seen a man so happy and so sad in the same day."

"I wish I could've known him." The tears were gone now and Lucy was left with nothing but the constant itch of 'what if.' Suddenly, another question popped into her mind and without restraint, she blurted it out, "What is the other kind of vampire?"

"When I said that, I was referring to our vampires versus the vampires that society is used to. They either find vampires sexy and moody, or old and dusty. The real ones that we are up against are blood-thirsty killers that can die, but are nearly impossible to kill. They heal like we do, but severe blood loss will do the trick; beheading or fire, too.

"Why can they die?"

"The draculicous venom feeds off of blood and without it the venom dies and is unable to sustain the life that vampires need. Therefore the charade of youth and power disintegrates and the vampire dies. Whereas, society's vampires are afraid of garlic, holy water, and sunlight, or they are near indestructible unless you have a wooden stake and great aim. Very false indeed." Cyrus seemed amused by his facts, but at least he was telling the truth. Sebastian wouldn't have been as straight forward with her. Lucy didn't know why he felt the need to protect her and wished that someone would tell him that she had grown since her first vampire encounter. She felt helpless, but was glad that Cyrus was on her side.

Just as another question snaked its way into her mind, a knock came from the door. Almost immediately, it popped open and Syrina poked her head through. She waited for Cyrus to wave her in before she greeted them both and asked that they come downstairs. Without another word, Cyrus stood and allowed Lucy to exit ahead of him.

They ventured to the back of the main room where the hidden staircase door was. Lucy followed the wolves down the stairs until the familiar glass doors appeared. Beyond them, she could see three individuals. Mitchell was laying on a table with Allegra tending to the gashes in his face and Kieron joking with him as he mashed something with a mortar and pestle.

Sebastian was sitting nearby simply watching Kieron cook his remedies. His face was pained as if he had similar experiences with the paste. As they laughed at something unknown, Kieron scooped the paste into his hand and slapped it onto the gashes in Mitchell's face. The goop stayed in place as it dried and Kieron grumbled threats before his brother had the chance to refuse the treatment.

"What is that?" Lucy asked as she gawked over the odd remedy. A subtle grin crossed Kieron's face before his answer finally came.

"This is a mixture of various herbs and serums that together help to speed the process of healing. It is quite simple and doesn't work on every wound, but the paste is all that we can do for him."

Lucy nodded as she sauntered to the young wolf's side and placed her hand on his shoulder. "If it's any consolation, thank you for helping defeat the coven. You're an amazing fighter." Mitchell didn't reply. He closed his eyes and sighed before rising from the table and wrapping Lucy in a hug. Tension overwhelmed her senses briefly and then it disappeared. Lucy didn't know why, but she was suddenly filled with a sense of satisfaction and hugged him back. They remained so for a couple of minutes until Mitchell broke the connection and passed by her to exit the room. No one spoke in the next minute or so. The lab had become silent with the exception of running machinery that sent a low hum through the room.

"Lucy," Kieron finally mumbled.

With the shock of Mitchell's affection still on her mind, Lucy couldn't find the words to say anything so she simply nodded.

"After what happened in the cave, I think it would be wise to run another series of tests to assess what effects Lucian's venom has had on your body. It would involve a blood draw and simple monitoring tests to measure your sight, smell, and other things; quite simple."

Kieron's Scottish droll caused Lucy's heart to race. She found it incredibly hard to say no to him and soon cleared her throat with a quick nod. With her permission, the room nearly erupted with motion. Syrina followed Allegra when she exited the main lab and into the accessory room that had been purposed as a hospital. For unknown reasons, Lucy was anxious for them to return for the tests, but they didn't.

Kieron wore an unreadable expression as he prepared the supplies necessary for phlebotomy. He collected a couple of tubes, some syringes, a tourniquet, and some antiseptic.

Lucy had become accustomed to the pain associated with needles, but it was the thought of losing blood for the purpose of discovering what no longer mattered that bothered her. She was perfectly content with the knowledge that venom wasn't a final situation and that she would be able to live her life without vampire needs. Lucy knew how she felt, but if the information was important to the wolves she would have to allow them to take her blood and run whatever tests to help them sleep securely.

A sharp pain interrupted her train of thought as Kieron's needle dove into her skin and hit a large vein. He pulled back slowly and retrieved the sample needed before filling the tubes and entering the same room where the women had gone only moments before.

Sebastian didn't speak. He licked his thumb and wiped the smeared drop of blood from Lucy's healing arm before standing and helping her to her feet.

"What other tests are there?" Lucy asked as she followed Sebastian along tables filled with machines of all sizes. He said nothing but did finally stop next to a desk covered in papers. Just as Lucy wondered what the tests might be, she caught a lightning-fast motion out of the corner of her eye. As quick as it had happened, she found herself snatching a tennis ball out of thin air. In shock, she dropped the ball and took a step backward. It had come out of nowhere. How had she stopped it?

"That was a test. It's all right," Sebastian explained as he held the palms of his hands out in surrender. His face told her more than his words. Sebastian had been surprised at first, but that primary feeling had been replaced by fear. He was afraid of her. Lucy saw Kieron peek around the corner. He smiled and gave a quick nod. He had thrown the ball and seemed pleased with the results of the test.

"That was amazing. I've never been that fast before. I didn't even see the ball coming. I just reacted," Lucy explained as she tried to ignore Sebastian's odd response.

"Your reflexes have been altered. Other things have also changed." The seriousness in his voice caught her attention. Lucy knew there was something he was hiding from her.

"What aren't you telling me?" She knew that the question was premature, but Sebastian acted as if he hadn't heard it. His eyes shifted from side to side anxiously before he turned away from her. With a grumble, Sebastian searched the drawers of the desk behind him. After a few moments, he paused to look at whatever was in his hand before turning to face her again. He was holding a small mirror.

Fear suddenly surged its way through Lucy's body as she accepted the mirror from Sebastian. "It's your eyes, Luce. They've changed." After a deep breath to calm her nerves, Lucy held the glass up to her face and sighed. The color in her eyes was drastically different. Where the edges had once been a gorgeous deep blue, they were now painted over in a glittering green. Luckily there was still blue near the pupil, but the green color that had become associated with vampires was staring her in the face, a sight that was literally nauseating. What else had Lucian done to her?

"Why?" was all that she could get out as Sebastian returned to her side. Lucy could feel his eyes on her and before he could move again, she wrapped her arms around him and held on for dear life. Almost immediately, she could feel Sebastian's strong embrace and they held each other until Lucy felt safe again. She couldn't trust her own body now. It was a strange place to live.

"I can't answer that. I'm only grateful that I still have you. Whatever may change, I will always be glad for that." Lucy had never seen him so serious. Without another word, they sat on the desk and held hands until Kieron approached them. The papers shook in his tense hand as he cleared his throat and sat atop the table across from them. Lucy gripped Sebastian's hand tighter as she waited for the results of the tests. A lump formed in the back of her throat and she hoped they didn't have to wait long.

"Well," Kieron began as his quivering hand held the papers in front of his face, "in every zephyr there is an extra gene that is incomplete, as you know, and in your DNA, I found that Lucian's venom has completed that gene. In all reason, you should be a vampire right now, but the genes that you got from your father have allowed you to stop the change."

"Is that possible?" Lucy's mind was reeling in the possibilities.

"I suppose it will have to be. You should know that your existence has been viewed as an impossibility in our world. A vampire cannot have children. Their entire body is kept alive by their venom and offspring are normally killed upon conception. You have changed things. Something unique about your parents is the key. You are the answer and the vampires cannot have an answer. If it is something that they can change, hybrids will take over. They will be viciously strong and fast. We will lose. The entire world will lose." Kieron was nearly begging for her compliance. He didn't seem to realize that he already had it. Lucy only nodded, but it was all that he needed.

"Now, onto more pressing matters. We were followed here. I smell the death that accompanies vampires. They are respecting our territory for now, but you aren't safe here anymore." His concern was obvious.

"How could we escape?"

"I think there will be a lot of running involved, but we will have to split up." His plan was simple and Sebastian already had a problem with it.

"That makes me incredibly nervous."

"It may not be a good plan, but I don't see another one." Kieron was certain and he didn't say anything else. Moments later, Cyrus appeared from the other room with the same frown on his face that Kieron had been using.

"We need to leave this place. All the time and work that I've put into this property and we are being forced out by two vampires," his voice trembled in anger as he paced before them.

"Who is it, Cyrus?" Sebastian asked as he stood and took a step toward the angered wolf.

"Eodin has sent Cecily and Eliza to retrieve Lucy. They will stop at nothing. Eliza is ruthless and no doubt he has placed her in command," Cyrus growled.

"Aren't there rules between vampires and werewolves that they have to honor?" Lucy's questions penetrated the air like knives.

"They will be considered mercenaries and vampires with such a purpose are very dangerous. They don't adhere to the rules of the world. The only way to stop them is to kill them," Kieron answered.

"How do we do that?"

"Drain them of blood, stab them in the heart, or remove their heads. Those are the three simplest ways and the ones most often used, but we can't worry about it now. First we need to leave this place. I will not fight a war in my home." Cyrus had grown angrier by the moment. His feelings were nearly suffocating Lucy's mind. It didn't take him long to realize this and pull them back in. How he knew about her sensitivity, she was unsure.

"Where do we go?" Lucy's questions spouted out once more. She was clearly unable to hold them in.

Just as Cyrus was about to answer, a loud bang came from upstairs and after a few silent seconds, Mitchell appeared at the top of the stairs. He didn't have to say a word. There were various scrapes and new bruises apparent on his body. The vampires had chosen to attack. In less than a second, Syrina was at his side and helping him down the stairs. An obvious pain tore at his side as he hobbled toward them. With a wince accompanying every step, Mitchell limped with her help until he got to Cyrus. His deep breaths obstructed any speech that came.

Cyrus didn't wait for him to say the words. He, along with everyone else in the room, knew what was happening.

"Cyrus, what can we do? They are in the house," Sebastian whispered as he herded the group into the hospital wing. Loud crashes echoed above. The two lady vampires were ripping apart the upstairs, no doubt searching for where Mitchell had disappeared to.

"There are escape tunnels behind that wall. I've never had to use them, but there's a first time for everything." Cyrus's worried expression wasn't easily hidden. Lucy could feel his fear stronger than that of anyone else in the room, but a good leader keeps his worries hidden from his followers no matter how reasonable he feels. Morale is always the most important thing.

As another second passed, Sebastian whisked Lucy into the corner while his brothers proceeded to tear down the decor that had hidden a small crawlspace. Syrina helped Mitchell enter first and then she disappeared into the dark space. Allegra took a moment to kiss her husband before she too vanished into the dark.

"Aren't you coming?" Lucy screamed at Cyrus before Sebastian could successfully influence her to enter the escape tunnel.

"Not yet. It is my duty as leader to defend our home and ensure your escape. Go, Lucy. Your life is more important than mine." His mind seemed to be decided, but Kieron was instantly bothered by it.

"I will stay and defend what I can. You have a family that needs you. Allegra needs you."

"You are my oldest friend, Kieron," Cyrus frowned and grabbed his arm.

"That's why I'm staying. Even if I die, my life has been long. Be with your wife and protect her. Keep Syrina safe and tell her that I love her. Tell her I am sorry," his voice had begun to crackle with emotion. Lucy could feel his fear in the back of her mind. His thoughts became hers. Her head was flooded with worries for Syrina and satisfaction that he would give his life for a greater purpose. Beneath those stood an anger that made Lucy's blood burn in her veins. It was rage against the invasion of the den and the pungent death smell that came with vampires. She had never been able to feel that way about anything before and now the strength of his anger was burning its way through her brain like wild fire.

"I will," Cyrus finally said with a nod.

"And don't let her come after me," Kieron's request seemed odd, but Cyrus agreed. The leader even tried to hide his sadness and gave a hearty laugh as he patted Kieron roughly on the back.

"It will be all right," Cyrus reassured him.

"I have no fear." They were simple words that had a big impact. Saying that you have no fear is different from actually feeling that way. Lucy had lost her grip on Kieron's emotions as he reeled them back in.

"I believe you. God speed, my friend." Nothing else could be said. Sebastian exchanged glances with Kieron before entering the dark passage, followed by Lucy and then Cyrus. The small hole made Lucy imagine that she had just escaped from prison. The walls and floor of the tunnel felt like concrete that became quite painful to crawl on after a few minutes. It was almost too dark to see where

Sebastian was.

In silence they crawled the length of a football field until light shone in from the end of the tunnel. As they exited into an unfamiliar part of the forest, Lucy was pulled from the ground and held until she found her footing.

Mitchell had been the one helping her. His pain had become nonexistent and the slashes in his face were nothing but silvery scars. Lucy looked back to the tunnel just as Cyrus emerged. It had become immediately obvious that Kieron wasn't following him and a gasp suddenly came from behind them. Just as Lucy glanced to her side, Syrina flew toward the opening and was stopped before she could enter. An echo of screaming came from her direction when Sebastian helped restrain and drag her away from the tunnel. Lucy watched Syrina's dark hair flip around wildly as she tried to kick away from the men. In time they were able to stop her struggles.

"How could you let him do that?!" She frowned and slapped Cyrus across the face as hard as she could. Although Lucy thought he should've been mad or have disciplined her for the breach of rank, Cyrus let his head hang and apologized for what he had done.

"Syrina, he volunteered to stall them. He sent his love and had me promise to keep you from saving him. I hope that you can forgive me, but we cannot go back for him." As he revealed the last of what Kieron had said, Syrina broke into tears and sobbed for a few minutes as the other wolves watched. No one volunteered to approach or console her and for some reason that just didn't sit right in Lucy's heart.

Without thinking she stepped into Syrina's space and put her hand on her shoulder. As soon as Lucy touched her, Syrina whipped around with a clawed hand, but with her newfound speed, Lucy was able to duck under the wolf's arm and embrace her with a hug. It took a moment, but soon Syrina hugged her back and Lucy could feel all the tense energy leave the wolf's body as she nearly went limp. Lucy could feel her friends' tears dampen her shirt.

Finally, Syrina was able to stand again and with a sniffle she moved away from Lucy without a word. Though her emotion had crippled her in the worst way, Syrina was able to enter the dim forest. Slowly the others followed and tried to keep the angry she-wolf at a good distance. It seemed that no one was prepared to comfort her and at that realization Lucy felt proud of herself. She had done what the others were afraid to do.

With a piece of what she had come to see as family gone, the hike to civilization would be long and quiet. The wolves didn't appear to be in a hurry. They let their heads hang in sadness as if they were walking to his funeral. What happened after they left was unknown, but Lucy could've sworn that she could feel him.

She focused on the life that kept fading in and out of her consciousness. The harder she did, the farther it seemed to stray. Finally the source vanished completely and Lucy felt her heart briefly sink into depression. She hoped against all hope that it was only distance that disrupted the connection, or maybe it wasn't him at all. The hum that she had associated with invading emotions was gone. Lucy had never felt her mind so silent. It was an eerie quiet that had taken over and for some reason it was terrifying.

With a sigh, she simply followed the person in front of her and watched the trees pass overhead as they journeyed through the hills and to a place that, Lucy prayed, was familiar.

Chapter Ten

he journey quickly became a never-ending hike through an unfamiliar forest. Lucy and Sebastian were alone now and had been so for a while. Cyrus seemed to believe that splitting the group up would better their chances of confusing the vampires. Lucy hadn't heard from her companion for a long time. She wondered what was going on in his head. She hoped that he would make the mistake of letting his guard down so that she would be able to feel his emotions. Unfortunately, she realized that it would take another breakdown to have a chance of him letting her in.

Birds chirped quietly and the scampering critters tried their best to avoid the two of them as they hiked. It seemed like they traveled for hours before the sun began to go down and the pace picked up. Lucy didn't mind. After her encounter with Lucian, she found many different changes that even the wolves didn't notice. She didn't tire as easily and was also able to keep up with the ridiculous pace that Sebastian had set. When darkness finally overtook the woods, Lucy could see what appeared to be stars flashing through the trunks of the trees. Then she assumed they were fireflies, but they didn't blink as normal bugs would. Finally she realized that they were coming up on a small city and the lights she saw were actually street lights peeking through the trees. Civilization had, at long last, appeared.

Lucy even recognized some of the landmarks. They had arrived in a city that she had gone to often with Tryp and Rae. Together, the three of them had attended sporting events and other fun outings provided by their rival high school. They had emerged from the woods directly behind the school building. Lucy's vision was immediately obstructed by the football stadium in the back of the school. It was empty and dark, just like the school building.

Lucy didn't know what day of the week it was, but the entire area was quiet and gloomy as if it was about to rain. The air was thick with moisture, which was oddly distracting. Finally, something caught her attention. There was a scent in the air that Lucy knew she recognized, but for some reason couldn't place. She thought on the smell for a few moments until it came to her. Lucy knew exactly where she had smelled it before.

"Sebastian," she began, but was immediately interrupted.

"I know. I can smell it too. We need to run." He frowned and took her hand. Lucy was ready to go this time and as he sped off into the parking lot, she was able to keep up very well. Together they ran even as it started to rain. It must've seemed very odd to passing traffic to see these two people running along the side of the road in the rain. Lucy knew this, but she was having the time of her life with him. Somehow she had let herself forget why they were running. The truth that Eliza and Cecily had not been fooled escaped her mind and Lucy was able to enjoy the cool rain as it hit her face. They ran for miles, but to Lucy, it didn't seem like very far. When Sebastian finally stopped to rest at a gas station, she could feel the weight of her used energy begin to take its toll.

The glow that came from inside the building was warm and left a feeling of false security in the air. The automatic doors opened for them and they went inside. Lucy hadn't realized how cold her body had become until the heaters inside warmed her skin. The employee behind the counter eyed them for a moment and then returned to his magazine while simultaneously blowing large bubbles of pink gum. As she listened to the annoying popping bubbles, Lucy became bothered by the changes that Lucian had caused. The things that she was able to do now would have never bothered her before. She was unable to trust her own body. It was like living within a stranger and thinking, smelling, and hearing in the way that that person did. In some ways she wanted her old self back, but there were also many perks to the newfound abilities.

"Get something to drink and rest for a minute. The next truck that stops, we are hitching a ride." He didn't seem nervous or worried. Sebastian acted as if he had a plan and Lucy hoped that it wasn't just a charade. Without question, she did what he said. She removed a bottle of water from the refrigerated case and also snatched a breakfast burrito from the warmer, and as she moved to the counter to pay for what she had gotten, Sebastian stepped into her path with a frown. "Don't worry about it. Eat if you're hungry. Drink if you're thirsty. He won't stop you. He is with us."

"He's a wolf?"

"No. His parents were, but he is not," Sebastian explained.

"Is that possible?"

"Entirely. First generations usually give birth to other wolves, but his parents were a second and third generation. He's only human, but he's the best kind of human."

"How so?"

"Robert is a vampire killer when he isn't working here," Sebastian said it so casually that Lucy nearly missed the negatives in his sentence. She was speechless for a moment, but was then hit by several questions.

"Do you allow vampire killers?"

"We certainly don't stop them, usually. We have employed him on several occasions. Robert will be able to slow Eliza down so that we can get a good head start."

"I thought we got away from her." Lucy was worried.

"No. She is right outside. Cecily is very fast. They've been on our heels from the beginning, but she won't step foot in here. Don't worry," Sebastian smirked and got a bottle of water for himself.

"Why won't she step foot in here?" The question was simple, but Sebastian seemed to stumble over it. When he had finally gotten comfortable with his answer, Robert interrupted with his own.

"I'm in here," he shot her a cocky grin and blew another bubble.

"Okay," she grinned skeptically and stepped up to the counter to get a better look at the vampire killer. His shaggy brown hair nearly covered his eyes and he wore a baggy t-shirt with cargo pants and red converse. Somehow, his shoes catapulted Lucy back to memories of the man who had helped her find the bus terminal in the unfamiliar town when she had run away. She remembered both his kind face and willingness to help with reverence and hoped to see him again someday to thank him properly.

"Do you doubt my mad skills?" Robert's question brought Lucy back to reality. She didn't know if it was a rhetorical question or not, but instead of answering she opened the burrito and took a bite. The man behind the counter didn't persist. He calmly stepped behind the register and cleared his throat to get Sebastian's attention. "Did you leave in a hurry?"

"You could say that," he chuckled before opening his bottle of water and drinking half of it. Robert didn't ask any more questions. He dipped down and opened a trap door that Lucy had failed to notice before. She watched him disappear down a flight of stairs and then a light came on, illuminating the hole in the floor. She stared intently at the lit stairway until Robert's fluffy hair reappeared. It bounced wildly as he nearly stumbled over himself and set a small box on the counter before kicking the trap door shut. Sebastian met Robert at the counter before he could open the box. The small box creaked as he took the top off and placed it to the side. The wooden container was an old cigar box that was decorated in a red design, but inside there weren't any cigars.

With a grin, Robert pulled out a couple of stacks of hundred dollar bills. Sebastian also wore a mischievous grin that gave Lucy chills. He accepted the money and slurred a few words under his breath. Robert laughed at him and nodded as he held up one of his skinny fingers. With his other hand, the attendant ripped something heavy out from under the counter. It appeared to be a long-barreled pistol that appeared to Lucy to be very old.

"Very nice. Any sharps?"

"Of course; guns are nice, but nothing can beat the control of steel," Robert said, laughing through his teeth.

"Good and you'll need the firepower."

"I know." Robert's eyes shifted to Lucy before he returned the gun to the shelf under the counter.

"We aren't taking any weapons?" Lucy asked and nearly jumped when both men turned in place to look at her.

"We won't need any." Sebastian nodded with a smile before he sat across from Robert, the counter between them, and began talking. The seconds seemed to tick by slowly. They began to drag on in a way that started to make Lucy tired. She had finally let her head hang down when the sound of chair legs scooting across the floor caught her attention. The men were shaking hands now while Sebastian shoved one of the stacks of hundreds in his pocket and claimed it would be enough. With a smile he turned and reached for Lucy's hand. She nearly melted under the passion of his grip as he led her to the sliding door and it automatically opened.

The rain had not stopped. It was pounding the pavement so hard that Lucy could feel the ripple effect of each drop. Out in the dark, Eliza was waiting for them. Lucy could smell her. A scent of bubblegum and peppers filled her nose. Cecily was there too.

These truths impaired her confidence. She wasn't ready to fight Eliza, and defeating Cecily once hadn't earned her anything but the fear of revenge. All of these things made her tremble as her heart beat faster. However, with one squeeze of her hand, Sebastian brought her back to the present and his eye-squinting grin made her stomach flip into knots.

"There's your ride," she heard Robert shout before the headlights of a long semi-truck appeared as it rolled up to the gas pump. She was immediately intimidated by the size of the rig, but with Sebastian near, Lucy was able to act against what her human brain told her. Suddenly, Robert appeared in her peripheral vision and she tried not to seem startled. He was well-equipped now with a shot gun on each shoulder, an ancient sword at his waist, a pistol holstered on the other hip, and a grenade in one hand. She wasn't sure if he was overly prepared or understood what it would take to slow down a couple of vampires, but by the seriousness in his face she realized that he might have been just slightly insane.

The wind blew fiercely, but was soon blocked by the truck as it stopped for gas. The driver stepped out and was temporarily hidden by the vehicle. Lucy watched his feet under the truck. The man paced quietly as he topped off the truck's tank and after a few minutes he stopped and replaced the hose in its holder. The driver then returned to his seat, slammed the door, and gingerly placed his hands on the wheel before turning his head to look at the door. Lucy could feel his hard and consuming stare on her. She could sense his nervousness and anticipation. Goosebumps covered her arms. He wasn't an ordinary person; she was sure of that. Maybe that's why the vampires left him alone.

Sebastian's grip tightened suddenly. He didn't look down, though. His eyes were focused on the truck. The gas station door wanted to close and tried every so often, but then jerked back open after half a second. It became a constant and annoying cycle.

Then she saw Robert move. He walked into the rain and pulled one of the shot guns into his arms. The crying sky had him drenched from head to toe in less than a minute. The nose of the gun dripped as if it was drooling. Lucy watched him anxiously. The anticipation was excruciating, but finally Robert glanced back at them.

"Ready?" Sebastian asked, but didn't wait for an answer. With a pull, he jerked her out into the rain, causing her bottle of water to fall to the ground. Without stopping for it, Sebastian pulled her past Robert and into the long open distance between the gas station and the truck.

At first Lucy thought they would make it, but just as they reached the halfway point, she saw something out of the corner of her eye. From the darkness came a shriek and then Cecily flew out of the blackness around them. Like a falcon, she dove with talons and teeth bared. Fear swept through Lucy's body, but Sebastian didn't appear even slightly worried and she wasn't left to wonder why he was so calm.

A shot rang out and was instantly muted. The bang cut through the thick sheets of rain and echoed into the distance. A gut-wrenching thud came from Cecily's direction. The slug from Robert's shotgun had struck her in the side and knocked her out of the air. Lucy saw her fall to the ground as they ran past her and finally came to the semi's passenger door. Sebastian pulled it open with such force that Lucy thought the hinges might come loose. Without missing a beat, he lifted her into the seat as easily as if he was picking up a feather. It seemed effortless.

Immediately the driver turned the key and his truck roared to life. He then shifted into drive and punched the gas. The force of the sudden acceleration nearly knocked Lucy off of the seat. As if he had anticipated the force, Sebastian pulled her back into the chair and simultaneously slammed the door. The truck sped up slowly. It didn't gain power very well.

The man next to her shifted gears quickly to compensate for the energy needed. He didn't look at them or say anything. His task kept him busy. The features of his face and the way he manipulated his eyebrows made driving the truck appear difficult. Suddenly, a powerful and fearful emotion entered Lucy's mind. At first she thought it might be Sebastian and she worried for him, but upon closer inspection, she realized that it was Robert she was feeling. He was strong, but very afraid. Lucy could see what he was planning to do and she became fearful as well. His plan was dangerous.

"Go faster," she immediately demanded of the driver. He

glanced down to defy her, but quickly judged her face and without words, obeyed.

The semi sped down the road faster than it had ever gone before and just as they passed a road sign telling oncoming traffic of the gas station ahead, Lucy watched a large explosion fill the rearview mirror. The rumble rocked the truck and the heat from the flames raced after them. Sebastian watched in disbelief and then hung his head in remorse.

"He was a good man." He frowned and turned away from the window.

Lucy had not been accustomed to death, but now it seemed to be a regular occurrence in her life and something that she would have to get used to. She couldn't feel Robert anymore. He was gone, but something had replaced him in her mind. It was anger and determination. Lucy could almost taste the blood in her mouth. She then felt the need for revenge and instantly decided that Eliza had survived the blast. Something else was hidden in the vampire's mind along with the desire to kill. She was wounded badly. It would slow her down, but nothing except death would be able to stop her.

"Eliza is still alive, but wounded badly. Cecily too," Lucy mumbled to whoever was listening.

"I figured. We have a head start though. To heal, they will need to feed and we are in the middle of nowhere. They will have to hunt before they can chase us again, but Eliza won't just settle for anyone." His changed voice revealed a state of concern.

Lucy watched his eyes shift back and forth for a moment before she placed a hand on his thigh. His reflexes caught her hand at the slightest touch. His speed was incredible and nearly caused Lucy to jump out of her skin.

"What are you thinking?" she was finally able to ask as his arm went limp again.

"Eliza will hunt for someone who smells like you. She is vain and cruel. She will want to rip part of your life away if she can."

"Tryp and Rae?"

"They're safe. She won't backtrack, but we're coming up on the city I took you to when we confronted Lucian at the blood bank. When you ran away, did anyone talk to you or touch you? The smallest contact will leave a scent that she can pick up."

"I spoke with a man for a few minutes and he gave me money for the bus. Is he in danger?" Lucy's heart was racing.

"Possibly."

The man from her past had been so kind and understanding and she had condemned him to be slaughtered. "We have to warn him."

"I agree. We have a few hours. Eliza won't be able to use extra energy for travel. She won't risk it." Sebastian seemed so sure of his words.

"How do you know her so well?" Lucy couldn't help it. The question just popped out and she felt the need to cover her mouth. The look on Sebastian's face made her wish that she had stopped the words before they left or that she could take them back.

"I've known Eliza for a long time. She knows me as well as I know her." He didn't go into any further detail and Lucy didn't press the issue. He had given her more questions rather than answers, but the new curiosities could wait.

Lucy watched the world outside pass her window. The rain slowed to a drizzle after a while and finally city lights peaked over the horizon. They were returning to the place that she had escaped from.

As they entered the first brightly-lit road, Lucy felt her pupils shrink into near nonexistence. She blinked roughly at the pain it caused. Her eyes had become more sensitive to light and it started as a tickling pain that began in the center of each eye. Immediately, the strong street lights gave her a headache above each of her eyebrows. The pain wasn't excruciating, but it did bother her.

She watched the cars drive by and the people shake off their umbrellas as they uncovered their heads. It had rained there as well, but it had not been as heavy. At the next light, something caught her eye. It was a large building guarded by a gate that was twice as tall as she was. The large sign next to it read "College of Technological Sciences," which triggered a hidden memory. Lucy immediately grabbed the driver's shoulder and demanded that he pull over. The driver was shocked, as was Sebastian, but he did as she requested. The large truck stalled at the curb and the man inside allowed them to exit before he forced the vehicle to roar back to life.

"I hope there was a good reason for that, because we no

longer have a ride." Sebastian was angry, but Lucy knew that she had a great reason for abandoning the truck.

"The man that Eliza is after, he's a teacher," she smiled and gestured at the sign.

"Lucy, he could be an elementary school teacher for all we know."

"No. It was the way he said that he had to teach a class. I'm sure he's a college professor of some kind. Can we break in?"

At first, she thought that he might say no since he probably should have, but something in the logic must have made sense, or he had just begun to trust her. A grin stretched across his face and with a chuckle, he took her hand and led her around the corner. After glancing around for prying eyes, Sebastian gave her a boost to the top of the fence. Again his strength was impressive, and Lucy was over the fence in one swift move. She pushed past the trees and bushes before plunging out into a soft, grassy area. There was a small path nearby that was lit beautifully with hanging lamps. Many flowers and benches adorned the sides of the path. She could see a gazebo in the distance and a pond with a gorgeous fountain in the center. Caught in amazement over the beauty of the campus, Lucy had nearly forgotten about Sebastian.

She turned back toward the fence just in time to see the shadow of a figure drop down from a low tree limb. He took a moment to drink in the well-decorated ground before pulling her along behind him to the main building. They didn't walk on the main path in fear of being spotted, so instead the tree shadows became their cover. Sebastian crept up on the entrance as if he was stalking an enemy.

When they came to the foot of the staircase, Lucy allowed him to aromalize the area before they emerged from the shadows. Confident that no one was near, Sebastian strolled up the stairs and removed a couple of items from his pocket. Lucy watched him pick the lock. She had never seen it done so easily before.

"These old buildings have old locks. I grew up picking these. They are much easier than modern day doors." Sebastian seemed amused by his skills in breaking and entering. Together they entered the building and shut the door behind them. He even relocked it for good measure.

The halls were decorated with old pictures of former students and awards given for excellence by the state. Glass cases lined the intersecting hallway. They were filled from wall to wall with trophies and other awards that couldn't be attached to walls. As Lucy looked over the decorations, one plaque caught her eye. It had four rows of six pictures. Most of the people all seemed too old to be going to school. The beautifully carved piece caught her attention and she began to read the names below the pictures. After wondering about the importance of the people on this wall, Lucy noticed a title to the group hidden in shadow at the top. Upon closer inspection, she realized that this piece wasn't of former students. It held the names and photos of the school's current staff.

With a smirk, Lucy searched the pictures for anyone familiar, stopping on a twin of the man she had met on the street. He was even dressed the same. His feathered hair had been combed for the picture, but his bowtie and suspenders gave him away quickly. The brilliant blue eyes from before stared back at her from the other side of the glass, making him seem more real. The plaque below his picture was buffed to a shine and read 'Dr. John Smits: Department of Physics.' Finally this stranger had a name.

Lucy knew that she should alert Sebastian to her find, but for an unknown reason, she couldn't stop looking at the picture. In it he seemed happy and sad at the same time. His eyes were empty of emotion and still said so much. He was young and still older than her. John's attire added to the mystery. Suspenders and bowties were clothing of someone who had lived their life in a bygone period when those items were popular. The man staring back at her was intriguing. She found him to be odd, but there was a trace of loneliness in him too. Lucy was so engrossed in the photo that she hadn't noticed Sebastian at her side. Out of the corner of her eye she watched him judge the same picture.

"Is that him? John Smits?" His scrutinizing tone sent chills over her skin and Lucy was left with only enough free will to nod in response to his question.

"Let's find his room," Sebastian's suggestion rang through the empty hallway and before Lucy could dispute his proposal, he was too far away to hear her.

The corridors were long and wide with several doors on both sides. Lucy tried her best to see what was inside each room, but in order to keep up with Sebastian she had to sprint by and was unable to accurately judge the equipment within. He was in a hurry for an unknown reason and his willingness to find more information on Lucy's oddly dressed acquaintance filled her with confusion and anxiety.

After running the length of the hallway, Sebastian finally stopped at the last door and cupped his hands to look inside. Lucy watched him search the inside from afar. She couldn't believe how nervousness had impaired her. It was like she was unable to will her legs to go any farther. Lucy found herself swimming in a sea of doubts that quickly consumed her. As she drowned in her own thoughts, there was a split second of paralyzing fear. Her mind returned to all of the things she had forgotten about. She hoped that Avalanche hadn't been discovered by the vampires. She thought on the loss of Kieron and her grandmother's death. Lucy remembered her father's face and Lucian's demise. Even the scene of Viola's death struck her with nausea.

Just as she felt the gurgling that preceded vomit, Lucy saw Sebastian's head turn. She looked up to meet his gaze and found herself swimming in his blue eyes rather than drowning in her guilt and self-pity. The power of his stare seemed to give her the strength to overcome paralysis. She quickly returned to his side and gazed through the window. It was a large classroom shaped like an amphitheater with a desk and long blackboard at the front. There were several models hanging from the ceiling and a case of many odd-looking teaching materials at the far end of the room.

As she took in the clever, yet fun atmosphere of the room, the door clicked open and creaked out slowly as if the hinges were off kilter. Sebastian had been working like a mad man to unlock the door with the tools that he had used earlier.

She caught the swinging door before it passed her and allowed him to enter first. The knot in her stomach seemed to pull tighter as Lucy walked past the threshold and closed the door behind her. Sebastian glanced back when he heard the locking mechanism click. It echoed through the empty hall and Lucy almost thought that she could feel the vibrations as they hit her. The classroom was eerily quiet and with every step, Lucy could hear the floor creak. It was impossible to be completely silent in this room. She didn't know how old the room really was, but it appeared ancient compared with the rest of the building.

Sebastian didn't seem as distracted by the age of the room. He had already gone to the front and was attempting to break into the desk. Lucy approached cautiously while watching him become increasingly agitated by the fortitude of the simple piece of furniture. Finally, Sebastian abandoned the tools that had given him so much success in the past for a more reliable power. Lucy saw the muscles tense up in both of his arms as he wrapped his fingers around the handle and pulled. It only took a single tug for the lock to break free and the drawer to spring open.

Lucy was quickly at his side. The drawer held many books and documents, but nothing of great importance. Though she saw nothing of interest, Sebastian began going through the stacks of papers and after a while finally rested on a small post card. He didn't say anything at first, but simply read it over and over again.

"Why this?" Lucy finally found herself asking after waiting patiently for an explanation.

"We have his address." Sebastian grinned and handed her the card before standing and shutting the drawer.

"You are so clever." Lucy grinned after examining the paper and placing it on the desk. A smile flashed across his face before Sebastian headed to the door.

A small shock of frustration filtered down Lucy's body. She could feel it pass as if it were water falling over her skin. "Where are you going?"

"To his house; will you join me?" His cunning grin protruded through the dim light in the room. Sebastian held his hand out to her in hope, though he was sure that she wouldn't stay. Lucy stared at his open hand for a couple of seconds before pursing her lips with a sigh. Finally a grin broke the seriousness in her expression and she walked forward to take his hand.

As soon as they touched, a loud bang came from the windows in the back of the room. At a glance, they saw the shadow of a person jump out of view. Lucy didn't need to feel emotion to know what Sebastian was feeling or who had been watching them. Suddenly, the sound of breaking glass echoed from inside the building.

"They're inside. Come on." Sebastian groaned and pulled Lucy behind him out into the hallway. They scooted along the edge of the hall, trying to make as little noise as possible. Sebastian led her past door after door. She couldn't breathe and was unable to hear him breathing either. In the intensity of the moment, Lucy began to tremble. Her hands shook in Sebastian's steady grip and he looked back to reassure her, but his kind expression soon became fearful. Lucy watched his pupils dilate before he tilted his head slightly to pick up any noise. Sebastian cleared his throat and hesitantly placed an ear on the wall. Lucy watched impatiently as he listened. Seconds later he glanced back at her and pushed her shoulders hard enough to make room between them as a fist punched through the wall where Lucy had been standing. Dust and rubble spurted into the air before the fist vanished through the wall and Sebastian took Lucy's arm.

He pulled her to her feet and together they ran to the front door. It was still locked, but he made quick work of the door and the two of them left the school. Lucy remained on Sebastian's heels as they used the nearest tree to escape over the wall. She watched him climb the trunk like a squirrel and then jump to the top of the wall before sliding over to the other side. She shook her head in awe at the nimble skills he displayed before climbing the same tree the old-fashioned way and leaping to the top of the wall. Finally, she slid to the ground near him and they started to sprint down the sidewalk.

Rain had begun to trickle down from the sea of heavy clouds above. It was a light and refreshing shower, but to Lucy it was also annoyingly in the way. The drops stabbed her face sharply as Sebastian pulled her into a running speed that was faster than she had ever gone before. They crossed entire blocks in a blur, which made her wonder how he knew where they were or, more importantly, where they were going.

The way he drug her through the streets made it impossible for Lucy to see his face or judge the subject of his thoughts. She was certain of his determination, but there could've been fear or anger hidden under it.

It seemed like they ran for miles before shops and restaurants became apartments and homes. Finally, he slowed to a stop and let her rest briefly. Lucy felt as if she would collapse on the sidewalk. Not long after stopping she saw something out of the corner of her eye.

179

Eliza had paused at the corner of their street, followed closely by Cecily. The street light above them was the only direct light on that end of the boulevard. The bright glow of Main Street didn't shed much light on the side streets. Eliza's ruby hair was blazing under the lamps as if her head was on fire. It blew wildly in the wind while she took a long pause to assess the space around her. Almost immediately, she picked up on their location and began strolling down the alley, like a cat would hunt a trapped mouse. Cecily set a pace several feet behind her, trying her best to block the exit.

Sebastian, however, had no intention of running. He turned and snarled wildly as wolfish features became apparent in his face and claws extended out of his fingers. The tips of his ears tightened into points and his pupils dilated to the extent that the gorgeous blue color Lucy had come to love was nearly covered.

The two vampires changed as well. Their green eyes had been replaced by black pools of nothing and their sharp fangs had become apparent. Shimmering marks on their skin also began to shine under the dim light. Lucy didn't know what the marks meant, but she only remembered seeing them a few times.

Eliza sniffed the air gleefully and enjoyed the scents within. She glared at her prey. Her gaze fixated on Lucy, but was interrupted by Sebastian as he stepped into her view with a growl.

"Don't even try it," he warned with another snarl as he took a step forward.

"Try what exactly?"

"Attacking us; it would be a mistake," Sebastian responded to Eliza's nearly silent question. The vampire bit her bottom lip and thought on his answer. Lucy could feel the excitement and anticipation radiate from Eliza's position. Her emotions were spilling out into the air and Lucy was nearly drowning in them. In the midst of her thoughts, Lucy failed to notice that Sebastian and Eliza were already exchanging strikes. The vampire's clawed hands slashed through the air with such velocity that Lucy could hear the whirl of the wind as they cut.

Sebastian didn't seem to worry over her attacks and he quickly maneuvered around them with the dexterity of a snake. She swiped at his head and he ducked under her arm. The fluidity of the moves reminded Lucy of a martial arts movie. It was incredible that they could both dish out and avoid assaults with speed of such magnitude.

Suddenly, Cecily was at her side and Lucy could barely move fast enough to get out of the way of her fist. She could feel the slight breeze that came off of the near strike and tried her best to avoid wincing. The vampire tried several other attacks, all of which Lucy was able to avoid by only inches. She found herself ducking and side-stepping clawed hands and high kicks with speed that had previously been unobtainable. All appeared to be going well until she saw Eliza out of the corner of her eye. Sebastian was lying on the ground behind her, rolling in pain. The agonizing look on his face made her sick to her stomach. Cecily grabbed her arm furiously and pushed it into her back, twisting hard and trying to break it. The vampires had won and any resistance was over.

Eliza returned to them in the blink of an eye. She took a handful of Lucy's hair and pulled her head to the side so that she had control of her every flinch. Eliza bent over towards her as if she wanted to whisper in her ear. The vampire's misting breaths coated her neck in an uncomfortable wetness that felt as if there was water pooling on her skin. Eliza's closeness flooded Lucy's senses with the smell of peppers and a subtle hint of mint. A lump grew in the back of her throat as she realized her fate, but before the two vampires could act on it, Eliza's arms went limp and fell to her sides. Lucy didn't know why, but the expression on Cecily's face told her enough. Eliza soon fell to the ground and began convulsing, which was when Lucy finally noticed the man standing behind them. She didn't recognize him, but after studying his clothes, she decided it must have been John Smits, even though she couldn't see his face in the dark.

Cecily's rage grew and her cheeks turned red. The angry vampire leaped over her fallen sister, and dove at his neck with her fangs bared. Before she made contact, however, John managed to push up on her chin with one hand and then pushed her head to the side. The entire motion effectively closed her mouth before she could bite and also left her neck vulnerable. As Lucy watched him, she was left with the assumption that John was going to sink his teeth into her, but instead he glanced up momentarily before sticking the vampire with a syringe. In a few seconds, Cecily's pupils dilated and she sank to the ground.

Before Lucy could say anything, Sebastian had returned

to her side and was checking her over for injuries. The inspection quickly became annoying and Lucy stepped away from him, while simultaneously thanking the stranger.

"No problem. I'm John. Why don't we go inside?" He was quick to leave the defeated on the sidewalk and lead the way into the house behind a tall hedge and fence. The fight had taken place less than a yard from his front porch.

Smits led them into a study after locking the front door. It was a dark room lined with bookcases and several large chairs. The casually dressed man invited them to sit and then left to fetch a few glasses of water. He wasn't gone for more than a couple of minutes, but it was enough time for Lucy to take in what she had seen.

The room they were in was cluttered and messy, but it was filled with books, loose papers, and gadgets. John wasn't neat, but somehow Lucy could see past his oddness. She was happy to be in the presence of someone normal for a change. It was the first time she had made a point of ignoring Sebastian. He was uncomfortably jealous of John already and they had just met. His anger perforated the comforting aura of the house. Lucy glanced over to him. Sebastian's stare was focused on the doorway where John soon reappeared with three glasses of water.

"So who were your friends? They didn't seem too friendly," he casually struck up a conversation while making a place to sit among his stacks of books. Lucy watched Sebastian closely to see if he planned to answer. She hoped that he would, but instead his eyes met hers in a glare. There was something wrong, but Lucy just couldn't put her finger on it.

"What was in the syringe?" Lucy had forgotten what his question was. She was only trying to think through what had happened outside.

"Enough tranquilizer to kill a horse. Vampires tend to burn right through it, though," he said softly before clearing his throat and taking a drink.

"How did you get that?" Lucy asked, but John was quick to shake his head.

"You never mind how I got it," he smirked.

The reality of who she thought he was had been shattered. John knew about vampires and how to fight them, which also meant that he had encountered them before.

"How long have you known about vampires?" Lucy asked timidly as she approached him. John seemed confused by the question, but answered anyway.

"I've known since they came after me a few years ago. They called me a 'Zephyr' and tried to infect me. What they didn't know is that I'm a third generation wolf and can't be changed anyway." John took another drink. He didn't seem to be hiding anything like Lucy was used to people doing. Honesty was a breath of fresh air.

"You don't usually see vampires hunting in pairs since they either travel solo or in covens. Those two seemed to be hunting you for a specific reason, but no worries. They'll be out for a good half hour." He grinned and shook both of their hands.

"So how old are you then?" She finally asked after a few breathless moments.

"I am twenty-six," John answered quickly as if he was anticipating the question.

"No, really."

"Twenty-six; honest."

"Then how are you so accomplished?" Out of the corner of her eye, Lucy saw Sebastian perk up slightly. Apparently this was the answer he had been waiting for.

"I have done nothing but college since I was fifteen. I have an amazing memory and a lot of confidence."

"Oh, he's modest," Sebastian groaned.

"Why do you age?" Lucy finally asked as she compared the life of John to Sebastian's.

"What do you mean?"

"Sebastian ages slowly. Don't all of you?" Lucy could feel her face growing warm in embarrassment. John was even more confused now. She judged his expression one more time before turning to Sebastian for an explanation, which he was happy to give. He took her hand and cleared his throat before revealing more need-to-know information that had previously been withheld.

"Lucy, some third-generation wolves don't inherit traits that others do. The abilities are selective when the gene pool is thinned. His senses are strong and he could probably best me in a fight, but he will age and die just like a human."

"Why don't you rub it in," John scoffed at the way Sebastian spoke of him. It was clear that he wasn't entirely happy with the fact that he would die sooner than his species was meant to.

"I'm sorry, but she still doesn't know these things."

"Why not tell her everything then. Secrets only drive people apart."

"She isn't one of us and therefore she doesn't need to know." Sebastian didn't try to stop the truth and finally it was out. Lucy knew the answer to why he was censoring everything. They were divided by many things, but now the force behind him holding back was in the open.

"Why not change her then?"

"My family seems to think that introducing our venom into her body could have deadly consequences. I may not like it, but I would rather have her safe and alive than take the chance." Sebastian's transformation had begun in his anger, but he stopped it and scooted to the back of the chair to relax.

"That is rather odd since the only thing that could cause a shift to go awry is the bite of a vampire." John was skeptical for a minute until Lucy leaned forward and exposed the bite scar on her shoulder. He studied it for a moment before leaping out of his chair and running to the door. She didn't expect him to panic, but apparently Sebastian did. He sprang from his chair and darted out of the room. Lucy followed and rounded the corner just in time to watch John attempt to open the locked door before Sebastian jerked him away from it. Instead of fighting, Sebastian simply pushed him back into the room and grabbed his ear with one hand while holding his arm with the other.

Lucy closed the study door behind them and examined the situation cautiously. The men struggled for a couple of minutes before angry whispers were exchanged and Sebastian released his hold. The men returned to their seats in silence, leaving Lucy to wonder what was going on and why.

Panic ensued when John realized what had made the scar on her neck. Perhaps he put two and two together and thought that she was somehow a vampire. Maybe he feared that Sebastian was fighting for the wrong cause. Whatever it was, Lucy could see the fear in his eyes, but she felt nothing. His emotions were heavily guarded.

His pupils were constricted, and she could see his hands shaking from adrenaline. However, there wasn't even the slightest emotion of alarm coming from his direction. He was blank.

The Zephyr Gene

Chapter Eleven

Lucy watched John nervously. She wanted to know what he was thinking so that she could proceed with the proper intentions. Would he harm her to get out of this situation? As she watched him, his bottom lip began to quiver. There was a question on his mind, but he didn't know how to ask it. Lucy had been frequently blessed with that problem too. John's eyes eventually returned to their typical state and his shaking hands became still. His breathing slowed to normal until he was able to talk again. "Why is she still human?"

"We aren't entirely sure, but her father may have passed on an ability to resist venom." Sebastian's eyes had begun to shift. He was obviously uncomfortable with discussing her father. Or maybe it was the fear of the truth behind what her father represented.

"That's impossible!"

"We thought the same, but here she stands." Sebastian's nostrils flared as he spoke.

"Those bloodsuckers must be on your heels. You realize what she could become?" He exclaimed as he sat forward in his chair

"Of course and we've been through it once already. My brother, Kieron, believed that she was able to burn out the venom using the strength in her own body."

"Impressive. Have you given thought to joining a pack, Lucy?" The question bounced around through Lucy's mind. It was a powerful set of words that set a solid knot in her stomach.

"I want nothing else, but Kieron warned me that I could die if bitten by a wolf. A single body can't contain venom from both species."

"That is a pity, but you are on our side then?"

"Yes."

"Your father?"

"A vampire."

"Mother?"

"Human or maybe zephyr."

"Fascinating." His eyebrows crossed in doubt.

"I know." Lucy had come to terms with the impossibility of her existence.

"You're lucky then."

"Being hunted isn't exactly a luxury," Lucy said with a smile. The beats of her heart suddenly sped up. She couldn't believe it. She had begun to flirt with this stranger and right in front of Sebastian. He didn't seem to notice and she was thankful for that.

"I see. I would be happy to join you; extra protection and all that." He seemed to have made up his mind, but Lucy was quick to deny him.

"You're human. You could die."

"I'm very fast and I'm not exactly safe here."

"As much as I would like to believe that you could hold your own against a vampire, I would worry too much." The more Lucy told him that he couldn't join them the more he was determined to go.

"Then you will just have to trust that I will be fine because I'm going whether you agree to it or not."

"I suppose it will have to be all right, if we really can't stop you," she said with a smile.

"You could try," he growled and pushed her into a chair before leaping into a back flip. The center of the room was briefly a war zone. If either Lucy or Sebastian had stood up to stop him they would've been hit by a foot or flailing arm. Before he returned to the floor, John launched a straddle in midair before landing a solid punch into the hardwood floor. It was an amazing feat that splintered the wood, leaving a dent the size of his fist. Lucy saw Sebastian roll his eyes.

"Okay, I guess that is proof enough. I suppose it wouldn't hurt to have you along, especially since Eliza would be after you anyway," Lucy decided and heard Sebastian grumble. She knew he was mad, but she wasn't about to leave John as vulnerable as he was.

"And we can take my car then," John offered as he stood and took the glasses of water from the room. Lucy watched him leave before turning to Sebastian. His emotions were hidden, but she was sure of what they were. Though he was both angry and jealous, Lucy knew that she had made the right decision. John's red Nissan would serve as great transportation and would give them a great head start to wherever they were going.

Before long, John returned with a worried smile. He leaned casually against the door frame and cleared his throat. "We have less than five minutes before the tranquilizer wears off." As he finished his sentence, Lucy didn't have much time to think. Sebastian was quick to grab her hand and follow John out into the hallway. They went upstairs and into the first room. It was a large bedroom with a wardrobe, dresser, and bed. The color scheme consisted of reds and blacks that left the room in a gloomy state.

John didn't waste any time and immediately threw open the wardrobe and removed two large satchels. He tossed them on the bed and began throwing clothes inside. Lucy watched him closely as he tossed in men's clothing, but also feminine clothes as well. Lucy wanted to ask why he had them, but before she could he glanced back. "Behind the vase picture is a safe. The combination is 8141989. Get the money out and toss it in this bag," he growled and hastily threw her a smaller satchel.

Lucy looked down at the bag in her arms and pushed past the hesitation that hit her like a brick wall. She wriggled out of Sebastian's grip and approached the picture to her right. The lovely vase held small purple flowers highlighted by a black background. Behind the frame sat a safe that had been set into the wall far enough that it would be undetectable. Using a small keypad, she typed in the number sequence that he had mentioned and the door popped open. After a quick glimpse of the goings on behind her back, Lucy opened the door and peered into the darkness.

All of a sudden, she realized what was inside and a gasp left her lips. There were stacks of money; easily a couple hundred thousand was in the vault. She didn't know what to say, but did as he had asked and threw all of it into the bag. When the safe was empty of all currency, Lucy returned to Sebastian and waited for John to finish packing.

After another minute, he had finished and didn't even bother to zip the bags before he rushed past them and back down the stairs. Lucy could barely keep up. Sebastian pulled her behind him as they went through the side door of the garage. Inside sat John's red Nissan. The car seemed relatively new and was polished to shine.

John wasted no time. He threw the bags into the trunk and slammed it shut before heading to the driver side and taking out the keys. Before he could slip inside, Sebastian snatched the keys out of his hand and said, "I'm driving."

Lucy could see the surprise in John's face, but he didn't confront Sebastian like she assumed he would. The defeated wolf cowered under his superior and slid into the back seat. Lucy took the passenger's seat and Sebastian revved the engine before he pressed a button that pulled the garage door into the ceiling.

The world outside was darker than ever, but it didn't appear to be dangerous. As the car jerked onto the street, Lucy anxiously looked for any sign of movement. Thankfully there wasn't anything that caught her eye, but upon closer inspection she realized that Eliza and Cecily were not where they had been left. A shiver went over her entire body as she realized what that meant. Suddenly, Sebastian realized the same thing and John started to yell at him to go. In a panic, he slammed on the gas and the car sprang to life, but it was too little too late. A thud echoed down from the roof and a knife penetrated through it just above Lucy's head.

The blade was quickly retracted as Lucy sank into her seat to avoid any other attacks. They gained speed quickly, but it wasn't enough to throw off the attacker. The sound of shoes skidding across the roof reverberated through the car and made Lucy grind her teeth. Knowing that there was someone close by who planned to end her life became a sickening worry.

Sebastian drove like someone out of an action movie. The ways he was able to manipulate the direction of the car threw John around on his seat and had Lucy's knuckles turning white as she squeezed the door handle. Finally, as they sped around a corner, another thud came from the top of the car. This time the person who had attacked them fell off and onto the street. Lucy watched Cecily roll across the asphalt and into one of the street lamps. Seconds later Eliza was at her side. She didn't have to say much for her sister to spring to her feet.

Together they raced after the car as Sebastian pounded on the accelerator, trying to gain as much speed as possible. As their speed increased, Lucy became more confident, watching Eliza tend to her sister and seeing the distance between them increase.

The vampires' speed was formidable, but Lucy found their attempts worthless. She found herself scoffing at them as they pushed each other to run even faster. Later she would look back and know better.

Both vampires slowly leaned into their strides as far as they could without falling over or losing balance. Eventually their bodies were nearly horizontal, like a cartoon character would run to gain a significant amount of speed. As she reviewed the impossible scenario in her head, Lucy became dumbfounded when Eliza and Cecily began to gain speed and eventually started to edge closer to the car. The feat was incredible in a frightening way. Lucy couldn't wrap her head around the facts before her eyes. In awe she glanced over Sebastian's tense arm, at the speedometer. It read more than seventy miles per hour—another fact that was as confusing as it was absurd.

The car rounded yet another corner and its tires squealed painfully with effort. Hope that they would get away became a thing of the past as Eliza ran ahead of her sister and sprinted to the side of John's door. He quickly cowered to the other side of the seat and threw his hands in front of his eyes, preparing for the worst. Though she could've attacked the car, Eliza seemed to be content with just running after it.

Lucy watched her face with interest. There was something obvious in her expression, but Lucy couldn't name it. Something was wrong. Lucy saw her try to shake it off and continue on with the attack, but as soon as she tried to reach for the car, a pained look crossed her face.

Almost immediately she fell to the ground and held her head as she writhed in pain. Sebastian had seen this, but he only watched it in his mirror. Although Lucy assumed that he knew she wanted him to stop, the instinct to protect and escape was driven by the circumstances.

With another screech, their car sped around the last corner and exited the city. At the speed they were going, the lights behind them grew dim quickly until they were just a haze on the horizon. The road ahead was nothing but highway as far as the eye could see. It was absent of cars and was lit by only a few lights high overhead.

"So who are those two exactly?" John finally broke the silence with a sigh as he resituated himself in the backseat.

"Cecily and Eliza are assassins owned by Eodin. He has become one of Ella's counselors and has been tasked with bringing Lucy to the Forsaken," Sebastian explained with a grim look on his face.

"What! When did that happen?" The fact that important information was being kept from her had Lucy enraged. It was one thing to hold back on information about wolves, but there was an issue when life-threatening facts were being withheld.

"The day after Lucian's death. We thought it best not to tell you." Sebastian frowned.

"That was your mistake." She couldn't believe his arrogance. "When will you stop hiding things from me?"

"We really are doing it for you benefit. As much as you might want to know what is going on, once the truth is out, I cannot take it back. It is a dangerous concept that I don't want on your shoulders." Sebastian didn't look away from the road while he spoke. He couldn't look her in the eye.

"It is already on my shoulders and not telling me everything is more dangerous than you realize. If you want me safe, then the first step is sharing. I want to know what is going on. Did you know they had my father captive?" The silence in that car was thick and sickening to witness. Lucy watched his face anxiously. It was almost blank. Finally he nodded his head yes.

"I wouldn't have gone in the first place if you had told me where he was and why I should not try to save him." Lucy was lying to herself. After most of her life without a father, having one so close was too hard to resist, but convincing Sebastian otherwise couldn't hurt. Unfortunately, he wasn't buying her lies. He became agitated all of a sudden. His fingernails even lengthened into short claws.

"You still would've gone. You may be part vampire, but the human in your mind gives you impractical solutions."

"That isn't fair." She couldn't believe what he was saying.

"It doesn't have to be fair if it's the truth." Sebastian's words cut into her like shards of glass. Silence crept into the car and crushed them gently. The weight of his words stopped Lucy from talking. She held everything in tightly, trying her best not to cry.

They rode along in silence for a while before John broke it. Lucy had almost forgotten he was there, but was relieved when he interjected.

"You two argue a lot, but she is right. Sebastian, not explaining circumstances is worse than harm through naivety. "

"No one brought you into the conversation," Sebastian growled and gripped the wheel hard enough to leave indents.

"Well someone needed to stop you. If you care about Lucy at all, stop blaming her for mistakes that are directly your fault." John immediately cowered under his words as he sat back in his seat and stared blankly out the window. The dreadful silence crept in again and stayed even longer this time.

Lucy watched Sebastian struggle with his guilt. The last few days had created a type of self-loathing in him. It was difficult for her to watch this consume him. She didn't even have an idea of how to help.

"All right, Smits, you've made your point." Sebastian finally sighed and glanced back at John in the rearview mirror. Lucy could suddenly feel John relax. Until now she hadn't felt anything come from him. It was a short relief, but he quickly built the walls back up and Lucy was left feeling nothing from him as before.

"Where are we going?" John grinned as he scooted forward in his seat and rested both elbows on theirs.

"I haven't really thought about it," Sebastian revealed and was quickly interrupted.

"A good plan would be heading to Kansas."

"Do you think Piatt would be able to help us?"

"I think he would like to meet Lucy," John said with a wink that sent shivers over her body. Lucy didn't know why, but she was often mesmerized by him. He was attractive, clever, and very good at making peace. "Under his protection, Eliza wouldn't dare try anything."

"That's a great idea. Where can we find him?" Lucy was more

than happy to be in a place where she didn't have to worry about being attacked or kidnapped.

"Piatt is the alpha," Sebastian uttered as he quickly passed the car in front of him, causing the Nissan to jerk around.

"Of which pack?" Lucy began. Sebastian was obviously amused by her question, but after his smirk faded, he answered as seriously as he could.

"No, he is the alpha, the pure bred leader of every wolf in the country."

"Good plan," Lucy agreed when she finally realized their angle.

"I agree," Sebastian nodded. "The den is hidden beneath Mount Sunflower in Kansas."

"Mount Sunflower is a ridiculous name," John spouted.

"We didn't name it. The mountain is about ten miles from Weskan." Sebastian was trying his best to remember the facts buried in his mind. He couldn't seem to remember exactly where the city was.

"There is a map under your seat, Lucy. Find that city and plot a course," John said. Instead of asking questions, Lucy did as she was told and removed the map from under her seat. It was rather old and ripped in some parts, but still readable. As she struggled to find the needle-sized city, the men continued with conversation and she tried her best to eavesdrop.

"What pack are you of, Sebastian?" John began before he slid back into his seat.

"Alpha Joudin Kamerk."

"You are the vampire restriction pack of the East?"

"As some call it," Sebastian grinned and looked back at him through the rearview mirror.

"You must deal with vampires daily." John seemed impressed by the life he assumed Sebastian had. Lucy waited for the answer. She was anxious to know as much about him as possible.

"Not as often as you'd think. Their species is quite illusive."

"I'd imagine so," John sighed. The hum of the engine was all that filled their silence. It was a comforting rumble that nearly put Lucy to sleep. She finally found the point on the map that was called Weskan. It seemed like a continent away, but it was the destination of choice. Lucy pretended to be engrossed in her navigational duties, but kept both ears open to their conversation. She drank in every word.

"And what about you? Where is your pack?" Sebastian's question was simple, but appeared to give John something to think about.

"Don't have one; never did. I was born in Scotland. My parents abandoned me at a home for children when I was three. I escaped that wretched place at five and was on my own. I traveled, and learned whatever I could from anyone who would teach me. I spent a lot of time on trains and ships as cheap labor." John seemed to be holding back. He was clearly ashamed of his upbringing.

"Skills like yours take a lifetime and a good teacher," Sebastian confronted him with a statement that he couldn't avoid.

"At nine I was taken in by a nice Chinese man who let me stay in his attic while I taught him proper English. By thirteen he had taught me more than I could've ever taught him. For four years I studied tae kwon do under his guidance. He died a year after I started college." John didn't seem to be bothered by this part of his past. He quietly stated the facts and judged Sebastian's reactions through the help of the mirror.

"You've been on the move for so long," Lucy finally chimed in. She could barely contain herself.

"I've been running."

"From what?"

"Life," he sighed. "I always thought if I could stay ahead of whatever was coming to me that I could find a way around it, but bad things are inevitable. I'm living proof of what the world does to a child that is left alone."

"You seem as normal as any doctor I've met." She smiled and turned in her seat so that they were face to face.

"That is the biggest charade of them all."

"But, you really are a doctor though, right?" Now Lucy had begun to doubt him. She hoped against all else that he wouldn't be another liar.

"Sure, but if I wasn't would it matter?"

"I don't know. It would mean that I couldn't trust you to be honest."

"You can trust me; all right?" He was kind, but trust was a hard thing to just give someone. To Lucy, it was a gift to have someone's trust.

"It doesn't work like that," she denied his honesty. For some reason Sebastian didn't trust him and that was all Lucy needed to convince her.

"Give it time," John reassured her.

"What would time help?"

"I don't have any more answers for you." His voice had become harsher and Lucy flinched when she saw Sebastian tense up out of the corner of her eye. "Just do this for me as a favor; a favor for a complete stranger."

"Fine, but know that Sebastian will rip you apart if anything bad happens to me." Lucy spoke quietly and still Sebastian nodded in agreement.

"Is that how you usually start friendships? With threats? Not good," he said through his charm with a half-hearted smile.

"Shut up," Lucy ordered as she turned back around and crossed her arms.

"And rudeness too? Shame," John finished and received a humored glance from Sebastian. Lucy tried her best to retain the anger that stemmed from his sarcasm. It was difficult and she even crossed her arms to sustain the effect, but eventually they had all forgotten about witty banter and returned to the silence that had become very common in the car.

Lucy was left to the sting of her own thoughts once again. She was free to roam through the questions and memories that had happened all too fast. The visual of Sebastian murdering his own brother came to mind and she quickly pushed it away. Lucy tried to bring anything to the surface to replace that memory. She thought of her grandmother's body at the morgue and how sick she felt when Syrina used venom to disintegrate it. This recollection was even worse than the one before.

As she lost faith in trying to remember something pleasant, Lucy attempted one last thing. Regretfully, she thought back to the memories before Sebastian appeared. Though it seemed impossible, Lucy dug back to before the faceless people and even before high school ended. The simpler days flashed before of her eyes. They were like dreams. So many impossible things had happened since then and to her, the normal days of her past were nothing more than wasted time. Now there wasn't anything that could bring her back to those days. They were gone. The life that she used to enjoy had been replaced by one that she had learned to fear.

She glanced at Sebastian. He drove mindlessly to a destination that was inconceivable, to a mountain that she had never heard of in a state that she hadn't ever been in. Lucy watched cities pass as the turnpike turned into bridges that passed over other roads. She thought about the vampires that were no doubt following them. They were fast, but on foot it seemed impossible for them to keep up. At that moment she felt safe and that was one feeling that she had learned to savor.

As the long black roads slipped beneath the car, Lucy found herself becoming more and more exhausted. Thoughts that had been keeping her company became blurs against a blackness that was growing in strength. She couldn't remember the last time that she had slept, and at the moment, sleep sounded particularly appealing. It was like returning to the past and the pleasures that she had given up since meeting Sebastian. Although the passenger's side of John's car wasn't the same as a comfy bed, Lucy found herself drifting into unconsciousness. It was pleasant and safe and good.

Chapter Twelve

A sudden quake forced Lucy out of her comfortable, dreamless sleep. It took only seconds for her to return to reality, but as it sunk in, she was confused. The scenery had changed drastically compared to what she had fallen asleep to. Ahead of them wispy brown grass covered a plateau as far as the eye could see. The only greenery visible was behind an electric fence meant to keep cattle in. The fields to the right were bright, green, and healthy. It was a drastic difference when compared to the direction that they were heading.

Sebastian struggled with the wheel like he was playing a video game rather than controlling John's car. He allowed the backend to fishtail in the dirt while sporting the most devilish grin. Lucy instantly became worried for their safety and his sanity. She turned in her chair to inspect the backseat. John was sitting on the floor behind her seat with his feet stretched across to the other side. He had his arms over his head, cradling it like he was expecting a bomb. Inspecting the situation further, she noticed that there were several holes in the back window. Someone had been shooting at them and there was dried blood on John's shoulder. It was a dark brown color that had stained his white shirt. Lucy could see both the entrance and exit wounds, which made her feel a little bit better. He was wounded, but the bullet wasn't still in his body. The blood seemed to have stopped and these few realizations left her satisfied enough to turn around and inspect the environment beyond the car.

Green grass became a bright feature on either side of the road, which had now become a defined space with boundaries of dirt mounds on either side. The Nissan's tires sprayed a cloud of dust behind the car so thick that Lucy couldn't see what was following them. However, she didn't need to see. She knew what was following them. Lucy could feel John's fear and pain. Eliza had been the one who shot him through the window. Lucy could almost hear his thoughts. These feelings were new. His panic had painted a picture of what had happened.

They were in Kansas now. Sebastian had stopped for gas when they arrived in Weskan and that was where the vampires caught up to them. Eliza stole a handgun out of a police car and fired it as they drove away. She saw John's memories as if they were her own. When the officer confronted Eliza, she snapped his neck like a twig before running after the car. Lucy growled under her breath. She felt sick to her stomach and crumbled under the anguish for the death of a hero who had fallen under the hands of her enemy.

The quiver that raced over her body had caught Sebastian's attention. He continued on the road, but looked over her carefully and cleared his throat in a rough fashion to gain her attention.

"I'm fine," Lucy shot him a convincing grin and straightened herself in her seat.

"Liar," he groaned under his breath and took hold of her hand as the car fishtailed around a bend in the road.

"So much has happened. I can't believe I didn't wake up."

"Not much can wake a wolf once we've begun to sleep. Unsure if that happens to vampires, though," he chuckled.

"Good to know. I'll have to watch out for that." Lucy took it very seriously. She might not have been a wolf, but there were too many similarities between vampires and wolves to ignore any advice. They were both human hybrids and that was good enough for her.

"We are nearly there," Sebastian sighed with worry. "They won't give us much time to escape once we arrive. The den entrance isn't exactly car accessible."

"How far is it exactly?" Lucy asked after looking around once more to see if she could see their destination.

"A couple hundred feet, I guess," was his answer.

"What do you mean you guess?" John's interest perked up

then.

"I've never actually been there. It is more of an instinct, really." Sebastian shrugged off his doubt.

"Well that's good news," John grumbled loudly from behind Lucy's seat as she watched cautiously out her window.

The desert-like world passed by quickly. It was nothing more than flat and lifeless. Up ahead was a small mailbox that, strangely enough, didn't have a house to go with it. The single monument of loneliness burrowed its way deep into Lucy's thoughts. It was a sight she would never forget and always over-think. As the car sped past, she noticed a man-made sunflower on the other side. It was larger than a normal sunflower and grew sideways across a sign that read "Mt. Sunflower" in large copper-colored letters. Lucy was no longer confused by the mailbox's presence. They had finally arrived at Mount Sunflower without a welcoming face or mountain in sight. This flat and desolate terrain was the summit of a mountain? The den was either impossibly hidden or nonexistent, but Lucy was certain that there was nothing here.

Suddenly the road ended. It simply roped in a circle around the landmark and then went out the way that they had come in. Immediately, Sebastian slammed on the brake and John's car spun wildly off the road and into a grass-patched area next to a small shelter. As the vehicle slowed, Lucy heard John's moaning from the backseat. Either the damage to his shoulder was paining him or the handling of his car had made him queasy. Lucy believed he worried over his poor car and Sebastian's driving. She giggled softly when he emerged with a sour look on his face.

She couldn't help but find his reaction funny and turned her head with a smirk, only to have it ripped from her face. Out of the dust, two figures appeared and as it settled, the light lit their faces. Cecily's copper-colored hair blew effortlessly in the breeze as did Eliza's fiery locks. They didn't proceed, but waited patiently for their prey to emerge. It was over and they were willing to be patient. Sebastian exited the car and moved to stand in front of it. Lucy shook in anticipation. After all of their running, they were trapped and there was nowhere else to run.

Sebastian exposed his sharp teeth in a growl as his other side came to the surface. Hair covered his arms and claws grew from his fingers while his ears slipped into points. The vampire versions of Eliza and Cecily that Lucy had come to fear were revealed also. Their pale skin was made brighter by the black bottomlessness of their eyes. Each vampire had flesh-tearing claws and fangs that were barely visible from under their lips. These features took Lucy back to her first fear. The terror associated with the faceless people returned swiftly, and she wondered why these feelings still plagued her.

"Can't we get a break?" John groaned to himself as he joined Sebastian at the front of the car to defend whatever they had left. Lucy dug deep for her bravery this time and slowly left the safety of the car to join them.

"Do you have a plan?" she asked, as she took a defensive position between the men.

"Yes," Sebastian answered almost instantly, but something in his voice made her doubtful.

"Are you lying?" Lucy's question caused him to stiffen.

"Yes," his simple and defeated-sounding answer hovered on the wind. He didn't like admitting to a lie, especially when it was to himself.

"Oh," Lucy's faith was shattered. Hopes of escaping drifted even farther away.

"I figured that I would just wing it." The truth was out. He never seemed to have a solid plan.

"I would expect nothing less." Lucy couldn't help but be amused at his honesty.

"Flirting? Really?" John interrupted them loudly and nudged Sebastian in hopes of pulling him back to the pending fight. Eliza was eerily patient and waiting for the men to focus. She seemed prepared to linger as long as she needed to in order to best them in a fair fight.

"Are you ready to go then, mutt?" She crouched like she was prepared to tear him apart as soon as he moved. "You might as well put that away." To make the situation even more insulting, she implied that John was of no real threat. The vampires grinned at one another as John's face turned red and hateful.

"You aren't even a mutt. What's lower than a mutt, sister?" Eliza taunted him.

"He is a flea; less than a mutt and just above the dirt. He is a flea." Cecily flipped the copper hair out of her eyes and both women laughed hysterically.

The wolves stood firmly in Lucy's protection while their enemies had their fun.

After Eliza had caught her breath she took a step forward as another quiet giggle escaped. "Let's get this over with." Cecily soon joined her and both began strolling toward their cornered prey, closing the gap quickly.

"Don't you take another step!" A voice boomed from their left. The vampire women nearly fell to the ground under the power of the words. Lucy shuttered at the sight before her.

From all around came a hoard of wolves. All were larger than the wolves Lucy was used to. They were fearsome and beautiful. Their ears were flat against their necks and their teeth were bared in defense.

Sebastian returned to his normal human appearance and John's eyes searched the group in fear. The voice had come from a man amongst the dogs. He had long brown hair that was tied in braids, with red feathers and beads that made a clatter in the wind. He was a tall, bearded man who appeared to be rugged, like he had been wronged by the world. His bright blue eyes shone like gems in the sunlight, while his rippling muscles gleamed in the shadow of the mass that was his hair. Lucy had never seen a man with so much hair. It was so thick that dreadlocks looked as if they were seconds from forming.

"Your filth will not be tolerated here! Leave!" He roared at them in the calmest way possible, which gave Lucy goosebumps. Without another word, Eliza and Cecily retreated. Lucy watched Sebastian's stiffness leave as the death threat established by Eliza's presence faded. He was no longer tense or worried.

The leader of the pack moved towards them as majestically as a lion. His followers remained at their posts. No one moved to greet them or arrest them. It was strange to Lucy.

"Is everyone in one piece?" The leader's rough voice growled through his words. This man must have been Piatt. He spoke and acted like an alpha.

"For the most part," Sebastian explained as he motioned toward the bullet wound in John's shoulder.

The leader glanced at it and then nodded, "We will have that taken care of."

Under Piatt's guidance they wandered out into the desert-like plain, leaving the car and sunflower monument behind. Lucy didn't know where their destination was, nor could she see it, and for some reason that worried her. They hiked for a mile before Piatt stopped. They had gotten out of sight of the car and there was nothing ahead. It was an empty horizon.

Piatt seemed confident in his choice of direction and the wolves followed him without question. They traveled for a little while longer before a trio of boulders came into view. They formed a small triangle on the ground and seemed to be the only rocks around. Lucy focused on them as she hiked along with the group and came to notice that Piatt was heading toward them.

When they arrived, the leader dismissed his followers with a wave of his hand and the wolves dispersed in all directions. Lucy didn't realize the impact of an alpha until now. Cyrus hadn't really used his status to order his family around. He became a father figure whereas Piatt was an undisputed boss.

The four of them approached the rocks and Piatt leaped up to the top of the smallest one. With one final glance, he jumped into the center of the three boulders and disappeared into the ground. Lucy was taken back by the feat of magic, but was quickly relieved to find a hidden cavity below the surface. Piatt stood under the hole with a grin. He had landed in the belly of an underground cave system.

Almost instantly there was a group of four people around him. They aromalized his scent quickly and then backed away with a respectful bow. Lucy traded glances with Sebastian and John before she approached the hole and jumped in. Piatt stabilized her landing before moving aside to allow the men access. Sebastian and John followed her example and the three of them were immediately scented by the entrance guards.

Each of the four guards took a whiff of both John and Sebastian. Then they moved to Lucy. She watched them nervously. Personal boundaries were clearly avoided. Two of the male guards were satisfied with their inspection and then the female guards began. They were much more intrusive. Lucy was made to lift her arms and turn in a circle. From that experience Lucy took away two things: the wolves here were not very trusting, and they had an amazing sense of smell.

"She smells of bloodsucker," one of the woman decided as they both jerked away from Lucy with a growl. The male guards were then on alert as well. They surrounded Piatt instantly and snarled in defensive anger.

"Why do they not attack?" the same woman stated in shock as Lucy and the men only stood there terrified by what they were seeing. It took this question to enrage Piatt. He broke away from his guards in a rage and simply stared at them. Gradually, all four of the wolves backed into the wall with their heads low as they tried not to make eye contact while still watching their leader.

"Do not throw about insults at our guests, Adelaide. I have a nose and it works properly, thank you," he shouted at them as the accuser sank to the ground. "Had you gone further in your inspection, you would've noticed that she smells of human as well; a live human." Each of the male guards took one of Adelaide's arms and pulled her to her feet. They waited for the alpha's instructions.

"Clearly, you must be trained further, but for this insult I leave punishment up to your superior." He frowned as he passed them and entered a long tunnel. Lucy was speechless and wouldn't have been able to move if Sebastian hadn't grabbed her hand.

Without running, they caught up with Piatt as quickly as possible. He had taken a few seconds to calm down before speaking again. "I apologize for that. She is new to this post, but now maybe you can tell me why you smell so odd?" Lucy heard his question and tried to think of an answer, but was constantly distracted by John's limping and the sound of his pain.

"My father was a vampire when he met my mother."

"You are Cyrus's niece. I had a feeling that I would be seeing you soon," Piatt admitted happily as he took her arm and slowed his own pace.

"How did you know that?"

"Vampires across the country have become more active. The coven members from several cities in Kansas have begun to travel east. I feared they were looking for you. Once Ella found out she wouldn't have kept it a secret."

The difference between Piatt and Sebastian was amazing. The

alpha was more than comfortable telling the whole truth. He wasn't concerned about protecting her mind from their world. He understood the need she had to know what Sebastian felt didn't concern her. Being brought up as human, Piatt expected nothing less.

"That was what I feared," Sebastian unintentionally interrupted. Piatt was displeased with the interruption, but understood the concern in his voice.

"There is no point in fearing that over which you have no control. We must adapt rather than hide. It is our way. It is the only way." Piatt's voice vibrated in his throat as he tried to hide whatever emotions flared up.

"We can't stay here," John decided as he grabbed Lucy's hand and pulled her to his side.

Piatt was obviously aggravated by this, but he calmly turned and cleared his throat. "And why is that?"

"You say that vampire activity is increasing, and they have moved east to where Lucy was raised."

"I did," he nodded and waited impatiently for the point of all of this.

"You might find a trend developing. I guarantee they will return and those that live around this summit will begin to migrate inward. This den won't hold against an attack of that magnitude," John revealed his thoughts without fear.

Piatt listened to every word even though it was clear on his face that what a non-pack member said was irrelevant.

"This place was meant to withstand such an attack." The alpha's opinion was established and the conversation was over as far as he was concerned. Piatt turned away from the pending confrontation and began to advance down the passage.

Lucy pulled her wrist out of John's grip and followed Piatt into the darkness. Left without a choice, both of the men followed closely. Piatt's last sentence kept repeating in Lucy's mind as he led them. She could see the light on the walls drift farther behind them until it had nearly disappeared completely. The group walked in silence as if the recent darkness had stripped their voices from them. Lucy listened to Piatt's footsteps. His feet were firmly placed and didn't shuffle the dirt around like the steps of the men behind her. Everything about him was strong and powerful, even if he didn't mean it to be.

A few minutes of blackness passed before a bend in the passageway appeared and light filtered around the corner. Anticipation was almost overwhelming, but soon an opening came into view. The bright light beyond the hole soon faded and a breath-taking scene replaced it.

Beneath the surface of Mount Sunflower stood an entire civilization whose home had been carved into the rock around them. Human and wolf alike roamed along the spiral-like path that leveled out in certain places, where tunnels connected and drilled outward into the Earth. There were so many people inside that Lucy instantly felt crowded. Piatt stepped out into the passing traffic and trudged up the incline of the spiral. To avoid being left behind, Lucy found herself nearly attached to him as they climbed and the crowd split to allow them access. No one made eye contact with their leader. He wasn't visually assertive, but the human-looking pack members who passed them kept their heads low. The four-legged followers appeared to watch Lucy with disgusted looks, if that was possible. Many of them forced their ears flat against their heads and watched her hesitantly. She could feel Sebastian's breath on the back of her neck and smell his pungent fragrance that she had learned to love. As he grabbed her hand and leaped to her side, Lucy saw him growl at the wolves they passed and they quickly turned away.

"Don't pay them any attention. Humans and vampires are not permitted inside this place."

"Are they all wolves?"

"Yes; there are first and second generations mostly, but some young third generations still live with their parents. They don't usually stay around very long. Wolves that cannot convert tend to live among humans."

"Convert?"

"Transform so that the likeness of the wolf is displayed. First generations can become the four-legged beasts that you see and second generations usually remain human-like unless in battle. This makes them easy to distinguish from each other. Robert lived here for a time, but found the human life more appealing." Sebastian grinned as he led her along and they followed Piatt up the incline.

"What about you? What are you?" she asked as they pressed

on. Sebastian thought on it briefly and then cleared his throat.

"I was a zephyr first. I have no knowledge of the ancestry of my parents, but the fact that I become a monster probably makes me a second generation. Any wolf will tell you that it is a flimsy system. The rules don't always work the way you think they're going to," he explained to the best of his ability and oddly Lucy was satisfied with his answer.

After passing several of the platforms, the Alpha slowed down and waited for everyone to catch up. John soon joined them and together they entered another tunnel. It was lined with lit lanterns and flat rocks had been formed together to create a path. Piatt continued on and led them into a large chamber that was decorated in shining metals and colors of deep greens and reds. The breathtaking room left Lucy speechless. It reminded her of the main chamber in the coven. Werewolves and vampires decorated similarly and they both integrated spiral devices in their homes. Lucy laughed to herself at the humor of how they were alike.

"Make yourselves at home," Piatt said and offered the bow of a gracious host before he retired into his chambers, a room directly to the left, and slammed the door behind him.

Lucy should've been offended by his rudeness, but instead she decided that it would involve wasted energy. With a sigh, she joined John and reclined on one of the many sofas in the room. Together they watched as Sebastian paced in front of them. He was uneasy, but Lucy didn't know why. After a few more passes, she cleared her throat loudly and he shot her a glance. Sebastian paused briefly and then joined them on the large piece of furniture. Lucy squeezed his hand gently and placed her head on his shoulder. He was tense.

John appeared completely at ease as he hummed a melodic tune and tapped his thigh with his fingers. This quickly got on Sebastian's nerves, but he didn't say anything. They waited and took time to relax. Lucy watched the only clock in the room tick away minutes, which grew into hours. Oddly, she was perfectly content to sit there with the men and wait for whatever would come next.

As time crept into what must've been dusk, a loud bang came from behind the couch and then the door that Piatt had disappeared behind reopened. The wolf leader stormed out and stopped where they were sitting.

"Is everything all right?" Lucy asked as she studied his behavior.

"Yes, just wonderful, but I have some things I must attend to." His demeanor changed in that instance. He was relaxed and anxious at the same time. He contradicted himself.

"Can we help?"

"You are welcome to join me." Those few words barely had time to leave Piatt's mouth before Lucy was at his side. With no apparent surprise, Piatt nodded and walked on. He led the way out into the dimming light with Lucy at his heels.

There were hardly any people out now, but those they did pass offered him the proper respect. Children stared in awe, but weren't acknowledged. Piatt was the definition of what Lucy thought an alpha would be. He exuded strength and power over his people like a king would have. His outer shell hid well whatever was brewing on the inside, and for unknown reasons, Lucy was determined to know more.

"How long have you been this way?" She could almost see the hairs on Piatt's neck stand up in response to this question. He became tense and yet continued walking. Judging by these actions, Lucy was certain that he would not answer, but then he spoke.

"I was born here," he grinned back at her and reached out for her arm. Lucy gave it to him hesitantly and walked at his side, hoping that he would say more. A few minutes passed before he spoke again. They had arrived at another level and he stopped at the entrance.

"My family lines can be traced back to the first wolves, back to Ireland."

"Ireland?"

"Didn't Sebastian tell you his heritage?"

"No. Well, not much of it," she admitted as he released her arm.

"The first wolves came from Ireland and from there we have spread throughout the world just as humans have."

"How old are you?" A grin found its way across Piatt's face now and he chuckled briefly before concocting an answer.

"I am nearly three hundred forty-eight years old," he forced through soft laughter. Lucy joined in his amusement at the large number. To her it was still impossible for someone to be that age, and "still young."

Before she could ask another question, Piatt took her arm

again and led her into a tunnel. They began to pass many doors that were built into the stone. The passage was lit with lamps rather than torches like she had seen earlier. The change in lighting didn't make a lot of sense, but Lucy didn't ask. They wandered down the corridor until it ended with a door.

"What's in there?" she asked cautiously as he moved to open the door.

"Let's find out," Piatt commented before pushing away the door and inviting Lucy inside.

The bright room hurt her eyes at first, but once they adjusted, she could see that they were in some form of hospital. It was unbelievably clean for being underground and was also staffed with nurses and doctors who were busily checking on patient after patient.

"The last thing you expected?" Piatt wondered as he closed the door.

"Yes," was all that Lucy could get out. Without words, she followed Piatt to the very back of the hospital, where he paused at a curtain and then slipped beyond it. Lucy followed and was instantly exposed to a small, improvised room. An elderly man lay in the bed at the far side of the area. His face was aged with hundreds of years of living and his bright blue eyes were filled with wisdom beyond anyone's understanding.

"Lucy, I would like you to meet my father," Piatt nodded and allowed her access to the room. Lucy approached the man's bed slowly and studied him. Oddly, his eyes never left the ceiling.

"Father, this is Lucy. She is a hybrid," Piatt explained to no avail. The man didn't even look at her.

"It was worth a try. I figured that he might respond if I brought you," Piatt sounded defeated for the first time. Lucy was instantly sad for him, but she didn't say a word. Piatt waited a few more moments and then passed back through the curtain. Lucy followed him and was speechless when she noticed how upset he was. She didn't ask why, but didn't need to. Piatt straightened himself and led her out of the hospital wing of the den. As soon as they were out of earshot, Piatt began to explain.

"My older brother was the alpha. He inherited the position from my father by winning a battle against him and was a great ruler for a long while, but we had a small war with the vampires and he was killed. I took his command without following the proper protocol. We won, but I was forced by law to challenge the last leader for command. My father was quite old by this time and he suffered several blows that destroyed most of his memory. He hasn't spoken since the fight and frequently refuses eye contact," Piatt explained and was clearly troubled by the facts. Lucy had never been forced to harm someone she loved and hoped that she would never have to. There wasn't any possible way for her to understand what he was feeling and she wasn't going to try.

Without a word, she took his hand and led him back down the corridor to where it emptied out into the spiral walkway.

"It isn't your fault," Lucy comforted him with what might have been a lie. She didn't know what their laws were, but after knowing Piatt for this short time, she was sure that he would never do the harm that he had explained on purpose.

"I would like to believe that, but I know what harm I've caused and that cannot be forgiven."

"Are you a good leader?"

"I believe I am," he sighed and began to walk further up the path.

"Then you don't have to be guilty," she smiled and offered him a hug without even thinking about it. After a few moments, she was about to remove herself from the increasingly awkward gesture, when Piatt surprised her by taking the hug. The embrace was just long enough to make Lucy uncomfortable, but finally Piatt released her and they moved on. Confused, Lucy followed him and tried her best not to say anything.

Any thoughts of inappropriate gestures were forgotten as Lucy took in the sights while they walked to another unknown destination. She hadn't questioned his decisions yet and couldn't see doing so in the near future. His trust had yet to be earned, but Piatt had the qualities of a leader and intoxicating confidence. That was something that Lucy couldn't explain, not even to herself. His decisions were unquestionable and Lucy felt strength in his leadership. He didn't have to prove anything to her or gain her trust.

"You said that wolves came from Ireland," Lucy reiterated as she caught up with him. She couldn't look directly into his eyes for some reason. It was almost as if she didn't want to offend him.

Instead, Lucy took in their surroundings again, but this time she really looked.

The gorgeous architecture of the carved stone against reflected lantern light shone through the caves and cast an unnatural glow about the system. It was like staring into the night sky rather than gazing over a man-made, underground city. Lucy heard Piatt speak, but she was so distracted by the magnificent sight that she missed his words. Regretfully, Lucy asked him what they were.

"Are you okay? That wasn't what I said, but are you?"

"I'm fine."

"All right then. Yes I said that wolves come from Ireland," Piatt answered the question that seemed so far in the past. For a second, she had forgotten why she had asked him anything. Going back for a moment, Lucy finally recalled the looming curiosity.

"I wondered where vampires came from, since that is part of me."

"That's right. I had forgotten your parentage. Vampires come from Romania and the areas around it," Piatt stated with a worried grin before he cleared his throat and stopped at the side of the road where it bent to follow the natural curvature of the land.

Lucy feared for his safety and wondered if he was aware of his precarious position. The alpha of Mount Sunflower was one slip from tumbling down the side of a sheer cliff. It would be a short fall to a road that sat just below, but it would've been painful also.

"Lucy..."

As he spoke her name, she forced herself to look away from his feet and into his eyes. They were sparkling under the same light that splashed against the rocks. Piatt took a step away from the edge, but it was a step towards her. Lucy involuntarily moved back from the advancement, but he didn't seem to notice. He took another step and caused the same reaction. The last stride forced Lucy back once again and this time she was left against the rock wall. There was nowhere left to turn when Piatt's intense stare came to be only inches from her face. Lucy could feel herself tremble uncontrollably under the power of his presence. Piatt took in her scent and she was forced to take in his. It was indescribable, but she knew that she could never forget it. Every wonderful thing that she had ever smelled was instantly put to shame.

Lucy avoided looking into his eyes. Instead she focused on her own chest as it moved in and out. She tried to control her breathing. Lucy had never before felt so vulnerable. Then he spoke her name again, but quieter this time. He grabbed her wrist and moved it into her view. She noted the night and day difference between their skin colors. Compared to Piatt, Lucy seemed like she hadn't seen sunlight in years.

Finally, she built up enough courage to look him in the eye. Lucy wasn't able to breathe for a moment. She stared carefully into the depth behind his pupils. They stood close enough to one another that her reflection was clearly mirrored within the blackness. Soon her body decided that it needed oxygen and Lucy quickly resumed her breathing. A grin made its way across the alpha's face and he released Lucy's wrist.

"You confuse me, Lucy Gaskin," he finally said softly without moving an inch. She couldn't think of an answer to give him, but he wasn't expecting one. Piatt continued with his thoughts and didn't leave Lucy the time to ask questions.

"You are different; a hybrid raised as a human. Your instincts are lacking and you are falling in love with your natural enemy." He grinned and stepped away from her. Lucy was stunned by his honesty and was immediately denying the accusations.

"Not you!" was all that she could say. Lucy was adamant that their brief encounter hadn't meant anything, but Piatt chuckled loudly at her words.

"Not me indeed, darling," he said, laughing at the idea. "I admit that I enjoy closeness when it comes to personal space, but that was merely to judge what kind of animal you are." Lucy didn't have to respond to him. The look on her face was enough to further his explanation.

"Judging vampires and werewolves is usually an easy task because there are certain behaviors you can expect, but you're a mix of vampire and human. There isn't an easy way to determine how you will react to things. I wanted to see what you would do if I tempted you," Piatt explained his actions well as they continued up the path. Lucy tried her best not to blush or feel embarrassed for accepting him so easily, but she decided that it might have been a good thing that she was a lover and not a fighter.

"You sort of scared me," Lucy admitted as she joined him and watched the expression on his face change.

"I'm sorry. That wasn't my intent. Let's go this way," he ordered and pointed to the left side of a narrow fork in the road. The right side circled back up to where they had come from. It led back to where she had left Sebastian and John, which was where she actually wanted to go. Lucy almost defied his decision, but he didn't give her the chance. The alpha sped ahead into a darker area and Lucy reluctantly followed him. Shadows covered Piatt in spurts of time and nearly caused him to disappear at one point, but Lucy followed where he should have been and they came out on the other side of the darkened road together.

There was a glow without a source that filled the place. Lucy stood firmly on a ground of solid rock that was lit with the glow and appeared to be sparkling. It was a shine that came from inside the rock. She hadn't noticed, but Piatt was watching her, and as they finally made eye contact, a small grin appeared on his lips.

"It's silver. The farther down you go, the more you'll find. Come on." He smiled and offered her his hand, which she took. It was almost as if Piatt knew that she would follow him. Lucy came to the realization that he didn't even have to ask her anymore. She would follow wherever he went.

The direction that they were headed in seemed very deserted. In previous places there had always been another person or something that occupied enough space to take away the awkwardness. Piatt didn't appear nervous in any way and for some reason that didn't make her feel any better. The lamps on this path hadn't been lit and it was relatively dark. Lucy watched where his steps were and tried her best to step in the same places so as to avoid any slips. More than anything, she didn't want to fall. That wouldn't have been a good thing.

As they shuffled down the path, Lucy was finally able to see the end. It was a door with a small window on either side. There was a warm light coming from inside that was oddly soft and relaxing. It was a sign of safety, and although she didn't know what was inside, Lucy couldn't wait to enter.

Piatt was quick to grab the door knob and push his way past the threshold. Golden light rushed past him and into Lucy's face. It was warm and satisfying. Together they walked up a small stairway and into the foyer of a house that had been built into the rock. Wooden beams appeared to hold up the heavy stones above, which made Lucy uneasy. Her worry must've been evident on her face because Piatt took a moment to reassure her of the safety before he went further into the structure.

"It looks unsteady, but it was built by many fine craftsmen. It is safe," he said before shifting his weight to look down a few of the halls behind him. He seemed calm, but suddenly Lucy knew what he was looking for.

A young boy leaped down from a small perch above them and landed on Piatt's shoulders. He wrapped his arms around Piatt's neck and held on for dear life as Piatt tried to shake him off in a playful way. After a few moments, the boy let go and fell to the floor with a thud. He took hold of Piatt's leg and hugged it as they both growled in laughter. The boy looked to be about seven years old, had shaggy black hair, and was deeply tanned.

As she studied them, Lucy realized that they looked a lot alike.

"I want you to meet my youngest son, Roken," Piatt said as he smiled and ran his fingers through his son's hair. "Roken, this is Lucy. She is a hybrid, and a good friend of mine."

"You smell funny," the boy remarked with a strange look on his face as they shook hands.

"Now, that's not very nice. She is part vampire. That's why she has an odd scent, but she is a good person," Piatt explained to the boy before letting him speak again.

"I'm sorry." His sincerity caused an involuntary sigh to come from Lucy's mouth.

"Where's Mom?" Piatt asked him and allowed the boy to fetch his mother while they waited. In a few minutes a woman entered the room, followed by the boy. She immediately walked over to Piatt and threw her arms around his neck. They kissed passionately until it almost became uncomfortable for Lucy.

When they finally parted, the woman turned to Lucy and offered her a handshake. "Hello Lucy, I am Maria. It is good to meet you."

"Likewise," Lucy smiled back with a nod.

"I do wish I could stay and get to know you, but it is somebody's bedtime." She grinned and gave Piatt another quick kiss before she began a game of chase with Roken. Lucy laughed as they ran around and then sprinted out of the room with speed that seemed unnatural.

Piatt waited a few moments before offering Lucy a drink, which she refused. The sheer beauty of his home was all that she could focus on at the time.

"You said Roken was your youngest?"

"No, we have five children. He is our youngest boy. Kievre is our oldest daughter at fifty-three and Palkiana is our youngest child. She is seven years. I have two more boys. Twalan is forty-two and Hallion is twenty-three," he spoke the facts, but Lucy was thrown off by the strange ages.

"How old is Roken?"

"He just turned fifteen," Piatt revealed nonchalantly as he poured a drink for himself that both looked and smelled like bourbon.

"Sebastian told me that werewolves age slowly, but he said that the ratio was more like one year of appearance for every ten years lived. Roken looked like he was seven years old, so shouldn't he really be seventy?"

Piatt didn't laugh at the question, though she could tell that he wanted to. The amusement in his eyes was immediately buried and he cleared his throat before taking a drink. Lucy almost laughed at the face he made when the bourbon coated his tongue, but instead she made it clear that she was impatiently waiting for his answer.

"Wolves age closer to humans until puberty. At that point the aging process begins to slow down and it usually gets to the point you mentioned by age twenty-five to age thirty," he said with a smile before downing the rest of his drink. A soured pucker distorted his face before he swallowed and shook off any effect that the drink had had. "You seem quite obsessed with age. We really don't focus on that aspect of our lives because everyone is different. Most wolves don't even know their true age. It will be different every time you ask."

He looked around awkwardly, trying to think of another subject. Finally it hit him. "I suppose it is about time to get you back to the guys. I'm sure they're wondering where we've gone." With a quick glance at the glass in his hand, Piatt shelved the bottle of bourbon before stashing his glass in the sink. "Let's go."

Together they retreated out of the door and back up the dark path that was lit with silver rivers. Lucy didn't feel as afraid of the road as she had been before. Somehow, the weaknesses that plagued humans were slowly being stripped from her mind. Lucy was fearful of many things that she hadn't been before. She fondly remembered her fear of the faceless people and how that had transformed into a fear of vampires. Lucy recalled her fear of death and how that had now become fear of becoming a monster. Death would've been a sweet reprieve from the expectations and dangers that this life imposed.

The hike back up the spiral walkway was tiring, but it didn't seem to bother Piatt. Lucy did her best to appear normal even though it felt as if her lungs were being pushed into her throat. Apparently humanness still had an unwanted hold on her. It was frustrating being a hybrid and only being able to have parts of what the others had. Finally, the passageway to the alpha's quarters came into view.

"Why does your family live down there while you are up here?" Lucy hadn't planned on asking that question, but it had been burning her mind since they left.

"I live with them. My ruling post is up here, my charts and my books. My pack comes here to speak with me. Most are not permitted to enter or don't even know about the silver caverns unless invited. It is a law that the alphas before me cherished. It keeps my family safe as well," he explained as they entered the torch-lit tunnel. It was a comfort to know that Piatt wasn't trying to hide anything from her. Lucy knew that she could ask him a question and get the whole truth as an answer.

The doorway led back into the familiar hall. It was oddly quiet and Lucy's heart sank into her stomach before she saw a reclined blonde head on the arm of the couch. John was nowhere to be found, but Sebastian had fallen asleep. Lucy attempted to wake him, but as she shook his shoulder and he didn't stir, she was reminded that unless pain is involved it is nearly impossible to wake a sleeping werewolf. Lucy was about to stop her tries until she saw Piatt out of the corner of her eye. He was moving slowly toward the closed curtain that hid the study. It was almost as if he was stalking something. Lucy tried aromalizing, but nothing abnormal was in the air. Piatt moved the curtain aside slowly and stepped up into the large room. Nothing was out of place, but she now saw that John was standing at a table to their left, looking at various maps and graphs. He studied them closely.

"What do you think you're doing?" Piatt growled as John stepped away from the table and shuttered at the sound of his voice.

The alpha in Piatt had risen to the surface and Lucy was suddenly afraid. His demeanor had changed and every cell of anger within him was focused on John. With a low growl Piatt yanked the maps from view and threw them to the floor behind him.

John cowered slightly, but then Lucy noticed something change in him. His posture straightened and he made eye contact. Piatt seemed taken aback, but he wasn't able to confront John before he explained himself.

"Where are the rest of your guards?" John asked.

Lucy thought it was an easily answered question, but Piatt was immediately silenced. His eyebrows crossed as he thought of an answer and he stared at the ground as if John had the upper hand. "They aren't here," he finally grumbled a quiet answer to the small audience.

"Why aren't they here?" John took advantage of the upper hand he had over the alpha. He clearly knew something that he wasn't sharing.

"You already know the answer, so why don't you shed light on it instead of embarrassing yourself?" Piatt growled and regained his posture. He stood strong and stared deeply into John's eyes until he finally looked away.

"There are no guards to watch over this den. They've all gone!" John announced as he threw his hand wildly in anger. "We are all vulnerable here and you act confident when the truth is vampires could be within the city now and no one would know!"

Lucy could feel a lump form in the back of her throat as the men argued. She watched as the expression on Piatt's face became more wolf-like and he stood tall to tower over the inferior subject. She could see the dominance in his face and knew that a fight would likely break out soon. The tension between the wolves filled the room with pressure that Lucy could feel weighing her down.

In this short amount of time, Sebastian had awakened and was slowly moving in between Lucy and the arguing wolves.

"Stop it," Lucy ordered them. She had finally had enough.

"This is ridiculous!" As she spoke, the men instantly put away their attitudes and shied away from one another. Shocked as she was, Lucy took the opportunity to continue scolding them. "If what John says is true then why are you fighting over it when we can be looking at why the guards are gone?"

Piatt nodded casually and picked up the maps that he had thrown, then placed them back on the table.

"Normally there are around a hundred guards posted around the perimeter at any time of day. At the moment there are five still here. A month ago, my summer guards were supposed to be here to replace the spring guards. We have one group per season that are permitted to return home after their duties have been served." Piatt immediately appeared disturbed by his words and struggled for a moment to carry on. "I ordered the spring guards to wait, but after two weeks they became restless and I allowed those who wanted to leave to do so. Only five remained."

Everything became silent for a few moments and they all took this time to look at one another before Piatt stirred. He stretched the maps out and pointed to where the den was shown on it. Then he addressed a pencil-thin line around the area while he explained that it was an incredibly small perimeter.

"That was when I saw them last. I haven't heard word from the summer guards. I fear they were attacked." He sighed and rolled the map before returning it to the proper place.

"We need to leave," Sebastian told the group. "It was kind of you to take us in, but we must go as soon as possible."

"I've told you before that you are more than safe within these walls," Piatt assured him.

"Wake up! You are about to be attacked by a horde of vampires and there aren't any guards. We are leaving," Sebastian growled and took hold of Lucy's arm as he pulled her along behind him.

John didn't say any more. He followed them into the large living area and nearly ran into the couch on his way into the tunnel. They followed it out to the spiral road with Piatt following close behind, scolding them for placing Lucy in harm's way.

His eyes shone with anger as he stepped into their path and ordered them to stop, but Piatt never got the chance to say anything after that. The bustling streets were empty and silent. It was strange and eerie at the same time.

"Where is everyone?" Lucy asked what everyone else was thinking, but no one could answer her. Dissatisfied by their reluctance to speak, Lucy nudged Sebastian in the ribs and he grabbed her hand.

"I can smell them," she revealed and he nodded almost immediately.

"Me too," his answer sent a shiver down her limbs, which left goosebumps in its wake. Lucy knew why the den had become so quiet. It had been vacated. There were vampires near and the wolves had retreated.

The silence was almost overwhelming and the sudden absence of life reassured Lucy that they were definitely not alone. The peppery flower scent was thick in the air. Eliza and Cecily were near, but they had others with them now.

"Follow me," Piatt's whispered request echoed off of the rocks. Though she was certain he wouldn't lead them into danger, Lucy was hesitant to follow until Sebastian went with him. John didn't say a word, but she could see that he was just as aggravated with this as he had been with the lack of guards. He brought up the rear as they began their decent into the dark and quiet city.

The winding road seemed never-ending as Piatt led them down toward his home at the bottom of the cavern. They descended into the sparkling silver-lined tunnels, and soon the path narrowed between two large rocks. Piatt entered the space, but stopped almost immediately. He cocked his head and listened to something in what Lucy heard as silence. After a few seconds, he straightened to walk on when someone fell past the rock and into his arms.

Though he was slightly startled, Piatt cradled the person as he sank to the ground and began to groan.

Lucy was quick to join him on the ground. John and Sebastian hovered behind her as Piatt brushed the curly brown hair out of the fallen person's face. It was the young guard from earlier that day.

Adelaide stared into her leader's eyes and she smiled as she gently touched his face. It was obvious that she had been badly wounded. Her face was blood-spattered and pale while her eyes seemed sunken in and her dry lips trembled in pain. Tears began to drip out of the corners of her eyes and she tried to clear her throat before she whispered Piatt's name.

"Your family is safe. We got everyone out. Amos and James were killed at the south entrance." Adelaide's bottom lip quivered as her raspy voice revealed what had happened. "We evacuated the pack and then three of us made a stand at the north entrance."

Lucy winced at her every word. They were fluid-filled, and weak. "Cordelia and Marcus?"

"Wounded, but alive," she answered her leader when he asked about the remaining guards. The young wolf tried to appear amused, but her pain was too overwhelming. All that she seemed to muster was a wince.

"Can you walk?" Piatt's voice cracked in sadness as he tried to hold back emotion.

"Oh no, I will just stay here," Adelaide said as she smirked and grabbed his hand. She was defeated. "You need to go," she continued as she groaned and squeezed Piatt's hand. As she spoke, blood filled her mouth and sputtered in bubbles of dark red.

"Addie, where are you wounded? I won't leave you here." Piatt's emotions were filtering out to Lucy and nearly drowning her in sadness. He was overcome with mind-numbing grief. He knew Adelaide's chances were slim.

"I will stay, sir. You need to keep the hybrid safe. That fire-haired vampire is searching the catacombs for her," the young guard revealed as blood sprayed again.

"Any suggested routes, ma'am?" Piatt grinned as an expression of satisfaction came from the fallen soldier. She was clearly pleased with the respect he had given her.

"I would use the silver caverns," she whispered to avoid spitting blood on her leader's face. "The blueprint in their possession won't include those caves."

"Very good. Be brave now," Piatt mumbled into her ear. He bent forward and kissed her forehead as she exhaled her last breath. The light that was left in her eyes faded as her pupils dilated and her skin lost all of its color.

Though death now happened around her a lot, Lucy still hadn't grown used to it. After a minute or so, Piatt forced the guard's eyes shut and shifted her body into his arms. With a sigh, he lifted her off of the path. As Lucy watched him, she noticed a large pool of blood that had been absorbed by the loose, rocky soil. The young wolf had been badly wounded.

When Piatt was finally satisfied with how well he had hidden her body, Lucy could feel his emotions recede. She was no longer drowning, and was now able to stand after his sadness had weighed her down. Lucy watched him carefully. His eyes were wet and red with tears. She tried her best to ignore the signs of a fractured soul, but in time she was overwhelmed with guilt. It was because of her that the vampires had attacked. All of the death and sadness was indirectly her fault and this burden hurt more than any pain that she endured before.

"All right then. On to the silver mines," Piatt's quiet announcement woke Lucy from her destructive train of thought. To the casual observer, she might have looked fine, but Lucy was unable to see good in any of the situations that she was put in. Sebastian continued with his reassuring grins as if everything would be all right, but Lucy knew better.

After a while, they passed through the foyer of Piatt's home and he led them into what appeared to be an ordinary room. As John closed the door, where a small lamp was lit, Lucy was finally able to see where they were. The room was empty of furniture and instead of decorations there was only a hole in the wall that had been recently created. It appeared as if someone had broken through as if they knew what lay beyond. Piatt didn't seem worried, and without hesitation he led them on into an old cavern. As the lantern highlighted the walls, Lucy was able to see lines of silver that grew forward into the darkness ahead. The walls appeared to be alive with veins of silver and reeked of what smelled like rotten eggs. Though the smell was pungent, Lucy didn't comment and instead tried to focus on the tunnel ahead. She assumed that they would be running into trouble soon and was oddly ready to face whatever it was.

The small bubble of light they had didn't help much when it came to lighting the floor, and Lucy found herself tripping on uneven land as they marched onward. After what felt like miles, Piatt stopped and offered the group a quick rest. Lucy wasn't sure if he took the time for her or John, but she was grateful. As the men slid to the floor and each took sips from the one bottle of water they had brought, Lucy made her way toward Piatt. As she approached him, she noticed that he was checking the level of liquid in their lantern.

"Is it all right?" she asked, even though she really didn't care.

"The levels are fine. We will reach the cave's mouth before the lantern dies." He smiled and set the beacon on the ground before sitting against the wall himself.

"Are there a lot of caves down here?"

"There were. Over time they've deteriorated and crumbled into nothing. The silver-lined caves are the only ones that remain," he was quick to answer, and it was almost as if he really didn't want to talk. Lucy was able to pick up on this desire very quickly and they sat there silently in the dim light for a few more minutes. She watched the silver within the walls shimmer under the light of the lantern. The sight was so beautiful that Lucy was kicking herself for not seeing it before. The silver sparkled under the dim light like stars in twilight. The lines resembled veins that pulsed with life deep under the Earth's surface. Lucy was filled with awe at the sight.

Finally, the men stirred. One at a time they stood and began walking into the unexplored part of the tunnel. Piatt led the way with his lantern held out to light the path. The amount of tunnel illuminated by the lamp left John walking in the dark. Lucy assumed that he was only following shadows and couldn't actually see where he was going. Together, they hiked through the second half of the tunnel until a small light could be seen.

Piatt's grin widened. He had made it out of danger and his family was close. He hadn't been able to save Adelaide, but seeing his wife unharmed would be a comfort. Lucy found herself more than excited. She was exhilarated to enter the sunlight again. She didn't know how long they had been underground or what time of day it was, but that didn't matter. The warmth of sun on her skin would be a welcome feeling no matter how short a time it might have been.

As they exited into a wooded area, Lucy wondered how far they were from the den. She could remember back to the entrance and didn't recall a tree anywhere nearby. She took a brief look around and then decided to sit on a nearby rock, which was bathed in sunlight. The rough surface was so warm that she nearly fell asleep as she laid on it and allowed the rock to warm her insides. Lucy hadn't realized how cold that tunnel was until she was finally warm again.

When she ultimately decided to sit up, she could see that they were no longer alone. A few young women had appeared and were talking with Piatt. Lucy recognized one of them as Maria, his wife. She hugged him for a great length of time before opening one of the small, wooden chests they were carrying. At this point, Lucy had gained interest and walked over to the group.

Maria had pulled out swabs doused in disinfectant and had begun to clean the blood from her husband's skin. Lucy watched them for a while, but was soon distracted by Sebastian. He had begun to dig through the wooden chest full of first aid supplies. Lucy watched him for a few seconds until he found what he was looking for. It was at this point that she felt the need to understand where his mind was. Without hesitation, Lucy strolled to his side and touched his shoulder. His concentration was broken and he glanced over at her and then to the syringe in his hand.

"What is that for?" she asked.

There was a slight pause for thought before he nodded and turned away from her, without answering her question. It was at times like this that Lucy wished she could read his mind.

Curious, she followed him as he approached one of the other women and handed her the syringe, "Will you extract some of my venom?" It must have been an odd request because the female wolf gave him a strange look. She didn't seem to understand the question, but Sebastian insisted.

"Please. It may be a situation of life or death," he pleaded. The nurse thought on the question for a few moments before she scowled and then nodded. Clearly it wasn't a common request, but the woman did as he asked.

Using a low and almost inaudible voice, the lady asked him to lie on a nearby rock, which he did. The nurse exposed the sterile needle from its case and then placed it parallel to Sebastian's neck. With a steady hand, she inserted the bevel of the needle into the soft spot of his neck, directly under the far end of the right side of his jaw. Sebastian didn't seem bothered by the needle as much as Lucy was. As long as she could remember, needles had given her the willies. Her stomach twisted uncomfortably as she watched the nurse pull back on the plunger and a shimmering white liquid filled the syringe. To finish, the woman placed a finger over the puncture and removed the needle as she put pressure on his skin.

"Pressure," the lady said calmly and moved Sebastian's hand

to the spot while she recapped the needle. He held it for a while longer until the nurse nodded and handed him the syringe, saying, "Use it wisely."

Sebastian didn't say anything to her, but nodded gratefully and placed the venom inside his jacket pocket. Every possible question must have been displayed on Lucy's face because when he finally looked at her, Sebastian cracked a smile and chucked a little bit before passing by. The women looked over each of the men before coming to Lucy. They dropped a bag at her feet and the oldest of the women smiled as she looked around for any wounds.

"We managed to pack some supplies and clothing for you. We did guess your sizes, but you should find enough to help until you reach the next city." Any cuts or bruises had already healed, but the woman did wipe Lucy's skin free of Adelaide's blood, just as Maria had done to Piatt.

When she was alone again, the wolf leader approached. He was glowing now. The sunlight lit him like a candle and he burned dimly under its rays.

"We part here. I must go to my pack and you are bound for yours. Be safe and if you meet those vampires again," he grinned and took her hand, "give 'em hell." The farewell was bittersweet, but in time the wolves had disappeared into the woods and Lucy was left in the care of the men she trusted most. No words could be said as the trio entered a foreign forest. She could only hope that Sebastian's instincts would lead them in the proper direction.

Chapter Thirteen

The morning had drifted slowly into evening and Lucy had been forced to occupy her time by watching the sun hover overhead. The forest was thick and treacherous, but hadn't caused worry until strange sounds began to follow them. They didn't appear to be made by animals or by the wind. It was spooky and there was an eerie presence among the trees. Lucy tried to remain calm, but there was something within her that was panicking and she couldn't figure out why.

Then, without any warning, the reason came to the very front of her mind and she could finally decipher what her body was saying. There was a smell in the air that she knew. Sebastian stopped walking then. He lifted his nose to the sky. He could smell it too and no sooner than he could look back at her, a red-haired woman leaped from the trees above them and punched him hard in the face. She then took hold of his throat and threw him into the nearest tree before he could retaliate.

Lucy couldn't believe what she was seeing. A pulse of fear spread through her and before she could take a step to help him, a soft thud shook the ground behind her. Lucy was too afraid to look. She could feel the presence of a vampire and knew immediately that Cecily was close. Her strong scent gave away how close she was and Lucy could feel her muscles seize up. Chills drifted past her arms and to her cheeks. A knot formed in her stomach, but it wasn't enough to keep her still.

As fast as she could muster, Lucy whirled in a circle with her fist held out, hoping to land a solid punch to the vampire's face. It was, however a futile effort and Cecily was able to duck under the punch before it hit her face. She then took the opportunity to grab Lucy's exposed arm and, with little effort, flipped her overhead into the base of a nearby tree.

The force of the impact knocked the wind out of her, but Lucy was more than determined to fight this time. However, when she tried to stand up, she found that she was unable to move away from the tree. Probing further, she discovered that she was attached to it. As John began to occupy Cecily's attention, Lucy was able to search for what kept her from escaping. Frantically, she felt around and then discovered something wet. With a gulp she pulled her hands into her vision and saw them covered in sticky, red blood. Lucy's eyes followed her hand back down and found that a broken branch had stabbed her left side and literally impaled her. The injury was very superficial and didn't concern her, but she couldn't stand or escape the tree without assistance.

Both angry and helpless, Lucy watched both fights carry on. Sebastian had been tackled by Eliza and they were now exchanging blows. Cecily and John circled, but didn't attack. Clearly they were unfamiliar with each other and didn't know how to proceed. This hesitance didn't last very long. In time they began to fight as well, but they used more modern moves like marital arts, while Eliza and Sebastian were more than keen on just killing each other.

John and Cecily's fight grew more violent by the second. She fought with her teeth bared and Lucy soon realized that the ladies were here for blood. They were prepared to kill in order to get what they were after. The fight progressed without any real injury until Cecily moved to punch John's face. He observed the opportunity when it came and took hold of her wrist. She became infuriated and tried to bite him, but John didn't panic. In one swift movement, he released her wrist and captured her head in his hands. Following this maneuver, it didn't take much to snap her neck. A soft crack echoed off of the trees before Lucy watched her enemy fall to the ground. John had killed her without mercy, but he didn't even seem to care. Without looking back, he crawled to Lucy's side and examined the wound. She watched his hurried breathing and realized that her heart was beating just as fast.

"Are you all right?" he asked as he knelt next to her and pulled out a knife.

"Yeah," was all that she could say. After what she had witnessed him do, Lucy was thoroughly unable to say anything else. It was then that she knew why her heart was beating as fast as it was. Lucinda would have called it "fluttering." Lucy felt for him. She had never thought about it before, but she loved John. From the first words he spoke to her after she considered stealing his car, there was a connection that she wanted to deny. It was at the surface again and she wondered if he felt it too.

The knife he held made quick work of the branch and he helped her to stand before taking a closer look at the wound. Lucy could now focus on Sebastian, but it was difficult to watch his fight with John trying to remove the large splinter.

"It really doesn't look that serious and you've already begun to heal. I believe that removing it now would be the best thing." His words didn't make it to Lucy's mind. She was far too focused on Sebastian.

The elusive hunter side of the vampire had come forth. Eliza's large black eyes and sharp features were highlighted with silvery tattoos, her claws had extended, and her teeth were bared. The sight of her true form was sickening. Eliza's fiery red hair danced in the wind as she attacked Sebastian. He appeared worried, and this look wasn't very reassuring. Most of her strikes were making contact and he wasn't able to land a single blow. A knot dropped into Lucy's stomach and she felt as if she was about to vomit. Finally, Eliza leaped and kicked him in the face, which threw him to the ground. In less than a second she was on top of him and had both hands around his neck. Sebastian tried to fight, but he was oddly weakened and unable to push her off.

Lucy regained John's attention and told him to help Sebastian, but there was no time to do so now. Eliza bent down to bite him and Lucy couldn't bare the sight. She remembered him saying that vampire bites were dangerous for them and they could be life threatening, but she knew that Eliza wouldn't just stop there. Just as her mouth disappeared from sight on the other side of his head, she became stiff. She didn't move for the longest time. Lucy wasn't certain of what had happened. Did she bite him? Was he dying? Was she savoring the moment?

All her questions were answered as Eliza rolled off of him and began to convulse as she held her stomach. Lucy was unable to focus on that, though. She could only see the syringe sticking upward from Sebastian's stomach, where he held it firmly. As she watched, Lucy felt the stiffness in her abdomen disappear. John had removed the branch and threw it back behind them. Together they walked to Sebastian's side. John was oddly protective and watched her movements carefully.

Sebastian had a look of surprise and relief on his face. It was an expression that Lucy wasn't used to, but she was glad to see it anyway. Without thinking, she knelt to his side and took the syringe out of his hand before falling onto his chest. Then the tears came. Since meeting Sebastian, she had never been so emotional, but almost losing him was enough to leave her sobbing. When she was done, Lucy watched as John stabbed Cecily in the heart with his knife to assure that she was dead. Soon he returned with a bleak look on his face.

"I've never killed anyone before," he mumbled and then fell to his knees beside Lucy. Their enemies were gone for now and it was time to move on, but Lucy couldn't stand. They all needed time to collect themselves before traveling again. Together they rested and watched as the bodies of their enemies turned to dust, just as Lucian had.

As they relaxed, Lucy was faced with the memories that had continued to follow her. She remembered how easy it was for Syrina to disintegrate the bodies of people in the morgue and how the wolves were able to disconnect themselves from the pain of death. It seemed impossible to ignore such emotion as it rose to the surface. In a desperate attempt not to cry, Lucy took the locket from around her neck and held it tightly as she pushed back her tears. When she finally had control over herself, Lucy popped it open and looked over the photo of her parents. She remembered what the vampires had done to them and was instantly infuriated. If nothing else, she would find a way to save her father from them. Whatever it took, she was prepared to try.

The short rest was well earned and Lucy even found herself tired enough to fall asleep. She tried to refuse her body's pleading, but then a light snore interrupted her thoughts. Sebastian had fallen asleep and John was just about to join him. It took some time before she felt safe enough to sleep, but after the sun had finally gone down, Lucy was able to let go of her hold on reality. Sleeping was always an escape, even though dreams were a thing of the past. Lucy missed dreaming. That foolish human disability that could cushion the shock of reality was one that she would no longer have.

As she thought on these things, a startling wind erupted and she forced her eyes open to find the source. A small bird had landed on her knee and was studying her with curious black eyes. Its flapping wings must have been the cause of the wind. The bird was a bright red color with a darker grayish blue on the ends of its wings. It had an orange beak that was circled at the base with black. Lucy knew this bird well. It was a cardinal, but she had never been this close to one. It sat on her leg for only a few minutes before taking off for the trees.

The day had returned and Lucy hadn't noticed until now. She didn't realize that she had actually fallen asleep, but the amount of time that had passed was uncertain. She didn't know what time of day it was, and as she stood the men began to stir. While they joined her and stretched, she examined her wound from the fight. It had scarred and was no longer painful. The rest had been enough to allow her body the time it needed to heal itself. Her health quickly became John's first priority while Sebastian left to find some form of food.

John wasted no time in lifting her bloodied shirt slightly to check the wound. He examined the site carefully. Lucy could feel him run his hand over where the wound had been. Finally, he straightened to face her, saying, "That is amazing."

"So I've been told," Lucy commented as John moved toward her. He was close enough for Lucy to see her reflection in his eyes. The closeness didn't stop until finally John's lips met hers and they kissed. It was only a short peck and then it was over, but to Lucy, the moment was frozen. She had been given the time to stop him and to avoid the kiss, but she didn't. Lucy didn't want to stop it. In fact, the brief kiss was simply electric and she'd hoped that it would last longer or happen again, but at that moment Sebastian returned.

He didn't appear to have seen anything and John was quick to rush over to him like nothing had happened. Lucy, however, was unable to think about anything else. Her world was spinning and her heart fluttering. Sebastian had brought different fruits and berries with him, but there was obvious blood spattered on his forehead and shirt, indicating that he had caught a small meal and eaten it already to save his companions the horror of his animal instinct.

John nearly swallowed a handful of berries whole before starting on an apple, and Lucy ate a few apples along with some grapes. She immediately wondered where Sebastian had gotten these things, but knew that approving of his answer would be unlikely. She decided not to ask.

As they ate, Sebastian began to dig a large hole next to one of the larger trees. His reasons were unclear at first, but he did grumble that no human should find what was left of the bodies. When John had finished his food he helped Sebastian dig, and after a decent-sized hole was made, they gently placed the disintegrating skeletons inside. Tissue remains were still visible around Eliza's bones, but her skeleton was more gruesome than Cecily's due to the venom injection. Lucy assumed that it sped up the decaying process. Cecily's body was still intact, but her usual beauty was supplanted by the appearance of an old maid. Her youth had been destroyed by death.

Lucy recalled all of the terrible things that the two vampires had done to her and those around her, but now that they were dead, she couldn't hate them. She knew that hating them couldn't hurt, but it also wouldn't help and that was what stopped her negative feelings. No one deserved this life and Lucy wouldn't wish it on anyone. In her mind, it was strange to feel remorse for these vampires, but she saw them as more than what Lucian was to her. Cecily and Eliza seemed more human than he was.

Her stomach churned uncomfortably as the men buried the bodies, along with the branch that had impaled Lucy, and Sebastian's syringe. The only evidence of their fight was easily concealed and left behind.

Before filling in the hole, each of them searched through the bag they received from the lady wolves. The clothing they found wasn't proper in size, but it would do. The three of them changed their clothes and each took a bottle of water before chucking the old and bloody clothes into the hole and filling it in.

Soon after, they ventured onward and into the forest. Lucy marched between the men with Sebastian leading and John in the back. She had so many questions now, but was afraid to ask. This feeling was new. She had never been afraid of Sebastian before.

As time passed, John's strides grew larger for a short time and he jetted forward to hike at Lucy's side. They spoke casually about nothing of great consequence for a while until Lucy's questions built up such pressure that they forced their way out.

"Did Sebastian know we would be attacked?" Lucy watched their leader's muscles tense and then relax again. She knew that he had heard her whisper, but she still looked to John for the response. He seemed surprised by the question and hesitant to answer, but when Sebastian didn't confront them, he felt safe enough to speak.

"Of course not. Why would you think that?" His eyes shifted back and forth between Lucy and Sebastian as he spoke.

"He had that nurse remove venom from his neck like he knew he would need it. How did she get so much anyway?" This question sparked a twinge of excitement within John. It then became quite obvious why he had become a teacher.

"Humans have lymph nodes and during the change the nodes in a zephyr become useless. Our kind doesn't get ill and neither do vampires, so we don't need them. The nodes become pockets that produce venom and circulate it through our bodies. Sebastian had her extract some of his venom just in case he needed it. If he hadn't, he would be dead." John smiled and took her hand. Thinking immediately of Sebastian, Lucy loosened her grip, but John squeezed tighter. Confusing as this was, John gave her a reassuring smile, which oddly made the contact more acceptable. Sebastian either didn't mind, or didn't notice at all. A few more minutes of walking led them to the edge of the forest. The sight that lay just past the trees was astounding, and to Lucy, utterly thrilling.

There was an airport at the bottom of the hill that they were on. It held many different types of aircraft, but most of them were nothing like Lucy had been on before. On the left side of the airport sat a large field where a helicopter was fueling and a hot air balloon was deflating. In the center of the site, there were three long runways for the single engine planes, which seemed to be more common. Finally, to the right of everything was a long, oval, manmade lake that had four seaplanes docked near its shore.

As a whole, the sight was breathtaking. Lucy's stomach was suddenly filled with butterflies and she felt dizzy at the thought of flying. Sebastian, however, didn't linger very long. He was quick to duck out of sight at the right side of the hill. She didn't know why, but they followed his example and snuck down with him. At the bottom, he stopped and turned to face them. His expression was unreadable, but finally, he looked up and then over at John.

"Can you fly a plane?"

Lucy saw that question coming. She noticed the wheels in his head turning as soon as they got to the bottom of the hill. Sebastian wanted to steal a plane.

"Probably. Anything is worth a shot," John agreed, to Lucy's surprise. Her heart nearly jumped into her throat at the thought of flying, especially with someone who wasn't a seasoned pilot. The men didn't seem to notice Lucy's objection and took a moment to scan the area for security before they emerged into the open field between the hill and lake. Not wanting to be left behind, she tailed them closely and hoped more than anything that they would remain unseen. Sebastian led them along the shore of the lake, which was lined with rocks to make it more visually appealing.

When they got close enough, the men slowed down and straightened their posture. To her, it was amusing to see them both acting as if they had a shred of credibility when it came to flying. She knew better, but they seemed to be fooling everyone else. As they approached, several people eyed them, but didn't make a move to stop their thievery. Sebastian and John were putting on a good show, almost as if they had done so before.

Finally arriving at the dock, Sebastian stopped and observed the goings on next to each of the seaplanes. There were four men in white cleaning one of them and then two men dressed in nicer clothes seemed to be inspecting another. In a very nonchalant way, Sebastian managed to study them from over his shoulder and make a reasonable guess as to which plane he wanted to take. Meanwhile

John had taken more time to look around. Lucy watched his eyes move until finally he looked at her.

"I don't think this is an airport," he whispered and then glanced back to Sebastian. This assumption had Lucy looking around too. Finally, she nudged him, asking, "Why would you say that?"

"The facility isn't right and those people on the dock don't work here." He was quiet, but still sounded concerned.

"What is this place if it isn't an airport?"

John had her full attention. Was there something that she wasn't grasping? Did he notice something that she didn't?

"It's like a country club for plane enthusiasts. These men own and maintain their own planes. These places are very exclusive and very private. Everyone here has money," John answered with a groan. Lucy could almost hear his heart beating. Something about this place had him terrified.

"How much money?"

"Enough to not have to worry about anything. These people are wealthy enough to make people disappear. I don't think stealing anything from them is a good idea." His worry was reflected clearly on his face.

At that moment, Sebastian turned to them. He didn't say anything at first. His face was free of emotion and his eyes were sort of drooping as if he was on drugs. After only a couple of seconds, he grinned and cleared his throat. "If you know how to steal things from the rich then there isn't a worry. You just fly the plane. I will worry about everything else." His words were confusing and not reassuring in the least, but Lucy gave him the benefit of the doubt and hoped that John would do the same.

They waited quietly for a long time before Sebastian stirred. He was watching the men in white closely and when they finally headed away from the dock, he made his move. With his head held high, Sebastian strutted onto the dock and up to one of the planes. With a grin, he decided on a white seaplane with blue stripes that bobbed happily in the wind-whipped water. As smoothly as he could, John pulled down the boarding stairs that had been tucked neatly into the body of the plane. As soon as the platform touched the dock, John bowed his head as the two nicely dressed men approached them.

One of them was younger and seemed to be a second to the

larger man. His black hair and well-maintained beard had silver running through it, which reminded Lucy of a well-groomed pirate. He was rather rotund, but his blue suit was tailored to him with great care. He carried a large clipboard, which was layered neatly with many papers. The younger man seemed to stay back as the older one approached and cleared his throat.

"Are you aware that you are boarding Mr. Questen's aircraft?" the larger man wearing a blue suit asked Sebastian as he tapped him on the shoulder. Though Lucy found it rude, Sebastian didn't even bother acknowledging the man until he had assisted her in boarding the plane. Only when she was safely inside did he turn and greet the man.

"Gentlemen, I am aware of to whom this craft belongs. If I were not then I would not be assisting his niece in boarding. Also, I would check your records again because this aircraft belongs to Sir James Arthur Gillian," Sebastian finished with a grin. He seemed confident, but Lucy's heart was racing faster than it had ever gone before. There was a long pause as the man checked his clipboard and then glanced back up at Sebastian several times. Finally, he glared at them with a stern expression. Lucy could feel the sting of prison looming over her head, but as she thought on the impending doom, the blue-suited man grinned and slapped his clipboard lightly.

"You are very right, sir. That is our mistake and it will be corrected immediately. The plane has been fueled and is ready for your departure." With a tilting bow the men departed.

Sebastian watched them closely as they left and when they were nearly out of sight, he refocused on more important matters. He entered the plane and moved to the front as John followed him after latching the door closed. Together, they sat in the small cabin as Lucy took her window seat and fastened her safety belt. She noticed her own breathing quicken as the engines revved and the propeller began to spin. With a gulp of nothing except air, Lucy gripped her arm rests tightly as the plane backed away from the dock and to the far end of the lake. She watched the men as John instructed Sebastian on what a copilot's job was. They seemed to work well together and before long the plane was facing toward the end of the lake. As John walked through takeoff procedures with Sebastian, Lucy could do nothing but look down at the water. Besides the two small windows on either side of her, there was a large back window that gave a great view of the back of the plane. For people excited about the idea of takeoff, the window would have been a marvelous idea, but for Lucy it was terrifying. She immediately decided to look at the floor during launch.

When the men had finished, Lucy heard them pressing buttons and flipping switches. Before long the engine noises grew in magnitude and the buzzing below her feet became more powerful. She overheard John mention that this particular lake was rather short for the departure and return of these planes, but he was also confident that he could manage. Lucy didn't know whether to be thankful or fearful.

Finally, she could feel the plane moving. It glided through the water quite nicely, to her surprise. With her eyes glued shut in fear, she could only feel and listen to what was happening. The last thing she could remember about liftoff was John uttering some bone-chilling words that made Lucy sick, "We're out of room! Pull up! Pull up!" After that she couldn't remember anything else.

When her mind caught up with the rest of her body, Lucy became aware of her breathing. She was alive. Unsure if she had blacked out, she listened for anything that would give her a clue as to what had happened. She was incredibly nervous about opening her eyes. There was a ball of panic inside her that was ready to burst if it needed to. Since meeting Sebastian, she had been afraid of few things, but this happened to be the most terrifying. With a sigh, she sat back in her chair, took several deep breaths, and when she finally opened her eyes again they were in the sky.

The distance between the ground and the plane grew slowly, but Lucy was relieved that it was growing at all. She had soon mustered enough courage to look out of the window behind her and saw that the long lake was getting smaller as they flew away from it. Soon all that she could see were trees with cabins dispersed among them. Almost all signs of civilization had disappeared.

The excitement in the plane's cabin seemed to have gone and before long Sebastian stood out of his chair and went to the back, where Lucy was. He didn't say a word at first, but took a moment to look out each of the windows. Sebastian hummed lightly as he examined the ground below. Finally, he sat next to Lucy at the rear of the craft and took hold of her hand, "John seems to believe that we will make it as far as Indiana with the amount of fuel that we have."

"That sounds like a lie," Lucy thought aloud as Sebastian nodded to agree with her statement.

"I thought the same, but he knows a few tricks regarding the power and engine that will conserve fuel." He sighed and sat back in the seat while looking over his shoulder to the large back window. They had gotten high enough to see the wispy bottoms of the clouds above. They didn't look much like clouds now, but reminded Lucy more of fog.

"He knows more than he says; sounds like someone else I know." She frowned and nudged him playfully. "As long as we don't crash." She smiled as they took a second to laugh off any fear before gazing out of the back of the plane, and watched the world below pass by.

Chapter Fourteen

Lucy lost track of time after a while. Every town looked the same and the forests began to blend together. She didn't know how long they had been in the air, but the sickness she had at the thought of flight was long gone. Lucy was finally able to join Sebastian in rest. Many odd things had happened recently that had her questioning almost everything she believed in, and doubting everyone she trusted. There was more to Sebastian than what she knew and these mysteries in his past were confusing. How was he able to convince the men on the dock that he was allowed to take this plane? The answers to her every question felt so close, but Lucy wasn't ready to reach out for them. She was perfectly content in trusting with doubt. Still unsure of many things, she was prepared to be confused about most of the goings on until he was ready to talk about them.

Lucy spent most of the journey pressed up against Sebastian. She made sure that her side was firmly stuck to his so that she could do the strangest thing that she had ever done: She watched him breathe. In fact, she couldn't stop. With her ear set against his ribs, she could hear his heartbeat and watch him breathe out of the corner of her eye. It was satisfying and slightly uncomfortable, but she studied him that way for hours.

The plane ride seemed never-ending, but soon John took a moment to stand and stretch. The controls at his waist didn't shift at all, thankfully, and he soon returned to his post. A few minutes later, he turned his head and yelled back to them, "We are coming up on an airport. I need to land and refuel. It will be quick."

That was all that he said and there didn't seem to be any concerns from either of the men, so Lucy was all right with the idea. Then she started to wonder where they were headed. The curiosity slowly built until she finally sat up and walked to the front of the plane. John didn't notice her presence until she sat down in the copilot's chair and strapped herself in.

"You don't need to do that." John smiled as he addressed her insistence in a seatbelt.

"I know. It makes me feel better. So where are we headed?" Lucy tried to casually strip information out of him. To her surprise, he was very forthcoming.

"We're going to Greenland, but in order to get there we must stop for fuel a couple of times." He frowned as he studied the gauges and pushed forward on the controls.

"Why there?" The destination seemed odd and out of the way to Lucy.

"Sebastian told me that that is where Cyrus will go." John's answer forced butterflies to stir in Lucy's stomach. The thought of seeing her uncle again was very exciting. After everything that had happened since they parted, a familiar face would be more than welcome.

The plane soon began to descend out of the low clouds until Lucy was finally able to see where they were headed. There was a large body of water below them and it was getting closer by the second. Nervousness swept through her body and her stomach began to do flip-flops as John tried his best to land the plane. As they neared the choppy water, Lucy couldn't take the sight anymore. Knowing that she couldn't leave, Lucy covered her eyes and hoped for the best. She couldn't be sure, but a light snicker might have come from John's direction.

A few more minutes ticked by before John cleared his throat and touched Lucy on the arm. When she finally came out from her hiding place they had landed and John was already out of the plane. Lucy unbuckled herself and crept back to her seat. She watched the men carefully as Sebastian handed John a wad of cash before heading down to shore. John proceeded to give one of the men on the dock a small part of the wad before helping them fill the plane with fuel. They had gotten out of Lucy's line of sight so she waited patiently for the job to be done.

Sebastian returned after a while with a melancholy look on his face. Lucy wondered what was wrong, but she didn't ask. He strolled over, took a seat next to her, and proceeded to hold her hand.

"So where are we?" Lucy wondered as she leaned into him and rested her head on his shoulder.

"I believe we are somewhere in Indiana. There is a very large lake out there. I can't see the other side." His voice was comforting and didn't seem as sad as he looked.

"Do you think we will see Cyrus in Greenland?" Lucy was hopeful. She wanted the family to be reunited. In her mind, it was her fault that they were separated in the first place.

"I hope that we will. He owns a piece of property there that is completely out of the way and hidden among the mountains. You can only hike there or travel by sea, hence the plane." Sebastian grinned and hugged her close as they waited for John. The steel bird was quiet for a few more minutes before John boarded and returned to the front of the plane. Sebastian was quick to join him, and before long they had pulled away from the dock.

Take off was relatively uneventful and soon they were back in the sky. In time, Sebastian returned to her and they sat in the back of the plane together. Lucy was happy to sit with him. He was warm and his presence comforting, but in the back of her mind, Lucy was thinking about John. She watched the back of his chair, hoping that he would look back. It was a twisted form of torture, loving two men. The rest of their journey was met with a lot of silence and a few more stops for fuel. Though they stopped once in Maine and again in Canada, Lucy didn't leave the plane for longer than she had to. Whatever was happening beyond the safety of the plane didn't interest her.

As they left the cold shores of Ungava Bay, Lucy cuddled against Sebastian and fought the urge to fall asleep. It was a long trip over the ocean and the soft putter of the plane was more than she needed to drift off into the dreamless dark. She was able to keep herself from the weight of exhaustion, but barely. She focused on Sebastian's scent and breathing. Lucy tried to breathe when he did and even worked to synchronize their heart beats. This proved impossible. His heart thumped slowly and hers would flutter quickly. Still, she enjoyed listening to him. Before long, she found herself wandering back towards a nap.

She didn't stir again until Sebastian moved and she fell into the part of the seat that he had been in. She didn't know why he had moved, but when she found him, he was sitting in the copilot's chair and helping John guide the plane between two mountains. In between these giant masses was a bay of water that the men had begun to follow. Lucy nearly leaped from her seat and tried to look out of the small, round windows on her side of the aircraft. The lush, green hills that surrounded the cove created a green reflection on the ocean, which was the bluest water that she had ever seen. The rippled waves below distorted the plane's reflection playfully and had Lucy nearly giddy with excitement. As the bay's entrance faded into the background, she refocused her attention to the front of the plane and was able to see their destination just as the pontoons began to skim the surface.

In the distance she could see a two-story house. The second floor was set upon the cliff and when looking at the house from the perspective of the bay, there was a hidden first floor that was nestled inside of a former cave that sat about half way up the cliff. A beautiful diamond-shaped deck jutted out from the lower part of the house, making the home seem jagged in a way. Behind the deck was a wall of glass that had one door nestled in the very center. The house as a whole had a cabin style build, if the onlooker was discounting the odd first floor, which gave the structure a sense of awe and visual curiosity. The sight was breathtaking.

"Welcome to 'Occasum Sinus'—'Sunset Bay,'" Sebastian shouted so that the others might rejoice with him. Lucy had never seen him so happy. The buzzing of the engines soon faded as the plane washed up to the small sandy beach with a rumble that nearly knocked Lucy off balance. Sebastian was so eager that he ran back and threw the door open before John could even get his seatbelt off.

"Come on, Lucy," he repressed his enthusiasm to assist her in exiting the plane. The aircraft was still afloat in two feet of water so Sebastian carried her to shore. The house and its surroundings were ten times more breathtaking than what they had seemed when viewed from the inside of the plane.

"It's gorgeous!" Those seemed to be the only words that she could get out, even though there were so many more in her head.

"This is my most favorite place in the entire world." Sebastian's happiness radiated through his movements and expressions. It was almost as if he was a child again.

"When I was a young wolf, Cyrus brought me here to hide from Lucian. My brother used to be very keen on killing any wolf that came into his path. I was a special case and he felt the need to hunt me. We hid here for twenty years with the others. I have so many memories." For a moment Lucy thought that he was going to cry. The flashbacks in his mind must have been wonderful, but in seconds his excitement returned and he grabbed Lucy's hand as they made their way to a steep set of stairs that led up to the deck.

"Around the side of this cliff is a cave where we used to keep all kinds of boats and other equipment. We had a family of dolphins living here for a while too," he explained as they ascended the stairs. Lucy assumed the expressions on her face would have been amazing to photograph. All of the sights and smells left her tingling. When they reached the top of the stairs, she was surprised at how winded she was. The steep incline was exhausting, but the view was worth the climb.

Lucy found her jaw hanging open, a condition that she could not remedy. With a light sigh, she crossed her arms on top of the thick railing and rested her head on them. The view had her in a state that felt like an out-of-body experience. She was physically on the deck, but her mind was swimming in the soft ripples of ocean water and then flying within the colors of sunset that lit the sky.

When Lucy's mind returned to where her body stood, she finally noticed that John was standing next to her with Sebastian on his other side. She honestly could have stood on the deck with her boys and watched the scenery for hours, but after only a few minutes Sebastian stirred and invited them inside. He opened the door to the dark house and allowed them to go in first before he followed and then shut the door. He said 'Welcome' once more and flipped a single light switch that lit up the first and second floors, lit the fireplace, and turned on a selection of soft jazz music. The inside was decorated as a homey vacation house.

The room they had entered was purposed as a living room. It held a few couches and a few chairs, with a fireplace that seemed to light the décor on fire. The general color palate was honey and brown. The furniture maintained a gold and red theme. On each side of the fireplace was a staircase that arched upward, and led to a large loft that was part of the second floor.

"Upstairs you will find several bedrooms and some bathrooms. There are some game tables and a music room too. I don't think it really matters where you stay, but Lucy you should stay in Syrina's old room. She had the best view in the whole house. Find the purple door."

Sebastian smiled as he entered what appeared to be the kitchen, leaving her and John to do whatever they wanted. Out of the corner of her eye she saw John begin up the right side of the stairs and she immediately joined him. Together they explored the house one room at a time. The loft was decorated like the room below. It had many large rectangular windows that were close to the ceiling and had dark red drapes that would cover them if needed. In the middle was a championship-sized pool table that was carved out of redwood and lined with burgundy felt. A large flat-screen television was mounted on the wall, and there were several large armed chairs that lined the room.

Only one hallway led out of the loft and down to several wooden doors. Each of them had been stained a different color. The first one that they passed was a normal mahogany shade, while the other four were more wild colors. The second door was blue and the one after that was red. Finally they came to a honey-colored door that was across from a bright purple-colored door. Lucy glanced back at John once and together they headed to the end of the hallway. Oddly, the hall was empty of decoration. It was bare of emotion, unlike the warmth and joy seen in the rest of the house. She had expected family portraits or something of sentimental value, but there was nothing.

Lucy was the first to arrive at the purple door and with another apprehensive breath, she pushed it from its frame. The décor of the room was an obvious give-away of to whom it belonged. Syrina was known to be an advocate of purple. Lucy would have even gone so far as to say it was her favorite color. Three of the room's walls were a dark color with the other being a bright shade of purple. For some reason her eye was drawn to it. Hanging on the purple wall were several pictures that were all intermingled into a collage. There was a large bed on the other side of the room that looked like it had been made that morning. Several period items also adorned the room. They didn't fit into the décor, but these things must have meant something to Syrina if she had left them where they wouldn't be disturbed.

Finally, they finished looking over the magnificent room and focused on the view. There was a large pentagon-shaped window that Lucy remembered seeing from outside. It gave them a great view of the landscape outside. The beautiful sunset was barely hidden behind several small mountains, and the bay water lapped against the rocks that surrounded the small sandy beach below. The sky was painted in hues of pink, purple, gold, and orange. It was amazing.

As they watched, Lucy heard the door creak and she glanced back to find Sebastian. He seemed to be waiting for them to notice his presence. Lucy nudged John and together they stepped away from the window. Sebastian had a look on his face that made Lucy want to burst out in laughter. His cocky grin was coupled with mischievous eyes, which caused her heart to begin to race as they met him at the door.

"I am going into town. There isn't anything edible in the kitchen. Do you want anything?" Sebastian's funny expression had disappeared as John and Lucy thought on the question. Finally, John shrugged and passed into the hallway.

"Me neither, I guess." Lucy smiled and continued, "but be careful. I'm sure the terrain is anything but easy."

"I suppose, and I will be safe. I don't know how long I will be gone. I am not as fast as Mitchell, but if I'm gone longer than three days, you can start to worry." Sebastian spoke with a smile. Lucy knew he was trying to be funny, but there was little room to joke when it came to the subject of death. The absence of laughter must have gotten that point across.

"I will be fine," Sebastian reassured her before pulling her into his chest and kissing the center of her forehead.

"You'd better be." Lucy's reply was quick as she wrapped her arms around his waist and hugged him tightly. Letting go was difficult, but soon he had disappeared and Lucy was free to shut the door. This was the first time she had been alone in months and for some reason, Lucy didn't know how to proceed. She wasn't tired or really very hungry. There was only one thing that she could think of to occupy her time. With a sigh, Lucy entered Syrina's old bathroom and closed the door behind her. After locking the door, she walked straight to the large bathtub and started the shower. As the water heated she found a towel and some soap that had been stashed away in a small cupboard. As she placed the items near the tub, Lucy caught a glimpse of her reflection in the mirror. She nearly burst into tears.

Her face was beyond dirty and there was even splattered blood on her cheek. She couldn't begin to assume whose blood it was. Her eye color was vastly different as well. The beautiful blue color had become even stronger and the one green dash that had always been a reminder of her father had turned into a complete circle around the edge of the blue. This change had happened in both eyes and was strange, but wonderful also. It reminded her of her father. She saw the change and knew what she was, but also knew what she wasn't.

Her hair was in disarray, and her clothes were wrinkled and as dirty as her face. Trying to ignore the horrible state of her appearance, Lucy snatched a hair band from the counter below the mirror and pulled her hair back into a ponytail. When she looked back up to her reflection, she nearly swallowed her tongue.

With a shaking hand, Lucy ran her hand over the bite mark where her neck and shoulder met. It was still bruised slightly and she could see the dents where Lucian's fangs had sunken into her skin. The sight of the healed wound left her sick to her stomach and she fell forward into the counter while trying to support herself with her hands. Every ounce of strength she had was stripped out of her body and she was unable to erect herself. Lucy looked at her hands. They were the hands that had fought vampires, but now they could barely even support her. As she watched them, a tear fell onto the back of her hand and rolled down between her fingers. This sight somehow gave her the strength to stand again. In the mirror her face had gone red and both sides of it were wet with tears. They dripped off of her chin several times before she wiped her eyes with the back of her hand. Lucy could feel the scar left by Lucian's knife when she rubbed the remaining drops from the end of her chin. The disfigurements left by the vampire world hadn't been erased like she thought they would. Maybe it was her firm grip on the past that kept the scars from fading.

When she finally regained her composure, Lucy was able to step away from the sink and remove her clothes. Instead of throwing them on the floor, she skipped the formalities and tossed them directly into a small garbage can below the counter.

The water had become a perfect temperature and after removing the hair band from its place, she climbed into the shower. All the tension within her was immediately washed way, along with weeks of grime.

Lucy didn't know how long she had been in the shower, but even when every single body part had been cleaned, she stayed under the running water and just nearly let it drown her as she thought through the past few months.

Finally the water began to grow cold and Lucy was forced to turn the faucet off. She stepped out and used a large towel to dry off before wiping the mirror clean of fog. This reflection was far more appealing. She hadn't noticed before, but her features had changed since she had last looked in a mirror. They were sharper and her complexion wasn't as tan. Her cheeks were bright red, as if she was blushing. Her eyelashes seemed thicker and her lips had a rosy tint to them. It was almost as if she was wearing makeup right out of the shower. This was the strangest thing Lucy noticed about her appearance.

After shrugging off the strangeness in her reflection, Lucy brushed her hair and pulled it back into a ponytail. She used one of Syrina's many toothbrushes, something she had previously taken for granted, and then wrapped the towel around herself tightly before unlocking the door. As soon as she had assured herself the purple room was still empty, Lucy made her way to the only other unexplored door and she knew exactly what it was. She pulled it open and was pleased to find the largest closet that she had ever seen. Inside was a full assortment of underclothing, dresses, shoes, accessories, and so much more. All of the items were of different countries and ages. Lucy didn't know where to start.

Once a few minutes of shocked staring had gone by, she began at the dresses. There were some of all lengths and colors. Many of them were from obvious places like India and China, while others Lucy couldn't even begin to guess where they were from. It didn't take her long to choose a darker green dress that had a layered skirt and a halter top. It was light and flowing like chiffon and the most comfortable dress she had ever worn. The sundress fit like it had been made for her and instantly made her reluctant to try on anything else.

As she searched through the other items in the closet, Lucy chose a shade of nail polish to match her dress from a plethora of colors, and then proceeded to paint her fingers and toes. As they dried, she returned to the bathroom and searched through the cupboards in the back. Every beauty item that she could think of was stashed away inside. With a thankful smile, she took a curling iron and hair drier from the cabinet and stepped toward the mirror. For a while she focused on the task of drying and styling her hair. It felt good to be girly again. It was like the last few months hadn't happened.

In time, Lucy was happy with her hair and her nails had dried. She couldn't remember the last time that she had been able to relax and do the things that most girls enjoyed. When at last she finished and again looked into the mirror, Lucy saw that she had done well. She had thrown her curled hair up into a messy bun. When she was happy with her appearance, she returned the room to the way that she found it and then left to explore the rest of the house.

The plainly decorated hallway left much to be desired, and the other brightly colored doors didn't interest her. There were secrets to be discovered, but what she craved now was human contact.

Lucy followed the hallway back into the loft area and then down the steps into the living room. The fire continued to roll, but someone had stopped the smooth jazz. Lucy was again shocked by the sheer beauty of where she stood. No other place she had ever been could match the appeal, nor could she imagine that anywhere she would go in the future would. Before the striking splendor could paralyze her completely, she was able to venture into the kitchen. That room was just as beautiful as the one she had left. It was slightly rustic, and had high wooden beams that stretched the length of the room. There was a brick oven hidden in the corner across the way and the only lights in the room were hung high, which allowed them to give off only a hazy glow rather than brightness.

As she looked around, John came into the room. His clothes had changed too and his choice was more impractical. Lucy couldn't help but smile. He had obviously been raiding someone's closet. He still had a bowtie on, though it was a different one, but he also had on a waistcoat and a coat over it that had short tails. He now had trousers, but his feet were bare, just like hers. He was also wearing a top hat and he slid across the floor as if he was dancing. His smile was enchanting and, as he slid over to Lucy, he flipped his hat away with a quick snap. It landed only a few feet away, but Lucy didn't dare look. She was too focused on him.

John's advancement was subtle, but soon he had left only inches between them. Lucy didn't know what was happening. She could feel her heart speed up and chills fly over her arms. She didn't want to feel for him, but he was making it very difficult not to. At that moment she realized that Sebastian hadn't returned yet. When he said he would be gone for days she thought that it sounded like a joke, but maybe there had been some truth in the statement.

Lucy tried ignoring John, but when she looked away he used his finger to bring her chin back up so that their eyes could meet. His doe-eyed stare left her weak in the knees. John was perhaps the most handsome man she had ever met. Lucy wanted to love Sebastian more, but this unsupervised closeness was confusing and she was drowning in John.

Before he could get any closer, she did the hardest thing that she could think of and pushed away from him. Lucy made her way to the other side of the counter island and watched him as his posture straightened and he turned to face her, "Was it something I said?"

"You didn't say anything," Lucy managed the one thought that came to her lips.

"Then what did I do? Don't you trust me? " John smiled and rested his arms on the island.

Lucy could have tried to explain what she was feeling, but before she could, John interrupted with, "If you won't tell me then I guess I will have to convince you to trust me." His grin never left his face. John looked like Kieron when he smiled. They looked so much alike. The only large difference was that Kieron spoke with a deep accent. Otherwise, it was like the strange scientist was there with her.

While Lucy thought about the past, she watched John search the cupboards and then decide on a bottle of wine and two glasses. He read the label and nodded to approve of his choice before approaching her, "Will you join me?" Lucy didn't know whether to say yes or no, but she took his arm when he offered it to her and followed him willingly. John immediately knew where he wanted to go and proceeded to lead her outside. Lucy didn't know where they were going, but she soon found out.

They strolled around the side of the house until they got to the rocks. Then John stopped and handed her the wine and glasses before he leaped over the edge of the largest rock. Lucy's fear for his safety was quickly extinguished when his head popped back over the edge, and he asked for the items that he had given her. With a sigh, she handed him the bottle and glasses. She watched him set them aside and then he held his hands up to her. This sight was all too familiar, but despite her brain telling her how bad the idea was, Lucy leaped into his arms.

John caught her as if it was nothing and slowly lowered her to the grassy ground below. This closeness should have been as unappealing as before, but before pulling away, Lucy got caught up in his eyes again. They were so familiar and captivating. She got lost inside the deep pools of blue for a moment, before John cleared his throat and they parted. Lucy wondered how John knew that this little nook of grass was here, but she didn't ask. It was perfectly hidden away and simply marvelous.

There was a moment of awkwardness that soon disappeared when John popped the cork from the wine bottle and filled each glass halfway. He handed Lucy one of them and tapped his glass to hers before he took a sip. No words were said. She watched him stare out over the bay. So many things seemed to be going through his mind, but they were all hidden. He was able to keep all of his emotions tucked away. Lucy didn't know whether these were secrets that should worry her, or if she should be thankful that they were unknown. Whatever the answer, she was still tempted to know. Lucy tried her best to ignore his serenity, but then she saw something that caught her attention and made her forget about him for a moment.

The sun hadn't moved the entire time that they had been at

the house. It was still in the same position just behind the slightly taller mountains. The colors of sunset were still painted throughout the sky. Lucy knew that her beauty routine hadn't taken an entire day. Her gaze quickly moved from the odd sight of the sky to John's weird wardrobe. It struck her as silly, but in a good way. As she looked him over, he took another sip of his wine and Lucy noticed his watch. After a few seconds, she casually asked him for the time.

"It is a quarter of three in the afternoon," John replied before taking another sip. His odd way of answering the question didn't bother her as much as the answer itself.

"How is that possible?" she wondered aloud. John glanced over, but still acted as if he was a thousand miles away. When she finally made eye contact with him, he cleared his throat and began to explain.

"We are north of the Arctic Circle. This time of year, there is a summer solstice and a pleasant part of it is called Midnight Sun. The farther you are north the longer the sun remains present. In the winter, there is an excessive darkness that serves as the opposite of this constant light." John babbled through what he knew and then waited for Lucy to reply.

"You know an awful lot for someone your age." That response obviously wasn't what John was prepared for, but he took a deep breath and smiled.

"I can remember whatever I read. I've always been able to," he said as the pleased look on his face disappeared. "The winter months are cold, but they are rarely dark. The aurora borealis is a commonality during that time."

Lucy watched him as his eyes searched the orange-bathed mountains for anything out of the ordinary. He was happy. It was the first glimpse of happiness that Lucy had ever seen on his face, and it was so surprising that she didn't know how to proceed.

They sat in the never-changing scenery for a length of time that Lucy didn't bother counting. As far as she was concerned, time didn't have meaning here, and there wasn't a place for it. The day was at a standstill, and the only thing reassuring her that time was progressing normally was the rhythmic beating of waves below. The sea was free to move in and out just as it always had. It seemed to be the only thing here that was bound by the measure of time.

When John finished his glass of wine, he cleared his throat and set both the bottle and glass far in front of him. Lucy watched him out of the corner of her eye. She could tell that something was troubling him. There was something brewing within the limitless boundaries of his mind. Finally, his back straightened and he looked over to her. Lucy tried to make it seem that she hadn't been watching him and to her surprise he didn't mention it. She couldn't help but get lost in his gorgeous blue eyes again. They were shining like sapphires in the dim light.

"Do you ever think about being a vampire?" His question hit her like a ton of bricks. She didn't want to admit thinking of the consequences of her father's actions. Lucy feared what she could become. She was already afraid of what she was, but he couldn't have known that.

"I've thought about it," Lucy admitted to both him and herself.

"So have I," John sighed and began to pull at the grass between his knees. Suddenly, alarms went off in Lucy's head and she could feel her face grow red. She didn't know if the comment was meant to be positive or negative.

"You're afraid of me too." Lucy was sure of this, but when she said it John's head snapped in her direction and their eyes met.

"No! That has never crossed my mind! Lucy, I've fallen in love with you." As he revealed what had been bothering him, John took her hand and held it tightly. The confession was so unexpected that Lucy didn't have any words to say at first. She spent the next several seconds searching his eyes for any lie that may have been hiding. John didn't let much time go by before he tried to explain.

"I have never loved anyone as much as I love you. It is wrong to say this without Sebastian's knowledge, but I thought that you should know. For me it was immediate. After that day on the street when you tried to steal my car, I found that I couldn't concentrate anymore. All that I thought about was you. My teaching abilities suffered and I couldn't eat or sleep. Then you showed up in front of my house and I knew then that I would follow you to the ends of the Earth even if it meant that we could never be together." It seemed that John meant every word he said. It took time for her to process the confession and even after she understood what he was saying, Lucy couldn't look him in the face.

So many questions drifted through her thoughts that she was unable to rest on just one of them. She tried her hardest to see his point of view and admit to herself that she felt the same way, but buried in her was the realization that if she were to love John, Sebastian might no longer be in her life. This was something that paused any of her feelings toward him. She wouldn't give up Sebastian for anything in the world.

"There you are," shouted a familiar voice. Almost immediately, they both looked up to see Sebastian's smiling face. He looked over the situation and then grinned, "Are you stuck?"

"Nope, it is just a nice spot." John laughed through his disappointment before Sebastian disappeared behind the rock. As soon as Lucy had gotten over the shock of seeing his face, she realized that she was still holding John's hand and instantly released it. Without a word, she stood and proceeded to climb back to the top of the cliff. When she had almost gotten to the top, one of the rocks she was using as a footrest suddenly gave way and in a panic she hugged the wall as hard as she could. When the alarm of a potential fall faded she realized that John had kept her from falling with a hand pressed firmly to her butt. She didn't know if the site of his actions was on purpose or accidental, but instead of confronting him, she allowed him to push her to the top.

"Sorry about that. I just didn't want you to fall. It was an accident," he immediately explained when they had both gotten to the house. John opened the door with an apologetic grin and offered Lucy the chance to go ahead of him. This act of courtesy was lost amidst the embarrassing situation. Lucy simply brushed the dirt from her clothes and went inside without a word.

As they entered the kitchen, John placed the bottle of wine and glasses on the counter before sitting at one of the stools next to the countertop.

Sebastian was almost throwing his groceries to where they belonged. There wasn't anything gentle about the way he handled his purchases. Lucy wanted to ask him what was the matter, but John stopped her before she could get the first word out. A simple hand gesture was all that he made, but it was enough to get her attention. Then he completed the conversation with an expression that explained more than what his hand had. John was kind enough to save Lucy from an impending fight. It was the strangest wordless chat that she had ever been a part of, but she soon retired to Syrina's bedroom. The last thing she needed was a reason to choose John over Sebastian.

The bedroom was just as she had left it...immaculate. The palate of sunset hues shown through the window and lit the room beautifully. She was able to put the mess of relationships from her mind for a while and focus on other things. Lucy explored more of Syrina's closet, and then turned to a selection of literature. The wall opposite her bed was hidden by a large bookshelf that had been filled with hundreds of books. Many were old and worn from reading, but there were some new selections that had been added recently. Syrina had obviously visited this place more often than the others and was able to add to her collection. Several of the titles and covers depicted stories that involved either vampires or werewolves. Some of them even told stories about both.

For a while Lucy took the time to flip through several of the newer books. She was surprised to find whole sections of the werewolf ones marked in red ink. Many of the books had pages torn out and there even appeared to be blood stains in one of them. These findings were both shocking and illuminating. Lucy was able to see what Syrina did to occupy her years, but the question of why certainly stuck to every finding. Why would she do this? Lucy soon discovered that the literature involving vampires carried some of the same marks, but the reasons for them were baffling.

As she read through some of the harsh words that had been written, Lucy began to notice a couple of loud voices coming from downstairs. John and Sebastian were arguing over something that Lucy couldn't hear. She tried her best to make sense of what they were saying, but the floor muffled most of it. Lucy even tried to stop breathing, but it was no use. As quietly as she could, she placed the book in her hand on the floor and stood up. She snuck into the hallway and made her way to the top of the stairs. Lucy let her breath out slowly before she crouched behind the banister and eavesdropped on their argument. The emotion coming from the room was powerful, yet still minimal.

"It isn't something that you can plan," John tried to convince Sebastian of something, but he wasn't cooperating.

"I don't care what you think. I invited you along with the confidence that you wouldn't betray me. Especially like this." Lucy wasn't even in the room and she could feel how tense the atmosphere was. She imagined that Sebastian never blew up like this

"Think about things from my perspective. I thought this was what you wanted," John explained cautiously, hoping that Sebastian wouldn't lash out again. Instead he snickered.

"I never wanted this. I only expected it. That's what makes this hard. I had always feared that my life would come to this," Sebastian forced himself to stay calm. Lucy could hear the restraint in his voice.

"Come on now. You have an amazing life."

Lucy could hear the smile in John's voice as he tried his best to cheer up Sebastian. Their conversation had yet to make sense, but she hoped that it would soon.

"No. No, I don't," Sebastian sighed as he attempted to explain. "You see, to have a complete life, to have an amazing life, you must find that one person that you love more than anything in the world. Now I've found that one person, but she will grow old while I stay young. She will die and I will live. It's just…"

Lucy heard him pause and she wanted more than anything to run into the kitchen to console him. She knew that he was talking about her, and until now she had failed to notice the tears dripping off her chin. A knot formed in the back of her throat that she couldn't swallow. It hurt to breathe. She waited for him to finish his thought. It seemed like hours before he finally spoke again.

"My life is nice. My life is good, but it's just that one part of it that isn't fair. It's not fair to have the one you love so close and then have them ripped away from you…it's just not fair." Sebastian's voice trailed off then, but Lucy had heard all that she needed to.

Up until this point, she had been in complete denial about their age difference. In her mind he was her age, but in reality he was an old man in a mask. At that point she regretted every choice that she had made. Every decision that brought them closer together had been a mistake. It was her fault that Sebastian felt this way. She loved him, and in turn made him fall in love with her. Reason should have stopped her. There should have been a point where the relationship stayed platonic and went no further. It hadn't, though, and now she would have to live with the guilt of hurting the one person in her life who mattered most.

The chatter in the kitchen had now become quiet enough that snooping was impossible. Even if she could still hear them, the thought of listening to any more made her sick. As quietly as she could, Lucy crept back up to Syrina's bedroom and watched the world outside grow slightly darker.

The sun had dipped a little bit lower this time, but it never left her sight. The golden colors grew stronger in the low light. Lucy inspected the shadow of the waves as they licked the sandy beach and the bottom of the seaplane below. The sounds were completely comforting and soothed Lucy into a state of relaxation.

As she scanned the ground below, something caught her eye. It was only a shadow, but it was the shadow of a man. Curiosity struck, and she immediately left the room and made her way downstairs.

When she reached the first floor, Lucy noticed that both of the men were still in the kitchen. Then something tapped at the door. In no time at all Sebastian and John were at her side.

"It was the shadow of a man," Lucy told them as they approached the door.

"It must be Cyrus. Mitchell doesn't know where this place is," Sebastian whispered. Lucy's heart jumped when he mentioned her uncle's name. She hoped more than anything that he would be on the other side of the door. The wait was almost too much to bear. Finally, John took the door knob and pulled the door from its lock. Lucy peered hopefully out into the dim light, but the face that appeared wasn't the one she had hoped for.

A serious-faced Charles stood in the doorway. He didn't make eye contact at first, and it was this fact that kept Sebastian from attacking him, although he was prepared to. Charles took a few moments for the shock of his appearance to filter out before he decided to speak. "I am sorry to interrupt your evening like this." His striking green eyes glowed in the dim sunset light.

"Why are you here?" Sebastian wasn't interested in formalities. Lucy could tell that he was seconds from killing Charles and all that he needed was the right motive. Any negative glances or awkward movements and Sebastian was prepared to tear his heart out. Charles must have known this because he remained as neutral as possible.

Lucy grabbed a hand full of Sebastian's shirt and held it tightly.

She made sure to keep this from the sight of the vampire at the door.

"I have always been kind to you wolves," Charles began as Sebastian growled at him, "and I have no intention of changing that." As the words sank in, Lucy felt Sebastian relax slightly and she felt inclined to release him.

The men looked at each other and then John decided to speak, "Why are you here?"

"I have been sent by Ella to relay a message to you. She has been traveling for a fortnight and wishes to rest before coming here. She will bring a horde of vampires with her and you are not to resist or flee. These actions will result in the deaths of yourselves and several other wolves that you have met recently. Willingness to give up the Envy will result in a pleasant ending for all parties. Ella will arrive tomorrow evening." Charles made the instructions clear before he nodded and turned to leave.

"That's it then?" Sebastian shouted after him. "Is that all that you have to say to me? This is betrayal, Charlie! I should kill you where you stand." His voice was heavy with emotion, which might have been the reason that Charles returned. He came back to the door and smiled down at Lucy before glaring at Sebastian.

"I never stopped being your friend. Eodin has betrayed us all and he has given mental control over to the Forsaken. I cannot control my actions anymore. Before this damned zephyr war began, it was never like this. Brother against brother—that is the new way. That is where we stand." He frowned and scuffed his foot across the dirt.

"That is how it will end," John added as he stepped to the side and guided Lucy in. Sebastian didn't talk with him any longer. He watched until Charles's shadow had gone before he closed and locked the door. The three of them gathered in the living room.

Together they kept a time of silent thought. Lucy could feel both of the men as they combed through each emotion that was possible. After a while their constant changing made her ill. It was like being on a spinning carnival ride, which was reminiscent of the day this whole thing started.

In time, they moved over to the couch. The three of them reclined apart from each other and watched the fire sparkle below the mantle. Lucy didn't know how long they sat in silence. She could see the dim light grow slightly brighter, via the large window behind them. When visibility was finally decent, Lucy stood to go into the kitchen, but before she got there someone knocked at the door.

Both men were immediately alert, and Lucy shot them a glance before she headed toward the door. Sebastian and John didn't join her this time, though she could tell that they were both anxious to do so. With a shaking hand, she took hold of the doorknob and turned it, expecting to see another unpleasant sight. Her heart raced uncontrollably as the door swung inward, but it was quickly consoled when the man on the other side turned to face her. His smile instantly melted all of her worries and she leaped outside to hug him. Her uncle's deep-throated chuckle echoed through his chest as he squeezed her back.

Sebastian and John were suddenly at the door and the greetings began. They exchanged handshakes and hugs. John was introduced and immediately accepted as a brother. Not long after Cyrus arrived, a few other people came to the door. Lucy was relieved that her extended family had been reunited. Syrina and Mitchell followed Allegra inside and they shut the door. It was then that she realized Kieron wasn't with them. He would never be again.

It was obvious that Syrina still felt the tragedy as if it had just happened. She greeted everyone with a smile, but was still distant. Her mind hadn't left the day that they had fled the woods. She continued to struggle with Kieron's decision to stay behind, and it was clear that she wished that she could have saved him. Lucy remained aware of her feelings and tried not to pry, but Syrina wasn't even trying to hide how she felt. It was very distracting.

When the pleasant reunion had finished, the new arrivals dispersed throughout the house to eat, sleep, and change clothes. Lucy waited several minutes before she made her way up the stairs and to the end of the hallway. She stood outside the purple-colored door and waited nearly five minutes before knocking. It was another couple of minutes before Syrina answered. She didn't say a word when she opened the door, but stepped aside and allowed Lucy to pass into the room.

"I see you made use of my closet," Syrina stated with a nearly invisible grin. Lucy nodded and hoped that she wouldn't be angry.

"That dress looks good on you. I got that from a girl that I became friends with in Scotland. She was a good friend of mine in the late 1800s. I stayed at her farm for years until I didn't age and she puzzled together what I was. I had it on when she chased me from the premises." Syrina smiled as she reminisced.

Unsure why she was telling her the story, Lucy had begun to take the dress off, but Syrina stopped her.

"It looks good on you. I didn't mean that you couldn't wear it," she smiled and entered the bathroom.

"I assumed that it had sentimental value with a story like that," Lucy almost yelled after her as she pulled the straps back up and tied them around her neck.

"Sweetie, every scrap of clothing in my closet has a story like that," Syrina said as she laughed. "And I don't think any of them ended particularly well."

"Sorry to hear that," was all that Lucy could think to say.

"Don't be sorry. I'm not saddened by any of the memories in my past. I'm glad to have met all of the people, and am disappointed that the truth of who I really am affected them negatively. Such is this way of life," she revealed as she reentered the room and snagged a granola bar from its hiding place under her pillow. As she scarfed it down, Lucy felt herself compelled to ask how she was doing since Kieron's death, but she didn't know how to. After thinking through how to get past the impending awkwardness, Syrina spoke again, "I miss him, you know."

"I know," Lucy admitted as she joined Syrina sitting on the floor next to the bed.

"Kieron," as Syrina spoke his name Lucy could tell that she was trying her best not to burst into tears. "I cannot lose any more loved ones. My heart can't take it."

"You won't lose anyone else," Lucy tried to be helpful, but Syrina didn't accept her words.

"It is very wrong for you to assume that. Tomorrow Ella will come for you and my family will fight them. It is a war that we can't win. I suppose it is for the best though," Syrina shrugged and finished her granola bar.

"I didn't realize that you knew about that," Lucy said.

"Ella followed us here. We tried our best to keep her away, but Cyrus assumed that she would be able to find you eventually. Then we saw Charles leaving the house. It took only seconds to put two and two together. He delivered a decree of impending attack," Syrina revealed as the messy bookshelf caught her eye.

"Were you reading those?"

The question was simple and Lucy didn't have an answer right away. She had to think about it. After a few seconds, she seemed to be able to only get out one word: "Yes."

"I bet you're wondering about all of the red ink, then." Syrina smiled as she walked over and picked up the top book of a small stack. She looked through it silently for a moment and then waved it in the air as she explained why they had all been written in.

"I don't sleep much. This is a good way to take up time." She smiled again and tossed the book into Lucy's lap before picking up a second one. "Along with clothes, I collect these books also. They all depict either vampires, werewolves, or something like them. The red marks are falsified facts. There are a lot of them." She laughed before snatching the book from Lucy's hand and throwing them both into the stack to knock it over.

This sudden expression of anger was surprising, but Lucy wasn't afraid. She watched the fury consume her friend and then disappear, which left her trembling. She stared warily for a few seconds and then stood, but before she could comfort Syrina, someone knocked at the door. The sound immediately took hold of all of their senses. It was like a shock had gone through the room.

"It's me," rang a familiar voice. Syrina was quick to answer the door.

When the hallway was revealed, Mitchell's battle-scarred face appeared and forced a hesitant smile before entering the room. Lucy looked him over and was remorseful when it came to the shining marks on his face. She remembered that he had sustained severe blows. They had now become shining disfigurements that would be a constant reminder of what he had sacrificed for her safety. Before he said a word, Mitchell felt it necessary to give Lucy another hug. It was a long embrace, but at this point in time, she would take as much human-like contact as she could get. She didn't see them as wolves anymore. No matter how different their ages and parentage, these "people" were her family and she was unable to notice what was hidden from sight.

Though he was a little more rugged-looking now, Lucy still saw the young man from before. Mitchell's hair had gotten longer and he needed a quick shave to trim up his rough appearance. However, his smell was the same. Lucy couldn't explain it even to herself, but Mitchell had a familiar odor that gave her chills.

Finally she was brought back from her musings when Syrina took her hand and pulled her out into the hallway. Mitchell followed them and closed the door behind him. When Syrina let go, Lucy was made to follow her out into the recreation room and then down to the living room. She could hear the fire crackling beneath the mantle and was shocked to see the entire family gathered around the flames. They all looked over when she arrived. Immediately she knew that something had been discussed and a decision was going to be made.

Cyrus was the first to approach, when Mitchell and Syrina left her side to join the group. He gave a quick smile as he placed his hand on her shoulder and led her to the middle of the room. Lucy had never felt her heart beat so fast. She wasn't afraid of them, but their verdict on this senseless situation would decide how her life would proceed. She could tell that Syrina was already on edge.

"Lucy, the three of us have examined the circumstances and have argued over what course of action to take," Cyrus began, indicating that he had been talking with both Allegra and Sebastian. "We all have different solutions."

"We can either run, surrender, or fight. It is your choice," Sebastian divulged as he stepped forward. Lucy didn't need to think about it for long. She remembered all of the lives that were sacrificed because of her and all of the unnecessary running they were forced into. Everything she had put her family through made her sick to her stomach. She made the decision quickly.

"Surrender," Lucy said quietly as she tried to restrain herself from crying. Everyone in the room immediately had dumbfounded looks of shock on their faces.

"Why Lucy? We can protect you," Mitchell was quick to object.

"No. We've been at this for too long and I won't let them hurt anyone else. It's time to take a step toward your safety and stop worrying about mine. I hope you understand. I couldn't bear it if you lost someone else, and it was my fault," she admitted before anyone could defy her logic. "Tomorrow I will go with Ella and see my father again. They can't turn me if I concentrate hard enough, right?"

"I don't know about that. Lucian was one thing, but there are older and more powerful vampires out there," Syrina said with a frown and Sebastian winced under the mention of his deceased brother's name.

"You won't change my mind. It's done," Lucy growled and wrapped her arms around him. As they hugged, she could feel that John was losing control of his jealousy, so to avoid a fight, she released Sebastian and returned to the center of the room.

"You've all been like family to me and I love each one of you. Tomorrow will be a bad day, but I promise that the next day will be a relief to everyone." Lucy was uncertain if she was convincing enough. Inside she didn't know what she was doing.

She stayed with the family for the rest of the night. All conversation had died with Lucy's decision so she was blessed to be able to watch the midnight sun set the scenery aglow. The long window gave her the ability to see both the sea and the sky, along with the mountains covered in purple and white orchids. The sight was incredible, but it left Lucy with the realization that tomorrow her life would change for the worse, and she would no longer see her family or be with either of the men she loved.

 Chapter Fifteen

Glances were thrown, but nothing was said as the daylight hours crept in. Lucy could feel tension from each person in the room, and she wished that the reality from a month ago could have been the present now. She had never thought of herself as selfish, but now the only thing on her mind was every man for himself. Her heart was the only thing that kept her in place. She knew what would happen if she ran or asked them to fight. It was a battle that couldn't be won, even by the skills of the wolf pack.

Lucy watched the clock above the mantle as it ticked. She wished that time would move more slowly, even though the mood throughout the room wasn't pleasant. It reminded her of times that she wasted, and people that she missed. Significant moments in her past bubbled to the surface and she fondly reminisced through what she could no longer have.

Finally the clock chimed. It was nine o'clock now, and Lucy began to smell strange scents in the room. The vampires had arrived, and their odor was slipping through every crack that it could find. It seemed determined to ignite a rage within her and was succeeding. Lucy found herself growing angry, but she quickly put a stop to it. Getting mad wouldn't help anything.

As she scanned through the outside world, Lucy felt the presence of at least thirty vampires. Each of them popped into her mind as a dim light, as opposed to the ghostly white appearance of normal life. Lucy tried her best to focus on one of them, but when she tried, a more powerful form interrupted the connection and prevented any further exploration.

Gradually the wolves picked up on the odors in the room and they gathered at the door to face their enemy together. Cyrus took a moment to look behind him and into the eyes of each of his family members before turning the knob and opening the door.

The gorgeous sight of the midnight sun could no longer hide the tragedy that the day had brought. The long deck hid the group of vampires until they had gotten to the railing. There were about thirty of them, just as Lucy had thought. The dim light of their existence made her understand what they were facing. These creatures weren't human at all. The disease that made them vampires had stolen their humanity. The venom was a living creature that used their bodies like puppets. It didn't feel or have remorse. They played host to it, a terror that made them monsters.

After all that Lucy had seen, she decided what the truth really was. The wolves were superior in this fight because they were still human and hadn't succumbed to the power of the sickness that plagued them. They had overcome what the vampires could not. With regard to the past few months, Lucy was sure of many things. She was sure that she couldn't resist the vampires forever. She knew that love came in several different forms and she knew what true sacrifice was. The people around her had taught her more than she could ever hope to know and now it was her turn to help them.

Looking down to the beach, Lucy saw Ella immediately. She wore a blood-red dress that was caked with sand at the bottom. Her long hair was still in the wind and her green eyes glistened without need of light. She was the essence of power. At her side stood Charles and then another man was there. Eodin remained a man of mystery and power, but he had lost every shred of confidence. His smug nature was missing. He had given all power to Ella, and in losing his power, he also lost strength. He was different now. The vicious and maniacal man who had once terrorized her life was now broken into half the leader he had been. Though she still remembered the negativity that he had instilled in her life, Lucy felt sorry for him and for what he had become.

Lucy followed her family to the beach and they were surrounded heavily as they approached the lady of the Forsaken. She didn't seem surprised by this and confidently stood to the front of her followers as if she was threatened by nothing.

"Why do you still protect her? This fight is over and you have lost. Give her to us and you shall live. Protect her and I make no promises." Ella spoke in a creepy, but cheerful way.

"You have no power over us. We will dispose of you just as we defeated those you've sent after us before," Sebastian growled. Ella didn't seem fazed, but before she could say another word Eodin stepped forward.

"You destroyed my family! Eliza was so young and had such promise, but you don't see that. Monsters, all of you! I pray that you fall and that we cause the same pain that you have caused us."

At this point Ella held up her hand to stop him. Though he obviously had more to say, Eodin stopped and returned to his place in the formation.

"Now then, will she be joining us or will we be taking her?" Ella's words sent chills over Lucy's arms.

She began to step forward, but Syrina took her hand and stopped her. Lucy was confused for only moments before Cyrus spoke up, "You could never take her from us."

"Oh, I would beg to differ." Her voice had grown sharper. "Though you may be protected from the charms of my mind, her heritage is of my blood and cannot grant the same courtesy."

It didn't take long for Lucy to begin feeling light-headed. Then came a sharp pain as if someone was stabbing at her brain. She could barely find the strength to remain standing at first, but after a few more moments, Lucy was forced to her knees. In less than a second, Cyrus was at her side, but no one else was. She didn't have to look for them, though. The sounds of battle were quite clear. They must have tried to stop her, but Ella had brought the other vampires for a reason.

Though Cyrus was trying to encourage strength, Lucy couldn't find it. The pain that Ella was inflicting was unmatched by anything she had felt before. The stinging agony trickled down her arms and legs in rivers of torture that Ella seemed perfectly happy to inflict. Lucy suffered a migraine of epic proportions that crippled everything else and forced her into a ball on the ground. Cyrus hurried to hold her close and whisper words of comfort, but Lucy couldn't concentrate on them. She fought against the pain with all her might and then did something that she never thought she could do.

With a deep breath she briefly sacrificed her sense of sight to empower her sense of hearing. At that moment, Cyrus's words became clear as a bell and the visions of battle and her uncle's face became blacker than night.

"Lucy, long ago I told you that you are special and strong. Neither of these truths have ever let you down. It is right that you are not a wolf, but that doesn't mean that you can't fight her. Focus and push her out of your mind. You are an Envy and that means that you are stronger than she could ever be. Force her out."

His words continued after that, but Lucy stopped listening. Could she really do that? Was she strong enough to win a mind battle with someone who was centuries older than she?

After taking another deep breath, Lucy began to push, but not just with her mental strength, but with something else too. She gathered happiness and every scrap of joy that she could think of. These may not have helped against Ella, but the delight taken from the past made Lucy feel powerful. She remembered her grandmother, Rae, and Tryp, Sebastian and his family, even her father. In her mind she was able to create a wall of happiness, which kept Ella at bay for a few moments.

Immediately, Lucy sensed that this wall was confusing to the lady vampire. She might not have seen this before. Hesitant, Ella probed the invisible wall carefully as if she was intimidated by it. When she had finally discovered what had created this wall and what was sustaining it, Lucy felt the pressure return for a second time, but this time in anger. She felt Ella push harder than she thought possible. The wall held up for a time, but Ella forced her way through it, leaving nothing to protect Lucy's mind. She could feel her body begin to shake as her hearing faded into nothing. Both blind and deaf, she could do nothing but focus on what was happening within her thoughts.

Ella was there, mocking the defeat of her enemy. Lucy could see her grin and it was infuriating. Finally, the vampire ceased her arrogance and proceeded to take control of Lucy's mind. She could feel it. She could feel Ella envelop everything with thoughts of anger and vengeance. Lucy began to lose memories of her past and was only able to feel what Ella allowed her to feel.

The last thing she was able to hold onto were the words that Cyrus had given to her. He told her that she was special and that she was strong, but not once did she believe it. Lucy saw herself weak and helpless. She constantly needed to be saved by others like a distressed damsel, but now there wasn't anyone to save her. What is someone to do when there is no one left to save them? The question was to herself, but Ella felt the need to answer it.

"They must give in. There is no place for weakness in this world," her answer hissed through the dark recesses of Lucy's mind. She didn't believe that and couldn't as long as a piece of her was still able to resist Ella's attack. There was an answer to the question now. Lucy was sure of it. When there is no one left to save you...you must save yourself.

The revelation was instant. Lucy's memories returned in waves of happiness that flooded every edge of darkness with light. She felt her body stop shaking and finally her blurry vision returned. Cyrus hadn't moved. He was holding her tight and was still talking, but Lucy couldn't tell exactly what he was saying.

With control reestablished, Lucy began to push Ella clear of her mind. With her newfound confidence, it became easy to force her out. In seconds, Lucy had pushed her to the very edge of her memory and then with one final shove, Ella was gone. She was relieved, but now there was something else there. She pushed even farther and was suddenly confronted with many lights. They were dull and misshapen. It was then she realized what she was looking at. They were minds. Lucy was inside Ella's mind and looking out over every mind that Ella's was connected to. The sea of lights in front of her were the minds of every vampire in existence. It seemed impossible.

Suddenly her vision cleared and she was able to see both the inside of Ella's mind and Cyrus's desperate face. He helped her to her feet and kept her steady as she walked forward. Lucy could see the battle as it raged on. She watched her family fight for her and she watched as they struggled under the hands of her enemies. She felt her heart breaking and at that moment, Lucy knew she would be the one to stop it. She chose one of the lights in her mind and began to squeeze it. She watched the horde of people in view and noticed that when she held the light tightly, one of the vampire men fell to the ground, writhing in pain. Intrigued, she held it tighter and he appeared to seize. Finally she extinguished the light and the man went still. His light was gone and he was dead.

Lucy was surprised at how easy this was. Destroying these lights was as simple as snuffing a candle. She tried it once more with two of the vampires that were attacking John. The same series of events plagued them and soon they too were dead. At this point, the fighting had stopped and everyone was watching Lucy and Cyrus.

In one final experiment, Lucy reached out to every light that she could see. All at once, every vampire on the beach fell to the ground writhing in pain like the three before them. Lucy watched them and was displeased with the power that she had. It was wrong, but how could she not take advantage of this strength. She knew that had this opportunity been given to them, the vampires would use it to torture and then kill their enemies.

"Lucy, what are you doing?" Cyrus's voice was calm and clear.

"I can end them," was all that Lucy could say. She was shocked by the sound of her own voice. It was eerie and monotonous.

"All right, but before you do, look at them," he pleaded. The request was odd, but she did as he asked and looked out over the crowd. Every vampire was writhing and crying as they squirmed on the ground under the pain she caused. She looked over to Eodin. He was face down in the dirt and breathing heavily. She shifted her gaze to Ella. Her face was wet with tears and rather than being concerned with her own well-being, she was begging for the lives of her people. This was a new sight. Lucy never expected to see Ella begging for anything, let alone the lives of others.

"Cyrus, I can't make this choice."

"What do you mean?" her uncle's question made her skin crawl.

"I can see them all," her monotone voice explained, "every vampire. I see the lights of the royals and those overseas. I can end all of them and save so many lives, but somehow I cannot make the decision to do so." It was so confusing. Power of this magnitude should have been easy to use, but Lucy was unsure of how to use it. Cyrus took a moment to think and then took hold of her hand and spoke very quietly under the pleas of his enemies.

"Power is an awful thing in the hands of the weak. Lucy you are very strong. Stronger than I thought. You can choose, but be wary of the consequences. Their species, an entire species, will be gone. Your father will be gone. All vampires that choose to not feed on humans will die. You may be ending the existence of good people. In the end it will always be your choice." Though he spoke of choices, it was clear what needed to be done. Lucy squeezed back on his hand as her eyelids fluttered, releasing whatever hold she had over her enemies and those that she had never met.

When her senses finally became normal again, she came to realize that her face was wet with tears and her skin had gone cold and clammy. She looked over to Cyrus. His face was happy and proud as he hugged her. The relief of the moment was short and Lucy watched as her uncle turned his attention to the vampires. They were stunned by the ordeal and were gradually returning to the reality of the situation.

"Hear me!" Cyrus commanded their attention. "It would be wise to flee. This is over. Relay to your father that pursuing Lucy is no longer your place. She will be free of you, as will my brother. None of your kind is to set foot on this beach again. Now go."

Ella was quick to rally her troops and send them back over the mountains. As they left, she turned around only once and nodded in Lucy's direction. The wolves gathered and celebrated shortly. They were all impressed with Lucy's capabilities, and decided that they would be partying into the night on the high that came with this particular win. John was the only one who asked about Ella's strange behavior. Lucy grinned and was quick to say that she had warned the vampire not to pursue her family any more or there would be hell to pay.

It was a relief to know that vampires would no longer be a part of her life. The faceless strangers from months ago were now a vanquished enemy. Lucy had avenged the deaths of her loved ones and had become the weapon that she was destined to be. She looked back over her shoulder at the bloody sand and decaying vampires.

Lucy nearly cried at the relief she felt. Coming away from the battlefield with all of her family was a miracle that she wasn't going to forget. She loved them all so much that it would be impossible to lose anyone.

As she watched the last of the vampires disappear over the mountain, Lucy realized that it was time to let go of the lights of life. She could see them clearly even though the creatures that owned them were gone. It was time to move on and she would finally have her mind to herself again. It was a relief to be free of them, but a sudden pain took hold of her and she nearly collapsed. Luckily, the torment of pain was quick and Lucy gasped for breath as it disappeared.

Suddenly, the pain was followed by a time of clarity. Lucy was able to think logically and without distraction. She wouldn't have to fear the return of her enemies anymore. Their shadows wouldn't be a constant reminder of loss and Lucy could now live on with the knowledge that vampires would never threaten her or the people she loved ever again. She could live in peace, and live well.

Epilogue

Author's Note: As a reader, in most cases, I've wondered what happens to the characters of my favorite books when the last chapter is over, and there have been times that I have been unsatisfied in creating 'my own' ending. I want to know where the author would take the characters I've fallen in love with. As an author, I wanted to solve this uncertainty and tell you where I saw my characters after the events in "The Zephyr Gene." This part will be told from Sebastian's perspective.

Death is unpredictable, and completely unfair in most cases. None of us can see it coming, and we never seem to realize its merciless nature. Humans are a vulnerable race and many times they forget that, but I have seen other races become just as vulnerable. I never imagined that death would have such an impact on my life. When I was young, it hunted me with an eagerness that made me ill. Everywhere I went the people around me died; often times by my own hand. My life was never easy, even after I gained control of my instincts. I never knew that I could love someone so completely or that a chance for normality was within reach. Then again, where is the fun in being normal?

My name is Sebastian Balenescu. I was born in Romania as a zephyr, and became a werewolf when I turned seventeen. My older brother was made a vampire several years later. The rest of my family was human. He killed them. I traveled throughout Asia and settled in England for many years, but no matter where I went Lucian always found me and ruined whatever positivity there was in my life. He made sure that my friends knew what I was and then he would hunt them down.

After years of this, I met Cyrus and he put a stop to the torture that my brother enjoyed putting me through. Cyrus brought me to Switzerland with him and he was made alpha of a pack in the mountains there. We spent a great deal of time building and overseeing the success of that pack. He allowed another wolf to take his place as alpha and we moved several more times. Before finally settling in Ohio, we gained Kieron, Syrina, and Allegra. Mitchell joined us later. I never imagined that I would have a family that amazing. My entire life changed when I met them, and it didn't change again until the day that Lucian came to Ohio.

He hadn't come for me this time, which struck me as odd. I then discovered that he had joined a dangerous coven and that they were pursuing a specific human. Not only were they hunting her, but they were stalking her, which is not the vampire way. We monitored the coven for weeks before hearing whispers of a possible abduction. The night that I was sent to prevent it changed my life forever.

Everything that has happened since that day has led me here and to this place. I was always coming here. There was no way around it. There were whispers of different scents under my nose and hidden in the breeze. They all told me the same thing. I was close; close to her. Only a single deep breath was needed to point me in the right direction...so I took one. A slight step to the left would lead me where I needed to go.

The concept of instinct was the most appealing wolf characteristic to me. I always seemed to know where to go. Though following her scent was amusing, it wasn't always necessary. I knew exactly where she was.

It had finally gotten to be autumn again in Pennsylvania. The trees were beautiful and the falling leaves crunched under my feet. Suddenly, I stumbled upon the path that I was looking for. There was no need to wander around following a scent anymore. This path would lead me right to her. I began to think about what I would say when I saw her again. There would likely be nothing pleasant about my visit, but I simply needed to see her.

After another fifteen minutes of walking, my destination finally came into view. Hidden under a canopy of orange leaves sat a small cabin. It was a charming and peaceful house that had been nestled comfortably into the woods. Though I wanted to walk up and knock on the door, I made my way to one of the perimeter trees and stood behind it to watch the goings on.

Two men were working in the front of the house. They were of different ages, but both lived there. Gradually I came to realize that the man chopping wood was actually John Smits. This oddly brought a grin to my face. He had adapted well to life away from civilization. In some ways I was quite proud of him. The young and brilliant boy I had once known had grown into a man and as cliché as that sounds, it was absolutely true.

It took me a moment to recognize the man with him. After all, I had only seen pictures of him before. Craig Gaskin had been freed from the Forsaken's control and though his green eyes and sharp features revealed what he truly was, I could see that he was no more a monster than I.

The men chatted casually while John chopped several logs into smaller wedges. I soon grew bored with their conversation. It was nothing that concerned me. I tried to remain focused on my reason for being there, but as I watched the men laugh at a joke that I couldn't make out, someone behind me cleared their throat. I spun on my toes quickly and was ready to fight, but the gaze that met mine left me frozen.

Lucy radiated beauty just as she did the last time we were together. The same day that I told her the realities of a love like ours. It was the most difficult thing I had ever done. I looked into the eyes of the woman I loved and told her the most foul lie that had ever left my lips. The words I don't love you have haunted me since that day. In retrospect, I did what was best for both of us. John would make her a better life. I would've only been able to watch her wither and be unable to console her when she finally realized the impossibility of our love

Rage was the first emotion Lucy went to and she had every right to do so. I could see the anger in her face and she was fighting the urge to act on it. I wouldn't have stopped her if she did. I deserved whatever punishment she saw fit.

"Why are you here?" Her angelic voice was filled with hatred, but I still found it equivalent with a symphony.

"I came to say goodbye." It was the truth, but it wasn't what she wanted to hear. I watched her fight every hostility before she calmed herself and sighed.

"We've said goodbye. I don't want you here." Those words killed me inside, but I pressed on. She needed to know what I was going to tell her.

"I lied to you."

"Yes, I know." How I had missed those snarky retaliations.

"Several times."

"And?"

It was now or never. If I didn't say it now, I don't think that she would give me this chance again. "I am much older than seventy-six."

Lucy didn't speak for a minute. She was processing the information. It was like I could see the wheels turning in her head. Finally, she repeated my statement and then added, "How old are you?" I knew that this would be a shock, but I only had this one opportunity.

"I am three hundred and sixteen." The alarm of the high number was short as a familiar look of curiosity struck her face. "You don't look that old. I heard that the ratio of wolf to human years was one hundred to one. Was that a lie too?"

"No, of course not! That applies to most of us, but there are a lucky few with a gene that nearly pauses our aging. Syrina's like this too. She once told me that she is almost nine hundred years old." Though I tried to lighten the mood, Lucy wasn't about to give up on her resentment.

"Is that all?" Her being angry with me would make this part of goodbye even worse than I could have ever imagined.

"There is one more piece you need to know. Syrina and I have been offered an alpha position in Switzerland. I was there with Cyrus once and now they are having some vampire trouble. It will be a good change for both her and me. After today you won't be seeing me again." I could see that she was in denial, but I didn't try comforting her. There was a slight pause before Lucy straightened herself and stepped forward. I was honestly expecting something painful, but to my surprise she wrapped her arms around my waist and squeezed me tightly. As startling as this was, I hugged her back. How I had missed her. Lucy was my exact match in every way except for the one that had the power to keep us apart.

When she finally pulled away, I could see tears forming in her eyes, but she kept them from falling. This was the Lucy that I knew. She was strong.

"I will miss you," she finally said as we parted and stood awkwardly waiting for each other to say something. I watched her eyes shift back and forth, uncertain of how to proceed. A couple of seconds of thought was all that she needed before a sinister grin crossed her face and she took my hand.

"With all of my heart I want to thank you. Thank you Sebastian, for interrupting my life."

Her grin remained as I thought of a reply. It came to me quickly.

"Thank you for letting me." Lucy giggled at my witty response. Another pause took hold of time. I lost track of how long we were really standing under that tree, but finally she released my hand and we parted. She returned to the men and they looked up briefly to greet her before John left his post and blocked her path. He greeted her and they shared a kiss. I felt my face grow green with jealously and my stomach turn into knots, but I put a stop to this feeling immediately. I couldn't be resentful of this, because I had made it happen. It was my fault that it ended this way. I couldn't hate him, even though I really wanted to.

I didn't leave right away like I should have. For hours, I watched them talk and work. It wasn't that I couldn't leave, I just didn't want to. The thought of closing the book on this part of my life was eating away every good feeling that I had left. It was an idea that would take some getting used to. The fact that she would die before I would gain any more years left my soul crushed. That was my only real reason for leaving now. Having her close again and then losing her to death would be unbearable. She would never know how much I really loved her. It was by far the hardest thing I would ever have to do—love her enough to let her go.

Suddenly a wild breeze picked up and pushed a branch of orange leaves into my vision, but I caught it before it struck my face. I held it until the wind stopped and then let go with a sigh. It was time to go. I forced myself not to look back even though she was still on my mind. With a final deep breath, I turned on my heels and headed back into the wilderness with a broken heart. Our paths were different now and I would always have to live with the consequences of my actions. But in my memory there would always be Lucy, the only woman I ever loved and the only decision I can't regret.

About the Author

E.K. Arden grew up in Ohio. She graduated from Kent State University with a degree in veterinary technology. She lives in Brewster with her family. Find her on Twitter @ekardenbooks.

www.ingramcontent.com/pod-product-compliance
Lightning Source LLC
Chambersburg PA
CBHW050714180626
46814CB00002B/434